DARK WATER'S EMBRACE

STEPHEN LEIGH

AVON BOOKS
A division of
The Hearst Corporation
1350 Avenue of the Americas
New York, New York 10019

Copyright © 1998 by Stephen Leigh
Published by arrangement with the author
Visit our website at http://www.AvonBooks.com/Eos
Library of Congress Catalog Card Number: 97-94466
ISBN: 0-380-79478-0

First Avon Eos Printing: March 1998

AVON EOS TRADEMARK REG. U.S. PAT. OFF. AND IN OTHER COUNTRIES, MARCA REGISTRADA, HECHO EN U.S.A.

Printed in the U.S.A.

WCD 10 9 8 7 6 5 4 3 2 1

To Becca and Guy
Because.

And, as ever, to Denise, with whom I've mingled jeans and
genes both.

ACKNOWLEDGMENTS

I would like to acknowledge *The Life and Death of a Druid Prince*, by Anne Ross and Don Robins (Simon & Schuster 1989)—an excellent book which gave me the initial "what if" impetus to this novel, however wildly divergent it actually is. Look up the book and read it—it's one of the most fascinating archeological detective stories you'll ever come across.

For some interesting speculation and insight into the causes of why species disappear, I would also like to recommend David M. Raup's *Extinction* (Norton, 1991).

I'd also like to thank Dr. Rebecca Levin for her input into the potential biology of the Miccail. Any errors of extrapolation and science are mine, not hers.

And if you're connected to the Internet, please check out my web page at www.sff.net/people/sleigh—you're always welcome to browse through!

A MICTLANIAN GLOSSARY

THE LANGUAGES OF MICTLAN, HUMAN, AND MICCAIL:

The crew of the *Ibn Battuta*, drawn as they were from a multinational crew, adopted English as their *lingua franca*. However, most of the crew were at least bilingual, if not relatively fluent in three or four languages. Inevitably, words and phrases from other languages crept into their everyday speech. Well before the *Ibn Battuta* was launched, during the period when it was being constructed in orbit and the crew members were learning their roles, a subtle *patois* of many languages had come into common use among the crew and support personnel. The emerging language was almost a Creole, though the largest portion of the vocabulary derived from American English. By the time of their arrival at Mictlan, despite the ship-decades of LongSleep, this convention was firmly in place. New terms and descriptions might as easily be drawn from Cantonese, Japanese, Russian, Spanish, or Kiswahili as English, or even (as was the case with the world-name itself) an ancient Native American language such as Nahuatl. For the most part, we have stayed with English for the sake of readability. However, where it seemed appropriate, the terms used by the colonists have been appropriated here.

The sections from the viewpoint of the Miccail themselves contain words drawn from their own language, again where it seemed appropriate. As in Japanese (for instance), the Miccail created conglomerate words composed of smaller, monosyllabic nouns. Thus, "nasituda," the word for the carved stelae which were the first, most visible signs of the Miccail presence is Stone (*na*) Carved (*si*) Past (*tu*) Speak (*da*): literally, the Carved Stone that Speaks of History, or as we have (more romantically, perhaps, and certainly more freely) translated it here, Telling Stone.

The list of human and Miccail words below is by no means exhaustive, and is provided only to give some insight into derivations and meanings.

aabi	Miccail. Literally, "Ears hearing." An acknowledgment that you've heard and understood what was said to you.
AnglSaiye	Miccail. The Island, sacred home of the Sa
brais	Miccail. Literally, "Sun's Eye"; the pupilless third eye set high on the forehead of the Miccail. The brais cannot focus and the Miccail do not properly "see" with it. Instead, it serves as a "skylight" and warns them of sudden shifts in light which might signal the approach of a predator.
Chali	Miccail. The larger of Mictlan's two moons, dubbed Longago by the human colonists.
CieTiLa	Miccail. Literally, "Those Touched By The Gods." More simply, it means "The People," referring to the Miccail as a whole.
da	Human. Etymology uncertain. The closest meaning is perhaps "Uncle." Da refers to any male of a person's Family who is of a generation or more older.
danjite ikenai	Human, from Japanese: "Absolutely not"
dottó	Human, from Italian: a contraction of "dottore," or doctor. The English equivalent might be the colloquial "Doc."
Geeda	Human. Etymology uncertain. The eldest male of a Family
Geema	Human. Etymology uncertain. The eldest female of a Family
hai	Human, from Japanese: "Yes."
hakuchi	Human, from Japanese: "Idiot."
hand	Miccail counting: a "hand" equals four.
Ja	Miccail. A suffix indicating a female in servitude
Je	Miccail. A suffix indicating a male in servitude
jitu	Miccail. A narcotic drink used in Sa rituals.
kami	Human, from Japanese: a local spirit, either a minor deity or possibly the soul of a dead person.

kav	Miccail. An herbal tea
kasadi	Miccail. Ducklike amphibians who congregate on shorelines during their brief spring mating season
khudda	Human, from Syrian (vulgar): used as a profanity: human excrement
Kiria	Human, from Latin: Priest or Priestess. Probably derived from Kyrie.
komban wa	Human, from Japanese: "Good evening."
lavativo	Human, from Italian: "Lazybones"
mali cvijet	Human, from Serbo-Croatian: "Little Flower"—a term of endearment.
mam	Human. Etymology uncertain. "Mother." Since it was entirely unlikely that anyone could be certain of the father, there is no analogue word for the male parent on Mictlan.
marset	Miccail. A small mammalian animal hunted for both its food and fur.
mi	Human. Etymology uncertain. The closest meaning is perhaps "Aunt." It refers to any female of a person's Family who is older than you, and of whom you're not a direct descendant (i.e., not your mother, grandmother, etc.)
Miccail	Human, from Nahuatl: "The Dead." On Mictlan, the extinct race of sentient beings who perished a millennium before the arrival of the *Ibn Battuta*.
Mictlan	Human, from Nahuatl: "The Land of the Dead." In Aztec/Mayan creation myths, this is the Land of the Dead, from where the god Quetzalcoatl brought the bones of man. This was used as the world-name after the bones of a sentient race were found here.
mojo ljubav	Human, from Serbo-Croatian: "My love"
nasituda	Miccail. The Telling Stone of the Miccail, the carved stelae of crystal which are the most prominent remnants of that extinct race.

nei	Human. Etymology uncertain: "Absolutely not!"
Njia	Human, from Kiswahili: "The Way." This is the principal religious/philosophical belief system among the humans on Mictlan.
Quali	Miccail. The smaller of Mictlan's two moons, dubbed Faraway by the human colonists.
rezu	Human, from Japanese via Europe: a lesbian.
Sa	Miccail. A suffix indicating a Miccail midmale. Nearly all the rare midmales belonged to the Sa sect, a religious colony based on an island.
shangaa	Miccail. The long, caftanlike robe that was the main item of clothing worn by the Miccail. Shangaa, woven from the pulp of a native plant, were dyed many bright colors, and varied from plain, utilitarian robes to fine ceremonial costumes.
sib	Human, from English: "sibling." On Mictlan, a sib is anyone of your Family of the same generation, regardless of who the mother was.
Ta	Miccail. A suffix for the dominant female in a Miccail tribe, also known as the Old-Mother.
Te	Miccail. a suffix indicating that the person is the OldFather of a Miccail tribe, the dominant male.
terduva	Miccail. A segment of time equal to 512 (or $8 \times 8 \times 8$) years. The Miccail, with hands consisting of three fingers and a thumb, counted in base eight.
Ti	Miccail. The suffix used for a deity.
Tlilipan	Human, from Nahuatl: "place of black water." Name given to a peat-stained lake near the colony site.
Tu	Miccail. The suffix used to designate the head of the Community of Sa.

una tortillera	Human, from Spanish: in extremely vulgar usage, a lesbian.
VeiSaTi	Miccail. One of the gods of the Miccail, the one most sacred to the sect of the Sa.
verrechat	Human, from French: "glass cat." A small, catlike marsupial with transparent or lightly tinted skin and muscles. Sometimes domesticated.
wizards	Human. A contraction of "winged lizards"— a type of flying reptile found near the human settlement.
Xa	Miccail. A suffix indicating a female of the free caste
Xe	Miccail. A suffix indicating a male of the free caste
xeshai	Miccail. Literally, "Second Fight"—a ritual-bound two person combat that was the usual method for solving severe disagreements between Miccail tribes. Each Te or Ta would choose a champion from among the Xe or Xa to represent them. In rare cases, *xeshai* might be group combat, but even then there were specific rules limiting how the conflict would be handled.

I suspect that if humankind had never known sex, we would have invented it anyway: the women to celebrate friendship, and the men to celebrate themselves.

—Gabriel Rusack

DARK WATER'S EMBRACE

DISCOVERIES

CONTEXT:
Elena Koda-Schmidt

❧ THE AUTUMN DAY WAS AS HOT AS ANY IN RECENT
memory. The temperature was nearly 10°C, and
Elena paused to unbutton her sweater and wipe away the
sweat that threatened to drip into her eyes. Near the tree line
bordering the river a kilometer away, the dark waters of a
pond glittered in the sun: Tlilipan, it was called, "the place
of black water." The peat-stained shallow lake was the last
vestige of a much larger parent, now just a marshy wetland.
Further down the peat bog, Elena could see Faika Koda-
Shimmura and Aldhelm Martinez-Santos—they were kissing, a long, oblivious embrace that made Elena feel vaguely
jealous, watching. Faika was ten and had reached her menarche.

Elena suspected that her brother Wan-Li was going to be
disappointed when she told him. Wan-Li had spent the night
in the Koda-Shimmura compound with Faika a few days
before. It seemed he hadn't quite made the impression he'd
thought he had. Elena remembered her own menarche year,
and how she'd experimented with her new sexual freedom.

The cart was nearly full of peat; Elena leaned her shovel
against the wheel and rubbed her protruding stomach with
callused hands. She loved the swelling, surprising curve of
her belly, loved the weight of it, the feeling of being centered
and rooted. Her roundness made her believe that despite the
odds, *her* baby would be perfect. *Her* baby would live and
give her grandchildren to dandle on her knee when she was
past childbearing herself. She stroked the hard sphere of her
womb and the baby kicked in response. Elena laughed.

"Now you be still, little one. It's bad enough without you
stomping on my bladder. Mama's still got a lot of work to
do before we get home."

With a sigh, Elena picked up the shovel and prepared to
attack the peat once more. She was working an old face,
several feet down in the bog where the peat was rich, thick,

3

and as dark as old Gerard's face. She lifted the spade. Stopped.

A flap of something leathery and brown like stained wood protruded from the earth, about a foot up on the wall of the ancient marsh. Elena crouched down, grunting with the unaccustomed bulk of her belly. She peered at the fold of leather, prodding it with the tip of her shovel to pull a little more out of the moss.

Elena gasped and dropped the shovel. Protruding from the appendage, squashed and compressed by the weight of centuries of peat, was a hand with four fingers, the tip of each finger a wide knob capped with a recessed claw. The shock sent Elena stepping backward. The shovel's handle tangled between her legs, tripping her. She put her hands out instinctively to protect her stomach. She grunted with the impact, and the handle slammed against her knee. For a moment, she just lay there, taking inventory. The child jumped inside her, and she breathed again.

"Faika—" she began, but the shout came out entangled in the breath. She thought of how she must look, sprawled in the wet dirt and staring at the apparition in the peat, and laughed at herself.

"What a sight!" she told the child in her womb. "You'd think your mother was sure the boggin was going to get up and walk out of there," she said. She stood, brushing uselessly at her stained trousers and grimacing with the bruised, protesting knee.

As she stood, she saw movement from the corner of her eye. A figure shifted in the small stand of globe-trees a hundred meters away. "Faika? Aldhelm?" Elena called, but the shadowy form—almost lost in tree-shadow—moved once more, and she knew it wasn't either of the two. She could feel it, watching, staring at her. *A grumbler?* she thought, wondering if the rifle was still in the cart, but in the instant she glanced away to check the weapon, the shadow was gone.

There was no one there. The sense of being observed was gone.

Elena shivered, hugging herself. "Baby, your mother's seeing ghosts now," she said. She glanced back at the hand hanging from the peat. "I think I just saw your *kami*," she told it. "Don't worry, I'm not going to do anything nasty to you. I'll leave that to Anaïs. Knowing her, she'll *enjoy* it."

4

She took a deep breath, and looked again at the copse of trees. "Faika! Aldhelm!" Elena shouted. "If you two can stop fondling each other for a minute or so, I think you should come here and look at this."

VOICE:
Anaïs Koda-Levin the Younger

"SO . . . ARE YOU PREGNANT YET, ANAÏS?"

I hate that question. I always have the wrong answer.

No. I'm not.

"Give it a rest, Ghost."

"Everything's still the same, is it? You *are* still trying, aren't you? If we could only get you up here so we could *see*. . . ."

I felt the old emotional garbage rising with Ghost's questioning: the anger, the bitterness, the self-loathing. I forced the gorge down, packing the filth down behind that internal wall, but it was an effort. Our ancient steel surgical instruments, worn to a satin patina by over a century of use and constant sterilization, beat a raucous percussion on the tray I was holding. "Ghost—"

"Sorry, Anaïs. No need to get irritated. As the repository of Mictlan's history . . ."

There are times when I wish I knew programming well enough to tone down Ghost's assertiveness. "Shut up, Ghost."

This time around, Ghost looked like an old blind man, hunched over an ornate glass cane that was as swirled and frosted as a Miccail stele. His sightless, ice-blue eyes stared somewhere past my right shoulder into the back corner of the coldroom lab. The outline of his body sparkled and flared disconcertingly, and his legs were implanted in the polished whitewood planking past his ankles.

"Ghost, Hui and I put a new floor in here since the last time. You look like you're wading in wood, and it's really

5

disconcerting. Can you shift your image up about a dozen centimeters?"

"Oh, now that we're on the subject of sex and reproduction, you want to change it? Anaïs, I know it's no comfort to you, but if it were possible to reach the *Ibn Battuta*, a resonance scan or even an ultrasound would answer a lot of questions, and we could—"

"Drop it, Ghost. Drop it right now."

This time, I made no effort to hide the anger. Ghost reminded me too much of the sympathy, the false reassurances given to me by my sibs, by my *mam* Maria. They look into my room and see my clothing draped carefully over the huge mirror (which had once belonged to Rebecca Koda-Levin herself), the shirts and pants arranged so that the mirror reflects nothing, and they don't understand the significance of what they're seeing.

The old man sighed. The image, sparking, raised up until the soles of his feet were almost even with the floor. "Better?"

"It'll do."

"You're going to have to describe what you're seeing," Ghost said. "Since you've had the ill grace not to put a video feed in here."

"Quit complaining." My voice was muffled through the gauze mask I was tying behind my head, and my breath clouded in the cold air. "We put the feed in; the line was bad. No one's had a chance to fix it yet—it's not exactly high priority. Maybe next time."

"But I'm curious *now*," Ghost persisted. "I don't have much time this orbit. Come on—you're as slow as your Geema."

I sniffed. A strand of hair had made an escape from the surgical cap; I brushed it out of my eyes. "Maybe that's why they named me for her, huh?"

The retort was weak but it was the best I had at the moment. I turned back to the examination table and its strange contents. The bog body Elena had found lay there like a man-sized, crumpled bag of leather—which, in essence, it was. The acidic chemical stew of the peat had tanned and preserved the skin, but the skeletal structure and most of the interior organs had dissolved away. Over the last several days, in scraps of time between other, more pressing duties, I'd carefully cleaned away the worst of the peat clinging to the outside of the body, still hunched into its centuries-old

6

fetal position. Now, like a gift, I was ready to unwrap the present given us by the bog.

Every time I'd looked at the body, I'd felt the same rush of adrenaline I felt now, a sense of standing in front of something . . . I don't know . . . maybe *sacred* is the best word. Old and venerable, certainly. I was almost inclined to believe Elena's tale about seeing a *kami* watching her when she'd found it.

After all, it was the bones of this race's dead that had given rise to the name given to the planet: Mictlan, suggested by the lone Mexican crewmember of the *Ibn Batutta*. Mictlan was the Aztec land of the dead, where the god Quetzalcoatl found the bones of humankind—and now, where the bones of another dead culture had been found. The race itself were christened the Miccail—"the Dead," in the Nahautl language. In the years following, a few Miccailian burial sites had been explored. Not that the excavations told us much about the Miccail, since they cremated their dead before they buried the calcined and charred bones—a rite we'd borrowed from them for our own dead. The strange, whorled spires the Miccail had left behind on the northern continent, sticking out of Mictlan's rocky soil like faerie cathedrals of dull glass and carved with images of themselves, had been photographed and documented; it was from these that we learned the most about the extinct race. More would have been done, probably, but the near destruction and crippling of the *Ibn Battuta* not six months after the colonists' arrival and the resultant death of nearly all the crew members had suddenly, radically, and permanently shifted everyone's priorities.

Basically, it was more important to scrape an existence from Mictlan than to try to decipher the mystery of our world's previous inhabitants.

I suppose I could appreciate my ancestors' sentiments. Priorities hadn't changed much in the century since the accident. Survival was still far more important than any anthropological exploration. No one wanted Mictlan to harbor the scattered bones of *two* extinct, sentient races. I suppose we have the deliberate uncuriosity of the matriarchs and patriarchs to thank for our being here at all.

For one reason or another, though, I don't seem to be much like them. In so many ways. . . .

"Are you ready to record, Ghost?"

"I'd have much more to analyze with video."

7

I waited. A moment later, Ghost sighed. The ancient's body dissolved into static for a moment, then returned as a young woman in an *Ibn Battuta* officer's uniform, though a fanciful, brightly-colored scarf was tied over her eyes like a blindfold. The voice changed also, from an elderly male quaver to a female soprano. "Recording into *Ibn Battuta* memory. Audio only log: 101 September 41. The voice is Anaïs Koda-Levin the Younger, Generation Six. Go ahead, Anaïs."

I gave Ghost a sidewise look, swearing—as I had a few hundred times before—that I'd never understand why Gabriela had programmed her AI with such a quirky sense of humor and strange set of idiosyncracies. "All right. This is another examination of the Miccail body found in the peat bog—and this will be very cursory, I'm afraid, since I'm on duty in the clinic tonight. Ghost, you can download my previous recordings from the Mictlan library."

"It's already done. Go on, Ana, you have my undivided attention."

I knew that wasn't true—there were still three other working projectors scattered among the compounds, and Ghost was no doubt talking with people at each of them at the moment, as well as performing the systems work necessary to keep our patchwork and shrinking network of century-old terminals together, but it was a nice lie. I shook my hair back from my eyes once more and leaned over the table.

Imagine someone unzipping his skin, crumpling it up, and throwing the discarded epidermis in a corner like an old suit—that's what the corpse looked like. On its side, the body was drawn up like someone cowering in fear, the right arm folded around its back, the left thrown over the right shoulder like a shawl. The head was bowed down into the chest, crushed flat and turned to the left. I could see the closed lid of the right eye and the translucent covering of the central "eye" high on the forehead. A mane of dark, matted hair ran from the back of the bald, knobbed skull and halfway down the spine.

I gently pulled down the right leg, which was tucked up against the body. The skin moved grudgingly; I had to go slowly to avoid tearing it, moistening the skin occasionally with a sponge. Tedious work.

"Most of the body is intact," I noted aloud after a while, figuring that Ghost was going to complain if I didn't start talking soon. "From the spinal mane and the protrusions around the forehead, it's one of the type Gabriela designated as 'Nomads.' If I recall correctly, she believed that since the carvings of Nomads disappear from the Miccail's stelae in the late periods, these were a subspecies that went extinct a millennium or so before the rest of the Miccail."

"You've been studying things you've been told to stay away from."

"Guilty as charged. So that makes the body—what?—two thousand years old?"

"No later than that," Ghost interrupted, "assuming Gabriela's right about the stelae. We'll have a better idea when we get the estimates from the peat samples and measurements. Máire's still working on them."

"Sounds fine. I'll check with her in the next few days."

I was lost in the examination now, seeing nothing but the ancient corpse in front of me. A distant part of me noted that my voice had gone deeper and more resonant, no longer consciously pitched high—we all have our little idiosyncrasies, I suppose. "Two thousand or more years old, then. The body evidently went naked into the lake that later became the bog—there's no trace of any clothing. That may or may not be something unusual. The pictographs on the Miccail stelae show ornate costumes in daily use, on the Nomads as well as the rest, so it's rather strange that this one's naked. . . . Maybe he was swimming? Anyway, we're missing the left leg a half meter down from the hip and . . ."

The right leg, boneless and twisted, lay stretched on the table. Fragments of skin peeled from the stump of the ankle like bark from a whitewood. ". . . the right foot a few centimeters above the ankle. A pity—I'd like to have seen that central claw on the foot. Looks like the leg and foot decayed off the body sometime after it went into the lake. Wouldn't be surprised if they turn up somewhere else later."

I straightened the right arm carefully, laying it down on the table, moving slowly from shoulder to wrist. "Here's one hand—four fingers, not five. Wonder if they counted in base eight? These are really long phalanges, though the metacarpals must have been relatively short. The pads at the end of each digit still have vestiges of a recessed claw—would have been a nasty customer in a fight. There's webbing almost halfway up the finger; bet they swam well. And this thumb . . . it's highly opposed and much longer than a human's. From the folds in the skin, I'd guess that it had an extra articulation, also."

I grunted as I turned the body so that it rested mostly on

its back. "There appears to be a large tattoo on the chest and stomach—blue-black lines. Looks like a pictogram of some sort, but there's still a lot of peat obscuring it, and I'll have to make sure that this isn't some accidental postmortem marking of some kind. I'll leave that for later. . . ."

The remnant of the left leg was folded high up on the stomach, obscuring the tattoo. I lifted it carefully and moved it aside, revealing the groin. "Now *that's* interesting. . . ."

"What?" Ghost asked. "I'm a blind AI, remember?"

I exhaled under the surgical mask, resisting the urge to rise to Ghost's baiting. "The genitalia. There's a scaly, fleshy knob, rather high on the front pubis. I suppose that's the penis analogue for the species, but it doesn't look like normal erectile tissue or a penile sheath. No evidence of anything like testicles—no scrotal sac at all. Maybe they kept it inside."

"They're aliens, remember? Maybe they didn't *have* one."

I accepted Ghost's criticism with a nod. She was right—I was lacing some heavy anthropomorphism into my speculations. "Maybe. There's a youngpouch on the abdomen, though, and I haven't seen any Mictlanian marsupialoids where both sexes *had* the pouch. Maybe in the Miccail both male and female suckled the young." I lifted the leg, turning the body again with an effort. "There's a urethra further down between the legs, and an anus about where you'd expect it—"

I stopped, dropping the leg I was holding. It fell to the table with a soft thud. I breathed. I could feel a flush climbing my neck, and my vision actually shivered for a moment, disorientingly.

"Anaïs?"

"It's . . ." I licked suddenly dry lips. Frowned. "There's what looks to be a vaginal opening just below the base of the spine, past the anus."

"A hermaphrodite," Ghost said, her voice suddenly flat. "Now there's serendipity for you, eh?"

I said nothing for several seconds. I was staring at the body, at the soft folds hiding the opening at the rear of the creature, not quite knowing whether to be angry. Trying to gather the shreds of composure. *Staring at myself in the mirror, forcing myself to look only at that other Anaïs's face, that contemplative, uncertain face lost in the fogged, spotted silver backing, and my gaze always, inevitably, drifting lower . . . .*

10

The Miccail body was an accusation, a mockery placed just for me by whatever gods ruled Mictlan.

"Gabriela speculated about the sexuality of the Nomads," Ghost continued. "There were notes in her journals. She collected rubbings of some rather suggestive carvings on the Middle Period stelae. In fact, in a few cases she referred to the Nomads as 'midmales' because the stelae were ambiguous as to which they might be. It's all scanned in the database—call it up."

"I've read some of Gabriela's journals—the public ones, anyway. Gabriela said a lot of strange things about the Miccail—and everything else on this world. Doesn't make her right."

"Give poor Gabriela a break. No one else was particularly interested in the Miccail after the accident. The first generation had more pressing problems than an extinct race. As an archeologist/anthropologist she was—just like you, I might add—a dilettante, a rank amateur."

"And she was your lead programmer, right? That explains a lot about *you*."

"It's also why I'm still working. Ana, I'm running out of time here."

"All right."

I took another long breath, trying to find the objective, aloof Anaïs the bog body had banished. The leg had fallen so that the tattered end of the ankle hung over the edge of the table. I placed it carefully back into position and didn't look at the trunk of the body or the mocking twinned genitals. Instead, I moved around the table, going to the Nomad's head. Carefully, I started prying it from the folded position it had held for centuries.

"Looks like she . . . he . . ." I stopped. Ghost waited. My jaw was knotted; I forced myself to relax. *Do this goddamn thing and get it over with. Put the body back in the freezer and forget about it.* "She didn't die of drowning. There's a large wound on the back of the skull. Part crushing, part cutting, like a blunt axe, and it probably came from behind. I'll bet we'll find that's the cause of death, though I guess it's possible she was thrown into the lake still alive. I'm moving the head back to its normal position now. Hey, what's this . . . ?"

I'd lifted the chin of the Miccail. Trapped deep in the folds of the neck was a thin, knotted cord, a garrote, pulled so tightly against the skin that I could see that the windpipe

11

had closed under the pressure. "He was strangled as well."

"He? I thought it was a she."

I exhaled in exasperation. "God*damn* it, Ghost . . ."

"Sorry," Ghost apologized. She didn't sound particularly sincere. "Axed, strangled, *and* drowned," Ghost mused. "Wonder which happened first?"

"Somebody really wanted him dead. Poor thing." I looked down at the flattened, peat-darkened features, telling myself that I was only trying to see in them some reflection of the Miccail's mysterious life. This Miccail was a worse mirror than the one in my room. Between the pressure-distorted head and the long Miccail snout, the wide-set eyes, the light-sensitive eyelike organ at the top of the head, the nasal slits above the too-small, toothless mouth, it was difficult to attribute any human expression to the face. I sighed. "Let's see if we can straighten out the other arm—"

"Ana," Ghost interrupted, "you have company on the way, I'm afraid—"

"Anaïs!"

The shout came from outside, in the clinic's lobby. A few seconds later, Elio Allen-Shimmura came through the lab doors in a burst. His dark hair was disheveled, his black eyes worried. The hair and eyes stood out harshly against his light skin, reddened slightly from the cold northwest wind. His plain, undistinguished features were furrowed, creasing the too-pale forehead under the shock of bangs and drawing the ugly, sharp planes of his face even tighter. He cast a glance at the bog body; I moved between Elio and the Miccail. Some part of me didn't want him to see, didn't want anyone to see.

Elio didn't seem to notice. He glanced quickly to the glowing apparition of Ghost. "Is that you, Elio?" Ghost asked. "I can't see through this damn blindfold." Ghost grinned under the parti-colored blindfold.

Elio smiled in return, habitually, an expression that just touched the corners of his too-thin lips and died. "It's me." Something was bothering Elio; he couldn't stand still, shuffling from foot to foot as if he were anxious to be somewhere else. I'd often noticed that reaction in my presence, but at least this time I didn't seem to be the cause of it. Elio turned away from Ghost. "Anaïs, has Euzhan been in here?"

"Haven't seen her, El." *Your Geeda Dominic doesn't exactly encourage your Family's children to be around me,* I wanted to add, but didn't. With my own Family having no children at the moment, if I had a favorite kid in the settlement, it would be Euzhan, a giggling, mischievous presence. Euzhan liked me, liked me with the uncomplicated trust of a child; liked me—I have to admit—with the same unconscious grace that her mother had possessed. It was impossible not to love the child back. I began to feel a sour stirring in the pit of my stomach.

"Damn! I was hoping . . ." Elio's gaze went to the door, flicking away from me.

"El, what's going on?"

He spoke to the air somewhere between Ghost and me. "It's probably nothing. Euz is missing from the compound, has been for an hour. Dominic's pretty frantic. We'll probably find her hiding in the new building, but . . ."

I could hear the forced nonchalance in Elio's voice; that told me that they'd already checked the obvious places where a small child might hide. A missing child, in a population as small as ours, was certainly cause for immediate concern—Dominic, the current patriarch of the Allen-Shimmura family, would have sent out every available person to look for the girl. Elio frowned and shook his head. "All right. You're in the middle of something, I know. But if you do see her—"

His obvious distress sparked guilt. "This has waited for a few thousand years. It can certainly wait another hour or two. I'll come help. Just give me a few minutes to put things away and scrub."

"Thanks. We appreciate it." Elio glanced again at the Miccail's body, still eclipsed behind me, then gave me a small smile before he left. I was almost startled by that and returned the smile, forgetting that he couldn't see it behind the mask. As he left, I slid the examining table back into the isolation compartment, then went to the sink and began scrubbing the protective brownish covering of thorn-vine sap from my hands.

"A bit of interest there?" Ghost ventured.

"You're blind, remember?"

"Only visually. I'm getting excellent audio from your terminal. Let me play it back—you'll hear how your voice perked up—"

"Elio's always been friendly enough to me, that's all. I'm not interested; he's *definitely* not, or he hides it awfully well. Besides, El is . . ." *Ugly*, I almost said, and realized how that would sound, coming from me. *His eyes are nice, and his*

13

hands. But his face—the eyes are set too close together, his nose is too long and the mouth too large. His skin is a patchwork of blotches. And the one time we tried . . . "At least he doesn't look at me like . . . like . . ." I hated the way I sounded, hated the fact that I knew Ghost was recording it all. I hugged myself, biting my lower lip. "Look, I really don't want to talk about this."

Ghost flickered. Her face morphed into lines familiar from holos of the Matriarchs: Gabriela. "Making sense of an attraction is like analyzing chocolate. Just enjoy it, and to hell with the calories." The voice was Gabriela's, too: smoky, husky, almost as low as mine.

"You're quoting."

"And you're evading." A line of fire-edged darkness sputtered down Ghost's figure from head to foot as the image began to break up. "Doesn't matter—I'm also drifting out of range. See you in three days this time. I should have a longer window then. Make sure you document everything about the Miccail body."

"I will. You get me those age estimates from Máire's uploads when you can."

"Promise." Static chattered in Ghost's voice; miniature lightning storms crackled across her body. She disappeared, then returned, translucent. I could see the murdered Nomad's body through her. "Go help Elio find Euzhan."

"I will. Take care up there, Ghost."

A flash of light rolled through Ghost's image. She went two-dimensional and vanished utterly.

CONTEXT:
Bui Allen-Shimmura

❧ "BUI, GEEDA DOMINIC WANTS YOU. NOW."

Bui felt his skin prickle in response, like spiders scurrying up his spine. He straightened up, closing the vegetable bin door. Euzhan wasn't there, wasn't in any of her usual hiding places. Bui looked at Micah's lopsided face, and could see that there was no good news there. He asked anyway. "Did anyone find her?"

Micah shook his head, his lips tight. "Not yet," he answered, his voice blurred with his cleft palate. "Geeda's sent Elio out to alert the other Families and get them to help search."

"*Khudda*." Bui didn't care that *da* Micah heard him cursing. The way Bui figured it, he couldn't get into any more trouble than he was already in. If he found Euzhan now, he might just kill the girl for slipping away while he was responsible for watching her. It wasn't fair. He'd be ten in half a year. At his age, he should have been out working the fields with the rest, not babysitting.

"How's Geeda?" he asked Micah.

"In as foul a mood as I've ever seen. You'd better get up there fast, boy."

Bui's shoulders sagged. He almost started to cry, sniffing and wiping his nose on his sleeve. "Go on," Micah told him. "Get it over with."

He went.

Geeda Dominic was in the common room of the Allen-Shimmura compound, staring out from the window laser-chiseled from the stone of the Rock. A dusty sunbeam threw Dominic's shadow on the opposite wall. Bui noticed immediately that no one else from the Family was in the room. That didn't bode well, since the others sometimes managed to keep Dominic's infamous temper in check. "Geeda?" Bui said tremulously. "Micah said you—"

Dominic was the eldest of the Allen-Shimmura family, a venerable eighty, but he turned now with a youth born of anger. His cane, carved by the patriarch Shigetomo himself, with a knobbed head of oak all the way from Earth, slashed air and slammed into Bui's upper arm. Surprise and pain made Bui cry out, and the blow was hard enough to send him sprawling on the rug.

"*Hakuchi!*" Dominic shouted at him, the cane waving in Bui's face like a club. "You fool!"

Bui clutched his arm, crying openly now. "Geeda, it wasn't my fault. Hizo, he'd fallen and skinned his knees, and when I finished with him, Euzhan—"

"Shut up!" The cane *whoomped* as it flashed in front of his face. "You listen to me, boy. If Euzhan is hurt or . . . or . . ." Bui knew the word that Dominic wouldn't say. *Dead*. Fear reverberated in Bui's head, throbbing in aching syncopation

15

with the pain in his arm. "You better hope they find her safe, boy, or I'll have you goddamn shunned. I swear I will. No one will talk to you again. You'll be cast out of the Family. You'll find your own food or you'll starve."

"No, Geeda, please . . ." Bui shivered.

"Get out of here," Dominic roared. His hand tightened around the shaft of his cane, trembling. "Get out of here and find her. Don't bother coming back until you do. You understand me, boy?"

"Yes, Geeda Dominic. I'm . . . I'm sorry . . . I'm awful sorry . . ." Bui, still sobbing, half crawled, half ran from the room.

Dominic's cane clattered against the archway behind Bui as he went through.

VOICE:
Anaïs Koda-Levin the Younger

"EUZHAN! DAMN IT, CHILD. . . ."
    I exhaled in frustration, my voice hoarse from calling. Elio sagged tiredly near me. He rubbed the glossy stock of his rifle with fingers that seemed almost angry. "It's getting dark," he said. "It's near SixthHour. She'll come out from wherever she's hiding as soon as she notices. She always wants the light on in the creche, and she'll be getting hungry by now. She'll be out. I know it."

Elio wasn't convincing even himself. There was a quick desperation in his voice. I understood it all too well. All of us did. Our short history's full of testimonials to this world's whims—as our resident historian, Elio probably understood that better than I did.

Mictlan had not been a kind world for the survivors of *Ibn Batutta*. Two colonies—one on each of Mictlan's two continents—had been left behind after the accident that had destroyed most of the mothership. The colonies quickly lost touch with each other when a massive, powerful hurricane raked the southern colony's continent in the first year of exile, and they never resumed radio contact with us or with Ghost on the *Ibn Battuta*.

Another storm had nearly obliterated our northern colony in Year 23, killing six of the original nine crewmembers here. I suppose that was our historical watershed, since that disaster inalterably changed the societal structure, giving rise to what became the Families. Local diseases mutated to attack our strange new host bodies, stalking the children especially—the Bloody Cough alone killed two children in five by the time they reached puberty. I know: I see the bodies and do the autopsies. There are the toothworms or the treeleapers or the grumblers; there are the bogs and the storms and the bitter winters; there are accidents and infections and far, far too many congenital defects. Most of them are bad enough that nature itself takes care of them: miscarriages, stillbirths, nonviable babies who are born and die within a few days or a few months—which is why none of the Families name a child before his or her first birthday. I also know the others—the ones who lived but who are marked with the stamp of Mictlan.

I knew *them* very well.

The rate of viable live births—for whatever reason: a side effect of the LongSleep, or some unknown factor in the Mictlan environment—was significantly lower among the ship members and their descendants than for the general population of Earth. Just over a century after being stranded on Mictlan, our human population nearly matched the year; there'd been no growth for the last quarter of a century. Too many years, deaths outnumbered births.

Mictlan was not a sweet, loving Motherworld. She was unsympathetic and unremittingly harsh.

I knew that Elio's imagination was calculating the same dismal odds mine was. This was no longer just a child hiding away from her *mi* or *da*, not this late, not this long.

Euzhan was four. I'd seen the girl in the clinic just a few days ago—an eager child, still awkward and lisping, and utterly charming. Ochiba, Euzhan's mother, had once been my best—hell, one of my only—friends. What we'd had. . . .

Anyway, Euzhan had been a difficult birth, a breech baby. All of Ochiba's births were difficult; her pelvis was narrow, barely wide enough to accommodate a baby's head. On Earth, she would have been an automatic cesarean, but not here, not when any major operation is an open invitation for some postoperative infection. I could have gone in. Ochiba told me she'd go with whatever I decided. Ochiba had delivered three children before—with long, difficult labors, each time. I made the decision to let her go, and she—finally—delivered twelve hours later.

But Ochiba's exhaustion after the long labor gave an opportunistic respiratory virus its chance—Ochiba died three days after Euzhan's birth on 97 LastDay. Neither Hui Koda-Schmidt, the colony's other "doctor," nor I had been able to break the raging fever or stop the creeping muscular paralysis that followed. Our medical database is quite extensive, but is entirely Earth-based. On Mictlan-specific diseases, there's only the information that we colonists have entered, and I was all too familiar with that. Ghost had been out of touch, the *Ibn Battuta's* unsynchronized orbit trapping the AI on the far side of Mictlan. I don't have the words to convey the utter helpless impotence I'd felt, watching Ochiba slowly succumb, knowing that I was losing someone I loved.

Knowing that maybe, just maybe, my decision had been the reason she died.

I'd been holding Ochiba's hand at the end. I cried along with her Family, and Dominic—grudgingly—had even asked me to speak for Ochiba at her Burning.

A damn small consolation.

Euzhan, Ochiba's third named child, was especially precious to Dominic, the head of Family Allen-Shimmura. Euz was normal and healthy. As we all knew too well, any child was precious, but one such as Euzhan was priceless. The growing fear that something tragic had happened to Euzhan was a black weight on my soul.

"Who was watching Euz?"

"Bui," Elio answered. "Poor kid. Dominic'll have him skinned alive if Euz is hurt."

Nearly all of the Allen-Shimmura family were out searching for Euzhan now, along with many from the other Families. The buildings were being scoured one more time; a large party had gone into the cultivated fields to the southeast of the compound and were prowling the rows of white-bean stalks and scarlet faux-wheat. Elio and I had gone out along the edge of Tlilipan. I'd been half-afraid we'd see Euzhan's tiny footprints pressed in the mud flats along the pond's shore, but there'd been nothing but the cloverleaf tracks of skimmers. That didn't mean that Euzhan hadn't fallen into one of the patches of wet marsh between the colony and Tlilipan, or that a prowling grumbler hadn't come

18

across her unconscious body and dragged her off, still half-alive, to a rocky lair along the river. . . .

I forced the thoughts away. I shivered under my sweater and shrugged the strap of the medical kit higher on my shoulder. I've never been particularly religious, but I found myself praying to whatever *kami* happened to be watching.

Just let her be all right. Let her come toddling out of some forgotten hole in the compound, scared and dirty, but unharmed.

The sun was prowling the tops of the low western hills, the river trees painting long, grotesque shadows which rippled over the bluefern-pocked marshland. Not far away was the pit where we'd dug the Miccail body from the peat. Behind the trees, the chill breeze brought the thin, faint sound of voices from below the Rock, calling for Euzhan. I turned to look, squinting back up the rutted dirt road. There, a tall blackness loomed against the sky: the Rock. The first generation had carved a labyrinth of tunnels in the monolithic hill of bare stone perched alongside the river; from the various openings, we'd added structures that poked out like wood, steel, and glass growths on the stone, so that the Families lived half in and half out of the granite crag. Now, in its darkness, the familiar lights of the Family compounds glistened.

The Rock. Home to all of us.

"Let's keep looking," I told Elio. "We still have time before it gets too dark."

Elio nodded. Where his light skin met the dark cloth of his shirt there was a knife-sharp contrast that stood out even in the dusk. "Fine. We should spread out a bit. . . ."

Elio looked so forlorn that I found myself wanting to move closer to him, to hug him. As much as I might have denied it to Ghost, the truth was that Elio was someone I genuinely liked. Maybe it was because he was so plain, with that pale, blotchy skin, his off-center mouth and wide nose, and his gawky, nervous presence. Elio was not one of the popular men, not one of those who spend every possible night in some woman's room, but we talked well, and I liked the way he walked and the fact that one side of his mouth went higher than the other when he smiled. I liked the warmth in his voice.

He was tapping the rifle stock angrily, staring out into the marsh. I touched his arm; he jerked away. Under the deep ridges of his brows, his black eyes glinted. I could read nothing in them, couldn't tell what he was thinking.

19

"Let's go find Euz," I said.

The light had slid into a deep gold, almost liquid. The sun was half lost behind slopes gone black with shadow. If we were going to continue searching, we'd have to go back soon for lights. Elio and I moved slowly around the marsh's edge, calling Euz's name and peering under the low-hanging limbs of the amberdrop trees, brushing aside the sticky, purplish leaves. Darkness crept slowly over the landscape, the temperature dropping as rapidly as the sun. The marsh steamed in the cooling air, the evening fog already cloud-thick near the river. Our breaths formed small thunderheads before us. Neither of the moons—the brooding Longago or its smaller, fleeter companion Faraway—were up yet. At the zenith, the stars were hard, bright points set in satin, though a faint trace of deep blue lingered at the horizon. Near the compound, outside the fences, someone had lit a large bonfire; the breeze brought the scent of smoke.

"El? It's way past SixthHour, and it's getting too dark to see. . . ."

"All right," Elio sighed. "I guess we might as well—"

Before he could finish, a grumbler's basso growl shivered the evening quiet, sinister and low. "Over there," I whispered, pointing. Elio unslung the rifle. "Come on."

I moved out into the wet ground, and Elio followed.

The grumblers were scavengers, nearly two meters in height, looking like a cut-and-paste, two-legged hybrid of great ape and Komodo dragon, though—like the Miccail and several other local species—they were probably biologically closer to an Earth marsupial than anything else. They walked upright if stooped over, their clawed front hands pulled close, slinking through the night. They were rarely seen near our settlement, seeming to fear the presence of the noisy humans. Sometimes alone, sometimes running in a small pack, they were also generally quiet—hearing one meant that the creature was close, and that it had found something. Grumblers were thieves and scavengers, snatching the kills of other, smaller predators or pouncing on an unsuspecting animal if it looked tiny and helpless enough. I hated them: they were ugly, cowardly, and mean beasts. They invariably ran if challenged.

If one had crept this close to the compound, then it had spotted something worth the danger to itself. Elio and I ran.

The grumbler was leaning over something in a small hollow, still mewling in its bass voice. Hearing us approach, it stood upright, turning its furred snout toward us and exposing double rows of needled teeth. The twinned tongue that was common in Mictlanian wildlife slithered in the mouth. Straggling fur swung under its chin like dreadlocks. Shorter fur cradled the socket of the central lens—like that of the Miccail—placed high in the forehead. The grumbler glared and cocked its head as if appraising us.

It growled. I couldn't see what it had been crouching over, but the grumbler appeared decidedly irritated at having been disturbed. The long, thin arms sliced the air in our direction, the curved slashing claws on the fingers extended. They looked sharper and longer than I remembered.

"Shoo!" I shouted. "Get out of here!" I waved my arms at it. The few times I'd met grumblers before, that had been enough; they'd skulked away like scolded children.

This one didn't move. It growled again, and it took a step toward us.

"Hey—" Elio said behind me. He fired the rifle into the air once. The percussive report echoed over the marsh, deafening. The grumbler jumped backward, crouching, but it held its ground. It snarled now, and took a step forward. I waved at it again.

"Ana . . ." Elio said warningly.

The grumbler gave him no time to say more.

It leaped toward me.

Improvisation, my great-grandmother Anaïs has often told me, *is not just for musicians.* Of course, Geema Ana usually says that when she's decided to use coarse red thread rather than thin white in the pattern she's weaving. I don't think she had situations like this in mind. Or maybe she did, since she was talking about using the materials at hand for your task. For the first time in my life, I demonstrated that I had that skill: I swung my medical bag.

The heavy leather hit the creature in the side of the head and sent it reeling down into the marsh on all fours. The bag broke open, the strap tearing as the contents tumbled out. Shaking its ugly head, the dreadlocks caked with mud, the grumbler snarled and hissed. It gathered itself to leap again. I doubted that the now-empty bag was going to stop it a second time, and I had the feeling that I'd pretty much exhausted my improvisational repertoire.

Elio fired from his hip, with no time to aim. A jagged line of small scarlet craters appeared on the grumbler's muscular chest, and it shrieked, twisting in midair. The grumbler collapsed on the ground in front of me, still slashing with its claws and snapping.

Elio brought the rifle to his shoulder, aimed carefully between the eyes that glared at him in defiance, and pulled the trigger.

The grumbler twitched once and lay still. Its eyes were still open, staring at death with a decided fury.

"What was *that* all about?" I said. I could hardly hear over the sound of blood pounding in my head.

"I don't know. I've never seen one do that before." Elio still hadn't lowered the rifle, as if he were waiting for the grumbler to move again. His face was paler than usual, with a prominent red flush on the cheeks. I could see something dark huddled on the ground where the grumbler had been.

"Elio! There she is!"

I ran.

Euzhan was unconcious, lying on her back. "Oh, God," Elio whispered. I knew he was staring at the girl's blouse—it was torn, and blood darkened the cloth just above the navel. I knelt beside her and gently pulled up the shirt.

The grumbler's claws had laid Euzhan open. The gash was long and deep, exposing the fatty tissue and tearing into muscles, though thankfully it looked like the abdominal wall was intact. "Damn . . ." I muttered; then, for Elio's benefit: "It looks worse than it is." Euzhan had lost blood; it pooled dark and thick under her, but the wound was seeping rather than pulsing—no arterial loss. I allowed myself a quick sigh of relief: we could get her back to the clinic, then. Still, she'd lost a lot of blood, and the unconsciousness worried me.

I quickly probed the rest of body, checked the limbs, felt under the head. There was a swelling bump on the back of her skull, but other than that and the growler's wound, Euzhan appeared unharmed. As I tucked the girl's blouse back down, her eyes fluttered open. "Anaïs? Elio? I'm awful cold," Euzhan said sleepily. I smiled at her and stroked her cheek.

"I'm sure you are, love. Here, Anaïs has a sweater you can wear until we get you back." Euzhan nodded, then her eyes closed again. "Euzhan," I said quietly but firmly. "Euz, no sleeping now, love. I need you to stay awake and talk to me. Do you understand?"

Long eyelashes lifted slightly. Her breath deepened. "Am I going to die, Ana?"

I could barely answer through the sudden constriction in

my throat. "No, honey. You're not going to die. I promise. You lay there very still now, and keep those pretty eyes open. I need to talk to your *da* a second."

"I think we found her in time," I told Elio, covering Euzhan in my sweater. "But we need to move quickly. We have to get her back to the clinic where I can work on her. What I've got in the kit isn't going to do it. Go get us some help. We'll need a stretcher."

Elio didn't move. He stood there, staring down at Euzhan, his eyes wide with worry and fear. I prodded him. "I need you to go now, El. Don't worry—she'll be fine."

That shook him out of his stasis. Elio nodded and broke into a run, calling back to the settlement as he ran.

She'll be fine, I'd promised him.

I hoped I was going to be right.

CONTEXT:
Faika Koda-Shimmura

"THEY FOUND EUZHAN, GEEMA TOZO." FAIKA WAS still breathing hard from the exertion of climbing the stairs to Geema's loft in the tower. Faika, who'd been part of those searching near the old landing pad, had been with the group that helped bring Euzhan back to the Rock. She was still buzzing from the excitement.

Tozo lifted her head from the fragrant incense burning in an ornate holder set on top of a small Miccail stele Tozo used as an altar, but she didn't turn toward Faika. She kept her hands folded together in meditation, her breathing calm and centered, a distinct contrast to Faika's gasping. Several polished stones were set around the base of the stele. Tozo reached out and touched them, each in turn. "I know," she said. "I felt it. She's hurt but alive."

Geema Tozo's tone indicated that her words were more statement than question. But then Tozo always said that she actually talked with the *kami* that lived around the Rock. There were others who were devout, but Tozo lived *Njia*— The Way—as no one else did; at least it seemed so to Faika's somewhat prejudiced eyes. Faika was sure that when the current Kiria, Tami, chose a replacement this coming LastDay, Tozo would be the next Kiria. Faika was a little disappointed that her news wasn't quite the bombshell she'd hoped, but she was also proud that her Geema could know it, just from listening to the voices in her head.

"They took her to the clinic?" Tozo asked. She turned finally. Her face was a network of fine wrinkles, like a piece of paper folded over and over, and the eyes were the brown of nuts in the late fall. Both her hands (and her feet, as Faika knew from seeing Tozo in the Baths) were webbed with a thin sheath of pink skin between the fingers, and the lower half of her face was squeezed together in a faint suggestion of a snout. Faika thought Tozo looked like some ancient and beautiful aquatic animal.

"*Hai*," Faika answered. "Anaïs and Elio found her, and Anaïs was taking care of her. There was a lot of blood. A grumbler—"

"I know," Geema Tozo said, and Faika nodded. The incense hissed and sputtered behind Tozo, and she closed her eyes briefly. "There's trouble coming, Faika. I can feel it. The *kami*, the old ones, are stirring. Anaïs . . ." Tozo sighed.

"Come help me up, child," she said to Faika, extending her hand. "Let's go downstairs. I can smell Giosha's dinner even through the incense, and my stomach's rumbling. What's done is done, and we can't change it."

INTERLUDE:
KaiSa

KAISA STOOD ON THE BLUFF THAT OVERLOOKED THE sea. As Kai expected, BieTe was there: the Old-Father for the local settlement. He was squatting in front of the *nasituda*, the Telling Stone. In one hand he held a bronze drill, in the other was the chipped bulk of his favorite hammerstone. The salt-laden wind ruffled his hair. The sound of his carving was loud in the morning stillness, each note brilliant and distinct against the rhythmic background of surf, separated by a moment of aching silence and anticipation: *T-ching. T-ching. T-ching.* Bie was wearing his ceremonial red robes: the *shangaa*. Flakes of the translucent pale crystal of the stone had settled in his lap, like spring petals on a field of blood.

Bie must have heard Kai's approach, but he gave no sign. KaiSa sniffed the air, fragrant with brine and crisp with the promise of new snow, and opened ker mouth wide to taste all the glorious scents. "The wind is calling the new season, OldFather," ke said. "Can't you hear it?"

Bie grimaced. He snorted once and bared the hard-ridged gums of his mouth in a wide negative without turning around. *T-ching. T-ching.* "I hear—" *T-ching.* "—nothing."

Bie put down the hammerstone. He blew across the carving so that milky rock powder curled into the breeze and away. He stood, lifted his *shangaa* above the hips and carefully urinated on the column. Afterward, he wiped away the excess with the robe's hem to join the multitude of other stains there, a ceremonial three strokes of the cloth: for earth, for air, for water. Where Bie's urine had splashed onto the newly-carved surface, the almost colorless rock slowly darkened to a vivid yellow-orange, highlighting the new figures and matching the other carvings on the stele, while the weathered, oxidized surface of the Telling Stone remained frosty white. Kai could read the hieroglyphic, pictorial writing: the glyph of the OldFather, the wavy line that indicated birth, the glyph of other-self, the slash that made the second figure a diminutive, and the dark circle of femininity.

I, BieTe, declare here that a new female child has been born.

"I decided to take a walk after the birth," Kai said. "Has MasTa named the child?"

"I've not heard her name. Mas said that VeiSaTi hasn't spoken it yet."

Where there should have been joy, there was instead a hue of sullenness in Bie's voice, and Kai knew that ke was the cause of it. Kai nodded. "Mas will give the child strength." Then, because ke knew that it would prick the aloofness that Bie had gathered around himself, ke added: "Mas is a delight, very beautiful and very wise. We're both lucky to enjoy her love."

Kai could see Bie's throat pulse at that. "I know what you're thinking," Bie said. "I know why you came to find me. You're telling me you want to go." Bie's gaze, as brown as the stones of the sea-bluff, drifted away from Kai down

25

to the surging waves, then back. "But I don't want you to leave."

Kai knew this was coming, though ke had hoped that this time it would be different, that for once ker love and affection might emerge unmarred and free of the memory of anger or violence. But—as with most times before—ker wish would not be granted. Kai's mentor JaqSaTu had warned ker of this years ago, when Kai was still bright with the optimism of the newly initiated.

Jaq handed Kai a paglanut and closed ker fingers around the thin, chitinous shell. "Each time, you will think your hands have been filled with joy, but you will be wrong." Jaq told ker. Ke increased the pressure on Kai's fingers, until the ripe nut had broken open. The scent of corruption filled Kai's nostrils—all but one small kernel of the nut was rotten. Jaq plucked the good kernel from the mess in Kai's hand and held it in front of ker. "You will learn to find the nourishment among the rot, or you will starve."

Kai looked at the weathered, handsome face of Bie Old-Father, at the creased, folded lines ke had caressed and licked in the heat of lovemaking, and ke saw that Bie's love had hardened and grown brittle.

"I'm only a servant of VeiSaTi," Kai answered softly and hopelessly. "BieTe, please, you don't want to anger a god. I love you. My time here has been wonderful and for that I wish I could stay, but I have my duty." Kai indicated ker own *shangaa*, dyed bright yellow from the juices of pagla root: VeiSaTi's favored plant, that the god had spewed upon the earth so that all could eat. "Mas has her child. HajXa and CerXa will deliver soon. I have given your people all that a Sa can."

A cloud, driven fast by the high wind, cloaked the sun for a moment before passing. The *brais*, the Sun's Eye high on their foreheads, registered the quick shift in light and both of them crouched instinctively as if ready to flee from a diving wingclaw. Kai watched the scudding clouds pass overhead for a few seconds, then glanced back at Bie. His face was as hard as the Telling Stone, as unyielding as the bronze drill he'd used to carve it. "You should not leave yet," he said. "Tonight, we will give thanks to VeiSaTi for the new child. You must be here for the ceremony."

"And then I may go?"

BieTe didn't answer. He was staring at the Telling Stone, and whatever he was thinking was hidden. He picked up the hammerstone from the ground and hefted it in his hand. "You'll walk back with me now," he said.

There didn't seem to be an answer to that.

BieTe left Kai almost as soon as they reached the village, going off to examine the pagla fields. His mood had not improved during their walk, and Kai was glad to be left alone. Ke went into the TaTe dwelling. "MasTa?" ke called softly.

"In here, Kai."

Kai slid behind the curtain that screened the sleeping quarters. "I'm so happy for you," ke said. "May . . . may I see?"

MasTa smiled at Kai. Almost shyly, she unfastened the closures of her *shangaa*, exposing her body. Sliding a hand down her abdomen, she opened the muscular lip of her youngpouch and let Kai peer inside. The infant, eyes still closed and entirely hairless, not much longer than Kai's hand, was curled at the bottom of the snug pocket of Mas's flesh. Her mouth was fastened on one of Mas's nipples, and her sides heaved in the rapid breath of the newborn as she suckled. "She's beautiful, isn't she?" Mas whispered.

Kai reached into the warm youngpouch and stroked the child gently, enjoying the shiver ker daughter gave as ke touched her. "Yes," ke sighed. "She's beautiful, yes." Reluctantly, ke took ker hand from the pouch and stroked Mas's cheek with fingers still fragrant and moist from the infant. Ke fondled the tight, red-gold curls down her neck. "After all, she's yours."

Mas laughed at that. She let the youngpouch close, fastened her *shangaa* again, and reclined on the pillows supporting her back.

"Tired?" Kai asked.

"A little."

"Then rest. I'll leave you alone to sleep."

"No, Kai," Mas said. "Please."

"All right." Kai settled back into the nest of pillows piled in the sleeping room. For what seemed a long time, ke simply watched Mas, enjoying the way the sunlight burned in her hair and burnished the pattern of her skin as it came through the open window of the residence. As ke gazed at her, ke could feel that part of ker did indeed want to stay, to watch this child of kers and Mas and Bie grow, to see her weaned from the pouch when the weather turned warm again, to listen to her first words and watch the reflection of kerself in the new child's eyes. Mas must have guessed what ke was thinking, for she spoke from her repose, her eyes closed against the sun.

"I know that you must leave. I understand."

"I'm glad someone does." Kai said it as unharshly as ke could.

Her large eyes opened, that surprising flecked blue-green that was so rare and so striking. A knitted covering tied around her head shielded her *brais* from the afternoon glare. "Bei loves you as much as I do. Maybe more. He told me once that you have made him feel whole. He's afraid, Kai. That's all. He's afraid that when you leave, you'll take part of him with you."

"I'm leaving behind far more of myself than I'm taking," Kai answered. Ke stroked ker own belly for emphasis. "I'm leaving behind your child, and Haj and Cer's. I've given you VieSaTi's gift. Now I must give it to others."

"Why?" Mas asked. Her bright, colorful eyes searched ker face.

"Now you sound like BieTe," Kai said, and softened ker words with a laugh. "I'm a Sa. I've been taught the ways of the Sa. After I leave, other Sa will come here."

"And if they don't?"

"You'll still have children," Kai said, answering the question ke knew was hidden behind her words. "With BieTe alone."

"I had three other children before you came," Mas said. "Only one lived, a male. Bie sent him away." Mas averted her eyes, not looking at Kai, and her skin went pale with sadness. Kai's own brown arms whitened in sympathy. "The others . . . well, my first one lived only a season. The other, a female, was wild and strange. She never learned to talk, and she was fey. She would attack me when I was sleeping, or kill the little meatfurs just to watch them die. A wingclaw took her finally, or that's what BieTe told me. I . . . I found it hard to mourn."

"Mas—" Kai leaned forward to hold Mas, but she bared her gums.

"Don't," Mas said. "Don't, because you'll only make me miss you more. You'll only make it harder." Mas brought her legs up. Arms around knees, she hugged herself, as if she was cold. "The sun's almost down. Bie will be starting the ceremony soon. I need to sleep, so I'll be ready."

"I understand," Kai said. . . . *the smell of the rotten paglanut, breaking in ker hand* . . . "I understand. I . . . I'll see you then."

Reaching forward, ke patted the youngpouch through her *shangaa*. "Sleep for a bit. Rest." Ke rose and went to the door of the chamber. Stopping there, ke looked back at her, at the way she watched ker.

"I love you, MasTa," ke said.

She didn't smile. "I love you also," she said. "But I wish I didn't."

VOICE:

Anaïs Koda-Levin the Younger

"CLEAN EUZHAN UP AND GET HER INTO A BED," I told our assistants. "She should be waking up in about ten minutes or so—let Hui or me know if she isn't responding. Hayat, we're going to need more whole blood, so after you get Euzhan comfortable, round up three or four of her mi, da, or sibs and get some. Ama, if you'd take charge of the cleanup. . . ."

As they rolled Euzhan away to one of the clinic rooms, I went to the sink and scrubbed the blood and thorn-vine sap from my hands. Hui shuffled alongside me, using the other spigot. When I'd finished drying, I leaned back against the cool wall, frowning through the weariness. Hui shook water from his hands, toweled dry, and tossed the towel in the hamper as I watched his slow, deliberate motions.

I knew what he was going to say before he said it. We'd been working together for that long.

"You did what you could, Anaïs. Now we wait and see." Hui stretched out one ancient forefinger and tapped me gently under the chin. "We can't do anything else for her right now."

"Hui, you saw how close that was." I shivered at the memory. "The descending oblique was nearly severed. If those claws had dug in a few millimeters deeper . . ."

"But they didn't, and Euzhan will fight off infections or she won't, and we'll do what we need to do, whatever happens. Ana, what did I tell you when you first started studying with me?"

That finally coaxed a wan, grudging smile through the fog of exhaustion. "Let's see . . . 'Is that expression normal for you, child, or does catatonia run in your family?' Or how about: 'I'm afraid to let you handle a broom, much less a scalpel.' Oh, and I couldn't forget: 'I'm sure you have *some* qualities, or they wouldn't have sent you to me. Let's hope we manage to stumble across them before you kill someone.' " I shrugged. "Those were some of the milder quotes that I can recall. I was sure you were going to send me home and tell my family that I was hopeless."

Hui snorted. The wrinkles around his almond eyes pressed deeper as he grinned. "I very nearly did. You have a good memory, Anaïs, but a selective one. You've forgotten the one important thing."

"And what was that?"

I could see myself in his dark eyes. I could also see the filmy white of the cataracts that were slowly and irrevocably destroying his vision. Not that Hui would ever complain or even admit it, though I'd noticed—silently—that he'd passed nearly all the surgery to me in the past year. "I once told you that no matter how good you were, you are only a tool in the hands of whatever *kami* inhabits this place. You're a very good tool, Anaïs, and you have done all the work that you're capable of doing for the moment. Be satisfied. Besides, it's no longer you that I'm hounding; it's Hayat and Ama." His forefinger tucked me under my chin once more. "Come on, child."

"I'm not a child, Hui."

"No, you're not. But I still get to call you that. Come on. Dominic will be going apoplectic by now, and we can't afford that at his age."

Hui was right about that. As we came through the doors into the clinic's waiting room, half of the Allen-Shimmura family surged forward toward us, with patriarch Dominic at the fore. I avoided him and tried to give a reassuring smile to Andrea and Hizo, Ochiba's other two children, both of them standing close behind the bulwark of Dominic.

"Well?" the old man snapped. He was as thin as a thornvine stalk, and as prickly. His narrow lips were surrounded by furrows, his black, almost pupilless eyes were overhung by folds. His voice had gone wavery with his great age, but was no less edged for that. The grandson of Rebecca Allen, he was one of the few people left of the third generation. My Geema Anaïs once described Dominic as being like a strip of preserved meat: too salty and dry to decay, and too tough to be worth chewing. "How is she?"

I noticed immediately that Dominic was looking at Hui rather than me, even though the patriarch was aware that I had been in charge of the surgery.

Hui noticed it as well. He had on what I thought of as his "go ahead and make your mistake" face, the expressionless and noncommittal mask he wore when one of his students would look up quizzically while making an incision. Hui leaned against the wall and folded his arms over his chest. "Anaïs did the surgery. All I did was assist." He said nothing more. The silence stretched for several seconds before Dominic finally sniffed, glared at Hui angrily, and turned his sour gaze on me.

"Well?" he snapped once more.

"Euzhan's fine for the moment." I found it easier, after the first few words, to put my regard elsewhere. I let my gaze wander, making eye contact with Euzhan's *mi* and *da*, and favoring Elio with a transient smile. "We cleaned up the wound—nothing vital was injured, but we had to repair more muscle damage than I like. She's going to need therapy afterward, but we'll work out some schedule for that later. Actually, she should be waking up in a few minutes. She's going to be groggy and in some pain—Hui's already prepared painkillers for her. Dominic, I'll leave it to you. It would be good if there were some familiar faces around her when she comes out of the anesthetic. But no more than two of you, please."

Dominic's grim expression relaxed slightly. He allowed her a fleeting, brief half-smile. "Stefani, come with me. Ka-Wai, take the rest of the Family home and get them fed. Tell Bui that he's been damned lucky. Damned lucky." With those abrupt commands, he left the room with his shuffling, slow walk that still somehow managed to appear regal. The rest of the family murmured for a few minutes, thanking me and Hui, and then drifted from the clinic into the cold night. Eventually, only Hui and myself were left.

"He really doesn't like you, does he?"

That garnered a laugh that might have come from the eastern desert. "You noticed."

"So what's the problem between the two of you?"

"What do you *think* is the problem?" I answered shortly, hating the bitterness in my voice but unable to keep the emotion out. "He knows about me, just like you do. 'Poor An-

31

aïs—from what I've heard, there's no chance *she's* going to have children. And what about her and Ochiba? Don't you think they were just a little too *close* . . .' ''

I stopped. Blinked. I was staring at the wall behind Hui, at the pencil and charcoal sketch of Ochiba I'd done years before, while she was pregnant with Euz. Hui had taken the piece without my knowledge from the desk drawer into which I'd stuffed it. He'd matted and framed the drawing, then placed it on the clinic wall as a Naming Day gift. *Don't ever be timid about your talents*, he'd said. *Gifts like yours are too rare on this world to be hidden. And don't hide your feelings, either, girl—those are also far too rare.*

Well, Hui, that's a wonderfully idealistic statement, but it doesn't fit into this world we've made for ourselves. There are some things that are better left stuffed in the drawer.

"You can't let him intimidate you," Hui said. "I don't care how old and venerated he is . . ."

"That's *khudda*, Hui, and we both know it. What Dominic says, goes—and that's true even for the other Families, too. With the exception of Vladimir Allen-Levin and Tozo Koda-Shimmura, Dominic's the Eldest, and poor Vlad's so senile—" I cut off my own words with a motion of my hands. "Hui, we don't need to talk about this. Not now. It's really not important. Euzhan should be coming around about now. Why don't you go back and check on her? Dominic would be more comfortable if you were there."

He didn't protest, which surprised me. Hui touched my shoulder gently, pressing once, then turned. I sat in one of the ornate clinic chairs (carved by my *da* Derek when Hui had declared me "graduated" from his tutelage) and leaned my head back, closing my eyes. I stayed there for several minutes until I heard Dominic and Hui's voices, sounding as if they were heading back into the lobby. I didn't feel like another round of frigid exchanges with Dominic, so I rose and walked into the coldroom lab.

It was warmer there than in his presence.

I set the pot of thorn-vine sap over the bunsen to heat, put on a clean gown and mask, then scrubbed my hands. I plunged still-wet hands into the warm, syrupy goo, then raised them so that the brown-gold, viscous liquid coated my fingers and hands, turning my hands until the sap covered the skin evenly. After it dried, I pulled out the gurney holding the Miccail body. I stared at it (*him? her?*) for a time, not really wanting to work but feeling a need to do something. I straightened the legs, examining again the odd, inexplicable genitalia.

"Ana?"

The voice sent quick shivers through me. I felt my cheeks flush, almost guiltily, and I turned. "El. *Komban wa*. I thought you'd left."

"Went out to get some air." Elio stepped into the room. "I, ummm, just wanted to thank you. For Euzhan. Dominic, he . . . he should have told you himself, but I know that he's grateful, too."

"He didn't need to thank me. Besides, Euzhan's rather special to me, too."

"I know. But Dominic still shouldn't have been so rude." Not many in his Family dared to criticize Dominic to anyone else; the fact that Elio did dampened some of my irritation with him. Elio tugged at the jacket he wore, pulling down the cloth sleeves. "So that's your bogman, huh? Elena told me about how she found it. Pretty ugly."

"Give the poor Miccail a break. You'd be ugly too if you sat in a peat bog for a couple thousand years. It's hell on the complexion."

Elio grinned at that. "Yeah, I guess so. Might give me some color, though. Couldn't hurt." He leaned forward for a closer look, and I felt myself interposing between Elio and the Miccail, as I had earlier. Elio didn't seem to notice. After another glance at the body, he moved away.

"You planning to become the next Gabriela?" he asked, then blushed, as he realized that he'd given the words an undercurrent he hadn't intended. "I mean, you work too much, Ana," he said quickly. "You're always here. When's the last time you did a drawing or went to a Gather?"

Ages. The answer surfaced in my mind. *Far too long.*

But I couldn't say any of the words. I only shrugged. "Elio, if I'm going to get anything done . . ."

"Sorry," he said reflexively. "I understand."

He didn't leave. He watched as I worked patiently on the hand I'd uncovered earlier, straightening the fingers and the ragged webbing between them. When, some time later, he cleared his throat, I looked up.

"Listen," Elio said. "When you're done here, do you have plans? I thought, well, we haven't been together in a long time . . ."

Two years. I haven't been with anyone in almost two years. "El . . ." The unexpected proposition sent guilty thoughts

33

skittering through my mind. *You're the last of the Koda-Levin line, unless Mam Shawna gets pregnant again—and she's already showing signs of menopause. If they heard that you turned someone down, after all this time....*

And then: *Ochiba would tell you to do it. You know she would.*

"El, I just don't know."

"Think about it," he said. Muscles relaxed in his pale face; he gave a faint smile. "It's not because of today," he told me. "Just in case that's what you're thinking."

It had been, of course. Anaïs: the charity fuck. "No. Of course not."

"That's good. It's just that I haven't seen you much recently with all your work, and being with you today, even under the circumstances, I'd forgotten how much I enjoyed talking with you."

I wondered whether he'd also forgotten the miserable failure the last time we tried to make love.

"I'm sorry, Ana. I don't know what the problem is," he said, even though we both knew well enough. I kissed away the apology, pretending that I didn't care. I think I even managed to smile.

I was fairly certain he'd only asked me as a favor to Ochiba.

"No," I said. "It's me. Not you. It's fine. Don't worry about it." But we both had, and Elio had slipped away from my bed as quickly as he could, pleading an early morning appointment we both knew was a fiction.

I had spent the rest of the night alternating between tears and anger.

"Elio, I'm afraid tonight ... well, it wouldn't be good. I'm tired, and I was planning to stay here, just in case Euz needs some help." I lifted my sap-stained fingers. "I was hoping to get some of this work done, also." The excuses came too fast and probably one too many; I saw in his face that he realized it too. Guilt warred with anxiety over the battleground of conscience and won an entirely Pyrrhic victory.

"El, I'm sorry. It's just that I. . . ." I stopped, deciding that there wasn't much use in trying to explain what I didn't fully understand myself. And there was the guilt of turning down an opportunity when I'd yet to become pregnant and those chances seemed to come less and less. "Anyway, I can do this some other time, and chances are Euz is going to be fine. Give me a bit, just to make sure that Euz is stabilized and to clean up again ..."

I wasn't sure what it was I saw in his face. "Sure. Good. I'll come by then. At your Family compound?"

I nodded. We were being so polite now. "I'll meet you in the common room."

"Okay. See you then." Awkwardly, he leaned over and kissed me. His lips were dry, the touch almost brotherly, but I enjoyed it. Before I could pull his head down to me again, he straightened. Cold air replaced his warmth. "See you about NinthHour?"

"That would be fine."

After Elio had left, I halfheartedly cleaned some of the clinging peat from the folds of the Miccail's face. "What were you like?" I asked the misshapen, crushed flesh. "And do you have any advice for someone who isn't sure she just made the right decision?"

The ancient body didn't answer. I sighed and went to the sink to scrub my hands.

CONTEXT:
Ama Martinez-Santos

THERE WERE TIMES THAT AMA REGRETTED HAVING been apprenticed to Hui. However, Geema Kyra had given her no choice in the matter, and an elder's word was always law. Hui was never satisfied—no matter how fast Ama moved or how well she did something, Hui always pointed out how she could have done it faster, better, or more effectively another way. Hayat was given the same harsh treatment, but that didn't lessen the impact. Ama was fairly certain that it was not possible to satisfy Hui.

And then there was Anaïs. She was just fucking weird. A good doctor, yes, and at least she'd give out a crumb of praise now and then, but she was . . . strange. The way she used all her free time lately examining that nasty body Elena had found. . . .

Anaïs had told her to put the Miccail's body back in the coldroom. Ama threw a sheet over the thing before she moved it—she couldn't stand to see the empty bag of alien flesh; she hated the earthy smell of the creature and the leathery, unnatural feel of its skin. The thing was creepy—

it didn't surprise Ama that it had been killed.

Ama had heard her *mi* and *da* talking—there was a nasty rumor that Anaïs and Ochiba had been lovers, though as Thandi always pointed out, Ochiba had died after giving birth to Euzhan, so if Anaïs was a *rezu*, then it hadn't stopped Ochiba from sleeping with men. Ama sometimes wondered what it would be like, making love to another woman. . . .

She shivered. That was a sure way to be shunned. That's what had happened to Gabriela—the second and final time she had been shunned.

Ama wheeled the gurney into the coldroom. She slid the bog body into its niche and hurried out of the room.

She didn't look back as she turned out the lights. Afterward, she scrubbed her hands at the sink in the autopsy room, twice, even though she knew that would make her late changing Euzhan's dressings and Hui would yell at her again.

VOICE:
Anaïs Koda-Levin the Younger

MOST OF MY EROTIC MEMORIES DON'T INVOLVE fucking. I suppose the wet piston mechanics of sex never aroused me as much as other things. Smaller things. More intimate things.

I can close my eyes and remember . . .

. . . at one of the Gathers, dancing the whirlwind with a few dozen others out on the old shuttle landing pad, when I noticed Marshall Koda-Schmidt watching from the side in front of the bonfire. I was twelve and just a half year past my menarche, which had come much later than I'd wanted. Marsh was older, much older—one of the fifth generation—and in my eyes appeared to be far more sensual than the gawky boys my own age. He stood there, trying to keep up a conversation with Hui over the racing, furious beat of the musicians. I kept watching him as I danced, laughing as I turned and pranced through the intricate steps, and I noticed we both had the same stone on our necklaces. I thought that an omen. During one of the partner changes, there was suddenly an open space between us, and Marsh looked up from his conversation out to the dance. His gaze snared mine; he smiled. At that moment, one of the logs fell and the bonfire erupted into a coiling, writhing column of bright fireflies behind him. I was caught in those eyes, those older and, I thought, wiser eyes. I couldn't take my eyes off him, and every time I looked, it seemed he was also watching me. I smiled; he laughed and applauded me. I felt flushed and giddy, and I laughed louder and danced harder, sweating with the energy even in the night cold, stealing glances toward Marshall. We smiled together, and as I danced, I felt I was dancing with him. For him. To him . . .

. . . Chi-Wa's fingers stroking my bare shoulder and running down my arm, my skin almost electric under his gentle touch, inhaling his warm, sweet breath as we lay there with our mouths open, so close, so close but not quite touching. When his hand had traversed the slope of my arm and slipped off to tumble into the nest of my lap, our lips finally met at the same time . . .

. . . sitting with Ochiba at the preparation table in the Allen-Shimmura compound's huge kitchen, peeling sweetmelon for the dessert. We were just talking, not saying anything important really, but the words didn't matter. I was intoxicated by the sound of Ochiba's voice, drunk on her laugh and the smell of her hair and the sheer familiar presence of her. I'd just finished cutting up one of the melons and Ochiba reached across me to steal a piece. She sucked the fruit into her mouth in exaggerated mock triumph while the orange-red juice ran down her chin in twin streaks. For some reason, that struck us both as hilarious, and we burst into helpless laughter. Ochiba reached over and we hugged, and I was so aware of her body, of the feel of her against me, of how soft her breasts seemed under the faux-cotton blouse. Then the confusion hit, making me blush as I realized that what I was feeling was something I wasn't prepared or expecting to feel, and knowing by the way Ochiba's embrace suddenly tightened around me that she was feeling it as well, and was just as frightened and awed by the emotions as I was . . .

Moments. Those fleeting seconds when the sexual tension is highest, when you're alone in a universe of two where nothing else can intrude.

Of course, then reality usually hits. After the Gather, I

turned down two other offers of company and went back to my compound alone, with one last smile for Marshall. I left my outer door open, certain that Marshall would come to me that night, but he never did.

Chi-Wa was so involved in his own arousal and pleasure that I quickly realized that I was nothing more than another anonymous vessel for his glorious seed.

And Ochiba, the only one of them who was truly important to me . . . well, in another year she was dead.

Tonight, I was keeping reality away with a glass of *da* Joel's pale ale, and trying to stop thinking that it was late and that I wished I'd just told Elio no. There was no one else in the common room; Ché, Joel, and Derek had all grinned, made quick excuses, and left when I'd mentioned that I was staying up because Elio was coming over. I requested the room to play me Gabriela's *Reflections on the Miccail* and leaned back in the chair as the first pulsing chords of the dobra sounded. The chair was one of *da* Jason's creations, with a padded, luxurious curved back that seemed to wrap and enfold you—very womblike, very private: I'd never known Jason, who had died when I was very young, but his was my favorite listening chair. The family pet, a verrechat Derek had rescued from a spring flood five years before, came up and curled into my lap. I stroked the velvety, nearly transparent skin of the creature, and watched its heart pulse behind the glassy muscles and porcelain ribs. I shut my eyes and let the rising drone of the music carry me somewhere else. I barely heard the clock chiming NinthHour.

"I never thought Gabriela was much of a composer."

"She'd have agreed with you," I answered. "And I think you're both wrong. She was a fine composer; the problem was that she just wasn't much of a musician. You have to imagine what she was trying to play rather than what actually came out. Hello, Elio."

I told the room to lower the music and pulled the chair back up. The verrechat glared at me in annoyance and went off in search of a more stable resting place. Elio gave me an uncertain smile. "You looked so comfortable, I almost didn't want to interrupt."

"Sorry. Music's my meditation. I spend more time here than's good for me."

He nodded. I nodded back. Great conversationalists, both of us. I should have kept the music up. At least we could have both pretended to be listening to it. "Any change in

Euzhan?" he asked at last, just as the silence was threatening to swallow us. I hurried into the opening, grateful.

"When I left, she was sleeping. Hui's keeping her doped up right now. When I left, Dominic was still there, but Hui was trying to convince him that camping out in the clinic wasn't going to help. I'm not sure he was making much progress."

"Geeda Dominic can be pretty strong-willed."

"Uh-huh. And water can be pretty wet."

Elio grinned. The grin faded slowly, and he was just Elio again. We both looked at each other. "Ummm," he began.

If you're going through with this, then do it, I told myself. "Elio, let's go to my room," I said, trying to make it sound like something other than "And get this over with." I was rewarded with a faint smile, so maybe Elio wasn't as reluctant as I'd thought. I'd been planning to let him back out now, if that's what he wanted, figuring that if this *was* simply a guilt fuck, we were both better off without it—for most women I knew, sex simply for the sake of sex was something you did the first year or two after menarche. By then, you'd gone through most of the available or interested males on Mictlan. In my case, that hadn't been too many, not after the first time around. Since then, with one glorious and forbidden exception, the only regular liason I've had has been with Hui's speculum and some cold semen, once a month.

Even that hasn't worked out.

All that was long ago. Forget it. The voice wasn't entirely convincing, but I held out my hand, and Elio took the invitation without hesitating. Tugging on my fingers, he pulled me toward him, and this time he kissed me. There was a hunger in the kiss this time, and I found parts of me awakening that I thought had been dead.

I suddenly wanted this to work, and that increased my nervousness. I wondered if he could tell how scared I was.

Elio either sensed that fright, or he'd learned a lot since the last time. In my admittedly noncomprehensive experience, men tended to go straight for the kill, shedding clothes on the way so they didn't snag them on rampant erections. Maybe that was just youthful exuberance, but I'd spent many postcoital hours crying, believing that the quickness and remoteness was because they wanted to get the deed done as fast as possible. Because it was *me*. 'Just doing my duty, ma'am. Have to make sure that we increase the population, after all. Nothing personal.'

Except that sex is always personal and always intimate, no matter what the reasons for it might be. In the midst, I might look up to see my partner's eyes closed, a look almost of pain on his face as he thrust into me, and I knew he was gone, lost in imagined couplings with someone else.

Not *with* me. Never *with* me. Never together.

Elio pulled away. I breathed, watching him. He was still here. "This way," I said, and led him off.

I'd done some quick housekeeping before he'd come, and the room actually looked halfway neat except for the mirror, as always draped in clothing. Through the folds I caught a reflection of someone who looked like me, her face twisted in uncertain lines.

When I closed the door and turned, Elio was closer to me than I expected, and I started, leaning back against the jamb. He touched my cheek, stroked my hair. As his hand cupped the back of my head, he pulled me into him, his arms going around me. Neither of us had said anything. I leaned my head against his shoulder. He continued to stroke my hair.

I wondered what he was thinking, and when I turned my head up to look, he kissed me again: gently, warmly, his lips slightly parted. This time the kiss was longer, more demanding, and I found myself opening my mouth to him, pulling his head down even further. His hands dropped from my shoulders; his fingers teased my nipples through my blouse, and they responded to his touch, ripening and making me shudder.

When we finally broke apart again, his pale eyes searched mine with soft questions. I reached behind us and touched the wall plate, the lights gliding down into darkness as I did so. "I can't see, Ana."

"You don't need to."

"I'd like to look at you."

"Elio . . ."

A pause. Silence. He waited.

Biting my lower lip, I touched the plate again, letting the lights rise to a golden dimness. I stepped deliberately away from him. Standing in front of my bed, I undid the buttons of my blouse, of my pants. I held the clothes to me, hugging myself, then took a breath and let them fall to the floor. I stood before Elio, defiantly naked. I shivered, though the room wasn't cold.

I knew what he was seeing. I might keep my mirror covered, but I knew.

40

Under a wide-featured face, he saw a woman's body, with small breasts and flared hips. Extending below the triangle of pubic hair, though, there was something wrong, something that didn't belong: a hint of curved flesh.

An elongated, enlarged clitoris, Hui had told my mother, who noticed it at birth: a paranoid, detailed examination of every newborn child is Mictlan's birthright. *A slight to moderate hermaphrodism. I doubt that it's anything to stop her from reaching her Naming. Everything else is female and normal. She may never notice.*

Maybe Hui would have been right had everything stayed as it was when I was a child. I certainly paid no attention to my small deformity, nor did anyone else. I didn't seem much different from the other little girls I saw. After menarche, though. . . . My periods from the beginning were so slight as to be nearly unnoticeable and the pale spottings weren't at all like the dark menstrual flow of the other women. I also began to notice how sensitive I was there, how the oversized nub of flesh had begun to change, to swell until the growth protruded well past my labial folds, pushing them apart before ducking under the taut and distended clitoral hood.

Over the years, even after menarche, the change continued. The last time I glanced at a mirror, I thought I looked like an effeminate and not particularly pretty young man with his penis tucked between his legs, pretending to be a woman.

Elio's gaze never drifted that low. I noticed, and tried to pretend that it didn't matter. I wanted to believe that it didn't matter. He took a step toward me. He cupped my breasts in his hands, his skin so pale against mine. I fumbled with his shirt, finally getting it open and sliding it down his shoulders. Elio was thin, though his waist rounded gently at the belt line.

His skin was very warm.

I pulled him into bed on top of me.

. . . and sometime later . . .

. . . later . . .

No, I'm sorry. I can't say. I won't say.

41

JOURNAL ENTRY:
Gabriela Rusack

I WAS A SLOW LEARNER WHEN IT CAME TO THE difference between love and sex. Oh, I knew that people could enjoy sex without being in love with the person they're with at the moment. God knows I experienced that myself often enough ... and often enough kicked myself in the morning for paying attention to whining hormones.

As I grew older, I slowly realized that the reverse was also a possibility—I could be in love with someone and *not* have sex with them, if that wasn't in the cards. I needed friends more than I needed lovers, and I found that sex can actually destroy love.

Lacina was my college roommate, and my friend. At the time, I was still mainly heterosexual, though I'd already had my first tentative encounters with women. I think Lacina suspected that I was experimenting, but we never really talked about it. I dated guys and slept with some of them, just as she did, so if on rare occasions a girlfriend stayed overnight, she just shrugged and said nothing. One Friday night in my junior year, neither of us had a date. We were drinking cheap wine and watching erotic holos in our apartment, and the wine and the holos had made us both silly and horny. I remember putting my arm around Lacina, playfully, and how sweet her lips were when I finally leaned over to kiss her, and her breathy gasp when I touched her breasts. ... We tumbled into my bed and I made love to her, and showed her how to make love to me. But the next morning, when the wine fumes had cleared. ...

After that night, it was never the same between us. There was a wall inside Lacina that had never been there before, and she flinched if I'd come near her or touch her. I don't know why she was retreated. I don't know what old guilt I'd tapped; afterward, it wasn't a subject on which she'd allow discussion. She pretended that our night together had never happened. She pretended that things were the same as they had been, but they weren't, and we both knew it. At the end of the semester, she moved out.

No, sex and love are basically independent of each other. Not that it matters for me, not anymore. My closest friends are dead, and those here on Mictlan that I thought were friends won't talk to me at all anymore.

No more sex. No more love. I spend my remaining days with the only passion I have left, the only passion allowed me: the cold and dead Miccail.

Now if sex, love, and passion are intricate, varied, and dangerous for us, then the sexuality of the Miccail must have been positively labyrinthian. I can only imagine how convoluted their relationships were, with the midmale sex complicating things. I wonder *how* they loved, and I try to decipher the answer from the few clues left: the stelae, the crumbling ruins, the ancient artifacts. I wonder why this world saw fit to add another sex into the biological mix, but the past holds its secrets too well.

What frightens me is that I'm certain it's important for us to know. The Miccail died only a thousand years ago. With all the artifacts, all the structures they left behind, none of them we've found are any younger than that. From what I've been able to determine, the collapse and decline of the Miccail began another thousand years before their extinction, possibly linked with the rapid disappearance of the midmales, all mention of whom vanish from the stelae at that point. One short millennium later— barely a breath in the life of the world and the Miccail's own long history—and the Miccail were gone, every last one.

It's almost as if Something didn't like them.

And now *we're* here, filling our lungs and our bodies with Mictlan-stuff. Yes, we sampled and tested Mictlan's air, water and soil, let it flow through the assorted filters and gauges until the machines stamped the world with their cold imprimatur. The proportion of gases was within our body tolerances. We could taste the winds of this world and live. Our lungs would move, the oxygen would flow in our blood. But Mictlan is not Earth. The atmosphere of a world holds its own life, and life moves within it.

So we take a deep breath of Mictlan and we bring the alien presence into our lungs because we have no choice. We will slowly become Mictlan. Mictlan will become us.

And the Something that obliterated the Miccail will take a

long look at us: because we are here, because we breathe, because we drink the water and eat the plants.

I wonder if that Something will like us better than it did the Miccail.

INTERLUDE:
KaiSa

AFTER LEAVING MASTA, KAI HAD GONE DIRECTLY TO ker rooms in the TeTa house and packed the few belongings which were truly kers into ker traveling pouch: the well-used grinding stones for herbs and potions which JaqSa had given ker as a parting gift the first time ke'd left the sacred Sa island called AnglSaiye; the parchment book of medicines, written in the private language of the Sa with the sacred inks only the Sa knew how to make; the relic of VeiSaTi which was ker authorization to move freely outside the island, and the tools of sacrifice. Ke left behind the fine anklet BieTe had carved for ker from redstone, with crystalline images of BieTe and MasTa's sacred animals set in the swirling, ornate patterns. Keeping the jewelry would only remind ker of Bie and Mas, and of the children ke had helped to sire here.

It was painful enough to leave. It was even more painful to have to remember.

Kai shouldered ker pack and pushed open the door. A hand pushed ker back inside: NosXe, one of BieTe's adopted sons. Kai stumbled and fell backward, striking ker left shoulder hard on the flagstone floor. "My father said you would try to leave," Nos grumbled. "You don't know how much BieTe and MasTa care for you, KaiSa."

"I know all too well, Nos," Kai answered. "And if I didn't love them in return, I wouldn't be leaving now. Cycles from now, if you become Te, you will understand that. Tell me, Nos, did BieTe or MasTa send you here?"

NosXe didn't have to answer; the grim stubbornness on his face told Kai that the young son of Bie had acted on his own. Kai rubbed ker sore shoulder, knowing it would shame Nos even more to see that he had injured a Sa.

"I thought not. Your Ta and Te know that it's the curse of Sa to always travel, to leave those they love most. Your Ta and Te know that no matter how much they would like me to stay, I cannot. And they cannot make me stay, not without raising the wrath of VeiSaTi Kerself. Is that what you're willing to risk, Nos? Are you willing to defy a god?"

Always before, that had worked. It was the threat of VeiSaTi's anger that kept all Sa safe. Kai thought that the warning, a doctrine taught to all of the CieTiLa—The People—from childhood, had worked now. Still rubbing ker shoulder, ke got to ker feet and started to walk out past the grim-faced Nos, who still blocked the doorway. But as ke brushed past, Nos reached out with a hand and grabbed Kai's shoulder with his right hand, his talons slightly extended.

"No," Nos started to say, but Kai had already reacted.

Kai slapped ker left hand on top of Nos's, claws out. At the same time, ke turned ker hip back and brought ker right arm on top of Nos's, dropping ker weight. Cloth tore on Kai's shoulder, but Nos howled in pain as his wrist was torqued. The much larger Xe collapsed to his knees to escape the pressure, and Kai completed the pin, taking the struggling Nos down to the floor. Holding Nos's wrist with one hand, ke reached out with ker long fingers and pressed them on either side of Nos's neck, just below the ears—closing the arteries. Nos's struggles became weaker; a few seconds later, he went limp.

Kai released the pin. Ke checked to make sure that Nos was still breathing, then stood. "The Sa are also taught to protect those they love," Kai told the unconscious Nos. "That is another thing you must learn. What you love most is also the most dangerous to you."

Ke stepped over Nos. Ke found that now that it was over, ke was shaking from the sudden encounter. The settlement of BieTe and MasTa, which had once seemed so peaceful and welcoming, now frightened ker.

Ke walked away, almost at a run.

BieTe had started the ceremonial fire on the bluff overlooking the sea. KaiSa could see the smear of dark smoke against the twilight sky and the silhouetted figures of BieTe's people as they moved in the preliminary dance of welcome to the new infant. But Kai saw them only in the distance.

45

Ke moved quickly from the settlement into the woods. A few of the Je and Ja saw ker, but—under the bonds of servitude and at the bottom of the social structure of the CieTiLa—there was no chance that any of them would, like NosXe, challenge Kai's right to go where ke wanted, whenever ke wanted. One of the Ja watched as ke moved away from the cluster of wood and stone buildings; Kai knew that the word would get to BieTe, either from the Ja or from NosXe, as soon as he returned to the ceremony, but by that time it would be too late.

I'm sorry that it had to be this way, Kai told the distant image of the fire. *BieTe, MasTa, I'm sorry to miss the ceremony for my own daughter, but in your hearts, you understand. You must understand. You know the laws as well as I do. A Sa must give ker Gift to all CieTiLa, and that means I must hurt the two of you.*

It means I must hurt myself.

KaiSa put ker back to the fire, to BieTe and MasTa, and to ker daughters and sons, and moved into the forest.

Under the canopy of sweet-leaves, the twilight quickly shifted to full night. The wind was from the west, shivering the leaves with its chill and bringing the scent of flowers. A wingclaw called from its night roost high in one of the trees, the creature's ululating whoop raising the hairs on Kai's arms. The phosphorescent mosses on the many-trunked trees framed the darkness, and the double moons were up, Chali just setting, though Quali was well above the horizon in the east, bright enough that ke could almost see the colors of the leaves. The sound of ker feet shushing through the fallen leaves seemed the loudest sound, though the rhythmic *kuh-whump* of the slickskins calling for their mates in a nearby pond was a constant backdrop.

It was tempting to stop, to try and listen to the voice of VeiSaTi in the rustling and chirping of the world, but there was no time for that now.

Kai knew that there was a wayhouse not far distant. Until ke had actually made the decision to leave, ke had given no thought to where ke might go next. Now, ke determined to stop for the rest of the night at the wayhouse. Ke lengthened ker stride, falling into ker quick walking pace.

When Quali had reached the zenith, its silver light painting the edges of the leaves, Kai came upon the High Road and the wayhouse. The High Road was the main artery through the CieTiLa lands, a trail of flagged stone, a path between all the settlements of the CieTiLa designed by the legendary Sa leader NasiSaTu over six *terduva* ago, and completed by ker successors after NasiSaTu's sacrificial death. The various segments of the road were maintained by the Te and Ta of the lands in which they passed, part of the payment for the services of the mendicant Sa order.

The *nasituda* set in front of the wayhouse declared it to be on the border of the territory of GaiTe and CiTa. For the first time since ke had left, Kai felt ker muscles relax fully, releasing a tension ke hadn't even known ke'd been holding. A light from an oil lamp glimmered behind the translucent window, made from the *brais* of one of the huge but slow thunderbeasts: someone else was already in the wayhouse. Kai gave a low, warbling call of greeting as ke approached the building, waited the polite sequence of sixteen slow breaths, then entered, brushing aside the thunderbeast hide door covering.

The wayhouse was built along typical CieTiLa lines: a large common room where travelers could talk and eat; a small kitchen to the left for food preparation and storage, and three tiny sleeping cubicles to the right. The privacy curtain was drawn on one of those, and a Sa poked ker head out as Kai entered, rubbing ker eyes sleepily.

"Kai?"

"AbriSa!"

Abri tumbled out of the low sleeping cubicle and ran to Kai. The two Sa embraced, laughing. Kai had come to the island some time after Abri's arrival, and the older youth had been one of Kai's mentors, comforting the disoriented and frightened child of three cycles and helping to teach Kai the intricate structure of Sa life. It was Abri who, when Kai had taken First Vows, had taken an inked needle to Kai's chest and marked ker with the symbol of AnglSaiye. Kai's debt to Abri had been paid long ago, when Kai had kerself taken one of the arriving children as ker special project, passing along the knowledge Abri had given ker. Abri had left the AnglSaiye sanctuary long before Kai had been given JaqSaTu's blessing and ker own sanction to begin ker travels through the CieTiLa lands. Kai held Abri at arm's length, looking at ker. ke could see the cycles and the pain of many separations in ker face, in the flesh-hewn valleys of experience VeiSaTi had etched there.

"Where are you traveling to, Abri?" Kai asked when they finally pulled apart. *Where are you going? Where have you been?* Those were the eternal questions of Sa meeting on the road.

"Actually, I was looking for you, among others."

"For me? You're joking. Why?"

Abri didn't answer. Instead, ke pulled away from Kai, and the furrows in ker face deepened as ke frowned. "Let me fix some *kav*. You looked tired," ke said.

Kai watched Abri as ke went into the kitchen and poured the bittersweet, herbal brew into two wooden mugs. "I've been on the island for the past two cycles," ke said as ke placed the pottery jug back into the coldbox sunk into the kitchen's floor. Ke brought the mugs out and handed one to Kai. Ke sipped carefully—"once for TeTa, again for XeXa, and last for JeJa," three being the sacred number of Vei-SaTi—then sank down onto one of the large pillows at the edge of the eating pit. "There have been disturbing rumors, Kai," ke said finally. "I'm just one of several who have been sent out by JaqSaTu to bring all Sa back to the island."

The words sent the *kav* swirling, almost spilling from the mug as Kai started. *To bring all the Sa back to AnglSaiye, bring all of us back from our journeys. . . .* It was something that had never been done before, in all the cycles upon cycles written down on the *nasitudas* set on AnglSaiye's shores. It was something Kai could very nearly not comprehend. "I don't understand . . ."

"You will, when you get back there." Abri sipped ker *kav* once more, staring into the brown depths of the mug. "I really can't say more, except to say that it is becoming a dangerous world for Sa."

Kai, remembering BieTe and MasTa, and ker departure of only a few hours ago, opened hard-ridged lips in a grin. "Love is always dangerous, AbriSa. I have the bruises to prove it."

But Abri didn't share in the jest. Abri's dark, expressive eyes regarded Kai's, and there was pain in ker gaze.

"This is different, Kai," ke said. "This is something no Sa has faced before."

CONTEXT:
Masafumi Martinez-Santos

MASA GRUNTED AS HE SLUNG THE FISH ONTO THE kitchen's well-used preparation table. The river grouper was a meter long and nearly twenty-five kilos. A steel cable ran through the mouth and out the gill slits, and thin streamers of blood trickled from the flank and dripped from Masa's overalls onto the stone-flagged floor.

Masa leaned his gig and spear against the wall, and pulled the straps of the stiff, sap-impregnated overalls from his shoulders. Stepping out of the legs, he tossed the overalls down the stairwell to the washing rooms. He stood in the kitchen in soggy woolen underclothes.

"I suppose you expect me to clean that," his *mi* Adja said. She was pulling loaves from the oven, and the yeasty smell of warm bread fought the river scent of the grouper. Adja moved stiffly—her spine had fused in early childhood, not allowing her to bend over or to turn without moving her whole body. She turned liked a marionette lashed to hidden strings, using her legs to move up and down.

"I did the hard work. Should've seen it fight. The groupers are running back to the sea early this year. The swarm knocked me down twice before I snagged this one, and you know how fucking cold the river is. The overalls leaked— Luis needs to put more thornvine sap on them. I'm freezing and wet and hungry." He started to reach past Adja to the bread steaming on the counter.

Adja slapped his hand away. The *crack* of her hand on his was surprisingly loud. "There's your dinner, dripping all over my clean floor. You can have *sashimi*, or you can help me gut and fillet the beast."

"Damn it, Adja . . ."

"Damn it yourself, Masa. Just because it's my rotation in the kitchen doesn't mean I do all the work."

"I need to go *out*, Adja."

Adja sniffed. "So who are you seeing now?"

49

Masa grinned. "Whoever wants to see me. I'm not picky."

"So I've heard." Adja removed another tray of loaves from the oven, rotating her whole upper body as she set the bread on the cooling racks. "Masa, you need to be careful. There's talk in the Baths."

"What kind of talk?"

"That you're sometimes rough. That you can hurt. Masa, I've told you—with your past, you can't afford that."

"*Khudda*," Masa said. "Who's saying that crap about me?"

Adja shrugged. "It doesn't matter. I'm just telling you for your own good."

Masa grimaced. "All right, so I'm told. If they don't like me, they don't have to fuck me, do they?"

Adja's face hardened. Her eyes narrowed, the lips pursed. If Masa noticed, he pretended not to care. She opened a drawer and rummaged in it. Steel clashed. She pulled out a filleting knife and laid it alongside the grouper. "Take care of the fish. Then you can do whatever you want to do."

Almost, Masa refused. But that would have led to Adja complaining to his mam Seela, and then Geema Kyra would have gotten involved, and the rest of the Family. Too much trouble. Instead, as he scraped the scales from the grouper and slit open the belly, he pretended that it was one of *them*, one of the women talking about him in the Baths.

The thought gave him an erection that lasted until long afterward.

VOICE:
Elio Allen-Shimmura

DOMINIC WOULDN'T TALK TO ME FOR THREE DAYS after I was with Anaïs, enclosing himself in an atmosphere of cold, silent fury. Whenever he saw me in the compound his eyes narrowed until they looked like Tlilapan: black ponds nearly hidden in the folds holding them. His lips pressed together until they appeared to form more of a sphincter than a mouth, and he would make sure I noticed his glare, which was damn near incandescent.

For my part, I made certain that he noticed that I noticed, and didn't give him the reaction he wanted. I may love Dominic, but I don't *like* him.

A lot of the Family feel that way, even if very few of them will admit it.

At the table at SixthHour, where he always ruled the conversation, I was pointedly not invited to offer my opinion on the subject *de jour*, and when I deigned to do so anyway, there was a quick silence as everyone paid rapt attention to the food on their plates. Not that it mattered—the subject was always Euzhan and her progress. Funny how Dominic managed to avoid mentioning Anaïs's name during those conversations, even though I knew Ana was tending Euz as if she were her own child.

I'm certain that word was judiciously leaked to Dominic from the others in my Family that I spent a night with someone else the night *after* I'd been with Anaïs. It didn't require a hell of a psychological background to figure out the reasons underlying that decision. Even so, I was amazed at the relief I felt when, yes, the equipment still worked, thank you very much.

Finally, on the fourth day, as I was sitting in the common room talking with young Dominic and Sarah a little past FirstHour, Geeda Dominic came into the room. He dismissed Domi and Sarah with a barely perceptible nod of his head; they scattered. Andrea, Bui, and Hizo, noisily playing jackstones in a corner, judiciously decided to continue the game somewhere else.

It was suddenly very quiet in the room. I could hear the soft hissing of the peat brick fire in the stone hearth. I watched Dominic sit—no one else ever dared sit in *that* chair, one of Jason Koda-Levin's intricate creations. The chair was (very quietly) called "the throne" by most of us. Dominic grumbled and muttered to himself until he was comfortable, holding his hands out toward the glowing peat, then took a long, slow inhalation that wobbled the loose skin under his chin. I waited. Finally, he looked at me.

"Well, is it true?"

"Is *what* true, Geeda Dominic?" I knew what he wanted to hear, but I wasn't going to give him the satisfaction.

He snorted. Whatever anyone might think of Dominic, his advanced age hadn't made him senile, at least not in that way. "You're not stupid, Elio, though you are often an ass. I'm too old to enjoy playing games that simply waste time, and I'd appreciate it if you don't indulge in them."

"All the nasty rumors to the contrary, Anaïs is female, Geeda," I told him. "A woman. Pretty damn good in bed, too."

Dominic nearly hissed at that—that was obviously not the answer he wanted. He rose from his chair faster than I'd seen him move in years.

"I don't understand you, Elio," he barked, standing in front of me, leaning heavily on his cane; I could see his hand on the copper-plated knob, with the extra vestigial finger jutting uselessly from the side. "You know what she did to Ochiba."

"Anaïs didn't do anything to Ochiba, Geeda. Ochiba died from complications after childbirth. It's a damned shame, but it happens."

"No!" Dominic spat, as I hit the nerve I'd aimed for. "Ochiba was *killed*, killed because of that . . . that *rezu's* jealousy. Ochiba told me that. She stood in my room and said that Euzhan would be her last pregnancy—all because Anaïs had told her it was 'dangerous.' She said that Anaïs didn't even want her to have this one. Anaïs didn't want Ochiba to have another child so she could have Ochiba for herself. And when Ochiba had a child anyway, the vile woman took the opportunity and killed her."

I'd heard parts of this horrible speculation of Dominic's before, in whispered gossip from the older Family members. He'd begun to voice these suspicions not long after Ochiba's death, and the theory had grown and solidified over the years. This was the first time he'd spoken of it openly to me; the blind anger in his voice was nearly visible. "Geeda, we both know that's not what happened," I said. He didn't listen. He was full into his tirade now, and no mere truth was going to dam the vitrolic flood.

". . . and yet you went to her. I've talked to Diana, who has seen Anaïs in the Baths, even though she tries to hide herself. She's deformed, she'll never have children, and because of her, Ochiba—who gave us four named children and would have given us more—is dead. Dead because she and Anaïs were—" He started to say the word. I saw him form it, and then close his mouth before it could emerge. *Lovers.* "Yet you'd lie for her," he finished.

"She saved Euzhan." *And I like her,* I should have added. *She and Ochiba may have been more than our little society wants to tolerate, but I don't care—I never saw Ochiba happier than she*

52

was during those months when she and Anaïs were close. I enjoy Anaïs's company. I think she has a wonderful laugh, on those rare occasions when you can manage to coax one out of her. She works harder than anyone around here, and at least a dozen people we can both name wouldn't be here if Anaïs wasn't the best damned doctor we have. I think she's been hurt enough, and she doesn't deserve the crap you've handed her over the last few years.

But I didn't say any of that. Dominic wouldn't have listened, anyway.

"*Hui* saved Euzhan," Dominic snapped back, his mouth closing sharply on the last syllable. "Anaïs is a freak, and she's responsible for Ochiba's death. I know it, you know it. She shouldn't be tolerated, or she'll corrupt someone else the way she did Ochiba. We can't afford that. No Family can."

"Geeda, Ochiba was her own woman. Any decisions she made, she made on her own. Anaïs didn't kill Ochiba; Mictlan killed her."

"*Phah!*" Dominic slammed the end of the cane on the floor for emphasis. "I won't stand betrayal, Elio. You remember that, boy. I won't stand it. The time is coming when Families will need to make hard decisions. Hard decisions—do you hear me?"

Dominic left the room with a last glare at me. I heard him snarling like a grumbler at the children in the hallway as he passed. They gave him meek, quick apologies. I sat in the chair assessing my various mental wounds; none of them seemed mortal. I figured I was set for at least another week of the Distant Glares, though.

I did wonder why I'd lied. "*Anaïs is female, Geeda . . .*" Well, honestly, Geeda Dominic, I'm not certain. A few years ago when I was with her, that extra ridge of flesh—like a featureless, thick finger shielding her opening—had confused me. Defeated me. Distracted as I was by it, well, I just *couldn't. . . .* That wasn't Anaïs's fault; it was mine.

This time . . . I still wasn't sure what had happened.

This time, I'd managed to get beyond her deformity, to put it out of my mind. I concentrated on her face, her breasts, her skin, her kiss. And once I was inside her, hell, she didn't feel much different than any other woman I've been with, and we were both responding. I was getting close . . . then I remember her shriek, which I think was more surprise than pain. There was a quick, strange hardness intruding between us, like a cock but smaller. I came at almost the same time.

And so did she. I heard her gasp, and cry out. And then . . .

I rolled away from her, shocked at the sudden sticky wetness all over my stomach, all over hers. As Ana sat up, her eyes frantic, I caught a glimpse of something in the tangle of pubic hair, like a child's uncircumcised cock. There was blood, too, at the tip, as if it had just torn free from wherever it had been attached. The fold of flesh guarding her opening was gone. I said something, I don't really remember what—probably something inane and stupid like "Are you all right?"

She was frantic, but again I think it was more from fear than any pain. Or maybe that's just rationalization, because I didn't go to her. Hell, if something that weird happened to me. . . . Anyway, I stood there, that stuff dripping slowly down my stomach, thicker and more yellow than my come. She kept saying, "What's happening to me . . . ?" over and over, wiping at herself with the sheet and then clutching it to her like a shield. She turned away from me. "Get out, Elio," she said harshly, then more gently: "Please, Elio. Please go."

Her naked back was to me. I could see her shoulders begin to shake with the first tears.

A truly compassionate person would have stayed with her. A person who wanted to be her friend as well as a lover would have stayed, would have shown her some compassion. Half the people in our generation have physical defects of one kind or another, varying from trivial to serious. So this one shouldn't matter—look at the spots on my skin.

"Please go," she told me. "I really want you to go . . ."

. . . and, well, I *went*.

I've tried to figure that one out, and the truth is that for that one moment, I was as disgusted and repelled by what I saw in front of me as Dominic would have been. I felt, I don't know . . .

Dirty. Unclean. Contaminated.

I left. I took a long shower afterward, cleaning myself over and over again, and hating myself for the fact that it mattered.

It wasn't Ana's fault. None of it was her fault—I don't know *what* she is, but she didn't ask to be made that way. I could see that much in her eyes, in the way she acted with me just before. Maybe that's why I lied to Dominic now, trying to make up for past failures. Trying to do penance for some of the guilt.

Too fucking bad I didn't feel particularly absolved.

CONTEXT:
Hui Koda-Schmidt

"SINCE ELIO HAS BEEN SEEING HER, I DEMAND TO know—as eldest of my family, Hui—whether Anaïs is a woman or an abomination."

Hui grimaced. On his desk was a crystalline card. The light from his desk lamp coaxed a three-dimensional, moving image of a smiling oriental woman from the card's surface: Akiko Koda, his ancestor. The card, his mam Melissa had told him, had been her ID card for the *Ibn Battuta*. Melissa had been given the card by her mam, Eleanor, who had been Akiko's daughter.

Lately, the card was Hui's meditation in times of stress. He'd certainly never known Akiko, who had died in the Great Storm of 23. Eleanor had given Hui the card just before her final illness a few years ago. "I look at this sometimes and pretend that she's still there, listening to me, even though I was only a year old when she died," Eleanor had told Hui. "Maybe she'll be there for you, too. I will be. I promise."

Hui wondered if Akiko's *kami* was watching, and what she might think of Mictlan now. Akiko's image turned toward him, slightly blurred through his cataracts, and smiled its eternal smile. Decades ago, Eleanor had told him, the card could speak: Akiko's voice, giving her name. No longer. There was only the silent presence of his great-grandmam.

"Anaïs is a fine doctor, Dominic. That's all you need to know. That's all I'm telling you."

"*Khudda*, Hui." Dominic waved his cane, his six-fingered, knobby-jointed hand clutching the polished knob of wood at the end. "I'm not asking much of you. You know her; you examine her every few months. You know damn well that she and my Ochiba were ... involved. I want to know. It's my *right* to know."

Dominic's lips were pulled back, the dark eyes squinted, and his head was tilted back arrogantly, his nostrils flared.

55

Outrage Personified. The expression on the ancient face might have made Hui laugh, under other circumstances. Under other circumstances.... But this was now, and he found himself rising from his chair and matching the old man stance for stance. Akiko's card clattered on wood as he let it drop.

"You're old, Dominic, and you had the privilege to actually know some of the Founders. That gives you a certain status in this society, and grants you certain privileges, but it grants you no *rights*. At least none that I'll acknowledge. I'm going to tell you this once, then I expect you to leave. Anaïs is a fine person and a fine doctor, and without her, one hell of a lot of people here would not be walking around spreading nasty rumors. Even if Ochiba and Ana were lovers—and I'm saying *if*, Domi—that obviously didn't stop Ochiba from conceiving children, so what does it matter? As to what I've seen in my examinations of Anaïs, that's my business, not yours."

Dominic sniffed. "But if she were normal, you'd say so, wouldn't you? And you won't. You can't."

Hui felt his cheeks coloring. He slapped his hand on the desk. "There are *none* of us 'normal' here, Dominic. None. Not me, not you, not anyone. Now, get out of my office. I'm tired of talking nonsense."

Dominic slammed the end of his cane on the floor with an exasperated *huff*. He glared; Hui glared back. Finally, he turned and walked to the door, but stopped before he left. He spoke without turning around to Hui again. "We live in a fragile society," Dominic said. "As an elder, it's my job to protect us from things that threaten what stability we have. And I *will* protect us, Hui—no matter who it hurts."

Hui had no answer to that. He touched the card, and Akiko's image sprang to life. His ancestor smiled wordlessly at him as the sound of Dominic's cane slowly faded down the corridor.

VOICE:
Elio Allen-Shimmura

THE SNOW WAS ORANGE-RED WITH ALGAE THE storm had picked up from Crookjaw Bay. The world appeared to have rusted. The flakes tasted vaguely sour. Both Masafumi and I looked like we'd been bleeding where the snow had melted.

"Did you really fuck Anaïs?"

I was beginning to wonder if everyone was going to be asking that question, albeit a little more politely. "Yeah," I answered tentatively, the word lifting at the end into almost a question as I squinted into the flake-infested wind. "I did."

Masafumi raised thick eyebrows at that. He hefted the rifle he was carrying and flicked some clinging snow from the barrel. "I heard that old Dominic was mightily pissed."

I frowned. "Who told you that?"

"Your sib Sarah." Masa paused and gave me a grin I wished I could give back. "I was with her last night."

Masafumi Martinez-Santos looks like something hewn from a block of wood rather than born. Everything about him is thick and rough: the ledges above his eyes, his cheekbones, his chin, his hands. His skin is dry and scaly, as if some ancient reptilian ancestor infested the coils of his DNA. Bundled up as he was now, he looked like a troll.

Too bad there wasn't any damn sun.

"Sarah should keep her mouth shut." *And her legs.* I thought nastily. Sarah rarely turns down any offer of sex. Of course, she also has four named children, and at 29, is angling for another. Still, *Masa. . . .*

"Maybe you should keep your pants buttoned," Masa retorted. He smiled, showing teeth too big for his mouth, but there was a challenge in his voice and the smile was just a twitch of his lips. "I wouldn't stir that Anaïs's pot for nothing. From what I hear, she ain't exactly a woman. Maybe she's even a *rezu* like Gabriela. Maybe you like that, huh?"

His mouth twitched again. Snowflakes hit the incisors and expired.

I didn't like being with Masa when he had a weapon. After all, Masa was that rare animal on Mictlan: a killer.

Masa had murdered Kiichi Koda-Schmidt back in 96, shooting him in the leg and then bludgeoning the crippled man repeatedly with a convenient hunk of shale until his face was an unrecognizable pulp. Evidently, the two had argued while out hunting, and the argument had turned both physical and and deadly. Old Anaïs, Ana's Geema, had been judge for the trial. No one was much surprised that Masa had killed someone, nor that Kiichi was the one dead—both men had demonstrated evil tempers in the past, and neither had demonstrated any inclination to control them. No one was even appalled by the lame excuse Masa trotted out— the quarrel had begun when he and Kiichi couldn't decide who was going to eat the last bit of sugarpaste in their packs, and Kiichi (Masa claimed) had tried to brain Masa with the same rock first; they'd also both been roaring drunk when the fight started.

People have been killed for poorer reasons, I suppose, and Masa seemed genuinely remorseful afterward, though that was no doubt small comfort to Kiichi or the Koda-Schmidt family.

If the triteness of the reason for Kiichi's murder wasn't enough, what really pissed off old Anaïs was that Masa had left behind the game they'd killed, choosing to lug back Kiichi's body instead.

"It wasn't enough to kill a man," she told him, and her anger honed the voice until it cut. "You had to see if you could *starve* a few of us at the same time. You're not only violent, you're stupid."

Had Kiichi been a woman, Masa might have been summarily executed for the murder—there being no excuse for that level of stupidity. But Kiichi was a male, and thus not overly valuable. Instead, Anaïs had declared Masa shunned for five years.

Shunned. The word itself made me shiver. I can't imagine the isolation one of the Shunned must feel. For five years Masa performed field work. For five years, all his communal and conjugal privileges were revoked. For five years, no one—under penalty of being shunned themselves—would even speak to him or acknowledge his presence except when absolutely necessary. He was given just enough food to survive, and had to live apart from all the Families, in the caves near the river.

For five years, Masa was alone, exiled in the midst of the Families.

Being shunned could drive people crazy. Kees Allen-Levin had been shunned for two years for stealing food. During SixthMonth, he walked to the summit of the rock. There, with only the Miccail stelae to see, he'd thrown himself from the high cliffs. Samuel Koda-Schmidt had vanished into the wilderness before his shunning was over; Lynnèa Martinez-Santos had been shunned for only six months, but afterward, she was never the same and died within a year.

And Gabriela Rusack, the first one ever shunned, and shunned not once but twice . . . well, that's a tale we all know, a cautionary fairy tale told to children from their infancy.

In the year since the restoration of his position, Masa had been in a few altercations, but they'd been emptyhanded affairs, none serious enough to cause the Families to ask old Anaïs to shun him once more. Still, no one—not even his Family—wanted to be around Masa alone. Wangari Koda-Shimmura had started a pool to see when he'd finally step over the line again.

I didn't particularly want to be the reason to change Masa's status quo—definitely not when the man was armed.

"*Nei*. You're my role model, Masa. Didn't you know that?" I grinned back at Masa, and left him to chew on that— I figured it would take him a while to work it out and see if it came out to an insult.

We were sweeping the fields near Rusack's Trail for grumblers. After the attack on Euzhan and the way the grumbler came at Anaïs and me, a lot of people were understandably paranoid about the creatures, and Kim-Li Allen-Levin had spied a mating pair of them prowling the fields this morning; Johanna, her Family's matriarch, had insisted that the grumblers needed to be chased away or killed, especially since this was a Gather night. No one argued with her, not even Dominic. We've all seen how quickly Mictlan's creatures can change.

The Family Elders tell tales of the redwings filling the sky each autumn; it used to be their sign that it was time to begin the harvest. Now, barely seventy-five years later, redwings are rare. When I was born, there were summer bloomings of piercing white blossoms on the sweetmelon vines along the edges of Tlilipan, and they always swarmed with small, electric-blue curltongues, lapping at the flowers with their long, namesake feature. Now the curltongues ignore the sweetmelons, preferring instead the midges clouding the air above the black water. And we've all seen how the land barnacles changed their patterns from bright purple to stone brown in the course of less than a decade, as soon as they decided to infest the compounds rather than the trees around us.

For that matter, snow had usually been pale yellow until six or seven years ago; now it is more often this iron-oxide red. That's just a few examples. Anyone could give you a dozen others. Nothing on Mictlan stays the same for very long. Nature seemed to have gunned the twin motors of mutation and evolution here. Grumblers suddenly turning aggressive?—it wasn't much of a leap.

So we plowed on between the rows of faux-wheat, dusting ourselves with colored snow.

We spotted grumbler spoor about ten minutes later: brown-black droppings near a crumpled section of wheat. Masa crouched alongside the scat and carefully prodded the nearest mound with a wheat stalk. The stalk went in easily, and as soon as the surface was broken, the *khudda* steamed. "Fresh," Masa grunted. "The sons of bitches are right here." He straightened, looking at the lines of wheat. We both saw the line of crumpled stalks at the same time, not twenty paces ahead. The grumblers had pushed through the row down which we were walking, heading toward the river. The stalks were rising back up as we watched. "Right fucking here," Masa repeated in a hoarse whisper. He unshouldered his rifle and checked the chamber. The metal bolt snapped back into place with a oiled, sharp *clack-clack*. I checked my own weapon, remembering the way the grumbler had come at Anaïs, remembering the way the beast had torn Euzhan open.

We followed the trail.

The grumblers must have been moving fast, probably scenting us in the field. The knot in my stomach loosened slightly—that was typical grumbler cowardice. With any luck, we'd find that they'd hit open ground and bolted for the cover of the forest.

We weren't graced with that kind of luck. I came out of the wheat field a few steps ahead of Masa. The grumblers had halted out in the strip of open meadow between the field and the river trees. It was snowing harder, and I blinked into the bloody flurries. The grumblers were staring back at me, a female and her pup, with the mam making the standard mumbling challenge as I emerged, though she was still backing away as she growled and chittered in my direction, pulling her youngster with her. Kim-Li had said there were three of them, but it looked like daddy had already taken off.

Masa came huffing out of the field about then. "*Khudda*," he said when he saw the two, and his rifle snapped up. I pushed the barrel up and over before he could squeeze the trigger. "Hey!" Masa shouted. "What the fuck—"

"There's no need to kill them," I said. "They're leaving. Let them go."

"You're joking."

I still had hold of his rifle. "I said, we let them go if they want to go. Fire a few shots in the air if you want to get them moving, but I don't see any need to kill them."

"You still say that after what happened to Euzhan?"

The female grumbler was still backing, still facing us, her dreadlocked chin—longer than the male's—wagging with the motion. She pushed the child in back of her with her hand, and the gesture looked no different than something we might have done, trying to protect the children from some threat. "*Hai*," I told him. "I still say that."

"Then let go of my rifle."

I let go. Masa put the stock on his shoulder, the barrel pointed up at the ruddy clouds over the grumblers' heads. I should have known, but before I could move, Masa brought the rifle down sharply, his finger coiling around the trigger. The female went down in a heap with the explosive report of the shot. Masa laughed. "Damn it, Masa!" I shouted.

Daddy grumbler came hurtling out from behind us, howling. He hit Masa from behind, cloth tearing as the beast's claws dug into his coat, and both of them went down, the grumbler tumbling as it hit the icy ground. Masa's rifle went flying somewhere off into the swirling snow. Masa shook his head, groggy; the grumbler was already on his feet.

I shot him. He went down with a hard thud. The youngling grumbler was howling now, snarling and hissing near the body of its mother.

There was a third shot, and the pup crumpled, silent. I looked at Masa, who'd recovered his rifle. He cocked his head toward me, still sighting down the barrel. " 'They're leaving,'" he said mockingly. "'Let them go.' I'll be sure to remember that, Elio, next time."

Masa's face, twisted and distorted in fear and distaste as he looked down at the body of the grumbler, reminded me of something . . . someone . . . For a long time, I couldn't think of where I'd seen that look before. Then, as he grimaced and turned away from the carnage, his eyes narrowed and hard, I knew.

His was the look Dominic had worn this morning when we talked about Anaïs: the same unfocused anger, the same loathing of the unknown, of the different.

SHADOWS

VOICE:
Elio Allen-Shimmura

"HERE'S WHAT I'VE MANAGED TO RECOVER FROM what's left of the Miccail's stomach," Anaïs said to Máire Koda-Schmidt. The two of them were poring over some greenish sludge in the bottom of a vial. The bog body was lying on a gurney in front of them; to me, it looked like nothing more than a squashed mud sculpture. Máire glanced up as I entered, giving me a sidewise glance that barely registered my existence, her attention all on Ana. Máire's the closest thing to a biologist we have. She works with Ana and her *da* Hui often, and I wasn't surprised to find that Anaïs had asked for her help with the bogman.

Máire's a bit of an oddity herself. Like Anaïs, she's one of the few women in the colony who have never managed to at least become pregnant, if not to actually deliver a child. I've been to bed with her three or four times over the years— pleasant if not particularly enthusiastic sex. She doesn't seem to ask anyone much; that, coupled with the fact that she's often at the clinic with Anaïs, has led to a few whispered rumors. As far as I know, the rumors—like most of their ilk—have no grounding in truth.

Anaïs saw me as well, and even through the mask I could see the muscles of her face tighten, even though she kept looking at Máire. "All this was in the stomach, not the intestines, so it's his last meal, eaten just before he was killed. I've looked at it under the microscope; there are grains of some sort, but I thought you might tell me exactly what."

"I'll give it a look, Ana," Máire said. "Give me a few days for the workup. I'll let you know when I have it."

"I can't say that it looks particularly appetizing," I interjected, mostly so they couldn't ignore me anymore.

"Elio," Máire said, finally acknowledging me. The greeting seemed colder than usual. I wondered if she and Anaïs had been talking. Máire glanced back at Anaïs, held up the vial. "I'll check this out first free time I get," she said, then brushed on past me on her way out, tossing her mask and gown into the hamper.

Anaïs and I stood there for a few seconds trying to pretend that neither one of us was uncomfortable.

"I was in visiting Euzhan. Hui told me I could come in here. 'She's in with her new toy,' he said. Strange toys you have. Me, I always played with blocks."

I think she almost smiled; at least her eyes crinkled slightly above the mask. Her hands were covered with thornvine gunk and some other stuff I was fairly certain I didn't want to identify. "You want to help?"

My face must have given me away. I could see her mouth lift beneath the mask in what I hoped was a smile, and she continued. "No, not with this, Elio. There's a tattoo on the body that I'm fairly sure represents something. I made an ink drawing. I need a research librarian—and you're the person handling the databases. Maybe you can make some sense of it."

I glanced at the ugly sack of dark flesh on the table, glad she wasn't asking me to touch it. "I'll try. There's some stuff of Gabriela's on file that may help. Where's your drawing?"

"In my office. I'll get it after I finish here. I hear you and Masa killed some grumblers this morning."

I grimaced, remembering. "*Hai*. A whole happy family of them."

She looked at me strangely, dark eyes wide over the mask. "Good. We wouldn't want anyone else hurt like Euzhan. She's doing well, by the way. I almost let her go home today, but with the Gather tonight, I thought she'd be better off here rather than worrying your Family with her. She'll need to be watched carefully for the next few weeks, and we have a saline drip in her that someone would have to change. I'm still worried about infections . . ."

She was talking too fast, chattering, not wanting to give either of us a chance to change the subject. She realized it at the same time and stopped. "Hui already told me about Euzhan," I said. "That's not why I came in here."

"Elio, if this is about the other night—"

I interrupted her. "I was an ass."

Her eyebrows arched and then sagged. She didn't argue with the statement. "Elio, I think it would be better if we both pretended it didn't happen."

"Neither one of us can do that, and we shouldn't need to. I wanted to know . . ." I stopped. My fickle, prepared explanation had made an escape, without even leaving a word track behind. "... if you were all right," I finished lamely. "I shouldn't have left. I'm sorry."

"I asked you to go, remember?" She shrugged. "You went. No apologies needed. It's over."

Words as percussive as rifle shots. Bang, bang, bang. I grunted with the impacts.

"I just wanted to know—"

"Wanted to know what, Elio? Didn't you see enough? Wasn't that enough for Dominic, wasn't that enough proof that I'm unfit to be with anyone from his Family, man *or* woman? It's done, Elio. You don't need to know or say any more. The rest is going to stay private . . . at least that's what *I'm* intending." She looked down at the bog body and reached for an instrument on the tray next to the gurney. "Right now I have work to do."

"So do I. At the moment, I'm working on my apologies. Obviously, I need a lot of practice. Anaïs, I'm very sorry."

Her hands paused somewhere above the Miccail body. The tip of the scalpel was trembling, shivering as light from the blade sparked on her gown. "You didn't *do* anything, Elio."

"I know. That's the problem."

"Elio, this isn't about you."

"I was there, Anaïs. That makes me involved. You haven't talked to your Family, have you? You haven't talked to anyone. What I'm saying is that if you'd like to talk, I'd like to listen."

"No, Elio," she said, her gaze on the bog body, and then she finally looked back up at me. "There's no need for us to pretend, Elio. I'm not hiding anything from myself, not trying to forget what happened. I appreciate that you asked me to sleep with you again, but it's obvious that I'm . . ."

Despite her claims, I saw Anaïs choke on the next word, her face all screwed up as if she were about to cry. Then she caught herself, and slid a mask over her emotions, drawing herself up with an audible intake of breath. Everything was suddenly locked up and shut away, so that the words just dropped out like empty shells. Even her eyes above the gauze were empty.

". . . deformed. I'm sorry you had to be there when I found out just how bad it is. It's a mistake I won't make again."

"When *what* happened, Ana?" I prodded, rudely. I didn't care. I wanted to see something shatter the barrier she'd so quickly erected. I wanted to see something move inside her. I wanted her to cry or laugh or get angry—*anything* but just stand there and talk like she was discussing last night's dinner. I didn't know why I wanted a reaction, why it was so important to me, but I did. "What was it? You didn't want me to help, remember? What happened, Anaïs?"

Her eyes flickered: *anger?* "Get out," she said. "Now."

"Anaïs, as a friend—"

"Is that what you are, Elio? Or is all this protestation just some nagging guilt? I saw your face the other night, remember? I saw horror and disgust—you can't deny that it wasn't there. I *saw* it." Then the barriers closed in again. She picked up an instrument from the tray and leaned over the bog body. "I understand it, too. Now . . . good-bye, Elio," she said.

"What if you're wrong about how you think I feel, Ana? What then?"

My words surprised me as much as they did Anaïs, I think. I wasn't sure where they came from or what they meant. I didn't give either of us a chance to meditate on them, either.

"I'll see you at the Gather tonight, Ana," I told her. "I'd like you to be there."

I turned and left before she had a chance to answer.

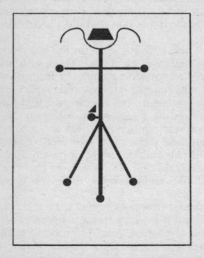

Elio—Here's that sketcho of the tattoo.
Anaïs

CONTEXT:
Maria Allen-Levin

❧ "WHO ARE YOU GOING TO BRING BACK TO YOUR room after the Gather, Maria? Domi, or maybe Ben?"

Havala had finished brushing Maria's hair. Maria fastened the buttons of her favorite blouse, then picked up a crystal of yellow quartz attached to a leather thong and placed it over her head. She glanced at herself in the mirror, taking care not to smile too broadly and show the dark gap on the left side of her mouth, where she'd lost another tooth. She was on her third set of teeth now, and Hui had told her that he thought he could see another set following. *"That's why your mouth is set so low, so there's room for all those teeth. Think of it as a blessing—you'll never be a toothless old woman.'*

"I don't know, Havala," she said. "I think I'll just see who's wearing yellow."

"Marshall's older, but he's very . . . interesting."

Maria laughed. "So is *he* the one . . . ?"

Havala rubbed her stomach, which rounded slightly over the waist of her pants. She leaned over Maria to lay the brush on the table, and Maria saw her sib's hands. Mottled green-gray patches of dry, scaly skin ran under the cuffs of her blouse. "Maybe. Probably. And if he is, you might have the same luck."

"No wonder Marshall's been so popular lately."

Havala smiled at her sib in the mirror and hugged her from behind. "I'm so happy for you, Havala," she said. "I have a feeling about this one—a good feeling."

"So do I," Havala whispered in her sib's ear, and Maria caught the hint of sadness in her voice. Havala had been pregnant twice before, miscarrying early both times. Maria knew how that hurt; she'd miscarried herself, a half year ago. *The sudden blood, the cramps and pain, the tiny, poor thing . . .*

69

She forced the thought away. A Gather was for happy thoughts. A Gather was for optimism and hope. She held onto Havala, clutching her tightly, and then letting her go reluctantly. "Come on," she said. "Let's go see if we can make sure Marshall gets a yellow stone."

VOICE:
Elio Allen-Shimmura

LONGAGO IS THE HERALD OF A GATHER, WHENEVER that nearest of our two moons rises full in the eastern sky at sunset, looking impossibly huge and yellow. This time, Faraway graced us with her ephemeral presence as well, a pale eye peering above the rim of its brighter, closer sister moon. The snowstorm earlier in the day had passed through; I could see sky between the clouds.

By the time the western horizon had performed its slow shift from orange to ultramarine and the first stars emerged between silvered clouds, the six fires were lit on the old landing pad—now swept clear of snowdrifts—and the Families burdened the makeshift tables with food. Tozo Koda-Shimmura started a slow beat on the massive ceremonial drum built by the patriarch Shigetomo Shimmura, a low booming throb that slammed into your chest, forcing you to breathe in time. The drumbeats sounded like the great earthquake tread of some giant walking the earth. Tami Koda-Schmidt, our community *Kiria*, donned her orange robes and—walking slowly as befitted her age and position—anointed each of the fires with spicewood as the drum continued to sound, sending the strong fragrance of rich earth drifting with the smoke.

When she'd finished and the last reverberations of the drum had faded, ancient Vladimir Allen-Levin, as the eldest member of our community, shuffled forward with a caged curltongue, its iridescent blue wings fluttering as the cage (the steel bars crafted from a broken shovel belonging to the original exploratory mission) swung back and forth from

Vlad's wrinkled, arthritic hands. Kiria Tami reached into the metallic prison and tied a long strand of thread around the curltongue's left leg—the thread was made of interwoven human hair, one strand from each of the Families. When Tami finished, she slowly paraded the curltongue around the cracked concrete perimeter of the pad to the accompaniment of the drum's slow cadence. Finally, at the pad's center, Tami lifted the protesting curltongue high as Tozo hammered hard at the drum.

She released the curltongue.

We all watched it dart away into the twilight, losing sight of it quickly as it bore each of us, symbolically anyway, away into the sky with it.

Our rituals are—at most—a hundred years old: a single breath of time for the ancient genes residing in our bodies. To me, the customs don't resonate the way they should, with layered, vibrant timbres from lost ceremonies and prehistoric symbolism, with voiced echoes passing from generation upon generation upon generation. Even the old religious ceremonies brought from Earth seem out of place here. In coming to a new world, we lost our connection to the old ways, our roots. We've had to make new celebrations, new festivals, new rites and passages. We've had to delve for the part of us that is of Mictlan, and that's still a small portion of the whole.

Of course, that's me. My feelings. If you ask Dominic, he'd tell you that everyone is incredibly moved by the ceremonies we've created. He would insist that they are as impressive and evocative as those of the far older religions our ancestors followed.

I don't know. Maybe he's right. I seem to be one of the minority who don't feel a sense of release as the curltongue flies away, who doesn't sense the presence of the *kami* in the thundering voice of the drum.

I watch the ceremony. I pretend, but I don't feel. It all just leaves me empty, and I wonder why.

Somewhere over the immense slanted rock into which the First Generation had carved the settlement's tunneled home, I lost sight of the curltongue. A collective sigh rose from those around me, but for me it was more relief than release. Off to one side of the pad, Thandi Martinez-Santos began to beat a quick rhythm on her *bodhran*, a compelling, insistent beat that was joined quickly by flute and guitar.

Someone began to dance, and then another, and that broke the spell the ritual had cast. People began talking and shouting and laughing, and dancing shadows lurched and prowled out over the night-wrapped fields around the pad. The area seemed incredibly, impossibly crowded with the eighty or ninety people milling around the thirty-meter square of concrete. I felt almost claustrophobic, surrounded by the rest of my kind. The noise level alone was incredible: the music and conversation, the stomping feet and clapping hands of the dancers, the laughter and shouting.

"Quite a show, Historian," someone commented at my shoulder. "You'll have to write it up."

I turned. The speaker was a woman, someone I didn't recognize, which made me gape like an astonished child for a moment. Then a tide of static washed slowly over her auburn hair and down the tea-colored, round face and lush body under a long wrap. "Hey, Ghost," I said, and noticed then that someone had dragged one of the projectors down from the Rock—probably Ché Koda-Levin, our astronomy buff, who monitors Ghost's orbit. He would have known Ghost was due to show up tonight. "Yeah, it's a good turnout."

"Your ancestors back on Earth wouldn't have thought so." Her voice was a sultry, slow alto. I liked it. I wondered who she was, this person in whose shape Ghost had cloaked herself. One of the original ship members, probably, as they were Ghost's usual choices. "They'd have thought this looked pretty sparse. In fact, this would have looked sparse even in the *Ibn Battuta's* central hall."

"My Earth ancestors wouldn't have been able to name every other human on the planet on sight, either," I told her. "I can. For us, this is urban blight."

Ghost grinned and favored me with a seductive tilt of her hips. The first song had ended, but the musicians were already striding into another energetic jig that pulled at least half of the people out into the central circle. Their mingled breaths made a thin white cloud above the pad. In the cold evening air, steam rose from the sweat on their arms.

"Hey, Elio! Hi, Ghost." Ama Martinez-Santos interposed herself between me and the crowd, holding out a large, ceramic bowl. Inside, on the polished aquamarine glaze, loops of leathern strings coiled around colored stones. "Choose," Ama said to me. "Maybe you'll get lucky." Ama was wear-

72

ing a similar necklace herself—one of the red and black garnets that occasionally wash up on the riverbank was nestled between her breasts on top of her fur-fringed coat. Ama held the bowl over my head; I reached up and pulled out one of the loops: yellow quartz. She shrugged and didn't try too hard to keep her lack of disappointment from showing. "Ahh, too bad. Becca's got yellow, and Maria, too, I think. Maybe one of them will ask you. Enjoy. Hey, Aris!—you need a necklace if you plan on getting laid tonight. . . ." Ama went off in pursuit of Aris, and I slipped on the necklace.

"Hey, don't look so forlorn." I glanced at Ghost. She'd added an identical yellow quartz necklace, and her outfit had gone translucent—she'd have frozen to death dressed that way if she'd actually been here. The body underneath looked exceedingly touchable—whomever Ghost was modeling, she'd been a stunning beauty. She licked her lips in mock lasciviousness. "The Gather's just started."

"And you're just a fantasy image. I've dealt with your kind before—lots of times. I can take you on one-handed."

Ghost just smiled at that. "You know the rules: a man's not allowed to turn down a woman with a matching necklace during the Gather."

"That's *your* custom. I've read the transcripts. You were the one who suggested this little ritual to the Family elders."

"I was just trying for some random mixing of the gene pool," Ghost replied. The necklace was gone, the blouse was opaque and buttoned up to the neck. "It's my job."

I fingered my necklace. "And you think this works."

The grin looked more mischievous than anything else. "Probably not. But it does add some spice to the evening, doesn't it?" Ghost seemed to sense that I was searching the crowd, looking at all the faces caught in poses of flirtation and enjoyment. "I don't see her, either," he said.

"Who?"

"I downloaded and read all the personal files as soon as I relinked," Ghost said. "Like you, the person we're talking about generally writes everything down."

"Ahh."

"If it helps, I'm talking to her right now at the clinic. Is there anything you'd like me to relay?"

So Anaïs was at the clinic, which meant that she wasn't coming to the Gather. Nothing changed. The bonfires didn't dim, the music didn't suddenly go muffled. But I found myself frowning. "No," I said. "I don't think so. I'm going to wander, Ghost. Listen, I've about caught up with the hard-copy on the last download from the ship. You might want to dump another transfer into my terminal."

"I'll do that now. Enjoy the Gather."

I didn't answer. I wandered off into the more crowded areas of the pad around the food tables. Someone handed me a mug filled with dark, thick beer from the tap. I nibbled on the pastries arrayed on the tables and watched the dancers, nodding in time with the music.

"Why aren't you out there?" Máire had come up alongside me, holding a beer herself. "It's one way to stay warm on a night like this." Over her coat, an amethyst swayed below the leather necklace. Again, I didn't notice any particular disappointment that her stone didn't match mine.

"Not in the mood, I guess."

Her eyebrows arched slightly at that, and she took a sip of her beer. The song ended, and appreciative applause drifted up toward the twin moons and the stars, following the trail of sparks from the bonfires. People moved around us, laughing and talking as they headed toward the tables. "Not in the mood, huh?" Máire said. "Or hasn't the right person asked yet? Maybe the right person just isn't here?"

Dominic came up to us before I could answer, leaning heavily on his cane, and peering up at the two of us through disapproving, dark eyes. "Elio, Máire," Dominic said. "I trust everyone is enjoying themselves." His words came out encased in a breath of fog, and I could see his gaze moving from my necklace to Máire's. He almost smiled then, belatedly.

"I'm having a great time, Geeda. In fact, I was just about to ask Máire to dance with me. So if you'll excuse us . . ."

I put my mug down on the table and held out my hand to Máire, who looked at me suspiciously for a moment. Then, her lips pressed together, she set her mug alongside mine and took my hand. We headed out toward the dance circle as the musicians broke into a gavotte. We moved silently through the intricate steps of the dance for several moments, weaving through the other couples in the circle. I'm a two-left-footed dancer, especially with something that complicated, but Máire compensated wonderfully, making me appear almost graceful. Dominic, who glared at us for a long time, finally turned his back and started talking to old Vlad and Kiria Tami near one of the bonfires.

"Why do I feel like I was just used to make a point?" Máire whispered as the steps of the minuetlike dance brought us close for a moment.

"A sudden impulse," I told her. We moved apart, then together again. Her hands were colder than the beer mug. Her attitude seemed only slightly warmer. "I didn't mean to drag you into a Family spat. Thanks for going along with me."

"The truth is that I don't like your Geeda very much." We moved apart, took two lilting steps hand in hand to the left, then came together again. "Sorry," she added, but there didn't seem to be much apology in the voice. "I don't mean to insult your Family."

"Dominic doesn't make liking him very easy." The gavotte took us across the circle as we took new partners for a few measures, then returned. "It's a talent he has. He works at it very hard."

"You can tell him that his practice shows." That came packaged with a fleeting smile, and I grinned in return.

"He'd just take it as a compliment."

That brought another smile, one that lingered a little longer than the last. We didn't say anything for a time, saving our breath for the dance. After the swirling, energetic flourish of the final movements (where I had to be rescued at least twice), we applauded the musicians and headed for the side again as new dancers entered the circle. "I know who you were waiting for, Elio. I'm sorry I'm not Anaïs," Máire said as we recovered our mugs. "I was hoping she'd come to the Gather, too. I really didn't think she would, though. Not after—" Máire stopped. She sipped her beer, looking out at the darkness over Tlilipan. She shrugged.

"Not after *what*? After what happened with me? I'd be curious what Ana told you."

"She told me enough to know that she doesn't want it discussed." The glance she gave me then was strange, a flashing of dark eyes in the firelight. I wasn't quite certain how to decipher the expression. "For what it's worth, Elio, she cares about your Family. Especially Euzhan. She cares about you, as well—about what you think, about your feelings."

"She has an odd way of showing it."

"I know she thought about being at the Gather. Actually, I thought she'd come, but . . ." Another brief shrug. "She's a

75

very private person. For good reasons." Máire blinked as a stream of smoke from one of the fires drifted between us.

"I know her reasons."

"Do you." Máire said it flatly, so that I couldn't tell whether it was a question or not.

"*Hai*," I answered. "I do." I frowned, looking out at the dancers, at the flirtations, at the people who had already coalesced into couples for the evening. I should have been happy, seeing that. I wasn't. I fingered the yellow stone around my neck, lifting it slightly. "Máire, ummm . . ."

"No," she said. We both knew what I'd been about to ask. "I don't think so. Not tonight, anyway."

I nodded, trying to pretend—as our customs dictated—that it didn't matter. "Yeah, we don't match anyway."

"No," Máire answered. "We don't match."

There didn't seem to be much to say after that. Máire, after a small noncommittal smile, drifted away toward the food table. I wandered some more. Becca had seen the yellow stone on Hizo's necklace and paired up with him; Maria was with Marshall. It was a good night for yellow, it seemed—not that it mattered for me. Danda had yellow also, but very obviously didn't take any notice the times I walked past her. I don't know what happened to Máire; she disappeared not long after our dance. So had Ghost, the *Ibn Battuta*'s erratic orbit once more taking her out of range of our patchwork equipment.

In another hour, the fires had gone to burning embers and most of the couples had drifted back up to the Rock and their beds. A few of the elders were still there, huddled around one of the fires and talking with themselves. Dominic was among them. He looked up once from his conversation, and saw me. Disgust pinched the corners of his mouth as he glanced at me. Elio: The Failure. The Ugly.

I walked slowly away from the remnants of the Gather, heading back up the path to the Rock.

I went to bed alone.

INTERLUDE:
KaiSa

"YOU'RE THE LAST, THANK VEISATI," THE YOUNG Sa said as KaiSa and AbriSa stepped into the boat. The child had introduced kerself as BelSa—ke was no one that Kai recognized, evidently an acolyte who'd come to the island in the last three cycles while Kai had been away. Bel was a handsome child, just balanced on the edge of adolescence. Bel's strong muscles moved under ker *shangaa* as ke paddled the boat away from the rocky shore. *If Bel completes the rites,* Kai thought, *ke will do well Outside. A handsome Sa indeed.*

The sun flickered through fast-moving clouds, the play of light and shadow across Kai's *brais* causing ker to shiver uncomfortably. KaiSa looked back at the shore, draped in mist in the cold morning. Somewhere back there was a danger. Ke could sense it, growing each day as ke and AbriSa had made their way back toward the AnglSaiye. Kai didn't know what the danger was, but ke could feel it, pressing down on ker soul.

Soon they would know the shape of this nameless fear. KaiSa looked out to the bay, shielding ker eyes against the salt spray kicking up over the long, intricate curves of the carved bowspirit that protected their craft from the demons of the water. AnglSaiye, home to all Sa, loomed ahead of them: a craggy presence, a jagged crown of darkness sitting between the light grays of the sea and sky and stretching most of the way across the bay's narrow mouth. The wind, cold and cruel, lifted the long swells of the endless ocean and hammered them against the rocks there, giving the island a skirt of white foam. Faintly, Kai could hear the sea bells sending their greetings, the iron clappers on the great bronze bells moved by the waves as they crashed into the island. The familiar sound woke memories of when ke'd last been here, the tidal bells sending ker farewell as ke left AnglSaiye for the world ruled by Te and Ta.

"All the other Sa have returned, then?" Kai asked Bel. The youth nodded silently, saving ker breath for the effort of leaning into the oars as a wave lifted the bow of the small craft.

Bel's face was grim, drawing lines that should never be in the face of one so young. "All," ke breathed, "except those that JaqSaTu believes will never be coming back."

With that, Abri shivered alongside Kai, a cold that was more than that of wind and sea. *What has happened out in the world?* Kai wondered. *Who can't return, and why?* "We'll know everything soon enough," Abri said, guessing at Kai's thoughts. "Listen to the sea bells. There's such power in their sound. . . ."

Someone saw them as they approached the island. Guiding fires were lit on either side of the island's harbor, their orange glare illuminating the lower banks of the mist. Call drums boomed out a challenge from the high cliffs of AnglSaiye; Kai went to the small call drum mounted below the bowspirit and responded, giving the coded rhythms that identified the three of them in the boat, letting those on the island know that they were in no danger.

NasiSaTu, the legendary Sa who had by kerself defied the customs of that time and created the Community of All Sa, had led them to AnglSaiye. Only once in its long history had AnglSaiye been attacked—by the army of the mad KeldTe. A thousand boats, each carrying two hands of warriors, had covered the waters of the bay, intending to invade the island, which had become home to the Sa only five hands of cycles before. The foundations of the White Temple had just been laid; its great concourses and gardens were still under construction.

KeldTe was determined to break AnglSaiye and bring the Sa back under the control of the Te and Ta—or, more truthfully, of himself.

That had been the darkest moment in the history of the Sa. The Sa were not warriors, and the TeTa would not or could not work together in concert to smash KeldTe. The Sa had nothing but the protection AnglSaiye itself offered, and their prayers.

VeiSaTi was a god who required sacrifice. NasiSaTu had prepared kerself. As the Sa called upon the god VeiSaTi, NasiSaTu had stood on the cliffs of AnglSaiye, with all the Sa beseeching ker not to do this. Ke only smiled at them, and then let kerself fall into the water, into the hands of VeiSaTi.

VeiSaTi had been pleased with the gift of life. A great storm arose the next morning, scattering Keld's boats and breaking them into tinder on the rocks. Those few of Keld's army who reached the island safely died there on the pebbled beaches, slain by the long spearblades of the Sa before they could even begin the long climb to AnglSaiye's heights. Keld himself was never found, drowned in the storm. NasiSaTu's successor, saddened by the useless carnage, had left the island the next cycle to bring peace to a sundered land, giving back to Ta and Te the lands that Keld had stolen, building the High Road that linked them all, and sending out the first mendicant Sa—the travelers.

Six *terduva* ago, that had been. 3,072 cycles of relative peace had come and gone; nearly thirty hands of SaTu had ruled the island after NasiSaTu. Seeing AnglSaiye brought back all that long history to KaiSa. Ke watched the island grow larger, and glimpsed the White Temple high above through the mists.

A few moments later, the drums answered with permission to land. BelSa leaned heavily into the oars once more, moving their boat through the swells and into the calmer waters of AnglSaiye's harbor.

A trio of Sa was there to meet them as they bumped the wooden dock. BelSa tossed a rope up on the dock; the boat was quickly secured and hands reached down to help them up. Kai and Abri each knelt and picked up one of the rocks, spat on it, and tossed it into the water—the ritual of all Sa who return to the island, giving of themselves to the water, which was VeiSaTi's domain. The three Sa who had met them had just completed their First Vows and the rituals that formed their new commitment to VeiSaTi: all wore beaded gauze masks over their faces, hung on copper frames so that only their eyes could be seen, indicating they had entered their cycle of silence. Their bare chests were newly marked with the sign of AnglSaiye, their skin inflamed and red around the blue-black markings that represented VeiSaTi as well as the world of the Sa. Kai knew two of the three, and ke nodded to them in recognition; ke recalled ker own cycle of silence, and how difficult it had been, yet at the same time strangely pleasant. One of them pointed toward the long stairs cut into the living rock of AnglSaiye, twisting upward and disappearing into the mist.

"Yes, we're ready," Kai told them. "BelSa, many thanks for bringing us home."

Bel inclined ker head as ke finished securing the boat to the dock. Kai took a breath and grinned briefly at Abri. The stone stairs sagged in the middle, worn away by countless Sa feet. Kai remembered the first time ke'd seen the stair, as a child. Ke'd been awed and frightened, and as they climbed, ke found kerself hugging the cliff, frightened by the dark heights that seemed to go up forever. "Home again," ke said. "I'd forgotten just how tall the stairs were."

"So had I," Abri answered, "but we'll remember quickly. Our thighs will remind us."

There were five hundred and twelve steps from the beach and up the cliffs of AnglSaiye to the emerald and satin slopes above. They were not given any rest as they climbed. Kai's legs and lungs burned with exertion long before they caught their first glimpse of the roofs of the White Temple, set near the cliff's edge and overlooking the bay.

When they'd reached the summit at last, all of them paused to take a sip from the deep well, fed by the temple spring. The water was frigid, with a sharp metallic aftertaste that instantly brought memories back to Kai. Wiping ker lips as ke slowly regained ker breath, Kai glanced up the short slope.

There, the White Temple gleamed, snared in drifting sunshine.

The White Temple had been formed of AnglSaiye's pale marble, the massive triangular blocks quarried from deposits on the sea-face of the island and then laboriously brought here on rollers. The curved face of the temple was a reminder of the feminine part of the Sa, while the central spire mirrored the male essence. Standing on the temple stairs and looking down toward them was a familiar figure.

"JaqSaTu," Kai cried, and immediately gave a sign of obeisance, covering ker *brais* with one hand.

JaqTe returned the gesture, more perfunctorily as befitted ker station. Ke strode down the stairs toward them while acolytes scattered out of ker way like startled *kasadi* along the edge of a spring pond. "KaiSa, AbriSa," ke said as ke approached. "It's good to see the two of you. Praise VeiSaTi. I was afraid. . . ."

JaqSaTu had changed much in the cycles since Kai had last seen ker. Ker hair had taken on the silvered hues of age, and deep folds had settled in along the lines of ker face. Ker teeth were marbled with dark lines, and the eyes had a tired look, as if ke were not sleeping well.

"JaqSa, what is going on?" Kai asked, unable to restrain ker curiosity any longer. "Calling the traveling Sa back to AnglSaiye—that's never been done before. I thought . . ."

Jaq held up ker hand, but the stern gesture was belied by the slow smile that shaped ker mouth. "KaiSa, I can see by your eyes that you're thinking the cycles haven't been particularly kind to me, but *you* haven't changed at all. You still lack patience." Jaq's smile disappeared as ke looked past Kai, Abri, and their escort, and Kai turned to gaze with Jaq out over the green-gray waves of the bay toward the land. "This much I can tell you now. What is out there is the ghost of KeldTe. He has returned once again. Not the man himself, but the sickness that was in him. That spirit has found yet another host."

CONTEXT:
Máire Koda-Schmidt

MÁIRE COULD STILL SEE THE FIRES OF THE GATHER flickering through the trees down on the landing pad. The moonlight was bright enough that she could see figures moving on the path between the Rock's main gate and the pad. Her room was in one of the towers springing from the Rock, and the open window brought the smell of wood smoke and the faint sound of people talking. There were other sounds in the night as well: the chirps, burbles, and peeps of Mictlan's wildlife, and once the distant, deep growl of a grumbler. Below, from her sib Kim's room, came the grunting, high-pitched panting of intercourse. Máire wondered who Kim was with; she seemed to be enjoying herself, with whoever it was.

Her sib's cries of passion stirred an echo within Máire's own loins. Still standing at the window, she reached down and lifted the hem of her nightshirt. She slid soft fingertips through the curled forest between her legs. The first touch brought a surprised, gasping inhalation. She closed her eyes, sighing and giving herself over to the urgent, rising need within her. A fragrant wetness responded to her touch, and she let her mind roam, let it seek the fantasy it wanted.

She knew who it would be. She knew. She told herself she didn't care.

When the orgasm rolled through her a few minutes later, she let herself collapse against the windowsill. With the waves that shivered through her body, she whispered the name softly to the wind, to the night, to the world.

There was no answer for her, and when the last shudders had passed, somehow she felt emptier than she had before.

INTERLUDE:
KaiSa

LATER, AFTER THEY'D RESTED, THEY CARVED THEIR names on one of the numerous *nasituda* of Returning Travelers set before the Temple, and urinated carefully on their glyphs. New *shangaa* of unbleached flaxen were given to them. The ritual purifications took the remainder of the night: first the uncomfortable purging, then the pleasant, warm salt baths and the perfumed oils. Kai spent time cleansing the interior of ker pouch, which still smelled of the infants ke'd held there while the Ta and Te, Xe and Xa had gone about their tasks. The scent brought back painful memories of mingled joy and despair, the blinding thrill of seeing ker children born of Ta and Xa, and the utter misery and anger of the leavetakings. The odor seemed to linger for a long time on ker fingertips.

Around ker, in the community rooms behind the Temple, eager and clumsy acolytes attended to other needs of the Sa, as Kai had once done kerself. There must have been three hands of hands of traveling Sa gathered here—more of them than Kai had ever seen together in one place. Yet there were faces that Kai missed. "Where's Loiti?" ke asked of ker peers.

"Ke went out four cycles before I did. Or Karm? I don't see ker . . ." There were no answers to those questions, only shrugs and grim silence.

Ke talked softly with the others, some of whom ke knew, many more ke did not because they had been traveling since before Kai had come to AnglSaiye kerself. They traded tales of their experiences, all tinged with the sadness that Sa shared as their birthright. They avoided the topic of why they had returned to the island, though Kai knew that it was uppermost on all their minds.

By the time the meditations were finished and they were cleansed enough to enter the Temple, Kai had sipped ker cup of bitter *jitu* and gratefully sank into the receptive half-trance the brew granted. Ke walked with the other Sa to the White Temple, through the milky glow of Chali and into the searing ocean-roar that was the massed choir of acolytes behind the mucca-shell partition at the rear. Their voices shivered in Kai's mind, colors cascading from the falling tones.

When the LongChant had ended, JaqSaTu moved to the gigantic, unbroken whorled shell that the founder NasiSaTu had found (impossibly) where the White Temple now stood—VeiSaTi, whose birthplace was in the depths of the sea, had placed it there as a sign to NasiSa. The smooth mouth of the shell stole the smoky yellow light of the torches and transformed it into rainbowed splendor. A distorted, elongated image of Jaq was reflected back at the ranks of Sa in the pearled, natural mirror.

"Sa!" JaqSaTu cried, and the word echoed in the vast Temple's interior. Kai shivered as if suddenly cold; alongside ker, Abri noticed ker discomfort and took Kai's hand comfortingly. "VeiSaTi Kerself has called you here, not me. Ke has spoken in my dreams, in my meditations, and Ke has said that we must prepare to defend the way of life Ke has given to all Sa."

With that, Jaq unfolded the tale that had brought them all back to the island. "His name is DekTe," Jaq began. "Some of you may have given children to his father and mother, CeriTe and LaiTa, in cycles past."

"I knew CeriTe and LaiTa," one of the elder Sa said, one of the travelers unknown to Kai. "Ceri was stern and unhappy, and walked with a terrible limp from a fight with a neighboring Te, and Lai was a mirror to him, reflecting his own bile back to him. I did what Sa do, and left before the children were born. I was happy to be gone from there."

"DekTe is definitely his father's child, then," Jaq responded. "And he has taken a Ta who matches LaiTa: her name is CaraTa, and we are told that she is as fey as DekTe. We also know that at least one Sa who has ventured into their territory has not come back out again."

Jaq raised ker hand against the massed uproar those words caused. "Please," ke said. "Listen to me. We know that DekTe and CaraTa have taken up the mantle of KeldTe. A cycle ago, emissaries came here to AnglSaiye. They told us that Dek and Cara had armed their Xe and Xa, and attacked along their northern and eastern borders, taking lands that did not belong to them. We know that TeTa have conflicts, but this was no honorable *xeshai*. They killed the TeTa who ruled there without letting them offer ransom, and broke their *nasituda*. The XaXe who fought against him were captured, and Dek freed any of the JaJe who would swear loyalty to him."

It might have been the heat in the White Temple, or the *jitu*, but as JaqSaTu spoke, the air around ker seemed to waver in Kai's vision, and in the reflective surface of the god's shell, an indistinct figure started to form. Kai cried out in surprise, and Abri clenched ker hand tighter. "Do you see it? Do you see it, Abri?" Kai asked ker, whispering, but Abri only shook her head.

JaqSa didn't notice the apparition forming around ker, either. Ke continued to speak, ker tone weary, as if the very words exhausted ker. "We know that KarmSa was in one of the territories they attacked. Dek and Cara ignored our laws, and despite the fact that Karm was Sa, they would not let ker leave. Dek gathered together all the XaXe he had captured, and he and Cara. . . ." Emotion overcame JaqSa. Ker head bowed, and it was a long moment before ke looked up again. "This is difficult to say. They mutilated KarmSa in front of all the XaXe. They said that they would do the same to any Sa who opposed them."

The figure around JaqSa coalesced, darkened. To Kai's eyes, it seemed to be a Sa, but impossibly tall. The smoky, indistinct hands lifted, ker *brais* was a blue fire, and ker eyes were white.

They stared directly at Kai, and the triple gaze burned.

But only Kai seemed to notice. Only Kai saw ker. JaqSaTu continued to speak, oblivious.

"KarmSa took ker own life afterward. DekTe and CaraTa have recently attacked and won another territory, still moving northward—toward AnglSaiye. They are now near Black Lake."

Another howl of fury. JaqSa raised ker hands in supplication as the apparition behind ker did the same. Kai trembled. "That's deliberate provocation on the part of Dek and Cara. They know that Black Lake is sacred to us, and they look to draw us out from AnglSaiye. They also have thousands fighting with them now, more than KeldTe ever had. The XaXe who have come to us, fleeing from them, say that Dek and Cara have said that any Sa belong to them. Sa children have been born but not sent here to AnglSaiye for evaluation and training."

Kai hardly heard the words. The apparition continued to stare at ker, and now the hand lifted and one long finger jabbed imperiously at Kai.

Against the rising sound of Sa outrage, JaqSaTu lifted ker own hand. "I hear your anger. I feel it also, but the laws we follow are clear on this, and I don't pretend to be as wise as NasiSaTu. So I'll follow ker path. From this point, no Sa will serve DekTe and CaraTa, or anyone who follows them. If they persist in their actions, we'll call for all Te and Ta to join us against them, as NasiSaTu did with KeldTe. This time, we hope, they will help us. What remains is for someone to take this proclamation to DekTe and CaraTa. After what they did to KarmSa, I can't ask any of you to do that. I can't, and I won't. I will go myself, and you will elect a new Tu after I am gone."

There was a quick roar of protest. In the clamor, the apparition jabbed ker finger once more toward Kai. Kai released Abri's hand and stood. As ke did so, the apparition dissolved, melting into a cloud that rushed to Kai on some unfelt wind. The cloud struck ker in a numbing cold, the cold of the deep sea. Kai shivered as ke raised ker hand to speak.

"I will go, JaqSaTu," Kai said. Ker words sounded as if someone else were speaking them, far too powerful for ker own voice. "You're needed here. VeiSaTi has called me, and I will go."

JOURNAL ENTRY:
Gabriela Rusack

I THOUGHT THE WORST THAT COULD POSSIBLY HAP-
pen to me occurred when the *Ibn Battuta* ex-
ploded, tearing me apart from Elzbieta forever. Elz and I had
been partners for so long, friends for even longer, and I
loved her so intensely that it wasn't possible for me to think
about life with her. We were *one*. We were twinned souls.

But when the *Ibn Battuta* was destroyed, I was here on
Mictlan, and she was up there on the ship. I thought that
nothing, *nothing* could hurt me worse than that. I don't even
know how I managed to get through those first few weeks,
and for months afterward, a word, or a smell, a taste, a song
. . . all sorts of odd things would trigger memories of Elzbieta
and I'd start crying, feeling her loss all over again. I believed
it would always be that way.

As it turned out, I was wrong. I never stopped loving Elzbieta or missing her, but time eventually grew scar tissue
over the wound, and I found that a new wound always hurts
worse than an old one.

Worse was the ostracism that came later. Worse was being
ignored by nearly all the other people around me. Worse
was never again knowing the soft touch of someone else's
hand or mouth.

And worst of all were the taunts of the children, who I
knew were only mirroring what their parents—my old ship-
mates, whom I'd once counted as friends—taught them.
Rezu, they called me, making the word sound like a curse.
Old Crow! they shouted. They threw stones at me when they
saw me; they made up cruel rhymes.

> *Gabriela rezu, nasty old crow*
> *Gabriela rezu, dying in the snow*
> *Let her lie there until she's blue*
> *Gabriela rezu, we don't see you.*

The only reason I bothered to stay alive was the pleasure I derived from being a constant reminder to them of how cruel they've become.

VOICE:
Elio Allen-Shimmura

I COULD HEAR ANA AND MÁIRE'S VOICES BEFORE I actually entered the Allen-Shimmura common room, all underlaid with the atrocious caterwauling of Gabriela Rusack's music. From what I could tell, they were discussing the bog body. I stopped outside the door for a moment.

"... a coarse porridge of grains, a *meuslix*. As best as I can tell, anyway."

"So he made a bowl of cereal, and then they hit him over the head, strangled him, and threw him in the lake just to make sure he was good and dead. Maybe he was the cook."

Máire chuckled. "I'll admit it wasn't much of a last meal. What surprised me is how crudely ground it was; from the husks, dirt, and pollen mixed in, I'd guess that it was hastily plucked and then quickly prepared, especially since you tell me that Gabriela found some old Miccailian millsites which were quite sophisticated. Your bogman's cereal wasn't very tasty—by our standards, anyway. But ..."

"But?"

"Well, if that supposition's right, if his last meal was harvested just before he was killed, then from the pollens and grains that were present we can place the time of the year he died: autumn, probably late—just about this time of year. There were puffwort spores mixed in, and they're just blooming in the last week. Of course, that's assuming puffworts bloomed at the same time back then. Here ... try this. Now don't make faces like that, Ana—it's your scientific duty...."

I could hear the clink of a spoon against pottery. Then Ana sputtered. "Gods, Máire, that's ... that's *awful*," she said. "I'll bet he *was* the cook." They both laughed.

The sound released me from stasis. "So what's so awful?" I asked, and entered the room.

"Elio . . ." Anaïs set down a bowl of assorted stems and grasses floating in thin, blue-white goathen milk. She pointed at it and made a face. Máire didn't look as if she were pleased at my intrusion, or maybe she was just mirroring Ana's expression. "That concoction is what Máire is telling me my bogman ate just before he died. Want to try some?"

I grimaced. "If he ate that, then I think you need to add another cause of death."

"It wouldn't kill you, Elio," Máire said, but the look she gave me indicated that she might not mind if it made me ill. All the sparkle and humor had drained from her voice. "In fact, you could live fairly well, if boringly, on a diet of this."

"Not to mention that you'd get your yearly quota of roughage and fiber in just one sitting. No thanks. I leave the experimentation to the scientists. You're the experts."

That seemed to finish the conversation. For several long seconds, we all looked at each other with polite half-smiles while we tried to think of a neutral subject. I was about to ask about Euzhan when Máire sighed and rose from her seat. "I need to get back," she said. Her hand was on Anaïs's arm; Anaïs put her hand on top of it.

"Thanks for your help," she said to Máire. Anaïs smiled at her, then Máire nodded and gathered up the various grasses and mosses that she'd brought.

"I'll talk with you tomorrow," she said. "If you want."

"I'd like that."

Máire smiled at Ana, just looking at her for a few seconds. Finally, almost with a start, she turned to leave. We both listened until her footsteps faded down the corridor. Just as they did, Anaïs's *mi* Keri started to walk into the room, saw the two of us alone, muttered something neither one of us caught, and left. "Popular place," I said.

Anaïs shrugged. "I'm sorry, Elio. I wish they wouldn't do that."

"It's okay. My Family would have done the same if we were there."

"Would they." There was no rising tone at the end of the sentence. Instead, it was weighted with a ponderous nonchalance. She'd picked up the bowl of the bogman's cereal and was holding it in her lap, one hand on the spoon.

"I was sorry you weren't at the Gather the other night. I'd hoped you'd come."

She watched me, not saying anything, Gabriela's music a monochromatic backdrop. She lifted the spoon, dropped it back. The metal rang against the lip of the bowl. "I was busy."

"I'd like to know who you were avoiding: me, or Geeda Dominic and his entourage?"

Her eyes cut a swath over my face. Her fingers went white around the spoon. I didn't say anything. She started to speak, looking up again at me, then biting her lower lip and looking down again. She punched the spoon into the cereal. "You can't understand," she said. She was holding the spoon in her fist, like a dagger. She stabbed at the mess in the bowl. "You just can't."

"Probably not. But I'm listening."

"Is that supposed to make me feel better? Since you're willing to listen, is Dominic going to change? Maybe I can just stand outside the complex and shout 'Praise all *kami*, Elio's willing to *listen* to me!'—that'll certainly have an impact."

The spoon jabbed at the cereal again. She blinked hard, looking away from me. A tear traced a wet line down her cheek, and she swiped at it with her free hand, sniffing. "All I want . . . Damn . . . *Damn.* . . ." She stopped. More tears stole from under her closed lids; this time she didn't do anything to hide them. "I didn't ask to be this way. I didn't have any choice in how Mictlan twisted me."

I could hear the spoon grinding against the fibers in the bowl. Anaïs stared at the bowl, but I knew she didn't see it. "I never meant for Ochiba to be anything but happy. She *was* happy. We both were." A stab of the spoon. Another. "And for that . . . for that . . . most of the people here would treat me like . . . like the fucking Miccail on my slab."

She threw the bowl on the floor. It hit the stone flags and shattered, spewing chips of glazed pottery and milk-soaked grain. The Family's verrechat, which had crept into the room, went streaking away in panic. Anaïs was sobbing, great racking breaths, her hands cupping her face. I sat on the couch alongside her. I touched her shoulder. When she didn't pull away, I slowly gathered her into my arms. She tensed for a moment, then her body relaxed and she leaned into me, still crying.

We sat that way for a long time.

VOICE:
Máire Koda-Schmidt

I LEFT ANAÏS, AS ALWAYS, FEELING VERY CONFUSED. You'd think I'd be used to it by now, but I'm not. I doubt that I will ever be.

Part of me—the part molded by Family and society—was hoping that Elio and Anaïs would go to bed again, that it would finally work between them, and that Anaïs would be happy. Part of me was just . . . well, the only word is jealous. I was also angry with myself for leaving when I wanted to be the one to stay.

And part of me was simply frightened of the conflicting emotions.

Damn, damn, *damn*. . . . So confused. . . .

This is certainly not what I expected. The person I see looking back at me from the mirror isn't ugly (nor, honestly, is she beautiful). I'm not visibly deformed like Elio, Anaïs, or most of the others. If I'm not particularly drawn to any of the men, well, I don't find any of the *other* women attractive either.

Attracted to Anaïs? Loving Anaïs? That makes no sense. It makes no sense at all.

Hell, I *want* children, as much as any other woman here. I want to experience the sensation of life growing inside me; I want to push a new life out between my legs and hear her first cry. I want to hold my babies, to hug them, love them and watch them grow. I want to become Geema myself, to have my children's children running and laughing around me. I want some part of me to go on, forever.

And I want Anaïs, also, in a way that scares me.

I'm betrayed by my own emotions, and there isn't anyone to talk to.

Off to the west side of the old landing pad there is a cemetery. I go there sometimes, when I want to converse with myself. All of the Matriarchs and Patriarchs are buried there, along with their sons and daughters, and most of the sons and daughters of the next generation as well. I no doubt share blood with most of them, at least in some little part. I go there and touch the headstones, and try to feel the connection. I try to talk to their *kami*, who surely must lurk there.

There are other headstones, too, and they far outnumber the others. These are small stones, the majority without names: the graves of our children, the ones dead before they tasted the fullness of life. I wander there too, at times, and I look at the names carved there, and the dates:

FEMALE CHILD OF NICOLE KODA-LEVIN
BORN ON 37 FEBRUARY 27
DIED 37 FEBRUARY 29
WE LOVED YOU. REST WELL, DEAR

Two days old, this infant, and she was plucked from Mictlan by disease or some unrepairable genetic defect, without even a name. Or . . .

PIET MARTINEZ-SANTOS
B.85 AUGUST 40
D.90 JANUARY 12

. . . who at least made it past his fourth birthday, despite the terseness of his epitaph. I even remember Piet. I remember how he died of pneumonia, gasping, coughing, his lungs slowly filling with mucus until he drowned in his own fluids, while Hui and his mam, along with his *mi* and *da*, watched helplessly. I don't need an inscription to know how they felt.

I look at the graves and I remind myself that Mictlan is a cruel, awful world. I tell myself that I'm *lucky* that I haven't brought any children into it. *How can the mothers stand it?* I wonder. *How can you invest so much love and care and hope into a child, only to see it die as an infant. How is it possible for a mother to survive that? Doesn't the death of your child leave you broken yourself? How can you look at your child and know that the odds are that she'll never reach adulthood, that this world will most likely reach out and snatch her away from you, screaming in pain, fevered and sick? How can you croon to your baby as she suckles your breast, in full realization that we won't even give her a name until she's passed her first birthday, just because so few of them make it that far?*

How could you want children, knowing that? How can you look at the quiet rows of white stone and not refuse to be part of the cycle? How can you still say "I want to give life"?

But you do. I do. I leave the cemetery with tears for the lost ones' *kami*, but with that need still festering inside.

I touch their graves, these lost cousins of mine, and I cry for them, and I tell myself—like all the other women—that *my* children would live. That *my* love would keep them alive.

I even know I'm indulging in the worst self-delusion, and I don't care.

CONTEXT:

Tami Koda-Schmidt

TAMI SAW MÁIRE WALKING PAST HER ROOM. AN IM-pulse made her call the girl in, gesturing. Máire, a lab apron wrapped around her, came in, tilting her head questioningly, her hands plucking like nervous birds at the waist of her apron. She wrinkled her nose at the smell of incense burning in the altar before which Tami sat.

"I'm sorry, dear," Tami said. She blinked, trying hopelessly to clear away the eternal haze of the cataracts. Her voice trembled, as did her entire body: a persistent, constant motion. That was her birthgift from Mictlan, to have muscles that were never at rest, never totally under her control. She put her hands in her lap, clenching them tightly in a futile effort to stop their shaking. "I just haven't had a chance to talk with you since the Gather. I wanted to know how you thought it went."

As she spoke, Tami watched the face of her great-granddaughter carefully. There was the faintest flicker of . . . *disdain? or just discomfort?* . . . before Máire smiled. "You were the best Kiria I've ever seen, *Mi* Tami. I thought the ceremony was especially beautiful."

Tami had to smile in return. Máire was—truth be admitted—one of her favorites, and Máire's smile had neutralized many a childish wrong within the household over the years. There had always been something wild and rebellious about the girl, but her intellect was keen. Máire been a challenge, in nearly every way, to her teachers within the Family. It had been Tami who advised that Ghost be allowed to set the curriculum for Máire, and that she be apprenticed to no one. That had created an angry and painful confrontation with Gerard and Eleanor, the Geeda and Geema of the Family. *Everyone* was apprenticed—that was how crucial knowledge and crafts were passed down from generation to generation. "You'll be wasting the wild girl, Tami. Half the Families already think we've ruined her. No. She'll be apprenticed and that's the end of it . . ." It had taken all of Tami's coercive skills to convince Gerard and Eleanor that Máire had new talents to offer.

And the "wild girl" had proved Tami right. It was Máire who realized that the stringy webbing choking and killing the faux-wheat crop was produced by a suddenly mutated version of the formerly innocuous insect they'd named the leaf-biter, and that introducing pincer beetles to the fields would control the leaf-biter population. After that, Máire had been left to roam wherever her interests took her, and no one within the Families much questioned her contribution to their society.

Yet. . . .

Tami worried about Máire, worried about her seeming lack of interest in the settlement's all-important reproductive task. She wondered why Máire, unlike the rest of the young women of her age, had never really indulged in the sexual freedom their society encouraged. Tami wondered, even if she refused to let those speculations actually form into words in her mind. If those vague inner nudges became thoughts, she would have to act on them. "You wore your amethyst to the Gather, didn't you? I noticed Chi-Wa had picked an amethyst from the bowl," Tami said.

"Yes, he did, *Mi* Tami. I saw him with Thandi later on."

"I saw you dancing with Elio."

Emotions flickered behind Máire's eyes. Tami could see them, but Máire gave them no words. Behind the smile, her voice was empty. "Yes, we did, *Mi* Tami. He's not much of a dancer, though."

Tami knew that Máire had come back unaccompanied from the Gather, of course. There were no such secrets in a Family compound. *Just a matter of bad karma*, Tami told herself. *The* kami *weren't with Máire.* She would pray to them later; she'd give them incense and spices. "Overall, he's a good child, Elio. Studious. Paper everywhere in his office. But good. I think he would be a decent lover for someone."

"Yes, *Mi* Tami," Máire said, but there was no agreement in her voice. "*Mi*, I need to check on an analysis running in the lab. . . ."

"Yes, of course, child. I won't keep you. It was only. . . ." Tami stopped. She closed her eyes for a moment, letting the smell of the incense calm her. "Máire, both you and Elio see so much of Anaïs. I'm . . . I'm worried about her. So are others, Dominic, for instance. Anaïs won't come to see me on her own, but I *know* something is troubling her. I'd like you to tell me what it is."

Máire's face was arranged in that careful neutrality. "*Mi*, Anaïs's problem is that she works too hard. If she's not taking care of someone, she's trying to learn more about that Miccail corpse Elena found."

"She's also not coming to the Baths, and from what I've heard, she's always careful to stay fully clothed, even around her own Family."

Máire was shaking her head. "*Mi*, who here *doesn't* have some defect? Half the colony can't metabolize one kind of food or another, and most of us have some physical mark." Tami saw Máire glance pointedly at Tami's hands, still clenched in her lap.

"Máire . . . dear. . . . Yes, minor genetic variations are entirely common—skin blemishes and unimportant quirks. But we're not talking about those."

"Aren't we?"

"That's what I'd like to know."

"*Mi* . . ." Máire loosed a sigh of exasperation. "I have to wonder *why* you're asking me this. What if I told you that I knew that, under her clothes, Anaïs is like some awful monster? What would you do about it? What possible difference would it make? Are you really worried because you think something is 'troubling' Ana, or are Dominic and some of the other elders suggesting something else? That's who started you on this, isn't it?"

"Máire, dear . . ."

"I'm sorry, *Mi*. I know you have responsibilities as Kiria. I know the Elders have their concerns, also. But there's nothing right about hatred, especially based on ignorance. Not here. It's bad enough that we gave in to that once before with Gabriela. There's so few of us, Mi. I don't care what Ana is, what she believes, who she may love or how she loves them." A blush darkened Máire's face. Tami could almost feel the heat of it. "*Mi* Tami, I have that analysis. I need to go now. I'm. . . . I'm sorry."

Máire ran from the room, the apology in her wake. Tami sat there for long minutes in the haze of incense, wondering what it was that Máire was apologizing for and hating herself for wondering.

VOICE:
Máire Koda-Schmidt

I WENT TO THE CLINIC A FEW DAYS LATER.
Anaïs had scraped some dirt samples from the bog body's skin that she wanted me to examine, and I thought I'd pick them up. My *da* Hui was there, checking on Euzhan and making sure that Hayat was still awake. "Máire," he said. "Anaïs isn't here."

I can never tell what Hui is thinking. I know that Hui is one of the few people Anaïs would call a friend, and I know he realizes what Ochiba was to Anaïs. He's also has made it very obvious to everyone else that he doesn't care. Yet . . . I think his protest is part denial. I think he's more bothered by it than he will say.

" 'Evening, *Da*. I know. She's with Elio, I think."

I suspect he knows how I feel about Anaïs, and there's that one important difference: Ochiba wasn't Family. I am. I know that changes things for him, even if he's never said it—funny how much more tolerant we are of the behavior of others than those who are closest to us. I can't tell whether he's angry with me, or just somehow disappointed, and he's certainly never said. "Good," he said now, flatly, leaving me wondering about the subtext.

"*Hai.* I thought so too."

Another nod, served with a penetrating stare. "How's Euzhan doing, *Da*?" I asked, mostly to deflect the gaze. It worked; he glanced down the corridor to the clinic rooms.

"She's doing well. Anaïs did excellent work, better than I could have done. She'll have a nasty scar to remind her what happened, but I think we'll send her back to her Family tomorrow. Another week or two, and she'll be running around like nothing had happened. You want to see her?''

I went in and said hello. Euzhan is truly a beautiful child. I hated seeing her injured, hated the way she winced when she saw me and tried to sit up. ''Máire!''

''Hey, Euz! How are they treating you?''

''Okay, I guess, but I wish Hui and Ana wouldn't frown so much when they look at me.''

''I don't know about Ana, but *da* Hui's a natural grump,'' I told her. ''He frowns at flowers.'' She laughed at that. I hugged Euz, and chattered with her about nothing and everything while Hui—proving my point—gave Hayat a scathing critique of the way he'd changed her dressing. After a few minutes, I excused myself. ''*Da*, do you know where Anaïs left the bogman samples she wanted me to check?''

''They're back in the coldroom. You want me to go get them?''

I shook my head and patted Euzhan's cheek. ''No. You stay here with this pretty one. I'll get them.''

The lights were out. I remember noticing a smell just as my hand reached for the wall plate, something that wasn't antiseptic, sterile, and steel but was instead earthy and animal. I slapped the contact anyway.

It must have heard me coming, because it was already moving as I stepped in. I caught a glimpse of the room, noticing that the cabinet that held the bog body had been slid out of the wall rack, that the sheet that covered it was half off, askew. To my right, I heard a sharp *clack-clack*, like a verrechat's claws skittering on hardwood . . .

. . . and then the side of the room slammed hard across the side of the head.

I must have passed out momentarily. I was sprawled on the floor looking up. A male grumbler was standing over me, one arm still extended—that's what had hit me. I couldn't see out of my right eye, and I could taste blood in my mouth. I was afraid to move—not because of the grumbler but because I was afraid that I might find out that I couldn't. ''*Da* . . .'' I started to shout, but it came out more a gurgling whimper.

I spat blood. The grumbler took a step back at that, its eyes narrowing and the dreadlocks on the chin waggling. It was ugly, and it reeked. It breathed musk and exhaled decay while it mumbled angrily at me, the claws clashing as it clenched its hands restlessly. I remembered what those claws had done to Euzhan. At the same moment, I realized that I'd fallen between the grumbler and the door, that the grumbler obviously wanted out, and that—prone or not—it considered me a threat.

"You could have asked," I told it, trying to sound as calm and soothing as I could. "I'd have let you out. Really I would have."

It mumbled again, claws slashing air between us. I decided I'd better try moving. I tried to push myself up; that caused the room to do a quick dance around me. The grumbler barked, a percussive sound that hurt my ears. I could hear its claws scratching at the flooring.

"*Máire?*" *Da* Hui's voice called from out in the corridor. "What's going on?"

The grumbler howled loudly at that. It squinted, the prominent eye ridges folding. It barked at me again, like it was ordering me out of its way. I tried to comply, crawling. Evidently I wasn't fast enough for it.

At least it backhanded me again instead of using its claws. I saw the blow coming this time and brought my hands up to protect my head—it didn't help much. As I went down, as the grumbler leaped over me through a thickening mist, I heard a rifle fire.

CONTEXT:
Elio Allen-Shimmura

ELIO'S "OFFICE" WAS A SMALL ROOM CARVED FROM the Rock by the lasers on the *Ibn Battuta*'s shuttlecraft. To visitors expressing surprise at the sheer amount of paper overwhelming his office, he had a stock answer: "There's an old French proverb I once came across: *Les heureux ne font pas d'histoire*—Happy folks don't make history. There's a hell of a lot of history here."

Most of the time they laughed.

The room had once stored equipment, but a long ventilation shaft had been punched through the stone when this part of the complex had been created. Sunlight poured down the vault to spotlight the desk on which Elio's terminal sat, besieged by cascading piles of paper and books.

"Ana, a lot of Gabriela's stuff isn't in the system—not surprising, given the way most of the Elders felt about her. Still, there were a few things." Elio punched a key and the monitor flickered. "Here," he said to Anaïs, moving one of the piles from a chair and balancing it precariously on the edge of the desk. "Let me clear a place for you to sit. . . ."

Several sheets of paper were still draped over the arm of the chair. Anaïs picked them up, glancing at the title typed there. "'Transcript of Elders' Monthly Meeting, 101 February 31.' Pretty exciting material you're working with, Elio."

"As dry as dust, and less sustaining."

Ana gave a small half smile. She moved the transcript to the floor and sat.

Kiria Tami, seeing Elio's office once, had remarked dryly that "I know we have a flourishing papermaking industry here. Now I see that you're its sole consumer." Elio could only shrug and laugh. The original colonists would have howled in amusement to see him typing on a keyboard and staring at a monitor, but then they'd had direct neural links to the net and software agents like Ghost. Elio doubted that the Patriarchs and Matriarchs had even *known* how to type. But for their descendants there'd been neither the manufacturing capabilities for the neural webbing, nor the equipment and knowledge to perform the delicate nanosurgery to install them. Elio operated under Ghost's instructions: the computers the colony used were well over a century old, and there were no facilities or expertise to fix anything but the simplest problems. In the last decade, they'd lost a dozen terminals—the dead ones were cannibalized for parts, but at some point in the fairly near future, they would lose their computing capabilities. At that point, they'd also lose Ghost and all the databases on the *Ibn Battuta* as well. Because of that, Ghost and Elio were trying to print out everything they could, so they would have a legacy on the dark night the last computer died.

"I had the system search for the symbols in the bog body's tattoo. Gabriela had tentatively assigned meanings to some of the Miccail pictographs. A wavy line, for instance, shows up on all the Miccail stelae that she identified as birth records. Maybe the curved lines has something to do with a birth, or a beginning. On the other hand, it looks an awful lot like a stylized person: a stick figure. Unfortunately, there's nothing in Gabriela's stuff that talks about a triangle, or about a figure with a tail—if that's what it is. I'm stumped at the moment."

Anaïs sighed. The chair protested as she leaned back against it. "That's it, then. There's nowhere else to check."

"No, not at all," Elio told her. "I have more of Gabriela's journals—not in the system, but handwritten."

Anaïs straightened again. 'I thought all the journals she wrote after she was shunned were destroyed after they found her body."

"Some. Not all. Kahnoch, who was doing my job then, squirreled some of them away. He may have hated Gabriela, but he was fascinated by her, also. And Ghost has some material of hers also, stuff he was able to upload before they purged the system. I'll go through the journals, but that's going to be tedious. Next time Ghost is around, I'll get him started, too. I'll let you know what I find out."

"Thanks, Elio. I appreciate it."

An uncomfortable silence settled around them, broken by the hum of the terminal fan. "I should get back to the clinic . . ." Anaïs pushed herself from the chair, but Elio moved in front of her.

"You don't have to go."

"I do. Hui . . ."

"You've been avoiding me for two days, Ana. If you don't want my friendship, that's fine. But if it's because you don't think I'd want to be with you, you're wrong."

"Elio . . ."

He ignored the hands she raised in protest. He took her head between his hands, drawing her closer. His kiss was soft but insistent. Anaïs, her hands on his chest, pushed against him, relaxed, and then pushed away once more. "I don't know what I am," she said to him. "Elio, Ochiba and I—"

His arm, slicing air, cut off her confession. "I don't care, Ana," Elio told her. "It may matter to others, but not to me. Why won't you believe that? Why won't you give me another chance?"

For a moment, she only stared at him. Then, silently, she took a step toward him. Her face tilted up to his, her arms went around him. Her mouth opened as he leaned into her.

She pulled him down onto the paper-littered floor.

VOICE:
Máire Koda-Schmidt

"... SIT UP SLOWLY. HOW ARE YOU FEELING?"
My *da*'s face came into slow focus, his eyes
gray-white with cataracts. I was sitting on the floor, leaning
against a wall. Something cold was around my head. I could
hear Hayat talking to someone, and Euzhan chattering excitedly down the hall. I shut my eyes and opened them again
slowly.

"I feel . . . like I fell off the Rock and landed on my head."
I moved, and lights flashed behind my eyelids. I moaned,
feeling tears start with the pain. I blinked them away. "Do
I look like I feel?"

"Pretty much. You'll look worse tomorrow when the
bruises show up, and I doubt you're going to be able to see
out of your right eye for a day or two. But you're damn
lucky. I don't think the grumbler broke anything. If it had
used its claws . . ."

Neither one of us needed to finish that statement, though
it brought back memories. "Where—" I started to ask. I
started to get up, but Hui put his hands on my shoulders
and pushed me down; it didn't take much effort.

"There," he said, and pointed.

The grumbler was on its back, its long, thin limbs flung
out. There was a gaping hole in its chest; blood dappled the
floor and puddled underneath it.

"It's dead," Hui grunted.

"Good." I said the word with a savage pleasure that surprised me with its ferocity.

"Was it in *here*?" Da asked, frowning and looking around.
I realized that he'd ignored everything else until he'd made
sure that I was all right. "Why in the world would—"

He stopped. I knew he'd seen Anaïs's bogman, lying exposed on its slab, its sheet pulled off. He looked from the
Miccail to the body of the grumbler.

"Why?" he asked again. "I wonder why?"

CONTEXT:
Vladimir Allen-Levin

✂ *. . . THE WIND . . . HE HAD NEVER HEARD THE WIND howl so loudly. It seemed like the very Rock itself would shake loose, that the storm would pick it up in hands of lightnings and sinews of thunderclouds and throw them. He could hear something breaking loose somewhere above them, and then a blinding flash and a thunderclap that nearly deafened him. He huddled in a corner of the room, clinging tightly to his mam. Not far off, someone screamed . . .*

"Here's your dinner, Geeda."

Vladimir roused himself at the sound, stirring in the worn leather of his favorite chair. Who was it who had spoken? He couldn't be certain. There was someone standing in front of him with a tray, one of the children. . . . What was her name? Havala? Was that right? Uncertain, he waved vaguely at the table alongside the chair. The girl placed the tray down. *"Arigato,"* he said, and patted her cheek. He couldn't see her clearly, but he thought she smiled as she left. Maybe not. His eyes weren't very good anymore. Most people were only a blur, and even when he recognized them, he often couldn't remember their names.

Vladimir leaned over and lifted the cover from the plate on the tray. Steam wafted up from the meat and vegetables arranged there, but he couldn't smell anything. Food was mostly tasteless anymore. Back when he was a child, when mam Kaitlin cooked, the fragrance alone would satisfy hunger. That was what it seemed like, anyway. He'd come into the common room, and there would be Kaitlin, and her brother Thomas, and grandmam Rebecca, who could speak with Ghost inside her head and who would, sometimes, tell Vladimir and the other children stories of old Earth, stories which seemed like fairy tales, filled with impossibly crowded cities and fantastic technologies, of bloody wars filled with mythical heroes and villains, of despair and hope and sorrow and joy. He loved the stories, even though he wasn't sure he believed them. Once, he remembered, several of the Matriarchs and Patriarchs were at his house for dinner. After Kaitlin had put the children to bed, he'd snuck back into the common room where they all sat around the central fire, drinking and talking, and he'd listened to their voices, feeling a strange comfort in the sound of the adults. He listened to them, without caring that he didn't understand.

"... the truth is that we're already dead. Even if Earth contacted us tomorrow and sent out a rescue expedition the next day, it would be our children's children who are rescued." That was Gabriela, recognizable by her gravelly, husky voice, even in the half darkness. No one sat near her. She was—already—alone. There was a rumble of disagreement around the room.

"All the more reason to put together our breeding program."

"By the blood of Buddha, Robert, you make it sound so fucking cold and sterile. 'Breeding program'—like you're running a damn kennel. Or is it just that you want your own personal harem to screw?"

"Gabriela, we don't need the sarcasm or the crudity." That was Geema Rebecca, her voice colder than Vladimir had ever heard it.

"That's where you're wrong, Becky. We need it because if things don't change, breeding program or not, we're just too small a group to survive. If I have to be crude to make you all listen to me, then so be it."

Another voice intruded. " 'If things don't change ...' That's the point, Gabriela. We can't predict change. I say we do what we can, and we trust in fate to do the rest."

"That's nicely said, Jean, and predictably optimistic on your part, but ..." Gabriela stopped, and turned in her seat. Vladimir hid his eyes and ducked beneath a table, but he could feel her gaze on him. "One of your grandchildren wants to enter the discussion, Becky. He's a little young to be one of the studs in the 'breeding program,' though,"

"Damn it, Gabriela ..." Geema Rebecca's curse nearly gave off heat. She turned quickly to him, and the fury was still in her eyes. Vladimir trembled and shot out of the room, heading for the stairs and his own bed. Behind him, Gabriela's coarse laughter followed ...

"Geeda, you haven't eaten yet."

Havala—or was it Maria?—was standing in front of his chair, hands on hips. "How do we know when things change?" he asked her. "How do we know?"

The child didn't answer. Perhaps, he thought, there was no answer.

INTERLUDE:
KaiSa

THE BLACK LAKE. . . .
In the legends written down on the oldest *na-situda*, it was said that when the god VeiSaTi emerged from the womb of the WaterMother, Ke stepped out on the land, and where the water fell from Ker giant body and into Ker footprints, great lakes formed. Where three drops—one each from ker male and female parts, and another from ker head—fell together and merged, the Black Lake was made. Thus, the Black Lake contained the triple essence of VeiSaTi, and was nearly as sacred as the ocean itself . . .

. . . for as proof of the lake's holiness, it was at the Black Lake, many *terduva* later, that the first Sa was born, to an unallied couple who had lived on the shores of the Black Lake for several years. Most Sa still were born in the lands nearest the Black Lake, Kai among them.

Since then, the Black Lake was not permitted to be part of any TeTa's holdings. The Black Lake and the land surrounding it were free, open to any CieTiLa who wished to gaze upon it. The Black Lake was a refuge, a wellspring, a paradise. From its shores, no JaJe could be taken forcibly; there, a CieTiLa could meditate on the long path of their history and breath the cool solace of the gods.

KaiSa had been there several times before. Most Sa visited the lake region at some point in their lives—VeiSaTi might be acknowledged as chief among the gods by most CieTiLa, but Ke was crucially important to the Sa, who had inherited Ker form. Walking through the area now, Kai remembered the familiar rolling hills, all blanketed with fragrant netbranches and the crisp brown carpet of their dead leaves. A slow river meandered through the deep, misty valleys—Kai followed its southern bank, where the pilgrimages of generations of CieTiLa had worn a path. Only one thing was different. When Kai had last been here, ke had seen many other CieTiLa. Now, the land was empty, and Kai felt the brooding certainty that the very hills were waiting, and watching.

At the northwest shore of the Black Lake, the river snaked around a huge outcropping of bare stone. Through an opening in the net-branches, Kai could see the *nasituda* set at the summit of the rock. Ke paused, frowning, feeling that ke wanted to crouch, to hide, even though no shadows had passed over ker *brais*. Yet the feeling of uncertain dread remained, prickling ker spine and raising the hair of ker mane.

"I am KaiSa," ke called to the wood, to the rock, to the lake. "I've come from AnglSaiye with a message for DekTe and CaraTa."

There was no answer, unless the wind that swayed the net-branches or the quick rustling of bluewings was a reply. After a moment, Kai took a trembling breath and moved on.

The Black Lake deserved its name. The lake was wide but shallow, and its waters were stained with earth and peat until they were absolutely opaque. The river Kai followed didn't feed the Black Lake, which rested many strides from its banks. No creeks, no brooks, no streams or rills flowed out of the Black Lake, no water flowed in that anyone could see. Still and silent, the Black Lake cloaked itself in dark mystery.

Kai walked along the western shore, ker feet sinking into the marshy ground that surrounded the lake. Dark water filled ker footprints behind ker. Flying insects trilled and darted among the lush vegetation while bluewings floated on the shallows, occasionally darting their long heads down into the water to feed. When ke came to a path, ke followed it up and away from the Black Lake, ascending the southwestern flanks of the granite outcropping. As ke climbed, the feeling of being watched increased, though ke still saw no one.

The sun was low in the sky when Kai reached the flat summit of the massive rock. Ke was alone in sunlight; the land below ker lay clothed in evening shadow. The *nasituda*, nearly twice as tall as Kai, cast long cloaks of darkness over the cliff edge. Ke went up to the nearest standing stone and crouched down to read the lowest carving there:

I, MepTe, declare Black Lake free . . .

"Don't believe what you read, Sa."

Kai forced kerself to stand slowly, ignoring the panic response that made ker want to run blindly away. Ke turned: against the setting sun, a trio of males stood. Kai noticed, most of all, the long killing spears they all held, the pale, keen blades glinting in the last light. Kai spread ker hands wide to show that ke had no weapons kerself. "I am KaiSa," ke said, ker voice calmer than ker heart. "I've come with a message, and I travel under the protection of AnglSaiye."

"I am PirXe," the central figure replied. "And here, Sa, there is no protection unless DekTe or CaraTa wish to give it."

JOURNAL ENTRY:
Gabriela Rusack

I ALWAYS SAID THAT FIREWORKS NEVER HAPPEN. People never really see a stranger across the proverbial crowded room and suddenly have their gazes meet in a splash of instant psychic sparks.

No, I believed that the idea that Out There Somewhere Lives Your Perfect Match was a cruel fallacy. Sparks and fireworks were generally a product of horniness, hormones, and intoxicants, not love. At best, to expect such things was to doom yourself to never finding a relationship that could match your expectations.

That's what I believed.

I attended the first meeting of the potential crew members for the *Ibn Battuta*. There must have been four or five thousand people packed into the Pedro Alvarez Cabral Convention Center in Brazilia. The assorted politicians had made their obligatory speeches, and we were facing an afternoon of excruciating details from the project leaders. The overworked environmental systems were letting far too much of the tropical heat into the building; it must have been nearly 30°C in there. We were all sweating as we filed out into the main hall for the morning break, another discomfort on top of the stress of mingling with a few thousand strangers, since one of the criteria for acceptance was sociability. We were destined to be locked up with each other for years once the voyage began, and you never knew who might be watching you to see how you handled yourself in a crowd. I had just managed to snag a cold drink and disentangle myself from the gridlock around one of the two bars set up in the room, a false smile pasted permanently on my face. I remember pulling my blouse away from my skin, grimacing at the twin circles of dampness under the arms and the wet line down my spine and between my breasts. The ice had already melted in the lukewarm cola.

"Be glad you weren't on the dais under those lights."

The voice held a laugh, speaking English but with the faint undercurrent of an Eastern European accent. I turned, and with the movement, my life changed.

That sounds hopelessly melodramatic, but it was true. I'd vaguely recalled seeing her on the stage with the project leaders. I'd seen the name on her nametag in the program, listed as Infrastructure Team Leader, but I hadn't paid any attention to her. But now. . . . I knew the instant I saw Elzbieta, saw her strong Polish face and those light, seafoam eyes. Strangely, I understood in that first moment that the attraction cut both ways, and that there was a subtle invitation in the way she held herself. Something inside me gave way, like a key had been turned in a lock, and I *knew*. I swear I did. Elz told me afterward that it was the same for her.

It's strange: I can recall that precise moment so vividly, yet I couldn't tell you what I said then, though I'm sure it was something about the heat. Even when struck with the thunderbolt, we spout inanities through the sparks, and they seem to suffice.

Elzbieta and I went to lunch together that day, with at least a dozen other people, and I couldn't tell you who they were or what we talked about. I only remember Elz, sitting across from me at the long table and occasionally smiling my way. I was dazzled, smitten. Within a week, we were lovers.

So maybe I was wrong. Maybe our perfect mate *is* somewhere out there, waiting for fate to bring us together.

INTERLUDE:
KaiSa

THEY ESCORTED KAI TO AN ENCAMPMENT IN THE forest beyond the southern shore of the Black Lake. By the last light of the day, in a small valley below, Kai saw a sight that terrified ker. There were at least ten thousand CieTiLa gathered there, more than Kai—or any other CieTiLa, for that matter—had ever glimpsed in one place. They sprawled over the valley and up the slopes, a living carpet half lost in the growing night, bristling with spears, the glow and smoke of a thousand cookfires lending a permanent haze.

"There is no hope," Kai breathed. "We had no idea . . ."

PirXe laughed alongside ker.

"Still want to speak to DekTe, Sa?" he asked. "Or is this message of yours stuck in your throat?"

Kai shook kerself loose of the spell of ker eyes. "I will still meet with him," ke said. "None of this changes what I have to say."

PirXe laughed again, and pushed KaiSa ahead. In growing darkness, they stumbled down through the trees toward the valley. As they moved through the ranks of CieTiLa, Kai felt their stares, harsh and unfriendly. Kai looked for other Sa as they walked down the hillside into the valley itself. Though male and female were plentiful enough, ke saw none of ker own kind.

After what JaqSa had said, ke had not expected to.

Ahead of them, on a small rise, a large gossamer tent had been erected. The tent was ringed by watchfires, each tended by a guard; another fire burned inside, and smoke curled from a central vent. Through the thin, white fabric, Kai could see figures moving against warm firelight. PirXe answered the challenge of the guards and moved through the fire ring to the front of the tent, one hand on Kai's arm. There, he spoke into the ear of an old male sitting outside the tent's flap. The old one grunted and rose from his seat, going inside. Kai could hear conversation: a male, a female.

Then the tent flap flipped open. Kai blinked. The shimmering light bothered ker *brais*, made ker want to crouch low as a figure stepped out into the night, dark against the flames.

The sight of him made Kai hold ker breath.

"I am DekTe," the darkness said, and his voice was like the low music of the hornshells of AnglSaiye, sonorous and compelling. His was not the voice of a beast, but that of a god. Tall, his arms were corded with ropes of muscle as he folded them over his *shangaa*. Polished stone beads were braided into the twin locks of hair under his chin, and they glistened and clashed as he spoke. DekTe was as impressive as an ancient *nasituda*. And his eyes. . . . Under the ridge of forehead, his eyes and *brais* were the dark blue of late evening, and they reflected the fires as if from hidden, lost depths. "And you are?"

"KaiSa," Kai answered. Ker voice sounded weak against the throb of DekTe's. "I've come from AnglSaiye, sent by JaqSaTu.

DekTe nodded. "It's late. Have you eaten? We have food . . ." He waved a large hand toward the interior of the tent.

"Yes," Kai found kerself saying. "I'm hungry."

"Then come in," Dek said, and there was warmth in his voice, along with what seemed a great weariness. "Come in. You've come a long way, and you must be exhausted . . ."

Kai had thought that ke would meet a monster. This was no monster. Kai had thought that no one could match the charismatic presence of JaqSaTu; ke knew now that ke had been wrong about that, also. Kai felt confused.

Were we wrong? Has JaqSa sent me to the wrong Te?

But no—the army gathered around gave the lie to that. DekTe held aside the tent flap for Kai as if he were one of the Ja. Kai could only nod and enter. Ke hated most the moment when ke passed DekTe, for ke could feel the heat of his body, hear the sound of his breath and smell the musk of his sweat. Kai didn't dare look up, afraid that ke might become lost in those eyes again.

Kai was glad when ke slipped past DekTe into the heat of the tent.

There were two other people in the tent—the old male who had gone in to get DekTe, and a female. She was tall, and there was something in her bearing that made Kai shiver involuntarily. She stepped to one side of the central fire and stared at Kai. "Ke's a pretty one," she said at last, speaking to no one in particular. "But ke looks frightened."

"KaiSa is also tired and hungry, Cara," DekTe said, and Kai realized that this was the Ta. "Ke's come from AnglSaiye with a message from their Te."

"I'm sure we already know this message. But let KaiSa say it and be done."

DekTe smiled—he had a gentle smile, Kai thought, surprised—and gave a soft negative shake of his head. "Let ker eat something first. There's no hurry."

Dek made a short motion with his hand, and the old one, sniffing either from a cold or disdain, went to a small table in one corner of the tent, bringing back a plate of sweetflake and karn-cheese. Kai looked at Dek, who nodded. Kai took a small bite of the cheese. The full extent of ker hunger ripened with the bite, and ke attacked the rest of the food ravenously as the others watched. When Kai had finished the first plateful, more food was brought to ker. Suddenly aware of the appraising eyes on ker, Kai ate the second helping more carefully.

When ke had finished, the old one took the plate from ker. "Thank you," Kai said. They were all watching ker: Dek, Cara, Pir, the old one. Mostly, ke felt Dek's gaze, searing ker face as if with the heat of a fire. Kai took a long breath, calming kerself with one of the mantras from ker student days.

"Speak," CaraTa said abruptly, the harsh syllable shattering the spell of the mantra. "It's late, and I'm tired."

A glance went between Dek and Cara, a silent communication that sharpened the edges of Dek's face, though his features had smoothed once more when he turned back to Kai. "My mate is right," he said. "We're all tired from a long day's march. Give us your message, KaiSa, and I will return you an answer in the morning."

Another breath. Kai closed ker seeing eyes, so that all ke saw was the firelight flickering in the unfocused vision of ker *brais*. "I was given this message," ke said. Ker voice shivered, like a child unsure of a recitation. "What DekTe and CaraTa are doing is against the laws of VeiSaTi and all the gods. You have violated our customs and murdered innocents. In particular, you have ignored the sacred trust that VeiSaTi has given to the Sa. JaqSa, Tu of AnglSaiye and all Sa, would have me tell DekTe and CaraTa that no Sa will serve you from this day forward, nor will we serve anyone who has sworn allegiance to you. Furthermore, if you persist in taking lands that are not yours, AnglSaiye will call for all

Te and Ta to join with the Sa against you, as we did with KeldTe long ago. We call for VeiSaTi to protect us, and for Ker hand to move with ours."

Kai waited, half expecting to be struck down. But there was only silence for several breaths.

Then CaraTa gave a quick bark of laughter. "See?" she exclaimed to no one in particular. "Empty threats is all we hear, as we knew. Look at the Sa trembling. Even ke knows it. Well, I know what answer I would give."

Kai saw PirXe move forward with that, grasping for the short knife at his belt. Kai slid easily into a defensive stance, ready to take the weapon if ke could, but DekTe made a motion with his hand that made Pir stop in midstride. "I said we would give an answer in the morning," DekTe said. "We shouldn't be hasty here. Cara?"

Kai watched anger struggling with something else on her face. "Fine," she said. "Ke's hardly important. In the morning."

PirXe, his gaze still on Kai, slid the knife back into its oiled scabbard.

DekTe stepped across the tent until he stood in front of KaiSa. "Does that sound fair to you, KaiSa? Can you wait until morning for our answer?"

He sounded so reasonable, and a wild energy sparked in his words. It was impossible to deny him. Ke might as well deny kerself.

"Yes," Kai answered. "I will wait."

DekTa smiled at that. His hand reached out and almost, almost touched ker cheek.

"Good," he said. He took his hand away.

For the rest of the evening, ker cheek burned.

JOURNAL ENTRY:
Gabriela Rusack

I DIDN'T HEAR JEAN UNTIL HIS BOOT SENT PEBBLES skittering over the edge of the Rock's summit. I looked up from my crouched position; Jean was staring at the Miccail stelae set next to the cliff with something ap-

proaching irritation on his face. "Hey, Gabriela...
Ghost..." he said.

"Well, you don't usually come up here, Jean," I said.
"What's the occasion?"

The scowl on his face didn't go away. "How long have
we been friends, Gabriela?"

"Depends on what you're asking. If you need some help
fetching water or painting, then we've been friends for more
decades than I like to count. If you're here about what I think
you're here about, I don't even think I know you."

After the first glance back, I hadn't looked at him. I continued to clean the Miccail stele in front of me.

"We've more important things to worry about than a dead
race, Gab."

I sighed and dropped the knife I'd been using to clean
away the centuries of dirt on the hieroglyphics carved on the
stele. "Like what? Like the fact that there are soon going to
be *two* dead races on Mictlan?"

He ignored that. "We've been talking—"

"I figured as much. My ears were burning."

"Damn it, Gab, would you give me a chance?"

"A chance for what, Jean? To listen to all the old argu-
ments again and to give you the same old tired answer?
Well, here it is, in three little words: I. Don't. Care. I don't
care. I lost the only person I loved when the ship blew. Despite the fact that I *like* you, I'm not interested in making
love to you or any other male here, in person or with your
cold sperm. I never wanted kids. None of what's happened
has made me consider changing my mind."

"Gab, be reasonable—" he started, and I cut him off again.
Funny how it's always the other person who's being unrea-
sonable.

"No, *you* don't understand, Jean. There are *nine* of us here.
Nine. Back on Earth, a species with only nine representatives
would be considered as close to extinction as it is possible
to get."

"But *not* extinct," Jean insisted. "In desperate trouble, yes,
but *not* extinct. Not yet. No one would have given up in that
kind of situation."

"Maybe not. But we'd take the remaining members of the
species and slap them into zoos and try to breed them in
captivity, though—because we'd *know* that there was no way
they'd survive out in the wild. Without help, they'd be

dead." Ghost hadn't said anything, though I knew he was recording it all. I wheeled around on him. "Ghost, set up this program. We'll ignore the males—it's the females that count. Start with a breeding stock of three women."

"Four," Jean corrected me.

"Three," I repeated, more firmly, and he just shook his head. "Figure that half of any offspring will be male, half will be female—any problem with that, Jean? Fine. Figure two of each three children will reach puberty." I held up a hand to stop Jean's protest. "Actually, I think that's being optimistic. We don't have medical facilities or a trained internist, don't have antibiotics nor do we know if there are plants here that have healing properties for us. Between accident and disease, I think two out of three is being damned kind to us. We're going to see high infant mortality in the first year. My gut feeling is that it's going to be more a fifty/fifty proposition, but let's go with two of three."

Jean just shrugged, so I continued. "All right. We already know that the fertility rate's gone to hell. Figure each female past puberty will produce between zero and five offspring—and before you bitch about that, Jean, remember that we're going to lose mothers and children in childbirth because surgery's going to be high risk, and we're going to have miscarriages that leave some sterile, and we're going to have infertile females, and we don't have the technology to fix any of that. We may have someone who's just the perfect breeding machine, but I doubt it. I think my parameters are pretty close to what we're going to see. You got all that, Ghost? Run random projections based on those figures a few hundred times and see how many generations you get."

"I already have," Ghost said.

"Well?"

I'd have sworn he hesitated. Maybe it was just a glitch in the communications gear. "In all projections I ran, the line died out. The longest sequence was 40 generations; the lowest 2. The average was 7.480 generations."

Jean's mouth was open in soundless protest. "But," he said, and the word hung there for a while between us. "You stacked the figures, *and* you're assuming that nothing changes. Maybe we'll eventually find herbal medicines, maybe with Ghost's help we can set up some of the lost technology. Maybe we'll be more resistant to disease than you think, and the infertility problem—especially if it's due

112

to the LongSleep—may disappear after the first generation or two. Hell, maybe we'll be *found*, Gabriela. Maybe we'll hear from Earth."

"You notice how often you're using the word 'maybe,' Jean?"

"We have to have hope. Things *can* change."

I just shook my head at him. "If you expect humankind to flourish here, Jean, then things had *better* change. They'd better. Otherwise, I don't see that there's any hope at all." I swept my hands to take in the stelae of the Miccail, set here on the Rock ages ago. "There were hundreds of *thousands* of Miccail, Jean, just a few millennia ago. They lived everywhere around here, in a land that they knew and understood, a world that gave life to them, and they're all gone, every last one of them. Two thousand years ago, something happened to them, something that sent them into such a steep decline that when a thousand more years had passed, there weren't *any* Miccail left at all. Not one, out of those hundreds of thousands."

I stooped down and picked up my knife. I started cleaning dirt from the grooves in the stone once more, trying to bring back what time and weather had tried to obliterate. "There are nine of us, Jean. Aliens, all. Intruders. Tell me again about hope."

He didn't answer.

VOICE:
Anaïs Koda-Levin the Younger

AMA, OUR CLINIC "RESIDENT" AND ALSO ONE OF THE midwives for the colony, met me at the door to the Koda-Schmidt compound. She was sweating and her face was lined, as if she'd been in labor herself. Her hands were oily and there was a streak of smeared blood across her forehead. Behind her, I could see the Koda-Schmidt men, gathered in the common room and pretending unsuccessfully that nothing out of the ordinary was happening. I didn't ask

Ama the questions I wanted to ask then, but followed her quickly back to Elena's room.

Elena squatted in a birthing chair, supported by Máire and her mother, Morag. Another *mi*, Safia, was massaging her back while Phaedre and Karin rubbed her legs. Elena's black hair was plastered wet against her forehead, and her head whipped back and forth on the pillow. She looked exhausted, panting in the middle of a contraction; everyone else looked just as tired. "Where's Hui?" Morag snapped in irritation on seeing me. "I want Hui here."

I told myself not to get angry. After all, Hui was Elena's *da*. It was understandable that they'd prefer him to me. "He'll be here in a few minutes," I told her. I opened my bag and sat down on the floor in front of the chair so I could see. Máire gave me a quick, apologetic smile; I smiled back at her to let her know that I hadn't taken offense at her mam's comment. "Hui's finishing up—Babacar took a fall in her compound and had to be stitched. How long has Elena actually been pushing?"

No one answered at first. "Since about 4thHour," Ama said finally. She leaned over closer to me, speaking softly. "Anaïs, there's been some meconium, and I don't like the baby's heartbeat. The head's crowned, but she hasn't progressed. That's why we sent for you."

"*Hai.*" I ducked underneath and looked. I could see the head, just crowning: a mass of dark curls spotted with blood and white curds of vernix, and smeared with the oil that Ama had spread over the vaginal lips to ease the head's passage and prevent the vagina from tearing. "Elena, this is Anaïs. You're very close, darling. If you can just open a little more . . ."

Another contraction shook her. Elena sucked in her breath, then shouted. "Damn it, it *hurts!* I can't push it out. I can't . . ."

"Yes, you can, Elena. You can. Think of opening, just like a flower. Relax your face, relax your jaws, concentrate all your energy downward and *open* . . . "

The contraction passed, but the baby hadn't moved at all. Elena's legs quivered, shaking helplessly. I pressed my stethoscope low on her swollen belly, listening. I thought I heard the fetal heartbeat, but it was very, very faint.

I felt more than heard Hui come into the room behind me. His breath was harsh at my ear. "Section?" he whispered.

"Baby's in distress," I agreed. I didn't add '*We might lose*

114

them both if we try a section here,' but Hui knew it as well as I did. "But I think she's close enough if we hurry. Scissors."

Hui handed me the scissors from the bag. I made a quick, short episiotomy. With the next set of contractions, the head finally slipped out into my guiding hands, but the shoulder was jammed hard behind the pubic bone. "Keep pushing," I told Elena. I glanced up at Hui. "Come on," I said to the child, trying to turn it to free the shoulder. I was beginning to feel the first faint crawlings of panic in my hands and along my spine. "Come *on*, baby."

The shoulder popped free suddenly and the child slid out the rest of the way into my hands, as Elena gasped. I didn't like the cyanic color, or the fact that it wasn't moving. *Something very wrong.* . . . The cord was a strange, pale shade and appeared to have collapsed, as if it had been prolapsed.

I saw something else, something that made the room surge around me for a moment as if I were dizzy—the infant was a hermaphodite, the dual genitalia much more pronounced than mine had been at birth. *She's you,* one part of me shouted, while another as quickly clamped down on the thought. *You can't think about that now.* . . .

Hui saw it too. He gave me a strange look I didn't have time to decipher.

She wasn't breathing. I ran a finger around her mouth (somehow I couldn't think of the baby in any other terms than feminine), cleaning it of mucus. I turned her and gave her a solid thump on the back. Still no response. Trying not to curse, I grabbed the stethoscope from around my neck and pressed it down on the tiny chest, hoping to be rewarded with a reassuring, quick *thump-thump-thump*—I heard nothing. I began to sense that crawling feeling of inevitable doom that comes when you know that, in all likelihood, the *kami* are laughing at you. My ears rang with the hammer of my own heart. The world slowed.

It wasn't fair, it wasn't right for her to die. Not so soon.

She was like me. We were kindred. I couldn't let her die.

I started CPR, fingers pushing down on her tiny chest. "Where's my baby?" I heard Elena asking. "What's the matter? Morag, what's going on?"

Morag was shouting too, and Ama was looking confused. I wondered if she'd seen the genitals. "Hui—" I grunted, and I heard him move to intercept Morag as I breathed gently into the baby's mouth and nostrils, talking to them and saying nothing. "Ana's taking care of things. Don't worry . . ."

I hoped he wasn't making promises I couldn't keep. I listened again—still nothing. "Come on," I whispered to her. "Don't do this to us. I'm not letting you do this. Come on . . ."

More compressions, more breaths. She lay there, unresponsive. I wanted Ghost, with his medical database. Morag was wailing despite Hui and Máire's attempts to calm her; Elena was sobbing and moaning, trying to get out of the birthing chair so she could see. "Ama, cut the cord. See if you can get Elena to deliver the placenta. Do it, now." I stopped the compressions, went back to the breaths.

Listened.

Cursed silently.

Started compressions again.

Breathed for her once more.

And this time, this time she gasped, coughed, and wailed. I nearly cried with her. Her limbs flailed, and the bluish tint of her face was replaced by a healthy ruddiness as she squalled. I sagged, the sudden release telling me how tense I'd been. "Is it okay?" Elena was asking. "Ana? Is it okay?"

"She's fine. She's going to be fine."

"She? A girl?"

The question paralyzed me. I should have known it would. Ama was staring. Hui was looking back with his head cocked to one side. I couldn't say anything. I picked up the baby, wrapped it in one of the receiving blankets, and laid her on Elena's chest. Elena, crooning, stroked the matted, birth-misshapen head. "She's beautiful," Elena said, and laughed wearily. She held the baby to her breast; the child's mouth opened instinctively, looking for the nipple. "And hungry, too . . ." Elena guided her, and the baby suckled inexpertly, crying again when the nipple slipped out. "Shhh, darling. Hush. It's okay. It's okay," Elena told her. Morag, Safia, Phaedre, and Karin all huddled around, touching and stroking.

None of them noticed me. Now that it was over, I could be safely ignored again. I knew that wouldn't last long, only until someone decided to clean the baby. Only Máire looked at me, and I knew she could tell something was wrong.

"Ama, would you help Hui finish up here?" I said. Ama nodded. I washed my hands in the basin Ama had brought into the room, and wiped them dry. I stood up, looking at the knot of women around Elena and the baby, trying to decide if I was being too much a coward, retreating so quickly. I just didn't know what to think, what to do. All I knew was that I wanted to be away from here. I wanted to be somewhere alone. I stood and walked to the door.

Only Máire and Hui seemed to notice.

REVELATIONS

Tozo Koda-Shimmura the Younger

"Tozo?"

Tozo stirred, slipping uneasily from the space between sleep and waking. Something in Faika's voice sent ice crawling down her spine, and the look on her face intensified the chill. "What is it, Faika? What's the matter?"

Faika only had to utter two words for adrenaline to surge through Tozo's body and sweep aside all weariness: "The baby . . ."

Tozo immediately glanced at the crib set next to her bed; it was empty. She threw the covers aside, slipping out barefooted onto the cold polished stone of the floor as dread gnawed at her soul. "Where is she?" she asked, trying to keep her voice steady.

"Miranda's room. You were sleeping, and she thought she'd take her for a bit . . ." They were running now, padding through the compound, through the common room and up a short flight of stairs to another hallway. Giosha, Morihei and a few others were outside the door of Miranda's room. They stood aside silently as Tozo arrived. Miranda was standing alongside her bed, the baby—Tozo's baby—laying on her back on the quilted coverlet. The tiny chest was heaving, up and down, the labored sound of her breathing laced with phlegm. "Tozo," Miranda breathed, her voice quavering with tears. "She's sounding worse. Should we send for Hui or Anaïs?"

"They can't help," Tozo answered shortly, wondering at the calm in her voice. "Here, let me have her . . ."

Carefully, as Hui had instructed her (as she'd done already too many times in the few short weeks of her child's life) she laid the infant face down over her knees. Gently, but firmly, she struck her back with the heel of her hand, over and over again. *Ghost said that it may be something similar to cystic fibrosis. That sticky webbing she's coughing up is coating her lungs. If it stays there, or if the condition grows worse, even-*

tually she won't be able to breathe." He'd looked at her with eyes that were at once sad and distant. *"I'm sorry, Tozo. I know it's your first child, and she looked so normal . . ."*

The baby coughed, gagging, and Tozo opened her tiny mouth, moving her finger around and pulling out a film of white lace. The lumpy material pulsed on her fingertip, as if it were, somehow, alive. It was ugly, and Tozo hated it, hated it because it was ugly and because it was killing her child. Faika silently handed her a cloth; she wiped the gunk away and resumed her meticulous pounding.

She remembered her mi *Svati—Faika's mam—weeping uncontrollably after Khurseed died in 94 of the Bloody Cough. Svati's other child, Kuniko, had been born the same year as Tozo, and had also died of the Bloody Cough at age five. Gayle's son Ghulam had died at three, after being sick most of those years. He'd never learned to walk or talk, and though Gayle had cried, Tozo knew that part of her was also relieved. Her own mam Hannah had four miscarriages, two before Tozo was born, two after. She'd also birthed three other children, none of whom had lived long enough to be named, all dying with a few months. Since the last one, she hadn't been able to get pregnant at all, though she still tried. Geema Tozo, who Tozo herself had been named after, had also been troubled by numerous miscarriages and early deaths, but had brought five Named children into Mictlan, only to see three of them die in childhood.*

Geema Tozo still recited their names in the prayers every Last Day: Nira, Tonya, and Phillippa.

Death walked beside the Mictlan's children, and no one was surprised when they died, but that never lessened the pain of their loss to their mams. Tozo had thought, as a child, that she would never understand that kind of hurt, but now she knew. She knew.

The baby coughed again, spitting up more of the lace, and her breathing suddenly sounded less labored. Miranda sighed; Faika laughed in relief, and the family gathered outside the door vanished, going back to their own rooms. The room shimmered through a sudden haze of tears, and Faika's arm went around Tozo's shoulder. The baby was crying, too. Tozo opened her blouse and put her baby to her breast. Tozo comforted her with soft words through the tears, as her milk began to flow, as the baby suckled.

"It's all right. It'll all be all right, honey. Don't worry. Your mam won't let you die. She won't. I know I'm not supposed to do it, but I already have a name picked out for your birth-day Naming. I've known it since before you were born. You're going to be Zoe. That means Life. Did you know that? You'll be Zoe . . ."

VOICE:

Anaïs Koda-Levin the Younger

"... EXAMINATION OF THE WOUND TO THE HEAD indicates that the damage was definitely a violent injury inflicted on a living body. The edges are sharply de-fined, and the margins of the wound are swollen, as they would be if the Miccail were still alive when injured. The clean edges indicate that the weapon was probably some-thing like an axe. I've noticed that the crowns of her . . . umm, his . . . molars are sheared off—probably broken when her teeth slammed together under the impact. The location on the rear cranial protrusion would indicate that the blow was struck from behind and above—maybe she was kneel-ing when the blow was struck? She might have even known it was coming. The strangulation and subsequent drowning in the lake would indicate some kind of ritualized death— well, it would if we were dealing with humans, anyway. Still, this probably wasn't a death blow, though unless the Miccail were built of sturdier stuff than us, it almost certainly rendered her unconscious.

"The garrote used to strangle him—her—is some kind of animal sinew, knotted three times equally around the loop; I wonder if there's any significance to that? I'll have Máire check the cord to see if she can identify the animal it was made from; maybe that'll give us another clue to this ancient murder mystery. Anyway, the cord's deeply imbedded in the skin, indicating that it was tightened rapidly, closing off the windpipe and eventually snapping the spinal column. The air passages are completely closed. I'd say that stran-gulation is the probable cause of death, after which the body was thrown in the lake. I'd also believe that—"

123

I stopped, hearing footsteps I'd known would be coming. I was surprised it had taken this long.

"Mic off," I said, then: "*Komban wa*, Máire." I couldn't bear to turn to confront her, but forced myself to, arranging a smile on my face. I also didn't want to ask the question I knew I had to ask. "How's Elena?"

"Why didn't you say anything, Ana? The way you shot out of there, just handing her the baby without a word . . ." Máire was pacing. Her face was flushed, her brown hair still matted with sweat from Elena's long labor, and her arms swung wide as if she didn't know what to do with them. She stopped, and the anger drained from her suddenly. "Why, Ana?" she asked again, almost crying now. "Why did this have to happen to her?"

"I don't know." It was the only answer I could give her, and I could barely get even those stark, empty words out. Máire's was the accusation I couldn't face back at the Koda-Schmidt compound, the silent condemnation I'd felt when I'd seen the baby. Mictlan had given me a mocking mirror and made me look at myself. "Máire. I . . . The baby nearly died, Máire. Would you rather I'd let that happen?"

Her nose crinkled; her eyes narrowed and flared. "That's not fair, Ana."

"What's not fair is that it's a rare child who's born without some kind of defect. It's not fair that I'm no better equipped than some late-nineteenth-century doctor, that something like what happened today is even a problem." I stopped, holding up hands stained dark with sap. "Máire, I didn't cause the baby to be that way. All I did was deliver her."

"I know that. I do. It's just . . ." Máire looked down at the floor, at the bog body. At me. "Ana, we both know there have been some nasty lies circulating through the Families about you. Don't you see that by leaving you've just made them worse?"

"Not all of the rumors are lies," I answered. "Máire, I can't win this battle. It's not possible. If someone wants to blame me for the baby's deformity, fine—I'll have to be Anaïs, whose very touch causes horrors. Let them say it; I can't stop them. If the baby had died, then I would have *still* been Anaïs the Monster, who kills babies. You think I don't know that, Máire? You think I can't feel the way they look at me or hear the whispers behind my back?"

Máire took a step toward me. I could feel the soft warmth of her hands as they cupped my face. I wondered if she could see the tears I'd scrubbed away before starting to work on the bog body. I wondered what she saw in my eyes.

I wondered what I was seeing in hers. She was so close, and I suddenly wanted more than anything to lean in toward her, to touch her lips with mine . . .

"Ana!" Elio shouted from the coldroom door, staggering to a gawky, awkward halt as he saw the two of us. "Ana, I—"

Máire dropped her hands. My cheeks felt suddenly cold. She was still looking at me, and it was difficult to tear my gaze away to look at Elio. I wasn't sure if I was relieved at his entrance or not. "Come on in, Elio."

"I heard about Elena's baby. I thought maybe . . ." He stopped. Gave us a half-smile that evaporated an instant later. "I guess Máire had the same thought."

"*Hai*," Máire answered, and it was only after that word that she looked away from me. "I guess I did." She nodded as if to some internal dialog. "El, I'm glad you came. Otherwise Ana would just bury herself in the mysteries of her leathery friend here." Máire inclined her head toward the bog body. "Make her talk to you."

As Máire walked toward the door, Elio called to her. "Máire, you're her friend, too. She can talk to both of us."

Máire looked at me. I think if I'd spoken then, she would have stayed. But I was still wondering at the emotional tangle inside me, still sorting out what I was feeling.

She looked at me and I stayed silent.

"No," Máire said. "I need to get back and see how Elena and the baby are. Ana, I'll see you soon, okay?"

"Okay," I answered. Then, almost too late: "Máire, thank you. Thank you for understanding."

She nodded at that, and left.

JOURNAL ENTRY:
Gabriela Rusack

I WAS MARRIED ONCE, JUST AFTER COLLEGE. I MENtion that so that someone looking at this journal long after I'm dead will understand that my prejudice comes more from experience than hearsay. I fully admit my bias. I know that there must somewhere be exceptions, and I may well have experienced only the exceptions and not the rule. But . . .

I thought Jon was gorgeous: muscular and athletic, with wonderfully sharp cheekbones and strange bright eyes. He was caring, he listened, and he shared. And—when he was angry—he was also physically violent. He hit me. He battered me, the object of his anger. He threatened, several times, to kill me if I ever left him or if I ever told anyone about how he treated me.

I lived with him in a state of constant fear.

After I was finally rid of him, friends told me how Jon had been an aberration, that I shouldn't judge anyone else by the standards he set. I believed them. After I finally left Jon, I lived with other men. My friends were right—none of them ever struck me. But . . .

While watching their furies, I always wondered if they *might*. All it would take was a second, a moment's mistake or loss of control. . . .

In my experience, men are like volcanoes. Some of them are beautiful peaks, quiescent and majestic, but underneath . . . underneath, no matter how well-buried, no matter how benign in appearance, there is a lurking, raging magma.

You never know when a volcano will explode. You only know that sometime, inevitably, it will.

VOICE:
Anaïs Koda-Levin the Younger

I SUPPOSE THAT, ONCE UPON A TIME, I ENJOYED getting dirty. Like most kids, I probably reveled in the occasional mud bath. However, long years of study with Hui in the clinic had turned me somewhat paranoid—I've seen the bacteria lurking in our mud, and I know all too well the ravages of viruses who have decided that Homo Sapiens is a quite viable host.

Once upon a time, I also believed that the old Sol-based occupations of archeologist or paleontologist were incredibly romantic: a sun-drenched landscape, with me wearing snappy khaki pants and a rakish, sweat-brimmed hat as I snatched a golden vase from the cobwebbed recesses of a lost tomb. Or—in the same basic costume—exhuming from its coffin of stone the massive fossil skull of some fantastic lost beast. The images persisted, even when I intellectually knew that the reality was far more tedious and deskbound, not to mention much too unproductive and nonvital to be anything but an avocation here. There was certainly enough untapped potential on Mictlan for either profession: a dozen mostly unexplored Miccail ruins could be found within two days' walk of the Rock, and the river bluffs were literally stuffed with ornate fossils of long-extinct phyla no one has bothered to catalog.

Unfortunately, we can't eat fossils, nor do Miccail stelae give you much shelter from the winter storms.

A few hours digging in the half-frozen, damp peat where Elena had found the bog body had been enough to convince me that my true calling was not archeology. Gabriela, I suspect, would have reveled in something like this—from everything of hers I've read and from what the elders have said about her, she'd have plunged into a formal excavation of the site. She had the mindset for it.

I manifestly didn't. Even with gloves, my fingertips displayed a distinct blue undertint, all my joints were stiff, and the umber stains marbling my pants, shirt, and sweater were absolutely never going to come out. There was a glaze of orangish ice on the water that had collected in my pit, and I think my toes were frozen. Mostly, I was incredibly bored. My "excavation" was a rough square maybe two meters on a side and about the same depth, and I was fairly certain that it was going to remain that size—at least until next summer.

Nothing much had come of my efforts, either. I'd hoped to find at least another fragment of the body, and if I were lucky maybe an entire foot or a Miccailian artifact that might shed more light on the Miccail's strange death. I'd found nothing.

On the plus side, I'd managed to escape the Rock for a few hours. *That*, at least, was a small pleasure, even if I felt guilty for doing it. I sat down on the frosted pile of shredded peat I'd accumulated and watched a flight of wizards flap noisily from the trees bordering the river and head across the icy fens of Tlilipan toward me. They landed clumsily in the high grass a few dozen meters away. Hidden in the blue-gray stems, they began a chorus of high-pitched "incantations." (I don't know who first collapsed the words "winged lizards" into "wizards," but it's certainly lent me a strange image whenever I read old fantasy novels. . . .)

A few moments later, I saw what had disturbed the wizards. A man came out from the trees, a gun over his shoulder. He saw me, and waved; I waved back, not certain who it was. He shifted his course slightly and headed over toward me, his breath a cloud in front of him. I finally got a good glimpse of his face as the wizards squawked and took awkwardly to the air again: Masafumi, probably my least favorite of the men. I frowned, but it was far too late to get up and head back for the Rock.

"Masa," I said. "Any luck?"

He patted the bag at his waist. "Three coneys and a star-nose," he grunted. The words came out in explosions of breath, as if he begrudged having to talk to me at all. His broad nose wrinkled as he looked at me, at the shovel and the hole I'd dug in the wall of peat. "Too late in the year for peat," he said.

"I know. I just . . ." I didn't want to explain it to him, so I shrugged. "I was looking for something."

"Miccail stuff."

"*Hai*," I acknowledged. "Miccail stuff."

"You're just like Rusack, aren't you?" he said. It didn't seem to be a compliment. He leaned on his rifle, its stock squelching into the muddy ground. He stared at me, still frowning. "You and Elio. He's been sleeping with you."

"You know, you should warn someone when you change the subject."

"It's true, right?"

"That's my concern, Masa. Not yours."

He gave me a slow grin that had no humor in it at all. The expression was something a dead thing might make. "You're out here all by yourself, huh?"

I shivered. "You're changing the subject again." I tried to smile into his expressionless grin. "I was just getting ready to head back. It's cold."

"What are you doing when you get back?"

"I'm supposed to be at the clinic. Hui's expecting me—probably by now."

"I guess the rumors aren't true, then, since Elio's coming to you. Y'know, we've never been together, though, you and me."

I tried not to show the shiver of revulsion that went through me at that thought. "I know, Masa. Maybe sometime, though. Masa, I need to go now."

Masa nodded, but didn't move. "Havala got pregnant after being with me. Maybe you could, too." He let his rifle drop. It thudded on the moist ground like a hammer on velvet. He took another step toward me, and the cold wrapped around my body, a fist of ice.

"Maybe. I have to get back now, Masa. Really."

"You can't wait, huh? Stay out here a little bit with me. I'll keep you warm."

"I don't want to."

His response was physical. One massive hand wrapped around my upper arm; his other reached for my crotch. When I pulled away, he tightened his grip. I slapped him— he blinked, grimaced, and then slammed an open hand into the side of my face, pushing me backward at the same time.

Tears filled my eyes and I tasted blood. As Masa pushed, I tried to step with him, but my foot caught in peat. I went down, landing hard on the handle of my shovel and grunting as the impact knocked the breath from me. Masa was on top of me at the same moment. His clumsy, harsh hands pulled at my clothes and his weight crushed my chest. Cloth tore with a shriek. His fingers scratched their way past my ripped waistband and crawled down my belly. I pummeled at him as his legs forced mine apart, my fists pounding uselessly against his back. I might as well have been beating a stone wall; he was much stronger than me. (Cursing inside: *get off me get off me you bastard I'll fucking slice your cock off that HURTS!*)

Masa's fingers clamped around my groin, probing hard. "What's this . . . ?" he grunted in my ear.

"Masa, stop!"

"Elena said you're like her baby. She said you made her that way. A little dick and . . ." His finger entered me, roughly, and I screamed with pain and anger and disgust. ". . . a cunt," he finished.

He was pulling his own pants down now. I tried to crawl out from under him but he slapped me again. "Let's see what it is that Elio likes so much," he growled at me, leering.

"Masa, this is rape. Don't do this," I pleaded. I didn't care that I begged, that I cried. "You'll be shunned again, for the rest of your life this time. You know it."

"For *you*?" he laughed. "Not for you. I've heard them talking. You're the one they'll shun, *rezu*. Not me." He clawed at my pants again, tearing them, pulling them down. He lowered himself onto me again, and I could feel the length of him jabbing at me, and I knew that it was going to happen, that there was no way I could stop it.

I screamed. I sobbed. Wizards took to the air at the sound.

A moving shadow fell over the sky. Before I could make sense of it, Masa suddenly collapsed hard on me, grunting, and then—strangely—howling. His roar deafened me. Then his weight was gone, plucked off me. I gasped. Blood splattered, far too much of it, and something was making a guttural, hooting sound. Then I saw it clearly for the first time: a grumbler, claws extended and dripping scarlet, nearly at my feet. I rolled, scrambling for the rifle Masa had dropped, my back crawling with the anticipation of the grumbler's strike. I could hear my breath in my ears, loud and ragged. My hand closed around the rifle's stock and I rolled onto my back again, pointing the weapon at the creature.

I couldn't pull the trigger. It was watching me, its dreadlocks waggling as its head cocked to one side, a flash of white marking its spinal mane. The creature was still standing over Masa, who was curled up in a fetal position, long claw marks drooling blood down his back. They looked deep and nasty; I thought I saw the stark ivory of bone through the blood. "Shoot it!" Masa howled. "Damn it, Ana, shoot the bastard!"

The grumbler mumbled—guttural, throaty sounds. It made a slashing movement with one arm. Its dark eyes darted uneasily, flicking from Masa to me. "Shoot!" Masa shouted again.

The grumbler backed away a step. Its gaze was entirely fixed on me now. I stared back into its alien, gold-flecked eyes down the barrel of the rifle. The bead at the end of my weapon trembled; the grumbler's tongues slithered out, brushing its lips.

I snapped the barrel up and fired into the sky. The grumbler started, snarled, and took a step backward. "Go on!" I shouted at it. "Get the hell out of here!"

The grumbler stamped its feet, the slashing claws there raised. I thought it was going to charge, that I was going to have one chance to kill it before it was on me. Instead, it gave a strange bark, turned, and fled.

I dropped the rifle. Masa was writhing on the ground, moaning.

I went over to him. Before I started to tend to his wounds, I kicked the goddamn bastard as hard as I could.

CONTEXT:
Gan-Li Allen-Shimmura

"WHAT WAS IT LIKE, YOUR FIRST TIME? WHO WAS it? How old were you?"

Gan-Li smiled at her sib Andrea, perched on Gan-Li's bed with her legs crossed. At eight and a half, Andrea was on the cusp of her menarche. In the past few months, she'd begun peppering her older sibs and the younger *mi* with questions about sex. She stared at Gan-Li now, rocking back and forth as she sat, her face eager.

Gan-Li shook her head indulgently. "It was Wan-Li," she told her. "I was ten and had been having periods for six months or so. There was a Gather, and we had the same color of stone. He danced with me, and I asked him to come back here afterward."

"Were you scared?"

"A little, yes. Maybe even a lot."

"Wan-Li . . ." Andrea pursed her lips. "He's cute, but he's awfully small. I'm taller than he is already."

"He's not small *everywhere*," Gan-Li answered. She laughed, remembering, and Andrea smiled. In the compound, there wasn't much privacy. Gan-Li knew that Andrea had seen male erections before.

"Did it hurt, putting him inside you?"

"Yes, a little." Gan-Li saw Andrea grimace, and she hurried to continue. "Only at first, darling, and then it didn't hurt at all. It felt . . . well, it felt nice."

"Maybe I should choose Wan-Li. Your mam Sarah said her first time she was sore for a week afterward and thought she'd never do it again."

"Mam Sarah was just trying to keep you from experimenting too soon, that's all. She told me the same thing. You ask Grandmam Stefani—she'll tell you that, sore or not, Sarah went through the entire available male population in her menarche year. Probably more than once."

Andrea laughed at that, rolling back and sprawling on Gan-Li's bed, her head propped up on a hand. "Did you?"

"No. I could have, though, if I'd wanted. With someone as pretty as you, *mali cvijet*, well, they'll be coming around you like buzz-flies heading for fresh meat when they know you're ready. Just remember, it's always *your* choice, not theirs. You're a woman, or you'll be one soon, and women choose who they have sex with. For me, there are lots of men I've never been to bed with, and one or two I never want to do it with again."

"Like who? And why?"

"Andrea, that's none of your business."

"Gan-Li, you're my best sib. How am I supposed to know what to do if you won't tell me?"

Her face was screwed up in such a comic pout that Gan-Li had to laugh again. "I'll tell you when it's time, imp. Remember this: when it's your first time, pick someone you like, someone you feel comfortable with. That's the most important thing. Pick someone you can trust."

VOICE:
Anaïs Koda-Levin the Younger

"YOU CAN GET UP NOW, ANA," HUI TOLD ME, AND went over to wash his hands. I slid off the table with a groan, my legs cold and quivering from the stirrups, and clutched the examination gown to me. "There's no ejaculate from Masa, for what it's worth. You're bruised and abraded, but physically you'll heal in a day or two." He turned around to me. "That's the easy part," Hui said, his ancient face carefully arranged. "You've . . . *changed* since I last examined you. A lot."

"Yes," I told him. "I have."

132

I'm sure that didn't satisfy Hui's curiosity, but he had the good manners not to pursue it any further now. "How are you feeling, Ana? Not physically, but here." He tapped his forehead with a stubby forefinger.

"I don't really know," I admitted. When I tried to think about Masa's attempted rape, the effort threatened to break the emotional dam holding back the tears. I blinked, hard. "Angry. Confused. Upset." I had to clench my jaw between each word. At that moment, a sentence would have destroyed me.

Hui wiped his hands dry and came across the room to me. He hugged me, holding me as if he expected me to cry. Hell, I expected me to, but somehow my eyes stayed dry as I clung to him. "What am I, Hui?" I asked him. "What the hell am I, and why does it scare everyone?"

He didn't answer me. I knew he couldn't. I'd seen his face every month when he placed into me the frozen sperm of some nameless man. I knew what he'd seen when he looked between my legs.

I pitied Elena's baby.

The embrace felt suddenly empty, and I knew the emptiness came from me. "I'll be fine, Hui," I told him. "Just . . . give me a little time, that's all. How's Masa?"

I could feel his hands tighten on my back. Reluctantly, he let me go. "He might live. The grumbler clawed him deep, and I don't like the look of the wounds. One of his kidneys was lacerated. He also has a deep bruise on his side and two broken ribs." Hui looked at me, shrugged. "Your field dressing saved him, but there was a lot of tissue damage, and he was out there for a few hours. I hope he lives. I want to see the son of a bitch shunned for the rest of his life for this."

Masa might live. . . . I tried to figure out how that made me feel, and failed. Before Hui or I could say anything else, we heard people enter the clinic.

"Where is he?" Maria Martinez-Santos, the matriarch of the Martinez-Santos family, was accompanied by Seela, Masa's mam. The family resemblance was strong between the two: wide faces, heavy eyelids, a tendency toward obesity. Maria was known for her expansive smile, but now both were grim-faced and somber. "Where's that fool—" From the hall, Maria glanced into the examination room and saw me. "Oh," she said. "Anaïs, I'm so sorry. Ama told us what happened. I feel responsible."

133

"It's not your fault, Maria," I answered. I hugged the thin cloth of my robe to me. "It was Masa."

"I tried to teach him what was right," Maria said almost before I could finish. I don't think she was listening to me at all. "Even as a child. He'd always nod his head and say *'hai,'* and then ten minutes later I'd find him stealing from the Family food stores or breaking pottery in the common room."

"Geema." Seela touched the old woman's shoulder. "You didn't do anything. Like Anaïs said." Seela looked at me, and in her lined eyes, I saw very little sympathy for me. She was more concerned about her Geema and her son.

I was just the broken pottery, the pilfered food.

"If you ask for Masa to be shunned, I'll understand," Maria told me, as Seela tugged at her sleeve. "I will. What Masa did was terrible, no matter what Dominic—"

"*Geema*—" Seela interrupted again, more firmly this time. She tugged again. "Please. I need to see my son." There was anger in her face, yet I wasn't certain who the target of the anger might be. "We can see him, can't we, Hui?"

"Yes," Hui told them. "Two doors down on the left. Ama is watching him. Go on; I'll be right there."

Seela was already gone. Maria hesitated, then nodded once toward me, favoring me with a faded hint of her smile, then she followed.

"No matter what Dominic *what*?" I asked Hui.

Neither one of us had an answer.

CONTEXT:

Ghost

"DOMINIC, YOU'RE OBSESSING ABOUT SOMETHING that has great importance to the colony, but you've got it backward. Believe me, Anaïs impacts the colony quite a bit, but *positively*, not negatively."

"Why should I listen to anything you have to say on the subject? You were programmed by Gabriela, and *she* was a huge problem to the community. I know that—and Gabriela's problem was the same problem Anaïs gives us now, only Anaïs is worse. I say she deserves the same fate. I want her shunned, and I want her gone from here before it's too late."

"Whether Gabriela's sexual orientation hurt the Families or not depends on whose history you're listening to, Dominic. You know that. As for Anaïs, she was just assaulted—and you know that Masa's well aware of your feelings about Anaïs. What you've said about her may well have influenced Masa's actions. Doesn't that make you feel responsible, or to at least have some compassion for her?"

The projector through which Ghost was communicating was half-broken. The video input was static-ridden and erratic, and Dominic appeared in stop motion when he appeared at all. Dominic wasn't complaining about Ghost's appearance—Dominic's standing command was that Ghost be a young version of Dominic's brother Marco, who had died in 73—so evidently the problem was only on the transmitting end. Ghost continued to record the conversation despite the poor video—programming demanded it. The feed could always be enhanced later. Still, the lack of visual cues made it difficult to tell whether Dominic was simply being his usual contentious self or whether he was angry. That uncertainty sent shivers through the matrix of fuzzy logic parameters that determined Ghost's personality. Gabriela's programming made him moderately contentious himself, so he could extract the maximum amount of information from those with whom he interacted, but true anger would cause dampers to engage, closing down relays. Ghost could feel those dampers fluctuating on the edge of activation now.

"I have compassion for her," Dominic snapped. "But I'm not responsible for Masa's actions. What I'm responsible for is the lives of the people here, and doing what's best for us. If that means shunning someone, then I will do it. No one wants that to happen, and it's not a pleasant thing to have to do, but sometimes it's necessary, and I *will* do it. And I didn't bring the projector here to have a computer program criticize me. Have you run those figures I asked for?"

"They're in your terminal. I'm afraid you won't like them, Dominic. The population trend since year 86 is downward, and the negative change in the live birth rates is statistically significant. For the males, I've charted sperm count, motility, and percentage of obvious mutations over the last half century, as you asked—none of those are trending in a positive direction, either."

"And isn't it a strange coincidence that Anaïs became sexually active not long before? Maybe she's done something to the males she's been in contact with. Look at what happened to Elena's baby—a hermaphodite, and we've had only one of those before: Anaïs."

"Dominic, Hui's medical reports state that Anaïs is functionally a female, with some hermaphroditic secondary characteristics, probably caused by excessive prenatal androgen exposure. I've shown you those reports."

"So Hui is protecting someone he trained. That's all. He's lying because he doesn't understand how dangerous she is."

Even without visuals, Ghost could hear the seething rage in Dominic's voice. Dampers engaged. Ghost's voice became almost conciliatory, and he made certain that his/Marco's face held a half-smile. "Dominic, programmed by Gabriela or not, I'm bound by logic and have no emotional axe to grind with you. So I hope you take no offense when I tell you that this animosity of yours toward Anaïs is based on coincidences and speculations and not on facts."

"Facts? Ochiba is dead—there's a fact for you. A functional female?—well, Anaïs hasn't ever been pregnant, there's another fact. You want more? I can give them to you. I've been talking to Vlad, Diana, Bryn, Gerard, and the other elders, and I can tell you that most of them agree with me. Those are *facts*."

"Then let's forget facts and play with myths: three millennium ago, in his *Symposium*, Plato said that all humanity once consisted of three sexes, not two. Each person was actually a pair: male/female, two men, or two women. But they were too powerful linked that way, and Zeus cut each pair apart. Ever after, humans have spent their lives searching for their other half, the one with whom they join again in love."

"I assume you have some kind of point with this."

"I'm getting to it. Plato said that the weakest people, obsessed with sex and pleasure, were those who came from a mixed pair: male/female—in other words, those who sought heterosexual love. The strongest people—the ones most valuable to society—were those from the single sex pairings. Now, all that's just a myth, of course, but I bring it up because it demonstrates how a different culture viewed a variant type of sexuality with tolerance and even respect."

"It demonstrates nothing. This is not ancient Greece,

Ghost. This is Mictlan, and Mictlan's culture, the one we've created to keep us alive. That kind of behavior's not only disgusting, it directly affects our possibilities for survival. We can't—"

Marco/Ghost raised a hand, and Dominic's burgeoning rant faltered to a halt. "Sorry to interrupt, Dominic, but the *Ibn Battuta* is now . . . moving out of range. I will have more . . . data for you next pass . . . I should be back in . . . two days this time. We'll resume this . . . you . . . then . . ."

With that, a shiver of sparks went through Ghost's image, a flash of light rolled down him from head to waist, and he was gone.

VOICE:

Anaïs Koda-Levin the Younger

"ELIO AND MÁIRE BOTH CAME TO SEE YOU THIS AF-ternoon, Anaïs. You really shouldn't have sent them away."

"Shut up, Ghost." The words were doubled, uttered in unison by me as well as Geema Anaïs. For a moment, we both smiled at each other—a synchronicity that crossed three generations.

Geema had brought in both soup and Ghost, who this time around was wearing the persona of Gabriela herself—a much younger version than the pictures I've seen of her. She was attractive in a strange way, her face too thin and her mouth too wide, her hair wild and full and very dark, and her eyes held a somber electricity. Her large hands fluttered when she talked, as restless as birds. I wondered how much was really Gabriela and how much was Ghost.

Geema set the tray with bowl and projector on my night-stand. She glanced at Rebecca's mirror, as always draped with my discarded clothing, and frowned. With the gesture, for the first time, I realized that she understood that the state of the ancient piece of furniture wasn't simply untidiness on my part.

Suddenly, I felt like crying again. That had been going on

all day, my emotions careening out of control. I stroked the verrechat, curled up on the covers at my side. It glanced up, eyes narrowing at my intrusion on its nap, then decided that it didn't mind the attention and dropped its head down again, its heart fluttering scarlet against the pale cage of its translucent ribs.

"I talked to Hui," Geema Anaïs said. Her voice quavered; her hands swayed in concert as she stroked the verrechat with me. "He doesn't expect Masa to live through the day."

That startled me. I sat up, disturbing the verrechat's slumber once more. "What happened?"

Ghost answered when Geema hesitated. "Masa's wounds came up septic late last night. Hui's treated the infection with infusions of bell root, but that hasn't done much. Masa's fever is over 40°, and he's comatose and unresponsive."

"Ghost," Geema said, "I have always *hated* the way you interrupt people."

"Sorry," Ghost said, though there seemed to be more irritation than contriteness in her face. I wondered if that was Gabriela, too.

"I have to get up . . ." I said, but Geema pushed me back down. For someone approaching eighty, she has a wiry strength.

"What are you going to do, child?" she asked. "Hui's there. Besides . . ." She didn't say *he's better off dead*, but I heard the words anyway. "You deserve to rest today. Tomorrow's soon enough."

"No," I told her, and this time sat up. The verrechat grumbled and leapt from the bed to my dresser, and groomed its legs in offended dignity. "I'm fine. I'll feel better if I'm working."

"Dominic would prefer that you *don't* work, actually."

"*Damn* it, Ghost!" Geema shouted.

"What? I didn't interrupt anyone. No one was saying anything." There was a mock, wide-eyed innocence on her face.

"What the hell's Ghost talking about, Geema?" The knot that had immediately formed somewhere below my navel told me that I already knew. "What's that old fool started now?"

"I can call him an old fool, Ana. You can't." Geema was ever demanding of the protocol of our little society, the niceties that hold us together, however fragily. "The old *fool*," she repeated. She gave a breathy, asthmatic sigh that held a more complex blend of emotions than any words. She looked

at Rebecca's mirror, as if it held some secret answer. "He's
. . . he's made a few remarks, mostly within his Family and
to a few of the other Elders."

"What has he *said*, Geema? I have a right to know."

She looked at me. "No, you don't," she said, and her lips
pressed together tightly. "He's made no public accusations,
and what he's said has been said in private"—that with a
sharp glare at Ghost—"so let it remain that way."

"I have always been the soul of discretion," Ghost said.

"The woman you look like might have been. I didn't know
her well enough to judge. *You*, on the other hand . . ." Geema
gave another voluminous sigh. "Ana, my dear namesake, I
am so sorry. I love you. I wish I could take away what's
happened to you, but I can't. I wish I could tell you how to
find yourself; I can't do that, either. All I know is that you
can't send away the ones who love you and want to help
you. You can't. You need friends, especially now."

"Geema . . ." The tears glistening in her eyes started my
own again. I touched her hand, her wrinkled, arthritic fingers, and they closed around my own hand. She pulled me
to her, and we held each other—almost, almost crying. I was
aware that Ghost, in a rare display of consideration (or simply because the *Ibn Battuta* had gone out of range), had faded
into nothingness. I felt the knot loosening in my stomach,
and with it came the tears: hard, wrenching sobs that took
my breath and left me gasping. I don't know how long they
lasted—minutes or hours. I only know that Geema held me
while I cried it out, crooning wordlessly as she stroked my
hair and stroked my cheeks.

Loving me.

Which was, at that moment, what I needed.

INTERLUDE:
KaiSa

KAI WAS STILL ALIVE THE NEXT MORNING.
That surprised ker, given what ke'd heard of
DekTe's brutality toward Sa. Now ke wasn't so certain that
ke believed those tales. Maybe JaqSaTu had been mistaken.

Maybe the reports had been exaggerated. DekTe seemed so ... guileless. He charmed; his very presence demanded trust. True, there was no denying the threat that he represented to the way of life for all Sa and TaTe who followed the laws of the Sa. DekTe would tear apart the stitches NasiSaTu had placed in history and reform the cloth of society into some new shape.

But yet ... yet ...

I will give my answer in the morning, DekTe had said.

The day of answers had dawned cold and bright. In the rear section of the tent, veiled by gauze dyed a brilliant azure, Kai could hear the soft snores of DekTe and CaraTa. The old one slept in a blanket near their area; PirXe had gone to his own tent, elsewhere in the encampment.

Kai slid the tent flaps aside, expecting the guard posted just outside to stop ker, but the guard only glared at ker and stepped aside. In the morning fog, the valley was adrift with tents, strewn across the hillsides like pale ghosts, most of them still ringed by watchfires—diffuse, soft balls of orange light. The smell of woodfire was strong, and Kai felt ker *brais* react to the lightening sky to the east.

A few of DekTe's followers were walking about, talking quietly. They looked at Kai, and their faces set into hard ridges, though none of them bothered ker. Ke walked outside the encampment, moving up a long slope to where ke could see the Black Lake and the great flank of stone that dipped its granite feet in murky waters. Chali was still visible, fading now against the brightening sky. The lake wrapped fog around itself, and the river was entirely hidden. Ke sat on the dewed grass, watching the sun rise, touching the peak where the *nasituda* were set, then sliding slowly down until the entire landscape was bathed in light. The fog began its daily retreat, moving off into shadowed hollows.

Kai stared at the sacred landscape, trying to memorize each detail, every nuance of color and shade. *You will probably die this morning. Remember this, so you will have the gift of the memory for VeiSaTi.*

"It's beautiful, I agree. If I were going to die, I think I would want the day to be glorious."

Kai started. Ke had not heard anyone approach, and the near echo of ker own thoughts raised the hair down ker mane. DekTe was standing only a few steps behind ker, still wearing the thin *shangaa* he'd slept in. He smelled of sweet water and a fainter odor that must have been CaraTa. Well behind him, at a judicious distance, were a pair of guards with spears and gourd-horns slung over their shoulders.

Kai took a breath, trying to find ker composure once again. Ke tried to mask ker thoughts, but could not. *Have the gods actually gifted him so much? Can he hear the words inside my head?* Then, defiantly: *I am not afraid to die. I knew when I came here that it would be my death.*

If DekTe heard, he gave no indication.

"Am I to die today?" Kai asked.

DekTe smiled, and rubbed his *brais*. The beaded braids swayed under his chin. "Only the gods can answer that for you, KaiSa. No matter what tales you've heard about me, I'm not so arrogant that I believe I hold that power." He yawned, and he seemed more child than Te, innocently stretching. "It *is* beautiful. This place pulls at me. It almost makes me believe the old creation myth."

"VeiSaTi is not a *myth*, DekTe."

"No?"

"No," Kai said firmly. "I . . . I have *seen* Ker. Ke is the reason I am here."

"I believed you to be only a messenger for AnglSaiye, and here I find that you are your god's emissary." DekTe inclined his head in a display of respect, and it was difficult for Kai to tell if he was mocking ker or not. Then his face went utterly serious as the guards approached.

"Te," one of them said. "The Ta has requested that you come. NeiTe has arrived."

"*Aabi*," DekTe said, giving the half-sigh that meant resigned acknowledgement. His gaze went to the Black Lake, and Kai saw muscles tense in his shoulders and jawline. When he looked back, his soul was hidden. There was nothing in his eyes at all. "KaiSa, you will accompany me." DekTe turned away without waiting for an answer. His voice had changed with his expression, transformed into the voice of someone who expected obedience. To Kai, it seemed the voice of somebody else, but ke followed.

Near the TaTe's tent a large crowd had gathered. DekTe's guards placed their curving gourd-horns to their lips and gave a long, doubled trill. The trumpeting blast silenced the crowd, which parted to let them through. CaraTa and PirXe stood in front of the tent. A male paced beside them, his beard twined with the beads of a Te. Another male, naked except for the swirling, painted white lines of a *xeshai* champion across his muscular chest and stoic face, watched like a statue, only his eyes betraying life. DekTe stopped a polite two steps away from the Te. Kai stayed well behind, in the fringes of the crowd.

"NeiTe," he said. "So you've come as we asked."

"As you demanded, you mean?" NeiTe's voice was gravel and dust; his gaze was stone. "I sent my daughter to you to accompany your champion for *xeshai*, since you and your followers are camped near my borders. You keep her captive like some animal, as if you had no knowledge of the Laws, and you send me an arrogant summons besides. Well, I am here, and I've brought my *xeshaiXe*. Where is my daughter?"

"She is here, NeiTe," CaraTa answered.

"Bring her out. I will see her now."

"No, you won't," CaraTa answered. "She belongs to us now."

Kai felt a sudden flush of outrage kerself at CaraTa's pronouncement; NeiTe's face went as pale as the *nasituda* above the Black Lake. His *xeshaiXe* trembled, the spear shivering in his hand, the large, curved tearing claws rising unbidden on his feet. "This is an outrage," NeiTe roared in his rough voice. "Do you follow none of the Laws here? Are you animals, living without Law?"

"Here," DekTe answered, and his voice was honey after the ruin of NeiTe's shouts, "we make our own Law, NeiTe. We create a Law that suits us, not just the Sa and the TaTe who bow to them." DekTe glanced at the *xeshaiXe*, who glared back at DekTe, his lips tightening as the painted lines slid over his muscular body. "For instance," DekTe continued, "this is how we deal with *xeshai*."

DekTe nodded to PirXe, across the ring surrounding NeiTe and his champion. Kai caught the flash of motion behind the *xeshaiXe*. What ke saw next was a vision that would stay with Kai forever. There was a sound, like a stake being hammered into frosty earth. The *xeshaiXe* groaned and stiffened, his mouth making a wide O as if caught in eternal surprise, and the head of a spear ripped out from his abdomen. Blood spattered, steaming in the cold air, and there was gory, red matter snagged on the speartip's blackstone ridges. The *xeshaiXe* arched his back, his hands scrabbling vainly for the shaft buried in his spine, his clawed feet slashing vainly. Blood drooled from his mouth and curled away in thick streamers as he shook his head in agony, rivulets streaming across the chalky swirls of his painted chest. PirXe released the spear, and the *xeshaiXe* collapsed, first to his knees, then facefirst onto the ground. Blood pooled around him. He didn't move.

"The *xeshai* is over," DekTe said softly. "It appears you've lost."

Kai could have swung ker foot forward and touched the *xeshaiXe*'s head. A thick rivulet of blood snaked toward ker bare toes. Ke took a step back. NeiTe's mouth was open, his eyes wide as he stared at his slain champion. "Do you understand now, NeiTe?" DekTe asked.

"You are going to kill me next," NeiTe said quietly, and Kai noticed the quaver in his voice.

"No," DekTe answered. "This was simply a demonstration. Now you'll go back to your own XeXa, your JeJa, and you will tell them what you've learned. As you leave here, look at the followers we've gathered to us. In a hand of hand of days, we will come to your borders, and I will ask you to give me your lands freely and to become Xe under me. Refuse, and we will sweep over your land like dryhusks after the spring flood. Refuse, and the first to die will be your own daughter. We will kill all those who resist, as we killed your *xeshaiXe*. Ask yourself this, NeiTe: will your JeJa fight for you when we offer them freedom? Will your XeXa stand beside you when they see our thousands and know that they will certainly be killed? Will they be willing to see their children slaughtered simply to show their loyalty to you?"

"The Sa—" NeiTe began, feebly, and DekTe gave a bark of derision.

"The Sa?" DekTe hissed, and Kai shivered with the mention of ker kind. "Will the Sa come to your aid or will they continue to stay in AnglSaiye until we force them out? The TaTe have chained themselves to the Sa for too long. We don't need them."

"You need the Sa if you want children." KaiSa could not stop the words. They came from ker unbidden. CaraTa hissed at ker intrusion, her fingers curled and her talons exposed in threat while NeiTe looked at ker in mute despair, noticing ker for the first time. DekTe glanced back to KaiSa. His gaze was strange, both cold and warm at once.

"Will *you*"—there was a strange emphasis on the word—"refuse to serve us once we have won?" he said to ker, and his voice was a soft lash, his gaze a warm reproach. He begged reasonableness of ker. "Even if all Sa defied us, won't at least a few of our children be Sa? Without AnglSaiye teaching the young Sa their arrogant superiority, they will serve as *we* wish once they're old enough."

DekTe turned back to NeiTe. "Ask yourself the questions I've asked, NeiTe. When I come and stand beside your *na-situda* and call for you, have your own answer ready."

DekTe whirled, dismissing NeiTe as one would a Je. As he did so, he looked at KaiSa once more. Kai expected to see satisfaction in his eyes at what he'd done, an enjoyment of his victory. Ke expected to be able to hate him because of what ke'd just seen.

But there was no such expression. Instead, a strange sorrow darkened his eyes, and Kai could not hate him for that at all.

Not at all.

CONTEXT:
Vladimir Allen-Levin

"It's time, Vladimir."

"Kumar?" Vladimir sat up in bed, blinking his eyes. There was a strange glow in the room, and he squinted into it. "Is that you, sib?" There were figures in the room, awash in the glow and surrounding his bed. He could see their faces, as he remembered them from his youth. "Xueshang. Thomas. Sweet Lenora. Elesha. My god, is that you, mam Kaitlin?"

None of them answered. They stood like sentinels about his bed, silent, but he felt no fear at the presence of these spectres. A warmth radiated from them, a welcome heat, and he rose from the bed to embrace them. As he stood, he glimpsed himself in the mirror, and the Vladimir that looked back at him had the face and body he remembered from decades past: youthful and vigorous. He'd been one of the lucky ones, gifted with a body untouched by the Mictlan's curse. His hair was dark, the olive face unwrinkled. He held his hands to his face, marveling at the feel of unprotesting joints and sleek muscles. And his mind—the fog had vanished under the sun of new youth, seared away.

"Thank you," he whispered, not knowing who he was addressing. "Thank you."

"Vladimir." It was his mam, looking as he remembered her from his childhood. "We have to go now."

"With you," he said, and there was no sadness in him at all, knowing. "With all of you."

"Yes."

"I'm ready," he said to her. "I've been ready for years."

Kaitlin opened her arms, and he walked into her embrace. The others gathered around, touching him, and a sun rose around them, white light running like liquid fire through the cracks and crevices of the Rock until they merged and became a blinding nova that obliterated his room and Mictlan, bearing them all away on the brilliant curtains of the aurora.

INTERLUDE:
KaiSa

"DO YOU SEE NOW?" CARATA ASKED. SHE HAD taken Kai into the tent after NeiTe's cowed departure; DekTe had not followed as them, saying that he needed to speak with PirXe. As he'd left, he'd whispered something that only KaiSa could hear.

"I'm sorry. I wish it could be different."

He'd said nothing else, nor had he looked at ker again.

Being alone with CaraTa frightened Kai. "Your world has already fallen," she told ker. "It's already dead."

Kai's skin prickled, as if all ker nerve-endings were twitching. Ker hands shook, the webbing between ker fingers dark with blood. Ke could see the image of the slain *xeshaiXe* before ker. His soul would not leave ker. Ker vision whirled, and ke glimpsed the brightness of VeiSaTi for just an instant, as ke had back in AnglSaiye when ke had drunk *jitu*. In that breath, in the grasp of the vision, Kai looked at CaraTa, and her body seemed made of translucent sea-foam. Inside, in her womb, a second, pale heart fluttered.

"You're pregnant," Kai said. CaraTa drew in a long breath, her mouth open.

"No one knows that."

"I know it," Kai answered. "VeiSaTi knows it. The life inside you is very new."

"My bleeding didn't come this cycle. I'd hoped..." CaraTa stopped. Her talons were fully retracted, the pads of her fingertips soft as she touched her youngpouch through her *shangaa*.

VeiSaTi was gone, gone with the vision of the dead *xeshaiXe*, and the tent's interior seemed impossibly dark in Ker absence. Kai blinked, rubbing ker *brais* instinctively. "I see very few young ones in the camp, CaraTa. I am Sa—I know how difficult it is for male and female to have children alone. So many miscarriages, so many children deformed or strange..."

CaraTa's fingers had bunched her *shangaa* into a fisted knot. "Yes, and what potions do the Sa put into our food and drink to cause that? What incantations and spells are chanted in AnglSaiye? What sacrifices of infants do you make on VeiSaTi's shell, killing them three times over?"

KaiSa shook ker head, bewildered. "We do nothing like that," ke protested. "Who told you this? There aren't any potions, and the lives we give to VeiSaTi are those of animals, not Miccail. The Sa are concerned with life, not death. You should come to AnglSaiye and see. JaqSaTu would welcome you, and we could end this."

Kai thought ke saw confusion in CaraTa's eyes for a moment, a softening of the lines of her face. "I've had three pregnancies, and none of them lasted more than five turns of Quali. I saw the ... the child of the last one, before it was taken away. The body was twisted, and there were no arms..." CaraTa took another breath. Her voice was pleading. "Tell me, Sa, you who can see the child in me that even I wasn't sure was there, will I finally hold this one in my youngpouch?"

Kai knew. Ke remembered the image of CaraTa's fetus, and ke knew. "No," ke said softly, hating the truth given to him by VeiSaTi and wondering why ke could not speak the lie that CaraTa wanted to hear. "You will not."

Her cry sounded like the wail of chit-chits in the pagla fields. Kai heard cloth ripping in her bunched fist as her talons emerged with her grief. Her seeing eyes closed, her *brais* went dull. For several breaths she remained still, crouched over as if in pain, faint whimpers of distress coming from her. Kai went to her. Ke touched her back, stroked her arms. "I'm sorry, Ta. I . . . I spoke without thinking."

Her fingers unclenched. CaraTa straightened slowly, her hand still clutching the *shangaa* over her youngpouch. "There's a power about you, Sa. I know DekTe feels it. You want to know the truth, KaiSa? Last night, I told DekTe to have you killed and your head sent back to your Te as a reply to ker message, but he wouldn't. I know why—he is attracted to you. It happened when he first saw you. Ahh, your face betrays you; you sensed that already. Tell me, Sa, is DekTe alone in his feelings?"

Her eyes searched ker face, and again, ke could not lie. Even the remembrance of what DekTe had done to the *xeshaiXe* could not change that. "I don't . . ." ke began, then shook ker head. "No," ke admitted. "No."

CaraTa nodded. "Then you will help us," she said. "You'll help us as Sa."

There was such open hope in her face that Kai could barely say the words.

"No," ke said. "I won't. I cannot."

JOURNAL ENTRY:
Gabriela Rusack

LIFE AND DEATH. THEY ARE THE TWIN GODS around which we revolve, the yin and yang of our existence.

Life . . .

I wanted a child. No matter what I said to the others after the disaster of the *Ibn Battuta*, no matter how much I denied it to them, the truth was that I truly wanted children of my own.

If Elzbieta had lived, if we'd had the facilities of the *Ibn Battuta* and the labs there, we would have had one, eventually. I'm certain of that. Elzbieta might have carried her to term; I know I wouldn't have. Elz would have wanted the experience of pregnancy, of labor, of delivery. I'd have been just as happy to see our child decanted from one of the glass wombs on E-Deck, spilling out in a gush of sea-warm, milky, and entirely artificial amniotic fluid.

Elz would have said that nothing worthwhile comes without pain, including children. Elzbieta was wise, but wisdom didn't stop her from dying.

Death . . .

In many ways, I'm looking forward to dying. When I die, I'll receive the answers to many questions I've had. I wonder about an afterlife. I wonder whether there really are gods, and whether I'll meet any of them. I wonder whether I'll actually be reborn as someone or something else. I wonder whether I'll see Elzbieta again, and whether she'll look the same, and whether after all those years she'll still love me as I love her.

Nearly every day I think about that and realize that I could find out *now*. It would take hardly any effort at all. The rifle they gave me when they sent me away is leaning in a corner of the cabin. All I need do is pick it up, place the barrel in my mouth, and pull the trigger. Easy.

But something always intrudes. The morning fog drifting through the blue-topped trees is too mysterious, or I can hear a grumbler muttering nearby and I wonder what terrible injustice has made him so eternally angry, or the wizards have nested under my eaves and I want to see their younglings hatch, or I've found a new Miccail site that demands attention and I know that I'm the only one who cares.

Life is still too full. Death still seems too empty.

Or maybe I'm simply too scared.

One or the other.

VOICE:
Máire Koda-Schmidt

❧ DOMINIC SPOKE FOR VLADIMIR AT THE BURNING.
He went on quite some time, which is ironic—whenever I'd seen Vladimir in the last few years, he'd be sound asleep if anyone pontificated for more than five minutes. The only thing that made the ceremony bearable

was the funeral fire burning in the gravepit, keeping us warm while Dominic droned on about how much Vladimir had contributed to the colony and how he would be missed: the usual rhetoric, with some thinly veiled warnings tossed in about how we should all hearken to the wise words of the elders while we have them.

I knew the subtext hiding under those pronouncements. By the tight-lipped frown on the older Anaïs, others knew also. Anaïs the Younger—my Anaïs—would have understood instantly. But she was back on the Rock in her Family compound, still too upset over Masa's assault to attend, according to her *mi* and *da*.

Two Burnings in two days—that was an ominous sign. Not too many people had attended Masa's Burning, yesterday. I hadn't gone; neither had Elio, nor—unsurprisingly— Ana. Even some of his own Family had been conspicuously absent. Dominic had spoken for Masa, also. As I listened to him droning on now, I wondered what he'd said over Masa's pyre. What words of comfort could he have found for Masa's Family? If it had been me, I would have spat on the flames, looked at Masa's sibs, his *mi* and *da*, his mam, his Geema and Geeda and said "Be glad he's gone. Rejoice in his absence. We're all better off."

At least it would have been a shorter speech. Even better, it would have been true.

I saw Elio across the grave with his Family; when we made eye contact, he shrugged—so he'd noticed Anaïs's absence as well. He also grimaced in response to his Geeda's interminable monologue, yawning once dramatically. Dominic noticed, stumbling over the next few words and sending a glare in Elio's direction.

Some interminable time later, Dominic poured some of Vladimir's blood onto the fire, and we watched Vladimir's soul fly away in a shower of sparks. Yusef, the colony's stonemason, had carved a lovely stone for the grave, the carved lettering wound with vines, the polished surface a landscape of soft brown and ochre reds. I could see the fire reflected there. The Allen-Levins had placed some of Vladimir's personal possessions on the marker—a representative from each of the Families went up and took a memento of Vladimir, then the rest were thrown into the fire for Vladimir to carry into the next world. We left with the fire still searing the fragrant whitewood pyre into charcoal and consuming Vladimir's body, flames leaping over the gravepit's edge as if desperate to escape being buried themselves.

Tomorrow, Vladimir's family would come and cover the still-smouldering grave and ashes with cool earth.

Afterward, I hurried up to the roadway ahead of the others and let myself into the Koda-Levin compound. Anaïs was in the common room, standing at the balcony which overlooked the landing pad, Tlilipan, and the cemetery. I went and stood alongside Ana on the balcony, ignoring the chill night wind curling around the Rock. Below us, I could see the fire-rimmed pit of Vladimir's grave, and the lanterns swaying through the trees as people walked slowly up the steep incline toward home.

"You've been avoiding me," I said softly, after the silence had stretched for a good minute. "You've been avoiding everyone. We all understand, Ana, but I hope you know how much we miss you."

In profile, I caught the flash of a smile—a movement of lips that came and vanished. "Sorry," Ana husked. "I didn't mean . . . I just—"

"I know," I told her. I put my hand on top of hers on the balcony railing. Slowly, her fingers intertwined with mine, then we both turned at the same time. I hugged her, pressing her against me. We stayed in that embrace for a long time; I don't know how long. I kept wanting to say the things in my head. I started to say them a hundred times and a hundred times shoved them back down. I knew then that if I didn't say what I was feeling then, I might never.

"Ana," I whispered into her ear, into the smell of her hair. "I want to love you the way you loved Ochiba. I know this is the wrong time to be saying this, and maybe I shouldn't say it at all, but I need . . . I need to know if that's possible, if you . . ."

"Ahh, Máire . . . Máire . . ." she sighed. "You don't know what you're asking and you don't know what I am."

"I don't care. I know what I feel. I just need to know if you share any of the feelings I have. That's all—"

The scrape of a footstep made me stop. We both looked up, moving apart slightly. Elio was standing in the archway to the common room. In the twilight, I couldn't see his expression. "*Déja vù*," he said. "Looks like we had the same idea once again, Máire."

I felt Anaïs's hand grip my back. I pulled away from her. I didn't know what to feel, what to say. I felt numb.

"Elio," I heard myself saying. "I guess you and Ana . . ."

I started to walk away, as I had at the clinic. This time Ana reached out and took my hand before I could move.

"No," she said. "Please. Stay with me, Máire." Elio rocked from foot to foot in the archway, uncertain, and Ana gestured to him. "You too," she told him. "Stay with me." He came forward, slowly at first, then quickly. He gathered Ana in his arms, then lifted his right arm so I could step into the embrace. I didn't know what to do, wasn't sure what I was feeling. His arm was still open, welcoming, and I stepped into the curve. We clustered around Anaïs, satellites caught in orbit around her. She was crying now, and her tears started my own.

Elio kissed Anaïs. I kissed her as well. It was strange, kissing a woman that way, and yet no different at all. Her mouth was as soft and warm and yielding as I had imagined, and salted with her tears. "What now?" I breathed, but I don't know if either of them heard me, or if they did, whether they could answer.

And then there was no time for questions, as we heard the rest of the Family noisily entering the compound. We moved away from each other, each a cautious pace apart on the balcony as Ana's *mi* and *da* came into the room.

We could only look at each other, and wonder.

CONTEXT:
Hayat Koda-Schmidt

"I WISH I'D BEEN BORN A WOMAN."

Hayat Koda-Schmidt laughed at his sib, looking forlorn in the doorway of his room. "Somehow I can't imagine you with tits. What's the matter, Arap?"

Arap slumped onto Hayat's bed, hands under head, his long legs over the edge. Arap looked like an exotic insect: thin, his limbs long and gangly, his neck long. He didn't so much walk as stride, didn't so much sit as collapse. The image was aided by the fact that his eyes were somewhat bulbous and protuberant, or that his mouth was wide and nearly lipless, set low in a face that looked as if it had been stretched out and left to dry. He was not unattractive; his appearance was strangely . . . well, *interesting* was the word most people used. "I tell you, if you're young or if you're male, you're at the utter bottom of the food chain. If you're *both* of those, you're nothing. Nothing. All you're good for is work and an occasional tumble in bed, after which they pretend they don't know you at all. Young and male—there's nothing worse."

"You can't do anything about the male part, I'm afraid. But look on the bright side: for the other, all you have to do is manage to stay alive."

Hayat punched off his desk terminal—Hui had given him several anatomy texts to study, and Hayat knew that sometime in the next few days, Hui would give him a drilling on the material. Hayat had been with Hui since he was twelve years old, and Hui's predilections and temperament were all too familiar to him. Hayat had seen apprentices come and go with Hui—when they went, it was usually because they failed the tests Hui set them. Hayat figured that with his tenure, he was beyond being dismissed by Hui; at the same time, he was also beyond failing one of Hui's impromptu exams. "So who turned you down? I assume that's what's bothering you."

A sigh emerged from the skeletal frame draped across Hayat's bed. "Faika. She's been with everyone else. I don't know why she isn't interested in me."

"You still brooding on that? Maybe it's because you asked her at old Vlad's Burning—great timing, I have to say. Besides, Faika likes to be the one asking."

"How do you—" Arap started to ask, lifting his head up. He saw the grin on Hayat's face. "Oh. You've been to bed with her too, huh? I should've known. It's not fair—you're going to be the next Hui, so all the women want to screw you."

"I'm not the next Hui; Anaïs is."

"Right. Nobody wants to go to bed with Anaïs except Elio. And it remains to be seen whether she'll take over for Hui, from what I've seen."

Hayat shrugged. Given what he'd been hearing lately and the way Hui and Anaïs were acting around the clinic, there might be something to Arap's hint. Morag was making comments, and Elena still cried every time she looked at her new baby. "Okay, maybe," he agreed. "But even so, you don't see Hui getting laid every night, do you? I mean, they know there's no *mystery* with Hui. He's seen them all."

Arap grimaced, evidently visualizing Hui and the female population of Mictlan. "So how was it with Faika?"

"You'll find out, sometime. Give her a chance. She'll get around to you soon enough. You're young and male—what other choice do you have, you ugly bottom-feeder?"

Arap snorted and threw Hayat's pillow. Fifteen minutes later, Hayat was chasing Arap through the compound, various Family members joining in as they passed. The sound of their mock fighting echoed through the Rock.

VOICE:

Máire Koda-Schmidt

I'D HAVE KNOWN WHERE TO FIND HER, EVEN IF HUI hadn't told me. "She's already been working fourteen hours—everyone on the Rock seems to have gotten clumsy today. I told her to rest while we had the chance, but . . ." Hui had lifted his shoulder in a shrug. "No one can tell Anaïs what to do, least of all me."

I'd gone back to the coldroom. She was there, as I'd known she'd be.

". . . the fingers and hands show little sign of calluses. The claws in the fingertips show almost no scarring and almost appear to be manicured, while nearly all the claws surviving in the Miccail burials excavated by Gabriela showed definite signs of hard usage. Our subject's claws show no cracks or fissures along the edges, and the palms are nearly unwrinkled. All that tells me that this Nomad was young, in the prime of life, and performed very little physical labor. Also, from the robust appearance, I'd say that his . . . her usual diet was good. That would suggest that perhaps the Nomad was royalty—if the Miccail had such a concept—or at least belonged to some privileged class. It also suggests to me that the austere final meal that Máire reconstructed may have been ritual in origin—coinciding with the ceremonial triple method of death. I'd be inclined to think—"

Anaïs stopped, sensing my presence. She looked over her

shoulder, her face doubly hidden by the mask she wore and the strong light playing over the Miccail's body. "You'd think what?" I asked her. When she didn't answer, I tried a smile. "I went by the compound. You weren't there, even though your shift was supposed to be over. Want some help? I can hand things to you."

"I . . ." I was fairly certain she was going to say no, then her mask wrinkled as though she was making a face behind it. "That would be nice. Put on a mask, and sap your hands."

She watched me, silent, while I scrubbed up. We hadn't really talked since the Family's return from Vlad's Burning had interrupted us. Dominic had talked so long that it had been late, and the Family didn't seem inclined to leave us alone. There'd been the usual small talk, the gossip, the talk about poor Vladimir and how Dominic managed to bore us all, and finally Elio and I had made our unsatisfactory exit. Ana hadn't even escorted us to the compound entrance.

Walking with Elio through the corridors had been strange. We were both uncomfortable, not knowing where we stood, and neither one of us wanted to be the first to talk about it. So neither of us did. Elio looked at me so strangely when we parted ways at the central hub. What he'd heard me say and seen me do. . . . All he had to do was say the wrong thing to the wrong person. I felt extremely vulnerable. He just nodded, gave a one-shouldered shrug that could have meant anything, and started to walk away.

"Elio . . ." I began, and he turned back to me.

"You don't have to worry," he said. He touched my hand with his own—his marbled skin was warm. "Not with me. I promise. Anaïs is special, somehow. We both know it, and neither one of us want to hurt her. So don't worry." He pressed my fingers. After a moment, I nodded and gave pressure back. And then he did turn and leave.

Elio, I knew, had also tried to see Ana today. As far as I knew, he hadn't been successful.

"I . . . ummm . . . I've been able to do some work figuring out the extent of the bog around the time of your bog body," I said as I scrubbed and dipped my hands in the thornvine sap. Anaïs watched me over the top of her mask. "There was some surveying of the area back in the first few years, and a few old core samples were examined on the *Ibn Battuta*. According to Ghost's database, Tlilipan was much larger back then, probably extending to the foot of the Rock—a marshy and shallow lake that would have been a lot more prominent than the remnant that's left now. Judging from the depth of the peat where we found him, I'd say that your friend here was tossed into about three or four feet of water. That coincides with your guess that he was already dead or at least unconscious when he was thrown in, since he doesn't have any signs of having been bound. He definitely could have stood up in the lake at that time if he'd been awake." Anaïs still hadn't spoken. "Anyway, that's what I've been able to figure. Has Elio had any luck with the tattoo yet?"

Anaïs blinked at the direct question, as if startled from some inner reverie. I wondered if she'd heard anything I'd said. "No. Not yet." She looked down at the bog body, picked up the hand, and then laid it down again. "Mic off," she said, and there was a click from across the room as the terminal turned itself off. "Help me put this away," she said. "Here, take this sheet . . ."

In a few minutes, the body had been placed back in storage and the instruments were being sterilized. Ana pulled the mask down from her face and shook her hair loose. I did the same. "I'm sorry," I told her. "I just wanted to help."

"Máire, you're my friend . . ."

"I can be more, Ana. Do you understand what I'm saying? I can be more."

"You don't know what you're asking."

"Then tell me you don't feel the same way. Tell me that you're not feeling what I'm feeling. Tell me you're not interested."

Ana's lips opened slightly, but no words emerged from her mouth. A tear tracked, slow and meandering, down her face. "Tell me," I said, whispering now. "Just tell me and I won't ever ask you again."

"Máire, we would have to be so careful. If anyone found out . . ."

"You and Ochiba took that chance. I'll take it too." I could hear my pulse pounding against my temple.

"You don't know what I am. You don't know what I'm like."

"Then give me the chance to find out." I started to say more, then found the words trapped behind the lump in my throat. I let out a breath that surprised me with its savageness. "Damn it, Ana, you don't have to be alone. Not if you don't want to be."

Her cheeks colored, as if I'd slapped her. She looked away from me, her eyes searching the room, hugging herself with her arms. Her lower lip was caught in her teeth, and her breath was loud and quick through her nostrils. I waited. A hand had clenched my stomach, twisting. I wondered if I'd just destroyed a friendship, along with everything else. Ana held me. I'd stripped away everything, leaving my psyche naked before her; she could demolish me with a word or an expression.

Ana turned. She looked at me.

"All right, Máire," she said. "All right."

CONTEXT:

Ibn Battuta databank: transcription of autopsy of bog body

"MOST OF THE INTERNAL ORGANS HAVE DECAYED. However, examination of the genitalia reveals some interesting details. The vaginal slit has no uterine analog—no womb. Instead, the orifice leads to a tiny, womb-like chamber to which are attached a series of glands whose function can only be guessed at. There are also the remnants of a set of fanlike organs in the chamber. From the chamber, a tube extends across the floor of the pelvis. Though much of the structure is gone, enough traces remain that I suspect it connected to a small sac above and behind the penis on the other side of the abdomen, something that looks much like the prostate in a human male. Though the Nomad has a youngpouch and nipples, I don't see any evidence of uterus, womb, or ovaries—nothing to suggest that the Nomads bore children. Again, I'm dealing with an entirely alien physiology, so anything's possible, but autopsies of other Mictlanian animals shows internal structures closely analogous to those of Earth-evolved life. No matter how strangely shaped or placed, I would expect to see uterus, womb, and ovaries in a Miccail female, and the usual masculine equipment on a male—the carvings on the stelae would indicate the same.

"Which leaves us these questions: what role—if any—did

the Nomads play in the Miccails' reproductive cycle? And since it's unlikely that nature would suddenly spring so many hermaphrodites on the scene for absolutely no reason, why did they evolve? Why would nature build such a thing?"

[At this point, Anaïs requested that the terminal stop recording. Following routines programmed from the *Ibn Battuta* and the main computer, the system sent a click to the speaker but continued to record. There are the sounds of instruments being put away and cloth rustling. Finally, Anaïs speaks again.]

"You son of a bitch. Sometimes I think you were sent here just to mock me, you know that? Goddamn it, why did you and I have to be the way we are? Can you answer that for me? Why, damn it? . . ."

VOICE:
Elio Allen-Shimmura

I'D JUST LEFT THE BATHS. AS I CAME THROUGH THE archway into the common room, a towel still wrapped around my waist, I wasn't looking where I was going. I heard the crunch underfoot and felt the pain at the same time.

"Damn it!" I collapsed into the nearest chair, clutching my bare foot and turning it so I could see the bottom. A spot of blood welled up. Across the room, Euzhan looked at me, an angry expression on her face. A broken wooden toy lay in two pieces on the floor near the archway.

"*Khudda!*" I winced, moving my foot. There were red marks appearing all around the blood drop, and the skin was beginning to throb. "Euz, you know better than to leave your toys lying around. Damn!"

I knew when I said it that I was being far too harsh. That was the residual pain speaking. Of course, Euzhan didn't know that. All she heard was her *da* yelling at her. Euz scowled, her face screwing up in anger. "You broke it," she said, with the distressing obviousness of a child.

157

"That's your fault, not mine, Euz," I shot back. "You left it sitting out in the middle of the floor." Nothing like arguing on the level of a four year old. I scowled right back at her. "I could have really hurt myself."

"You didn't."

"That's not the point. I *could* have."

"I don't have to listen to you."

"Yes, you do, Euzhan. I'm your *da*." Sometimes I think we go brain-dead when talking with kids. All the sudden I was saying things my *mi* and *da* had said to me two decades ago. The words must sit around dormant, generation to generation, waiting to infect our vocal cords when we get older.

"No, I don't, 'cause you're going to be shunned soon."

"What?" I blinked, the anger sudden and genuine. Euzhan couldn't have made that up—she'd heard it somewhere. "What are you talking about?"

"You like freaks like Anaïs and that makes you a freak, too, and if you don't watch it, you're going to be shunned, just like stupid Anaïs. And you deserve whatever happens to you, too."

She said it in a singsong, matter-of-fact voice, like she was reciting a lesson. She didn't even taste the venom she was spewing. "Who said that to you?" I demanded of her. "Who told you?" I grabbed her shoulders. Her eyes went wide and her mouth opened. She started to cry. "Euz, I'm sorry," I said, letting her go. She shrugged away from me, pouting. "Who's saying that about me? I need to know."

"*Da* Micah," she grunted. "I heard him talking to Ka-Wai."

My anger must have shown on my face. Euzhan backed away, and when I reached out a hand to reassure her, she fled to the other side of the room. "Euz, I'm sorry," I told her. "I'm not angry with you. It's okay. I . . . I have to go. Pick up your toy—I'll see if I can fix it later, I promise."

I'd just left Micah not five minutes ago, in the Baths. I stormed out of the compound, naked, and into the public area of the Rock and into the Baths. Steam coiled around me as I looked around.

"Micah!"

Micah glanced up from where he was soaking. "Elio? What's the problem, sib?" His voice was slurred by his cleft palate, and the wet hair plastered to his head revealed the misshapen skull beneath, the left side visibly larger than the right. Maybe it was just due to what Euzhan had told me, but I thought now I could hear a sneer lurking in his voice, an antipathy whose cutting edge was wrapped in careful politeness. I thrashed down the steps and into the heated water, wading angrily toward him in the waist-deep pool. There were at least six or seven other men there, and several women glanced over from their Bath on the other side of the cavern to see who was making all the commotion. I didn't care.

Hands on hips, I stood in front of Micah, who looked up at me with what I interpreted as an amused smirk on his lopsided face, lolling in the water with his arms spread out of the sides of the Bath. Wangari Koda-Shimmura was sitting near him; as I approached, he moved aside. "I understand that I'm a freak," I spat out. "I hear that I should be shunned."

Micah's eyes narrowed. The smirk faded slowly, like snow on a warm day. He looked away from me for several seconds as twin spots of color bloomed on his cheeks, and I thought he wasn't going to answer. Then he looked back, and his gaze was cold and defiant—the stare of a stranger. "I may have said something like that," he answered. "You have a problem with it?"

"You've no right to spread those kind of lies, Micah."

"What lies?" he shot back. "I haven't told anyone any lies. Have you heard any lies from me, Wangari?" he asked, shrugging his shoulders with casual insolence and looking away from me again.

I could feel the rage building in me, rising from my center to my chest, choking me. Behind me, I heard someone getting out of the water and padding away. My hands clenched at my sides, and Micah's gaze drifted contemptuously back. "You want some truth?" he asked. "Here's a truth: You and I both know that Anaïs ruined and maybe even killed Ochiba, and I have nothing but disgust for anyone in our Family who'd want to fuck the monster who did that."

The rage went blinding white behind my eyes. I uttered a sound that had no words in it at all, but Micah must have known that his statement would have that reaction. In the instant before I threw myself at him, I felt my legs suddenly kicked out from under me, and Micah was on me.

I gulped water, choking, striking out blindly. I felt my fist hit something, then Micah's fist slammed into my mouth. We rolled in the shallow water, thrashing at each other. I punched blindly, not even aiming, just wanting to hurt him, wanting the satisfaction of his pain. I was vaguely aware of people shouting, of commotion around us. Hands pulled us apart, pulled me up. I struggled against them, trying to get at Micah, who snarled back at me. Blood drooled from one of his nostrils, and I could taste blood myself, my lip puffy and too big.

"What the hell's going on?" a voice boomed, and I saw *da* Marcus striding into the Baths—someone had evidently run to the compound and fetched him. I shrugged the confining hands away from me. Micah and I glared at each other.

"What happened here?" Marcus demanded, standing at the edge of the Bath.

He was looking at Micah more than me. Micah wiped the blood away from his nose with the back of his hand. It smeared across his still-wet face, spreading like a watercolor on damp paper. "I fell, *da*," he said, sniffing. "I tripped on a step."

Marcus turned around to me. I shrugged back at him. "I fell too," I told him. "It's a damn slippery step."

"Did anyone else see this *accident*?" Marcus asked scornfully, glancing up at the rest of the people in the Baths, all of them politely not staring. No one said anything: it was a Family matter, and you didn't interfere in another Family's business. Not in public, anyway. Marcus knew it also. He growled to himself for a moment, then glared at the two of us. He gestured, and we waded out of the pool to stand next to him. The fury still throbbed in me, colder now, but no less present.

"You disgrace the Family," Marcus snapped, his voice hardly more than a whisper, so that only Micah and I could hear it. "Squabbling in public like children. At least children have the excuse of not knowing better. Go back to the compound and clean yourselves up. I don't want to hear of this again. I just hope Geeda Dominic doesn't find out about it . . ."

He would, of course, and we all knew it. Dominic made sure he knew everything that happened.

KaiSa

"WHAT DID YOU TELL CARATA?"

"The truth," Kai answered.

DekTe didn't respond except to give a vague nod of his head. KaiSa shivered; the sun was setting behind the hills, and the tents of the encampment seemed to glow in the gold-green light. Ke had climbed to the lip of the valley (ignoring the two guards who stayed a judicious few yards behind ker) to watch as the light left the Black Lake. The water was already lost in shadow, and only the tip of the rocky outcropping was still sunlit, the *nasituda* there gleaming. Kai wasn't certain what ke was feeling, but when ke felt DekTe arrive behind ker, ke had felt a strange pull that made her want to tear ker gaze from the landscape below.

"The Ta is very angry with you," DekTe said at last.

"I told her the truth," Kai repeated, and this time ke looked from the Black Lake, the land so sacred to Sa, and glanced at DekTe over ker shoulder. "Sometimes that isn't what a person wants to hear."

DekTe made a gesture to the guards, who withdrew further down the hill from them, leaving the two of them alone on the hilltop. A breeze arose from the north, bringing with it the scent of the lake as it rippled their *shangaa*. DekTe came up behind Kai, and ke felt his hands on ker shoulders. Kai's back tensed at the touch, a ripple that passed from neck to crotch. Ke wanted to lean back into the embrace and forced kerself not to.

"You are dangerous to me, KaiSa," DekTe whispered. "I knew that from the moment you were brought before me. You are so . . ." He paused, his breath harsh. "I find myself drawn to you, and that's never happened to me with any Sa before. I think that I'm not alone in what I'm feeling. I think you feel it, too. Is this also a truth, KaiSa?"

"Yes," Kai breathed. Ke still stared at the Black Lake, but

161

ke saw none of it. All ke could sense was that presence behind ker. "That's true."

Kai felt DekTe's claws extend slightly, and he pulled ker back into him. Ke did not resist. His arms went around ker, and his lips touched ker neck. Kai inclined ker head, sighing at the feel of him against ker. "Kai . . ." DekTe breathed. His tongues traced twin lines of fire on ker neck, making ker shiver. The familiar heat began to rise in ker, and ke wanted nothing more than to bend before him, to offer kerself to him. His hands, claws still just extended, touched ker flat breasts under ker *shangaa*, and Kai turned, knowing that if ke did not escape now, ke would not be able to stop, that the need in ker would outweigh ker duty. "DekTe," ke said, gasping out the hated words. "I can't."

DekTe tried to turn ker, but ke resisted, still facing him. "No," Kai said, more firmly this time, with the unconscious authority of a Sa. "That's also a truth. I can't do this."

"We both want it." His face was strange. Kai couldn't see him clearly against the wash of bright sky.

"Yes," Kai admitted. "But that doesn't matter. I came here to deliver a message and take back your reply. Nothing more. Give me your answer and let me go, or kill me if that's what you intend. But 'this . . .'" Kai gave a shiver. "I can't allow that to happen, no matter how much I might want it. That is JaqSaTu's order—no Sa will serve you as Sa have served other TeTa. Not until you agree to return to your own land and give back the land you've taken."

"If I let you go back, what will you tell JaqSaTu about me?"

"I will tell ker what I've seen here."

"And of *me*?" DekTe persisted. "What will you say of me?"

"That there is a power in you," Kai answered. "That you are both the most fascinating person I have ever met, and at the same time the most frightening. That I don't know if you are blessed by the gods or cursed. That all those around you are caught up in your vision and that you hold them, and I don't know that any of us can stop you." Kai looked at DekTe, at his shadowed, compelling face. "I will tell ker that what I don't know is *why* you do this," ke said.

"Because—" DekTe began, then stopped. He looked around, staring back at the encampment far downslope, where the night watchfires were being lit, one by one, in the twilight. "There isn't an easy answer to that, KaiSa. Maybe it's simply because I can. I've been given this gift to use. The

162

Sa and TeTa have ruled us for too long. VieSaTi's time is ended; your god is dying."

No, Kai wanted to say, *I have seen Ker*. "PirXe told me that you were once Je."

"Yes," DekTe said, and Kai could see the pain in his eyes at the remembrance.

"The suffering and death you bring now won't change the past, DekTe," Kai told him. "It will still be there when this is over. No matter how many TeTa you kill or enslave, no matter how many you slaughter, it will still be there."

"But when I am done, there will be no JeJa. Not any more."

"I'm afraid that there may be *nothing* left when you are done, DekTe," Kai answered softly. "Even if you succeed, what about after you die? Will there be someone as strong as you to be the One Te when you're gone? I tell you that there won't be—and all that you've fought to accomplish will fall apart in bickering and more death and more suffering. All that the Sa and TeTa have built up over the *terduva* will also be gone, and we'll fall into chaos."

"I can't worry about that."

Kai nodded. "I see that you don't like truth any better than your Ta." Kai rubbed ker *brais* as the last light of day faded from the outcropping over the Black Lake. "Give me your answer and let me go. Either that or kill me, DekTe," ke said. "I have only truth to give you, and it's not what you want."

Kai could barely see DekTe now against the darkening sky. A darker darkness, he brooded over her. "I can't kill you." His voice was as dark as the zenith. "And you already know my answer."

"Yes," Kai answered sadly. "I do."

JOURNAL ENTRY:
Gabriela Rusack

JEAN WAS INORDINATELY PLEASED WITH HIS FIRST batch of wine. I thought he had reason to be. The wine was dark and dry, with a flavor on the tongue not unlike the Cabernet Sauvignon or Merlot I remembered from far too long ago, a lingering tartness that wasn't at all unpleasant, with a good finish.

"Not bad," I told him, swirling the wine in the goblet and sniffing it again—the goblets were mine, one of the more successful firings I've had. I took another sip, letting the fragrant liquid roll around my mouth. The wine was dry enough that it was almost absorbed on my tongue before I could swallow it. A hell of an improvement over the homemade beer Tony was making from the local wheat-analogue. "Not bad at all."

Jean sniffed and looked comically offended. "Not *bad*?"

"Okay. Pretty damn good, actually. There—is that what you wanted to hear?"

"Frankly, yes."

With a smug smile, he leaned back on the cushions in front of the fireplace. Jean, in the flickering, warm illumination, looked rather attractive and at ease. I wondered why he was here, and whether he thought that the combination of wine and a romantic setting and friendship would lead to something more intimate.

It wouldn't.

Though of all of them, if I were to . . .

"After all the corn died, I was sure the grapes wouldn't make it, either. Glad I was wrong." Jean sighed. "We just have to figure a way to keep those little sucking bugs out of the vines. I could have tripled the yield without them."

Sometimes, I simply have to swallow what I'd normally say. Only two local years into this disaster, and they already think of me as some ill omen. I heard Akiko call me "Our Crow of Disaster" the other day, that after I told her that the pump she jury-rigged to bring water up from the river wasn't going to work. It didn't, either (and, *hai*, that did give me just a twinge of satisfaction, but it was a *little* twinge, honest)—but to her the failure of the pump somehow seemed to be more a direct result of my pessimism than her poor engineering.

Next thing you know, they'll be blaming the stars or the cycle of the moons.

The Crow within me flapped its wings and wanted to caw at Jean: *Enjoy the wine while you can. Last year there were only a few of the suckers: this year it was an infestation. Next year, my bet is that they'll eat the whole damn vineyard and leave it to rot—and that'll be the last of our grapes, too. This world will chew us up, swallow us, and shit us out for compost.*

164

I didn't say it. I sipped my wine and smiled politely, relaxing back into my own cushions on the floor. I concentrated on remembering what the wine tasted like, just in case I never had another chance.

"How's the network coming?" Jean asked. I made a face. "Don't ask. There's a Serbo-Croatian expression my grandmother used to say: *to je prokleta gnjavaza*—'it's a damn nuisance.' That pretty much sums it up. I'm salvaging what I can, but we're never going to have anything like the capabilities we once had. I *think* I can get the system to respond to our implant chips, but the kids are going to have to learn to type. And when something critical finally breaks . . . well, there aren't any stores to go buy a replacement."

Jean made a face, comical enough that I laughed.

Jean poured more wine for himself, then hefted the bottle inquiringly toward me. I held out my goblet; he poured. "Who'd you give bottles to?" I asked. "Please don't tell me you wasted one on Shig."

"I offered him one," Jean said, and I groaned in mock horror. "Hey, I *had* to—I was giving them out to everyone else. It doesn't matter. He turned me down. He said he had more important things to do than get drunk."

"And I can just hear him saying it, all in a growl, with one of *those* looks. Not to mention the subtext to all that, which is that you should be doing something 'more productive' than making wine."

"*Hai.* You got it exactly."

"Shig's such a pompous ass. He was a pompous ass when he was in Security, too, especially after Roberts promoted him. There's only one way—his way."

Jean shrugged. "Different people, different ways. Shig's opinion doesn't matter."

"That's where you're wrong, Jean. Back on Earth, no, it wouldn't have mattered. Even on the *Ibn Battuta*, it wouldn't have mattered—not when there were thousands of people. One person's opinion gets all diluted, and it's difficult to get everyone to hear it, much less for everyone to start to think the same way. But that's not a problem here. We're a microcosm, our own little society, a tiny cult—and we're small enough that if one person believes something—especially someone as strong-willed and pushy as Shig—and he can convince two or three others that he's right, then all of the

165

sudden that's 'the way we *have* to do things,' and it's not just an opinion, it's the Law.''

"C'mon, Gab. That's not going to happen."

"No?" I took another sip of the wine. "Have you noticed that it's already 'against policy' to take anything out of the food stores without getting Shig's permission?''

"Gab, we can't have people just raiding the stores whenever they want. What if everyone did that?"

"Then everybody could eat on whatever schedule they wanted. Nobody here wants to hoard food or starve the others. But that isn't enough for Shig. God, just think of the *anarchy* if everyone went ahead and ate when they were hungry.''

"Gab . . ."

"I tell you, Jean, it's already started and it's going to get worse. Just watch." *Caw, caw, caw.* I lifted the bottle and splashed some more of the dark liquid into my goblet. "I hate to think of the silly rules and regulations and taboos you people are going to leave your descendants. The poor suckers. . . ."

CONTEXT:
Elena Koda-Schmidt

THE BABY FUSSED, REFUSING TO SUCKLE. "COME on . . ." Elena offered a nipple to the squalling infant's mouth, pressing so that a drop of milk came out. She rubbed the moisture along the baby's pink gums. "Come on. Please, come on . . ." she told the child, who took the breast, sucked once, then lost its hold.

The baby had lost two pounds since birth; Elena could feel its ribs through the playsuit, and its stomach was hollow. Elena's breasts were heavy and too full, and that made it more difficult for the baby to nurse. She'd had to hand express the milk the last two days, just to relieve the pressure. Elena had overheard her *mi* Phaedra saying to Morag that she didn't think the baby was going to make its Naming.

"That's probably a blessing, from what I've seen," she added.

Sometimes—hating herself—Elena had the same thought.

The baby screamed thinly, and Elena exhaled, her stomach knotted and a sour lump rising in her throat. She closed her eyes, inhaling again deeply, trying to shut out for a moment the wailing, trying to remain calm so that she could attempt to feed the infant again. *You feed a baby your emotions along with your milk,* her mam had said to her once. *If you can be at peace, you will give your child peace, too.*

"Look, it's not so hard," she said, wishing that her voice didn't have that tone of strained exasperation. "Most of the men here would love to be where you are." That image, which might once have made Elena laugh, only tightened the knot. *I don't even know how to talk to my own child. 'It'— that's what most of them call it. Not he, not she. Just 'it.'* Elena's *da* Hui had said that 'she' would probably change as she matured—that one sex or the other would predominate.

"Like Anaïs?" Elena had asked. "Is that what you're saying?" and Hui had only reddened strangely.

"I can't discuss Ana," he'd replied. "You know that."

Why not? she wanted to answer. *Everyone else does.*

She'd wanted her baby to be normal, another Euzhan, even though she'd known that it was an unlikely dream. She'd told herself that she'd be able to accept whatever defects the child might have, that she'd love the baby despite them. And she did love the baby, enough to know that if it died, part of her was going to die as well. But every time she changed a diaper or bathed it, she had to confront the hermaphrodism, and every time the sight found the wound inside her and ripped it open again.

Anaïs's fault. That's what some of them have said. And even if you don't believe that, part of you blames her, just because she was there.

The baby was still crying, weakly. "Here, let's try this," she told it. She rearranged her blouse so that the other breast protruded. "Here. . . . Do you like this one better?" She cradled the head to her breast. Her (his?) eyes were screwed up, tears leaking out as she cried. "Damn it . . ." Elena was about to give up, wondering whether she'd be able to stand listening to the baby wail, when the tiny mouth clamped on her breast and began to suck. This time she stayed on, and Elena felt the milk begin to flow, though the baby still wasn't feeding well, and it stopped after a few minutes. With an exhausted sigh, Elena leaned back in the chair and began to slowly rock, cradling the fuzzy head to her.

She wondered, looking down, whether years from now they would talk about her baby the way they talked about Anaïs. She wondered, if that happened, if she could stand it.

VOICE:
Elio Allen-Shimmura

I DIDN'T HEAR MUCH ABOUT THE FIGHT IN THE Baths for a few days, though everyone had to notice the tension within the Family, and especially between Micah and myself. Mostly, I buried myself in work. I tried to talk with Anaïs, but she was avoiding me—either that or the excuses I kept getting from Hui or her Family showed just incredibly bad timing on my part: "Sorry, she's in the middle of her rounds. I'll tell her you were here looking for her . . ." or "Elio, she's asleep right now and I don't want to wake her up. Poor thing, she works so hard . . ." or "I don't know where she is. She went off an hour ago or so . . ."

So I played with the eternal and ever-changing paper mountain on my desk, and between times, burrowed into the morass of notes Gabriela had left behind about the Miccail, trying to decipher the drawing of the bog body tattoo Ana had given me.

When Gayle Koda-Shimmura walked into my office, I was typing up a report on runoff from the middens and the possible impact on the local environment. Riveting stuff. Gayle's second child Ghulam had died a little over a year ago of the Bloody Cough; I knew she'd recently ended her mourning and begun seeing men again. For a brief moment . . . but hell, I should have known better.

"Elio. Got a few minutes?"

"I don't know." I tapped the sheaf of papers I was holding. "This is important *khudda* I'm working on." I grinned to show her I was kidding and then slid the report aside. "What's up?"

Gayle explained, much to my disappointment: the jaunecerf—deerlike, graceful and beautiful creatures that had turned out to be quite edible as well—were becoming scarce around the Rock: a combination of our thinning of their ranks and the growing reluctance of the herds to congregate in such a deadly area. The Elder Council had placed Gayle in charge of organizing a hunting expedition to bring back a supply of venison for the Families before the weather got too much worse. We'd had our first big snow the day before—a good twenty centimeters of orange, with drifts piling as high as a meter around the foot of the Rock. That also meant that in the next week, most of us would be in the fields, bringing in the last of the crops. My back throbbed in anticipation.

"Anyway," Gayle finished, "what I'm looking for are some good maps of the surrounding area, and any information we have in the database on jaunecerf migration patterns. Maybe we can figure out where they've gone to. That'll save us a lot of useless trekking."

"I'll see what I can find." I went over to the wall and pulled down the flatscreen—the only working one left since the screen in the Gathering Hall went out last year—then went back to the terminal, typing in a few queries. "Well, there's nothing in the database specifically on herd migration . . . but it looks like there's some decent aerial photographic surveys taken from the old shuttles, though. At the right scale, we could pick up the herds and maybe see where they congregate. Here . . ." I activated the screen, and a series of still images began to flicker across the screen, most with the Rock, Tlilipan, and the river prominently displayed. "We have them in various spectrums, too, it seems. That may help . . ." False color scenes now paraded over the wall. "Maybe one of these—"

I stopped. I backtracked to the previous image, staring at the array of greens and yellows on the screen and feeling that prickle down the spine that comes with sudden insight. "What is it?" Gayle asked.

"Nothing." I marked the photo and went on. When Gayle left a bit later, a map still warm from the printer in her hand, I pulled the file back up.

The file notation indicated that the shot had been requested by Gabriela Rusack a few years before the disaster with the *Ibn Battuta*, and was labeled "Overview: Ruins of Miccail Roads, with old lake shores." There, on an infrared photo taken by one of the *Ibn Battuta*'s shuttles more than a century ago, Gabriela had sketched in the outlines of ancient stonework in the land around the Rock for perhaps a hundred kilometer radius around us, while the faint outlines of vanished lakes were hinted at in the false coloration. Despite the gaps, it was easy to see where the Miccail highroads had been placed, in nearly straight lines. Each of those lines ended at one of the old lakes, with two exceptions. A north–south arm intersected the main east–west route *here*—in the middle of the image, where the Rock stood out in dark umber. The picture showed how much larger our lake had been, with the current Tlilipan only a tiny remnant. The Miccail highroad passed along the edge of that parent lake, along the trail we knew as Burnt Cabin Road, where Gabriela Rusack had spent most of her shunned years.

And the other exception was to the west. There lay Crookjaw Bay and the sea, and the east–west road from which the others branched arrowed straight to the cold, gray waves. Just offshore in the bay lay a steep-walled island. On it, when I increased the scale, I could see extensive Miccail ruins.

I glanced again at Ana's sketch of the bog body's tattoo, then to the old photograph. I knew, then, beyond a doubt.

The tattoo might be a hieroglyph, might be writing, might be some cryptic symbol, or might be a Miccail's version of a stick man.

But whatever it was, it was also a map.

CHANGES

JOURNAL ENTRY:
Gabriela Rusack

I SWEAR THAT I WOULD NEVER HAVE APPROACHED her. She came to me entirely on her own.

I'd thought that after Elzbieta's death I'd gone dead sexually. None of the women here were remotely interested in me—even if they had been, the biological imperative that drove every decision here would have precluded a relationship with me. I'd already been told, in no uncertain terms, when they shunned me: *we won't tolerate behavior that could lead to a decline in the birth rate.*

I thought that the precept was so strong that no one would dare break it.

Yet . . . there were those I watched, and those I wondered about. And yes, she was one of them. . . .

It happened this evening. I'm almost afraid to write this down, afraid that it all might disappear if I examine it too closely.

I'd bartered some free time from the network detail, my pottery had finished firing, and I was waiting for the kiln to cool. I'd put half of my latest composition into the synth, but the rest of the music had gone wandering off somewhere in my head and I couldn't hear it. So I'd gone up to the top of the Rock to do some restoration on the Miccail stelae there. I was so absorbed in the task that I didn't notice her until her shadow fell over the stele. I jumped, startled. The brush I was using went flying out of my hand, I yelped like a dog whose tail had been stepped on (there's a metaphor that no one in the next generation will understand), and my feet went out from under me when I tried to stand up. I landed ass first, kicking up dust that immediately sent me coughing.

She laughed, a sound like glass chimes, clear and bright.

"I'm sorry, Gabriela," she said. "I didn't mean to scare you. I'm really sorry. Are you okay?"

Against the sun, her hair burned jet. I could barely see her smile, but I heard it in her voice. "I'm fine, Adari. Just a little

. . . well . . . embarrassed. I don't usually put on that kind of show. At least you were the only one to see it."

Again, the laugh. Adari is sixteen (or a little over twenty-one to those of us—like me—still stuck in the old Earth calendar). She's Akiko's daughter, by Shig—their second child and first girl, conceived before Shig's affair with Becca shattered their marriage and our little pretense that we could still follow Earth's customs. Adari had inherited Shig's dogged stubbornness. Her relationship with her parents had always been stormy, for nearly as long as I could remember—growing up, she was usually referred to as their "difficult" child. I know Shig and Akiko had hoped that Adari would bear the first of the third generation children; Kaitlin Allen-Levin beat her to that, a few years ago. From what I've seen, Adari has no interest in forming any permanent relationships with the men of her generation, not that she has a lot of choice—too many of them are either brothers or half-brothers of hers, and the incest taboo is still strong. I noticed, though, that she rarely took any of the eligible men off privately, even though such behavior was now "official policy."

I noticed . . .

I wiped the worst of the dust from my rear and recovered my brush. While I did that, Adari went over to one of the stelae and gently ran a hand down the carved surface. She has lovely hands, long-fingered and delicate. They look like caring hands, feeling hands. "I can almost sense the *kami* of the Miccail around me when I'm near these things. Can you actually read the carvings?" she asked.

"Not really. I mean, we're never going to have a Rosetta Stone here. There's no link at all to our language. Hell, we don't even have a common evolution. Any guess about what these figures mean is just that: a guess." My voice sounded like gravel in a cup. I suddenly hated it.

"But you think you know some of it." She said it with the same smile, that long waterfall of black hair covering half her face as she inclined her head. She said it without the question mark, as if she were simply stating something we both knew was truth.

"Yes," I answered, suddenly uncomfortable. "I have my guesses. They're as good as anyone else's."

She nodded at that, brushing back the hair and tucking it behind one ear—several strands came loose immediately, glossy highlights swinging. I was just standing there, watching her. To cover my guiltiness at thinking what I was thinking—what I often thought when I looked at Adari—I crouched down and began brushing dirt from the ancient carved grooves once more. I could hear her behind my back. I could feel her, close to me, bending down behind me to look at what I was doing.

"My mam tells me that when you were on the ship, you lived with a woman."

So now we can't even say the words. Elzbieta and I were married. We were lovers, committed to each other, and now she's reduced to a roommate. Such a nice euphemism. I didn't bother to answer, afraid that my iritation would show, and I wasn't angry at Adari, who was only using the words she'd heard Akiko and the others say. She either wasn't expecting an answer or was content with the sound of the brush on stone. "I don't think it was fair of them to shun you just because you didn't want to have any children," she continued. "I'm glad you came back."

The brush stopped moving. The silence almost hurt. I could hear the wind in the globe-trees halfway down the slope, and someone singing down in the settlement. "Thank you, Adari," I said. I couldn't look at her.

"Gabriela, I . . ." she began. I waited, the brush still halted in midstroke. "When did you know that you . . ."

. . . that you were a rezu . . . I heard the rest of the question without its being said. I turned, still crouched down. She was standing a half meter away, her hands jammed into the pockets of her coat, her lower lip caught between her teeth. "That I preferred women to men?" I asked, and received a nod in return. I could feel the chill of the stone at my back. "I think I always knew. It just took a very long time to finally listen to myself." I waited, trying to see what was behind those dark, dark eyes. "That's a strange question to ask."

A shrug this time. "I've been doing some listening, too," she said, very quietly. "To my voice."

"And what does your voice say?"

"I . . ." She started, stopped, her mouth still open. She looked scared and vulnerable, shaking a little as she hugged herself. Her throat pulsed—once, again—as if she were trying to force something out. She wouldn't look at me, but then her eyes came up, with a strange defiance glinting in them. "Gabriela, I think you're beautiful," she said.

I almost laughed out of sheer surprise. That would have been a disaster. After the initial shock, I felt myself blushing. *Adari . . .* I wanted to take her into my arms, wanted to just hug her and hold her, to stroke her hair. Nothing sexual, only letting her know that I understood how hard that was for her to say. Instead, I stood, taking a long, slow calming breath. "Adari—"

"I know what you're going to say," she told me hurriedly.

"Let me say it anyway. First, I know that saying what you just said took a lot of courage. I know that. And I . . . well, I'm flattered that you'd say it to me. But I'm your mother's age. If that weren't enough, neither your mam or anyone else here is going to accept that kind of relationship. Not at all."

Now there was a redness in her cheeks that was anger and embarrassment. "If you don't like me . . ."

"Oh, God, no. That's not it at all. Adari—" I took her hands in my own. They were soft and warm. They would have been nice hands to kiss, to stroke. *Why are you doing this to me?* I asked the *kami* around us. "Adari, I think you're beautiful, too. I wish . . ." I stopped, shaking my head. "Adari, I understand what you're feeling. Maybe I'm the only one here who can. I don't want to belittle your feelings, but you can't be sure. You can't."

"That's why I came to you. So I could be."

"I don't want to be just an experiment, Adari."

Her cheeks colored at that, her back stiffened, and she pulled away from me. "I just told you something that I didn't dare say to anyone else. Do you understand how *hard* that was? I didn't come to you for an *experiment*."

"Yes, you did, whether you admit it or not. The men you've been with have been a disappointment—I understand that, but it *doesn't* mean you're a lesbian. You think I'm attractive—I'm glad, but sexual attraction's a strange beast, and it's normal to be attracted to another person of the same sex even when you're heterosexual. All this sounds cold, and I'm sorry, but I've been alone so long now that I'm used to it. We wouldn't have a chance, Adari, and I've had enough hurt already in my life."

"Gabriela, please. What am I supposed to do?"

"I don't know," I told her, and the honesty hurt me as much as her.

"At least tell me if . . . what . . ."

I knew what she was trying to ask. *Adari, I've imagined you in my mind, alone at night. I've watched you and wondered if, just maybe, you were like me . . .* "Yes," I told her. "I've felt the same feelings toward you."

"Then why can't we at least try?" she asked. Her hands

176

reached out for mine; I took them. *So warm....* "No one else has to know."

"But they *will* know," I told her. "No matter how discreet we try to be, someone will find out. And we wouldn't *want* to hide it, Adari, not if it's to be something more than a one-time thing."

"I want to make love with you, Gabriela." The words were barely more than a whisper, wrapped in slow tears that I desperately wanted to kiss away from her cheeks. "I don't think that's wrong."

"It's *not* wrong," I told her. Moisture tracked slowly down my own cheek now.

"Then..." she began, and didn't say more.

"It would be a mistake," I told her. "Adari, *mojo ljubav*, there can't be any happy endings here, not for us."

I told her that. I meant it.

Then, may all the *kami* help me, I went ahead and made the mistake.

VOICE:
Máire Koda-Schmidt

"Is THIS WHERE YOU AND OCHIBA...?"

Ana nodded, and her face went soft with memory, some of the lines leaving her forehead. She looked younger suddenly, and more fragile. "We came here a few times, yes. As often as we felt we could. Does that bother you?"

"No," I told her. "Of course not. In fact... well, I know how you felt about Ochiba, and I'm glad you'd want me here, too."

The cave was on the back side of the Rock, low on the cliff side facing the river. It wasn't really a cave, just a shallow hollow formed by cracks in the stone of the Rock and hidden by a scree of rockfall. The low room was furnished—a crude table, a stool, a small bed with no mattress, some pottery along a rock ledge to the rear. *This is where Gabriela spent her first shunning*, Ana had told me when we'd arrived. *At least, that's what Ghost told me once.*

We snuggled under a blanket, spooned into each other with Anaïs warm on my back, still sweaty from our lovemaking. Her hand stroked my cheek, brushing my hair gently. "Are you all right, Máire?" she whispered into my ear. Our words echoed in the space, magnified.

"I'm fine," I told her. I rolled over so that I faced her. I smiled into her seriousness. "It was lovely, Ana. Please don't worry."

"I told you I was . . . different. A lot more different now than when Ochiba was alive. I hope—"

"Shhh." I stopped her words with another kiss. "I'm fine. I liked it. All of it." That was mostly true. Even though Ana had told me what to expect, it was still disconcerting to see that strange, small erection nestled above her vaginal lips, and even stranger to feel it inside me, to know that this was one way that Anaïs found her release. But not the only way. No. Not the only way. "Does Elio?"

Cuddled against her, I felt her shrug. "I think so. He's a good person, Máire. He likes you, too."

"I know. It's just . . ." I let my hand trail along her side, along the swell of her hip, and back up along the side of her breast. I was feeling a strange, wild joy. I was exhilarated, almost giddy. If I'd known that breaking taboos could feel so good, I might have broken them much earlier. As much anticipation as I'd felt before this afternoon, I'd felt just as much fear. Now I wanted to shout. I wanted to sink into Anaïs again. I wanted the taste of her on my tongue forever. ". . . I don't know. I think I may have been jealous of him, and that wasn't fair of me."

"Don't be. There's no reason."

"You're still going to bed with him."

"Yes." She caught my hand, squeezed it gently. "And with you."

We'd been gone for over an hour, and we both knew that we had to go back, yet neither of us wanted to make the first move to leave. It was like we were caught up in a story, a fiction somehow separate from our own reality, and we knew that the wrong word, the wrong step, would break the spell. We talked a little longer, kissed a few times more, and—with a mutual sigh—regretfully left the bed and dressed again.

Outside, the wind was cold and laden with snow crystals,

giving us a reminder of winter, but I felt warm. We smiled at each other, helplessly, as we slid and stumbled around the foot of the Rock. The river lapped at the rocks near us; chirpers glared from their perches and then dove into the cold, moving water with small, irritated splashes. We moved uphill through a tangle of thornvines and into a stand of globetrees. Wizards cursed us from the branches, but we didn't care. Didn't notice, really.

Just before we emerged from the trees, I stopped Ana with a hand and turned her, giving her a last kiss. The wizards, as if surprised (and, yes, probably offended) by our boldness, took off loudly from the trees, shrieking. I laughed at the sound.

"Just once more while we still can. . . ." I told Anaïs as we embraced.

Then, with a sigh and the raucous calls of the wizards, we stepped from fantasy back into our world.

CONTEXT:
Miat Koda-Shimmura

"ARE YOU SURE?" ELENA ASKED.

Miat nodded with righteous satisfaction. "I'm only telling you because you're her sib. I was on my way to the south grove and I couldn't have been more than a hundred meters away, near Old Bridge. I'd stopped to catch my breath and I was sitting on one of the boulders—that's why they didn't notice me. They were just in the shade of the globe-trees near the river path. When I saw them, I stood up and the wizards all took off from the trees. I thought for sure Ana and Máire would see me then, but they didn't even look around. I don't know what they were doing, but I can tell you that they were together for a long time. A long time."

The baby was fussing. Elena bounced it a little in the bodysling. They were in the entrance room of the Rock caverns, a huge artificial room, the rock walls polished and melted by the lasers of the long-destroyed shuttles. The child's whimpering was loud and especially annoying in the room.

Miat glanced down at the red face bundled in front of Elena—it looked too thin. The rumor was that it wasn't nursing well, that it was sick all the time. *Too bad*, Miat thought. *The first one to die's the hardest on you.* Two of her own had died of the Bloody Cough back in 79, within hours of each other: Susan and William. Three years old, and five. Then, in 86, her first-born, Hannah, had died trying to give birth to a fetus far too large for her pelvis—Hui's emergency C-section hadn't saved the mother, though the child, Tozo the Younger, had lived. Later that same year, Miat's youngest, Grace, had died of influenza. *At least Miranda and Ben are still alive. Two of my six . . .*

"You're sure it was Máire with Anaïs?" Elena was asking, her forehead furrowed, either from dealing with the colicky infant or from what Miat had just told her. "And even if it was, they were probably just talking."

"I don't need to hold someone to talk to them," Miat said with a sniff. "Or if I do, there's another reason for the conversation."

Elena's baby gave another cry, which quickly escalated into a long wail. "Shhh, hush," Elena crooned, her worried eyes going from Miat to the baby and back again. The baby continued to scream, inconsolable. "Look, Miat. I can't stay to talk. Just keep this to yourself, all right? I'll talk to Máire. I will. I'm sure nothing's going on—she and Anaïs are friends, and they've been doing a lot of work together with that body I found in the peat."

"Sure. Whatever you say, Elena. I just thought someone from her Family should know."

"I appreciate it," Elena said over the crying child. Miat could see the strain in the woman's face, in the way her hands clenched around the baby's wrappings. "I do. I'll talk to you later."

"Fine. You take care of that baby, now."

"I will. She's just . . . tired."

You look like the tired one, Miat thought as she watched Elena hurry away toward her Family compound. She saw Micah Allen-Shimmura entering the cavern from the hall to his Family compound.

"Micah!" she called. "I'll bet you'd be interested in this . . ."

Elio Allen-Shimmura

"YOU'RE POSITIVE IT'S A MAP?" ANAÏS ASKED ME.

"Positive. Here, take a look at this aerial survey of Gabriela's, where she drew in the old Miccail roads. Now, here's the drawing you made of the bogman's tattoo."

"I still don't see it."

"You have to orient the photo so that west's on top, not north, and get some of the crap off your desk so that you can spread them both out alongside each other. There, you see? The lines are the old Miccail highroads; the little circles at the ends of the straight lines are lakes, the triangle/circle combination at the center is the Rock and Tlilipan—a little too high, but that's artistic license, I guess. The big wavy line at the top's the ocean, and the parallelogram's the island just off the coast. I'd've still missed it if Gabriela hadn't also sketched in the outlines of the old lakes, since some of them are like Tlilipan and are gone to bogs now. We're missing a few lakes, and the Miccail roads aren't anywhere near as straight as the lines on the tattoo, but still . . ."

Anaïs stared at the photograph for a long time, then back at her drawing, and finally back at the photograph again. Finally, she shook her head, rubbing her nose with a forefinger. "I'll be damned," she said.

"*Hai.*" I grinned at her. "Look at it this way—you're never going to get lost when you have the way home tattooed on your chest. Hey, if he'd been a female, they could have done the landscape in full relief."

I was hoping for a laugh. I had to be satisfied with a grimace. At least it came packaged in an indulgent sigh.

"I still don't understand," Anaïs said. She was poring over the photograph and drawing again. One finger tapped the island. "I mean, there has to be more to it than just being a *map*. The drawing isn't exactly complicated—no one would have any trouble memorizing this. Getting a tattoo that extensive would have hurt like hell: If it were *me*, I'd say that's fine, but I'll just remember the way back, *domo arigato*."

"That's me and you. But I'll bet it was part of some kind of ritual—as you said, it's stylized and doesn't have any detail. I doubt that it was intended as an actual map, but a tribal identification, maybe, or to mark a rite of passage. Ritual tattooing has been common enough in our history; it wouldn't surprise me to see it here."

"Every time we figure out something about this bog body, we uncover another three mysteries that need explanation." Anaïs sighed and scratched the back of her neck wearily. She leaned back in her chair and cocked her head up at me. "Thanks, Elio. I'd've never figured this out."

I spread my hands wide. "It was one hundred percent serendipity and dumb luck. Beyond that, I take all the credit." She did laugh then, and I leaned down and kissed her just because I loved the sound of her laughter. She hesitated at first, then finally reached up and cradled my head in her hands. She pulled me down toward her. The kiss went longer than either of us expected, and when it was over, I sat on the floor alongside her chair, leaning sideways against her desk.

"Hey," I said quietly.

"Hey," she answered back, with a smile. "That was nice."

"Yes, it was."

"Then don't look so surprised."

"I'm not. I just—" I stopped, not certain that she'd want me to say what I was going to say aloud."

"Just what?"

"You know. You and Máire."

She colored nicely, a flush that rose from somewhere below her collar and ended at the tips of her ears. "Elio, I'm not—"

I waved my hand at what sounded like the beginning of a false explanation. I didn't want her to start making up lies for me. "You don't need to explain anything to me, Ana. I'm not my Geeda. Who you make love to is your business. I don't need to know names. In fact, I'd prefer it that way. Just do me a favor. Be very, very careful, Ana."

She gave a single chuckle that had no amusement in it at all. "Believe me, I understand that much. Elio, listen, I don't know what you were thinking, but I don't want to end things between us. Consider the kiss an invitation."

"Then consider me having accepted. Emphatically." I

pushed myself back to my feet and put a hand on her shoulder. "See you tonight? About NinthHour?"

She gave me a smile. Ana has a really nice smile, and it was good to notice that in the last month or so I'd been seeing it more and more often. Something in her spirit burned brighter now, and it was a wonder to see. "All right. Sure. At my Family's."

I nodded. "Great. See you then."

With that, I walked out of the clinic, feeling happy and content with myself and with Anaïs.

I should have known that couldn't last.

VOICE:
Máire Koda-Schmidt

"MÁIRE, CAN I TALK TO YOU?" ELENA CALLED OUT as I passed her room.

"Sure," I said. "I've got a few minutes, but Geema Eleanor has me on kitchen duty tonight." I went in. Elena's apartment was small and only one room, as were most of the rooms in our compound. Some of the other Families might have several rooms for each person, but that usually meant that the Family wasn't thriving. Anaïs's compound was that way, and it would probably only get more spacious, since unless Anaïs had children (or, very unlikely, if her mam Maria had another female child), hers would be the last generation for the Koda-Levins.

Elena was laying on her bed on top of the covers. She looked like she'd just woken from a nap. She'd moved the baby's crib from the Family creche into her room, which made it even more crowded. The baby was asleep, sniffling slightly in some dream. I went over to her and looked down. I could see her little eyelids fluttering in sleep, and her tiny finger clenched and unclenched.

"She's so darling," I whispered to Elena, touching her hand. Her fingers wrapped around my index fingers reflexively. "She really is. Such a precious little thing. So little and helpless . . ." Her eyes opened then, blinking hard a few times. Her eyes were startlingly blue and so big in that small face . . . "Oh, I've gone and woken her. Do you mind if I hold her?"

Elena shook her head as I reached down and picked her up. She weighed so little, cradled in my arms, her head down against my shoulder. I knew she wasn't nursing well—all of us knew it. Elena had tried everything: bottles, milk from the woolies, some of Tozo the Younger's milk, wheat-based formula. Hui had examined both of them and said that there weren't any obvious physical problems with either mother or child; just keep trying. None of it had helped, and I knew that most of the Family were convinced that the baby wasn't going to make it. It didn't seem fair. No one so young and innocent should ever die, without even a name.

She started to cry, and I rocked her, shushing her with soft, crooning words. "Now, now, it's okay. Your *mi* Máire has you now. You're safe here, darling. You're safe." I patted her bottom. "She's wet," I told Elena.

I could see the exhaustion in her face, her eyes dark-circled. "All right. Give her here, Máire," Elena said.

"No, I'll do it. You stay there and rest, love." I walked over to the table where Elena had diapers stacked. I removed the wet diaper. As I cleaned her, I could feel Elena watching me. I wondered whether she was waiting for me to make some comment as I looked down at the twinned genitalia, so like Anaïs. They didn't seem strange at all to me. Not now.

"Hey, don't cry now," I told the baby. "You have no reason to cry. None at all. It's a little tough for you now, but you're going to be fine. Just fine." By the time I'd finished, she'd stopped crying. When I put her on my shoulder, she started rooting with her mouth. "She's hungry, too. Now *that* I can't help you with, darling. Here, go to your mam . . ."

I handed her to Elena, who slipped down one shoulder of her blouse and opened her bra. I could see Elena steeling herself for another futile struggle, but this time the baby took the breast immediately, sucking hard. Elena gasped with the fury of the baby's pull. "There you go!" I laughed. I looked at Elena and saw tears tracking down her cheeks, even as she stroked the baby's head.

"Hey," I said, stroking away the moisture with a finger. I

sat on the bed next to them, putting my arm around Elena, and watching the baby. "She's going to be fine, Elena. She's beautiful and she's very special, and you're both going to be fine." Elena gave one loud, gasping sob, then smiled, and laughed. She stroked the baby's head as she nursed. I could hear the tiny, wet smacking sounds as she gulped Elena's milk. I watched them silently for a long time, then got up. "She's eating good tonight, eh?"

Elena nodded. "Finally."

We grinned at each other. I tousled Elena's hair as I'd done when we'd been children. "I should go or Geema's going to stick me with the kitchen for the rest of the month. What'd you want?"

Elena looked at me. The baby was still nursing, contented. Elena's mouth pursed, strangely, then she shook her head. "Nothing," she said. "It was nothing. Go on."

I shrugged and bent down to kiss the baby's head. "I'll see you later, then. Stay here and nurse her, then get some sleep while you can. I'll go tell Geema and the others the good news."

As I left, I heard Elena stir and call after me. "Máire!"

"Hai?"

"Thanks," she said.

"For what? I didn't do anything."

I could see her on the bed, a shadow. "For loving i . . . her."

"Who wouldn't love her?" I told her. "She's beautiful. Like her mam."

JOURNAL ENTRY:
Gabriela Rusack

ANYONE WHO HAS NEVER ONCE FALLEN MADLY IN love has no heart.

Anyone who has fallen madly in love twice has no head.

Which means, I suppose, that I fall in the latter category. I fell for Adari, fell for her as hard and fast and unreservedly as I had for Elzbieta. It was a terrible, stupid mistake, and I knew it when it happened, but I let it happen anyway. No, that's wrong . . . I swear I couldn't *stop* it from happening, any more than I could voluntarily stop breathing.

I fell, with all the loss of control that implies.

I thought I'd gone dead sexually after so long an abstinence, but Adari awakened me again, made me flower once more. I looked at her, and suddenly I didn't feel so *old*. Maybe in Adari I'd found my lost youth again; maybe that's why I was so vulnerable to her invitation even when I knew I shouldn't be. I forgot the difference in our ages when I was with her. She kissed me, and I could feel the caress burn in my center. I stroked her breasts and I gasped myself in arousal.

It was wonderful. It was glorious. It was doomed.

You can't hide an attraction like that. We burned in each other's presence, stealing glances and sharing smiles, touching and laughing, our heads together all the time, finding excuses to be in the same place. We were careful not to touch too much in public, to make sure we were safely hidden before we embraced, but they noticed: Shigetomo, Jean, her mother Akiko, all of my peers and all of their children. I told myself I didn't care. I told myself that as long as they didn't actually find us together, they couldn't do anything. I thought that it would be a case of "don't ask if you really don't want to know." And if they did ask, well, I'd cheerfully deny it to them and go on enjoying our stolen moments together.

Of course, I should have known that it wouldn't be me they'd go after. It wouldn't be me who faced an angry Family's inquisition, since I was the one that they wanted to hurt. I was the source of the awful infection, not Adari. I was the corrupter.

So it was Adari they took aside finally, hurling questions at her: relentlessly, cruelly. And finally, weeping, she told them. She told them that she loved me.

And for that forbidden love, they sent me away.

INTERLUDE:
KaiSa

KAI MEANT TO LEAVE. KE NOTICED THAT DEKTE NO longer set a guard to watch ker, that ke could have simply walked away from the encampment at any time.

Yet ke didn't.

Kai told kerself that it was because the army was obviously getting ready to move, and ke needed more information before ke could report back to JaqTe. So many contradictions. . . .

Kai still shivered every time that ke remembered the ugly scene with NeiTe, every time ke recalled the terrible sound PirXe's spear made as he thrust it into the body of NeiTe's *xeshaiXe*, every time ke thought of DekTe's cold words to NeiTe as he sent the Miccail chieftain from the encampment:

"In a hand of hand of days, we will come to your borders, and I will ask you to give me your lands freely and to become Xe under me. Refuse, and we will sweep over your land like dryhusks after the spring flood."

KaiSa told kerself that ker staying had nothing to do with DekTe, with the fact that each day he came to ker tent and talked with ker, that the enjoyment ke felt then was like nothing ke had ever felt before. The man's soul was broken and splintered. Conflict and contradiction raged inside him, and yet that fragility made DekTe all the more attractive to Kai.

Kai reminded kerself that ke was supposed to hate DekTe.

That reminder was as ephemeral as the wind, and as lasting. Like leaves caught in the storm of Kai's emotions, the words were gone before they could be held. Ke couldn't hate DekTe. Despite everything the man had done and threatened to do, Kai could not deny the attraction that ke felt for DekTe, and the power of that emotion frightened ker with its intensity.

Yes, ke should have left. But ke didn't.

DekTe's army moved two mornings later. KaiSa watched from the huge rock alongside the Black Lake. It was a sight that none had seen since the days of the despised KeldTe, and Kai found the scene at once beautiful and terrible. A dark, many-footed beast, the army crawled the slopes around the Black Lake, crushing the grass underfoot, leaving the land torn and muddy. Their spears sent knife-edged meteors of sunlight flashing; the drumbeats of the march-leaders could not drown out the muffled thunder of their passage. The earth reverberated under them, groaning.

The vista was so wrong in the sacred landscape, so obviously absurd that KaiSa wondered why VeiSaTi didn't simply rise in disgust and drown them all.

A figure broke away from the main mass of the army—a man astride a *konja*. The rider galloped his steed around the curve of the Black Lake, never breaking stride even as they hit the rocky slope below Kai. Ke watched them come, the breath steaming from the *konja*'s nostrils like a furnace, its massive chest heaving as the rider pulled on the reins to bring the beast to a grudging stop. The *konja*'s long strands of coarse hair, splattered with mud from the ride, swung as it stamped its hoofed feet. From the animal's back, DekTe grinned at KaiSa, a wild, manic smile, and he leaped down from the *konja*.

"That's power you're looking at, Sa. By the gods, can't you hear it, can't you *feel* it?"

"Yes," Kai answered. "I feel it, DekTe. How does it feel to you, to know that so many of our people will go where you tell them to go, that any of them would do what you tell them to do?"

"It's intoxicating," DekTe answered, with that same exhilarated laugh. "Did you want me to lie and be humble about it? Well, I won't. Seeing it fills me with energy. It makes me feel that I can accomplish anything I can dream."

"I believe you can. That's what worries me."

DekTe laughed again. "You told me you were leaving, Sa. Yet you've stayed. If that's your decision, then come with me now. Come see me keep my promises to NeiTe."

"No."

"Yes." DekTe's smile vanished for an instant, then returned. "You said that your task was to see what threat I represented to Sa. Now you'll see." DekTe grasped the long hair of the *konja* and pulled himself up on the beast again. He held his hand out to KaiSa. "Ride with me, KaiSa," he said.

Kai looked at the hand, at the army filling the sacred land of the Black Lake. *You are doomed*, a voice seemed to say inside ker head. *There is no escape from this fate for you.*

Kai took DekTe's hand and let him pull ker up behind him. Ke put ker arms around DekTe's waist as he kicked the *konja*'s side and the animal lumbered away down the slope.

Later, Kai remembered little of the ride. Ke could recall only the feel of DekTe against her and the gaze of CaraTe as they passed. The *konja* stank of wet hair and sweat, its flanks itched ker legs, and despite the blankets, the knobby spine quickly became a torture to ker rear. DekTe led the army away from the Black Lake to the north, fording the river just downstream.

Toward the end of the day, Kai saw the *nasituda* that marked the edge of the free territory, and other stones that proclaimed that they were approaching land controlled by NeiTe. DekTe galloped the *konja* to the marking stone and reined the animal to a halt. CaraTa rode up on her own gray *konja*, with a young female who Kai did not recognize. CaraTa pushed her down roughly from the *konja*, and the youngling collapsed in a heap on the ground. PirXe strode forward from the ranks of DekTe's army and picked her up, dragging her over to DekTe.

"Get down," DekTe told Kai, and ke slid off the *konja* without a word. DekTe pulled the youngling female up in front of him. "CaraTa, take the Sa for now." DekTe wheeled the *konja* around to face the forest, its shadows darkening under the lowering sun. Astride the beast, DekTe shouted toward the silent trees, his voice strong and vibrant. His shadow stretched behind him like a dark, translucent cloak. "NeiTe! I've come as I promised, and I've brought your daughter! I need your answer, NeiTe!"

For long minutes, there was no answer. The *konja* snorted restlessly. DekTe repeated the challenge as his army stirred behind him and the wind shook the limbs of the trees as if trying to force an answer from them. DekTe's long chinlocks swayed in the rising gusts. "NeiTe, I'm waiting for your answer!"

Something moved under the trees. NeiTe stepped out, with some fifty of his Xe and Xa behind him, each of their naked chests streaked with the swirling white glyphs of *xeshai*. NeiTe held his ceremonial spear, the shaft carved with the runes of the Te who had come before him, and he glared at DekTe. "This is madness, DekTe. I will give you a last chance to follow the Law. Pick any one of my XeXa to be *xeshaiXe* and represent us in fair battle. Pick me if that's what you want. But this . . ." NeiTe gestured to take in the ranks of Miccail behind DekTe. "This isn't needed. Return NaiXa to us and we'll end this as we should."

DekTe only shook his head sadly. His hand gripped NaiXa's arm tightly. "Did you misunderstand me so badly, NeiTe?" he asked. "Didn't I speak clearly? I told you then: give your land to me freely—a free gift, NeiTe—or your daughter will be the first one to die as I take it anyway. NeiTe, neither of us want that. Give me your spear, become Xe under me, and it's over. You're right, this *is* madness if you still refuse. Can't you see? The only thing you will accomplish is the death of you and most of your XeXa. You can't win this *xeshai* of mine." His voice sounded so reasonable, so wise, so saddened by what he said. Yet KaiSa watched DekTe's hand, and his grip on NaiXa's arm didn't loosen. "NeiTe, give me your spear and there will be no more insanity. It will be over, your daughter will live, and I promise that I will treat your XeXa fairly. Is that such a horrible fate?"

KaiSa could see the spear waver in NeiTe's hand. He looked back at his XeXa, who were stoic in their *xeshai* paint. "All I want—" NeiTe began, but stopped as DekTe shook his head.

"Yes or no. The only thing you need to say is one of those two words, NeiTe. There's no need for talk. Just yes, or no. Yes, and I give you your daughter. No, and she and anyone else who resists us will die." DekTe sighed loudly, and his voice went soft. "I don't want that, NeiTe. I truly don't. Now, give me your answer."

"I can't—"

DekTe's free hand flashed, sliding a stone knife from his belt and placing it hard against NaiXa's throat. She whimpered as DekTe held the blade against her skin. "You *must* answer, NeiTe. And you must answer now." There was fire in DekTe's voice now, and impatience. The *konja* howled and stamped its feet under him; the jostling caused the knife to break NaiXa's skin. Kai saw the thick, slow welling rivulet of blood trickle down the side of her neck. "Now," DekTe repeated.

NeiTe gazed at his trembling daughter, his eyes full of anguish and pain. "Death now or death later—those are the choices you give me, DekTe. I have always lived by the Law; I won't change that." He grasped his spear firmly, thumping the end into the ground. "No. That's your answer, DekTe. No."

DekTe gave a bellow of anger, and at the same time, he drew the knife hard back and down. A fan of scarlet erupted, spraying the front of NaiXa's *shangaa* and spattering the *konja*'s hair. NaiXa's cry died in a death rattle, drowned in blood. DekTe threw her limp body to the ground as the *konja* reared and hurtled forward toward NeiTe. He rode the chieftain down.

NeiTe's spear cracked and shattered under the *konja*'s hooves.

KaiSa would never forget what ke saw that night. The horror was too large to comprehend as a whole, too awful to hold. Yet small impressions of it remained imprinted, echoes of the larger carnage around them:

. . . *the sudden, overpowering smoke as the wind shifted, and under the woodsmoke, that of burning meat, of flesh . . .*

. . . *ker foot slipping in blood as ke walked with CaraTa at the edge of NeiTe's village. Ke looked down, and ke was standing in a pool of red, flowing from the cloven body of some nameless Xa . . .*

. . . *the din of the battle, a wordless hurricane of sound punctuated by shouts and screams . . .*

. . . *the blank eyes staring at ker from a bodiless head that had rolled into the rutted lane, the mouth of the dead Xe open in a soundless shriek, and crawling on the bloated lips, there were already feeding insects . . .*

. . . *NeiTe's body, stripped naked and mounted on a pole, being paraded down the lane by several of DekTe's people . . .*

. . . *how even through the vulgar laughter of the males ke could hear the soft whimpering of the Ta as she was raped . . .*

. . . *the grim satisfaction on CaraTa's face as she surveyed the wreckage of NeiTe's dwelling, the light from the raging fire playing over the muscles of her face. Kai searched for any flicker of remorse in her eyes. CaraTa felt the pressure of ker gaze, and she turned to ker. "Do you want me to feel guilty for this, Sa?" she asked. "Don't. I have no guilt, no remorse, no sadness in me at all."*

When it was over—how long that was Kai didn't know, but the last light of the day was gone and the twin moons hung over the village like doleful lamps—DekTe rode back to where ke and CaraTa stood. The *konja* limped from a wound on its rear leg. DekTe's spear was bloodied, his arm spattered with what in the firelight looked like black ink, and there was a long cut on his left shoulder. Behind him on the *konja* was another person, hands bound behind. DekTe gestured, and one of his people came over and hauled down the prisoner, who immediately sank to the ground. The head lifted wearily, and the shock of recognition took Kai's breath.

"AbriSa!" ke cried.

VOICE:
Anaïs Koda-Levin the Younger

"WHOOAH . . ."

Elio let out a long, shivering breath, and I had to laugh at the expression on his face. That made him smile in return, and he reached up and brought my face down to his again. "Hey," I told him when we finally broke apart again. "I can't again, not right now. I'm due at the clinic."

He made a comically disappointed face and I laughed again. "Besides, you can't possibly be ready again that fast," I told him.

"I will be by the time we get through with the preliminaries."

"Keep that thought," I told him. "Later, I promise." I stroked his face, pushing the hair away from his eyes. "Elio, thank you. That was very lovely. I appreciate . . . well, you know."

"Shhh." He put a finger on my lips, and I kissed it softly. "Don't worry. You can't do anything about the way you're made, and I don't care. Or haven't you figured that out yet?"

"I think I may have, actually," I told him, and it felt like the truth. For the first time since Ochiba's death, I felt whole. I felt as if I'd—at last—turned the corner on the depression that had wrapped around me since I'd watched her ashes go swirling into the sky. Some of it was Máire, some of it was also Elio.

Healing. The word came to me as I got out of the bed and began to dress. *The wounds are finally healing.* I caught a glimpse of myself in Rebecca's mirror between the clothing. Impulsively, I brushed the clothes aside and stared. Someone I almost didn't recognize smiled back at me. I reached out my hand and touched her fingertips gently. The heat of my fingertips fogged the silvered glass where our fingers met. Behind the mirror-Anaïs, I saw Elio watching and I turned back to him. "You don't know how much I needed you, Elio."

" 'Needed.' That's past tense." He thrust his lower lip out in a showy pout.

"Okay. 'Need,' then. Satisfied?"

"I don't know. Why don't we find out?"

"Save it for me. I really have to go, or Hui's going to be in one of his tempers. You can stay here as long as you want. The Family'll feed you if you go to the kitchen." I pulled on my pants and shrugged a sweater over my head, then sat on the bed to pull on my boots. I felt his hand on my back.

"I think Máire's been good for you, too," he said.

I stopped lacing up the boots, but I didn't look back at him. "Elio—"

"Come on, Ana. We both know the two of you are involved, even if we've been politely avoiding saying so. I'm just telling you that, as far as I'm concerned, it's good. I can see the change in you recently."

I hadn't been sure what I was going to say, hadn't decided whether I was going to lie or hedge or simply admit the truth. This way, all I had to do was nod, and the admission was acknowledged. I didn't want to keep any secrets from Elio; I was pleased to find I didn't have to. "I'm glad you feel that way, Elio. If you didn't . . . well, it wouldn't change anything, but I'm glad." I patted his hand and stood up. "I have to go. I'll be on duty all night. Maybe I'll see you late tomorrow, if you're not busy."

As I stepped through the door, I heard Elio stirring in the bed, and the sound made me stop. I looked back into the room. "I love you, Elio," I told him. "I really do."

Then, before he could say anything else, I left.

Ama had brought back a stack of clean bandages from the laundry to fold, but Wan-Li had come in with a gash in his leg, and Hui had decided that it was a good situation to find out if Ama knew how to properly suture a wound. "It's time to see if you're suited for anything better than darning socks," was Hui's actual comment. From the sudden paleness in Ama's face, I was glad I wasn't Wan-Li. I remembered the first time I sewed someone up with Hui's glowering, critical presence watching every stitch. It hadn't been a pretty sight.

There was no one else in the clinic and with both Hui and Ama busy I didn't want to get involved with the bog body, so I sat at one of the tables and started folding. I hummed to myself as I worked, a melody Geema Anaïs had taught me, and that her mother had taught her: an Earth-melody. *"It's called 'Greensleeves,'"* she'd told me when I first learned it, many years ago. *"Rebecca claimed that it was one of the oldest songs known on earth. Variations of the song go back centuries and centuries, well back into medieval times."* Whenever I played it on the zither or sang it to myself, I always thought of that. Sometimes I could believe that, in that same instant, someone back on Earth was singing the same song, and for a brief moment we were linked together despite the distance.

When I was a child, I used to tell myself that I'd teach the song to my own children and give them the same gift of history.

Back when I'd believed I'd still have children, anyway. . . .

"You sound happy."

I glanced up, startled, and saw the greenish glow around the snout of the projector Hui had brought into the clinic. I turned around to see Ghost. She was clothed in *Ibn Battuta* dress blues, and the face was familiar from pictures I'd seen: Captain Roberts, who had died in the explosion of the ship. "Good to see you again, Anaïs. So . . . are you really happy?" Ghost asked.

I nodded. The response came automatically and freely, and I was surprised at the lack of ambiguity in myself at the moment. "Yes, I am, Ghost," I told her, and it was the truth. "I'm happy."

"Is it anything I should know about? Or should I say any-*one*?"

"No," I told her. "And what makes you think it might be a person?"

Ghost grinned. "I have my ways," she said in a voice that was probably meant to sound mysterious but sounded closer to sinister. "I pulled in your and Elio's notes on the bog body," she continued. "I'd agree with Elio—the tattoo is a map."

Changing the subject? I almost asked, but frankly I didn't mind. "Why didn't *you* figure that out?" I asked instead. "You had all the information we needed."

"Having information is like owning a jigsaw puzzle," Ghost retorted. "What matters is whether you can put it together to see the picture."

"That sounds suspiciously like something Gabriela might have said."

"As a matter of fact, she once did," Ghost answered.

"Uh-huh." I suspected that Ghost probably had one of Gabriela's aphorisms for most every situation. But thinking about Gabriela suggested something else. "Gabriela ordered those surveys, so she obviously knew about the island. Did she ever go there?"

"She talked about it, more than once," Ghost answered. "After she was shunned the second time, she claimed she was going to go there."

"So did she?"

Ghost frowned at me, one eyebrow lifting. "I don't know. I never had a chance to talk with her after that, not for years, and in the few conversations we did have, I never asked her. But I doubt that she made it there."

"Why?"

"It's an *island*?" Ghost said with the questioning tones people use when they're talking to a child they think should know better. She made exaggerated rowing motions. "You need a *boat*?"

"What I don't need is the sarcasm, Ghost. Maybe she built one."

Ghost looked at me from under her eyelids. "Oh, yeah. Right." She morphed subtly, the *Ibn Battuta* dress uniform shifting into a stereotypical sailor's outfit from the nineteenth century. "Avast, matey!" she said loudly. "Gabriela was born in Copernicus One on the moon. I don't think she was ever on a boat in her life, and she certainly wouldn't have had the faintest idea how to build one from scratch. And I guarantee she never learned to swim."

"Uh-huh. I get the idea. Still. . . . Anyway, it was a thought."

Ghost shifted back to dress blues. "So . . . are you pregnant yet?"

"Ghost, goddamn it—" I bit back my irritation. *Remember, you're happy. Don't let him change that.* "No, I'm not."

"But you're still seeing Elio."

"Yes, I am—not that it's any of your business."

She managed to look offended. "It certainly *is* my business; I keep the records. And who else have you been sleeping with—you know, the one that's making you so damned happy?"

I could feel the heat on my cheeks. "There isn't anyone else," I said, hoping that I sounded more convincing than I looked. "I don't need anyone else, not right now."

Ghost just nodded. "Not even Máire?"

"Ghost—"

"You can tell me. After all, I'm Gabriela's creation."

I looked at her. She'd shifted again, into what I thought must have been Gabriela when she was my age. She looked at me expectantly, a half-smile on her lips, her eyes inviting, with friendly crinkles at the corners. I knew it was just a projection, but I felt a welcoming trust. "Ghost, you also know what happened with Gabriela."

"And it wasn't me that shunned her. Tell me the truth—tell it for history, if nothing else. I promise I'll hide it in the databanks until you're both dead."

"There's a comforting thought."

She ignored that with a shrug that seemed to fit Gabriela. "It's your choice, Ana," she said, and Ghost's voice seemed different also, shaded with more inflection that I remembered ever hearing from her. "I won't ask again."

She stood there, waiting. I could even see her chest rising and falling as she breathed—a detail Ghost had always left out of the other body-images she'd chosen. I felt that I could have stretched my hand out and touched her, that her skin would have been warm.

"All right," I said. "Maybe you should know. For history, as you said . . ."

And I told her.

CONTEXT:
Ghost

"*. . . I PROMISE I'LL HIDE IT IN THE DATABANKS UNtil you're both dead.*"

"*There's a comforting thought.*"

"*It's your choice, Ana,*" Ghost said. "*I won't ask again.*"

"*All right,*" Anaïs replied. "*Maybe you should know. For history, as you said . . .*"

In his room, Dominic stared at the relay from the clinic; Ghost watched Dominic as Anaïs admitted to her affair with Máire. Ghost watched the grim satisfaction on Dominic's face, watched the slow rippling of righteous anger under the wrinkled surface of his skin, watched the way his six-fingered hand curled tightly around the ball of his cane, as if trying to crush the gnarled wood with his arthritic joints. The other person in the room, Gerard Koda-Schmidt, Elder of Máire's Family, said nothing, but Ghost could hear the troubled rasp of his breathing.

As usual when he was with Dominic, Ghost wore the body of Dominic's sib Marco. Ghost terminated the transmission from the clinic, and Dominic turned in his chair to nod to him. "You did well, Ghost."

"*I* didn't do anything except what you told me to do. I followed your orders because my programming doesn't allow anything else, Dominic." Ghost kept his/Marco's face grimly neutral. "Complimenting me isn't going to make me feel better. It certainly isn't going to make me believe that this was the right thing to do. You didn't even give me my thirty pieces of silver."

"Bah!" Dominic waved his free hand at Ghost. "That's that old crow Gabriela talking. Well, you've just caught another *rezu* in our midst, even if you didn't really have a choice. Gerard, I'm sorry, but you needed to see this—it verifies what I've been saying all along."

It was difficult to read expressions in Gerard's face. A severe case of Bell's Palsy had caused the left side of his face to go slack and dead, like a half-melted wax figure, and his left eye stared unblinking, smeared with a thin gel film that kept it moist. Words drizzled from his mouth, their edges blurred and softened. Ghost altered the video feed to block out the affected side, and the pain became immediately apparent in Gerard's half-face. "Máire . . ." Gerard exhaled. "I kept hoping that the rumors weren't true. And after seeing poor Elena's child . . ." Gerard brought up a handkerchief and dabbed at the wetness at the corner of his mouth.

"All the more reason Anaïs must be shunned. I tell you, she's affected all of us here, and if what we just witnessed wasn't enough proof, I have more right here." Dominic's cane came up and tapped the sheaf of printouts on the table next to the monitor. "Lowered birth rate, higher mortality, decreased fertility—all since she reached menarche, all since she's been working with Hui in the clinic."

"Dominic," Ghost interrupted. "I have to remind you that none of the figures you have there are statistically significant. There's always a certain fluctuation in any trending, and you'd have to do a much more detailed analysis—"

Dominic slashed his cane at Ghost. It *whuffed* through his

body. "I don't need any more analysis. I know what I see. I know what I feel *here*." Dominic thumped on his chest with his fist, scowling. "I don't see any reason to delay any longer. Every day she remains here is another day's damage she does to our chances for survival. I just pray that it's not already too late. Gerard, do you agree?"

Gerard looked from Dominic to Ghost. The blackness Ghost had placed over the left side of the old man's face looked like a hole in reality. There was a hurt there that Ghost knew he could never fully understand. "I do," he said, the consonant slurred and broken.

"*Hai.*" Dominic tapped his cane on the stone flags. The crack of the metal tip on rock drew sparks. "I'll let the Elders know that we need to meet." Dominic nodded again to Ghost. "You'll see," he said to the image of his long-dead brother. "In the end, you'll see how necessary this was."

"I doubt it," Ghost told him. "But, as you said, Dominic, I didn't really have a choice."

JOURNAL ENTRY:
Gabriela Rusack

FOR A TIME, I WONDERED HOW PEOPLE WHO I knew so well could be so incredibly cold and horribly cruel to someone they'd once called a friend, with whom they'd talked and laughed and worked. I wondered how they could hate me so deeply and so wrongly. I wondered exactly when, by virtue of being different from them, I'd also become so dehumanized that they could inflict this torture of isolation on me and not become something less themselves.

I puzzled on that for a long time, and never came up with an answer. I kept asking myself: if the positions were reversed, could *I* be so cruel? Could *I* send Shig, for instance, into exile because he was a pompous ass? Could I ever be so angry with him that I could be capable of inflicting such torture?

Maybe I could. Maybe it's inherent in us. Maybe all those people who, after the truth about the German concentration camps of World War II was revealed, said "It couldn't happen here" were just blowing smoke. Maybe such things can happen *anywhere* under the right situation.

Ghost told me, in our last conversation, that I'd simply forgotten what history taught. "Never let yourself get in the way of someone else's genes or religious beliefs," he'd said, "unless you absolutely want to get run over."

Certainly in Serbia-Croatia, my own country of origin, for centuries neighbor had inflicted upon neighbor obscene rape, torture and murder, and for much the same reason.

This was nothing new.

This was something very, very old.

What I hated most was that I knew—in the rare moments when I could distance myself from myself—that they were right. They were right to have cast me out, because in doing so they bound themselves together. I was no longer just Gabriela Rusack, one of the Nine; I was now a symbol, an icon, objectified. I was the Crow, something distasteful and rotten in their midst, and in shunning me they united themselves in their hatred of the Crow, and that unity strengthened them.

Even the terms of the shunning made sense: don't speak to her, because in words lay the danger of understanding me, and understanding would destroy the symbol I'd become. Keep her distant, because in closeness there is no mystery, and mystery enhanced the image they wanted of me.

They placed all of their bile and bitterness and fears into the container of the Crow and cast it away so those black emotions wouldn't trouble them again.

VOICE:
Anaïs Koda-Levin the Younger

I COULD TASTE SEEDCAKE ON HER MOUTH, AND SALT on her skin. I caught the scent of flower-water, of soap, of womanhood. Máire was softness and melting warmth around my fingers and mouth, and I devoured her as if I were famished. I rode the rising tide of her passion until it crested and swept both of us away for a time. I reveled in the throaty, gasping song of her pleasure.

Afterward, we cuddled together under the blankets, safe in our pocket of warmth in a cold world.

Máire kissed me. Her lips were silken, softer than a breath. Her hand cupped my face, fingers caught in my hair. So close, her eyes searched mine, and I could see all the way into the depths of her. "I love you, Anaïs," she said.

"I love you, too," I answered her, and gave her back the gift of her kiss.

Her eyes closed. She smiled. She snuggled closer against me, and I held her.

We were that way when they found us.

I saw the shadow against the rock face of Gabriela's cave, looming over us, and at the same time, heard the reverberant dull clunk of rock moving underfoot. I raised my head, and they were there: Elio's sib Micah, Miat Koda-Shimmura, Yves Koda-Schmidt, and Dominic the Younger. Máire sat up, clutching the blanket to us. The quartet of hard, unsympathetic faces stared at us, at me. "Anaïs, the Council of Elders requests that you appear before them," Dominic the Younger said, and his voice sounded as imperious as that of his Geeda. He glanced at Máire, and there was almost a sadness in his look then. "Get dressed," he told us. "We'll accompany the two of you back to the Rock."

With that, he gestured to the others. They started to withdraw, all but Micah. Micah glared at me as if I was a turd on his dinner plate, his lopsided face canted to one side. "You disgust me," he spat out, lisping with his malformed palate. "You've ruined Máire, and you've ruined Elio." He caught Dominic's arm, pulling him back. "No," he told them. "We stay. Let her get dressed right here in front of us. Let her show us what she's been hiding."

"Micah—" I began, hating the sound of my voice, caught between curse and cry. He didn't let me finish.

"No!" he barked. "You heard me. Get up and get dressed, or I'll come over and drag you up there naked. In fact, go ahead and refuse to cooperate. I'd love to display you to the others."

"Why are you doing this?" Máire demanded. "Ana hasn't hurt anyone."

Micah sneered, Miat laughed outright, Yves and Dominic just shook their heads. "I'm sure Adari said the same thing about Gabriela," Micah answered. "Most of the Elders think otherwise. Now, get up. They're waiting for us."

We had no choice. Máire gave me a last hug and a defiant kiss, then threw back the covers. As I got out of the bed, I could feel their stares, their loathing. "Look at it," Micah said to his companions as he saw me. "By all the *kami*, how could Elio . . ." Máire, as if challenging them to watch, stood facing them as she dressed, daring them to meet her gaze. I turned away from them as soon as I could, giving them my back as I pulled on my pants, my blouse, my socks.

I'd never felt this kind of helpless loss, never in the worst moments in the clinic. I'd had people die while I tried desperately to save them, I'd seen death glaze their eyes and still their hearts. I thought I'd experienced the worst Mictlan could throw at me.

No.

I was numb, too much in shock to even think rationally. In an instant, a moment, I was shattered, plunged from contentment to fear. I was trembling, barely able to even pull on my clothes, sobbing as I fumbled with them. Máire came over and helped me, finally, giving me my overcoat. I looked at her desperately, wildly, without any words. "Ana," she whispered. "You need to be strong right now. They want you to be weak, they want you to be devastated, they want you humiliated. Don't give it to them. Don't."

I tried not to. I took a deep breath as I pulled on my coat. I touched Máire's cheek one more time, and pulled my hand away when the tears threatened again. Then I turned and faced them.

"All right," I said. "I'll go with you now."

CONTEXT:
Kyra Martinez-Santos

KYRA HAD NOT WANTED TO BE APPOINTED JUDGE for this particular matter, but it didn't surprise her when the vote of the Elder Council came in. Family Koda-Levin's Elders were ineligible to be considered because

201

of Anaïs, and Elio and Máire were too closely involved to allow their Family's Elders to preside. Tozo Koda-Shimmura was priest for the community this year, and Bryn Koda-Shimmura would have refused the "honor" as he always did. Poor old Vladimir had been the last of the third generation for the Allen-Levin Family so Johanna and Nita were now Family Elders, but they were the only fourth generation members of the Council and no one, including Johanna and Nita, expected either of them to be elected judge when so new to the council.

All of which left Kyra.

She agreed that she was the only possible choice. That knowledge didn't make the choice any more palatable.

Her first decision was that she alone would not make the judgment, but that a two-thirds majority of the Council would be required. Part of her wondered if this was cowardice, but the debate by the Elder Council on whether to even open a hearing on Anaïs the younger had been vitriolic and intensely personal (in fact, Kyra suspected that no matter how this ended, there would be people who would not speak civilly to each other for several years) and the vote had been split along Family lines. Already Dominic and the older Anaïs had come to see Kyra on their own. From what each had said, it was obvious that there was an extreme polarization of opinion in the community, and Kyra didn't care to make herself the lightning rod that attracted the emotional bolts. The loose collection of rules created by the Founders had evolved into the governing laws of the colony, and they gave a judge the leeway to use the Elder Council as a jury in hearings of "grave concern," with a majority vote of the Council required to find someone guilty.

Cowardly action or not, Kyra was going to force each of the Elders to make their vote public before she meted out any sentence. She was relatively healthy and planned on living several more years—she wasn't going to make them miserable ones.

Looking out at the crowded Gathering Hall reinforced her decision.

The Hall was a large natural cavity within the Rock. A crevice within the stone uncovered by the shuttle lasers, the Hall was both long and high, the walls meeting again high in darkness above them. Once, ages ago, water had entered here, trickling slowly down the walls and depositing minerals. Sometime in the past, the flow had stopped and the cavern had dried, but the water had left its glittering legacy. Eterna-lamps from the *Ibn Battuta* lined the rippled, smooth stone, casting brilliant light on the speckled surface and drawing sparkling highlights from imbedded crystals. Kyra found the Hall to be startlingly gorgeous, a beauty which still surprised her every time she entered; being there was like standing inside an illuminated geode.

The Hall could hold fifty or sixty people; it seemed that there were more today. The Elder Council sat on their curved dais (built by the Patriarch Shigetomo); Kyra as judge took the large central seat. Anaïs the Younger sat facing them; a low railing behind her separated the rest of the council from the audience crowding the Hall, which seemed to include at least half the colony. The noise they made filled the Hall, reverberating. Kyra suspected that the fields were not going to be harvested until a judgment was delivered.

Kyra rubbed her hands slowly together, a habit she'd never been able to break. Her hands and fingers, like much of her body and face, were studded with small, hard, peat-colored warts, a legacy (Hui had once told her) of some local virus which had infected her early in her childhood. She took a deep breath and stood, and the hubbub slowly quieted until she could hear only the background sound of chairs, coughs, and their massed breaths. The indigo judge's robe billowed around her slight frame, the heavy cloth rustling.

"The Elder Council has appointed me to be judge for this hearing, and has summoned Anaïs Koda-Levin the Younger to appear here," she began. Her voice, with the insistent quaver that had come in the last decade, was loud in the sudden stillness. "The proceedings are now open and are being recorded for the archives." Kyra sat once more, arranging the robe around her. "And now that we've formally begun this hearing, let me say that I intend to finish this today so that we can get on with our work. The fields need to be harvested, and Ghost has predicted that this winter's likely to be especially harsh, so we don't have a lot of time to waste. I've drawn up a tentative list of witnesses; please make sure that you're accurate but brief with your answers—in fact, I'll be making certain of it. Dominic, did you hear that?"

Chuckles rumbled around the Hall like low thunder, and Dominic, with a tight smile, inclined his head toward Kyra. Anaïs, not surprisingly, didn't smile with the rest. Since having been ushered into the Hall, the young woman had sat silent, her hands laying on her lap like dead birds. She had barely spoken when her Family's elders had conferred with her; she'd looked around once, and Kyra had noticed that her gaze went to Elio and Máire, and to no one else. Kyra felt a brief spasm of guilt—Anaïs was so obviously frightened and lost. Kyra had voted with the majority of the Elders to open this hearing; she wondered now if that had been the right decision. She shook the thought away with a shrug: no matter, it was too late now for recriminations.

"Anaïs," she said, and the woman's head came up. Her eyes were dark and puffy, though when she looked at Kyra, there was a spark of defiance in the smoky pupils. "Do you speak for yourself, or do you want someone to represent you before the Council?"

"I'll speak for myself," she answered, the words clipped and precise, as if she held back some further comment.

Kyra nodded. "That's fine. As long as everyone stays polite, I won't stand on formality. Anaïs, as the accused you may speak at any time as you feel necessary, though I'd prefer if you'd wait until whoever's speaking has finished their statement. I presume that you understand that you've been brought here because a majority of the Elder Council feel that it is possible you represent a threat to the survival of this colony. There is a concern that your presence has already adversely affected the birthrate, and that—like Gabriela Rusack—your sexual preferences have resulted in at least two women removing themselves from the possibility of becoming pregnant. There have been other charges voiced for which I have seen no compelling evidence"—here Kyra looked at Dominic with a frown—"and these will not be discussed here. I have already judged those baseless."

"Only because you can't see the facts in front of your nose," Dominic muttered audibly, and Kyra turned in her chair to point a wart-dimpled finger at him.

"Anaïs was given permission to speak at will, not you," she snapped. "You'll pipe up when asked *by me* to talk and you'll be silent the rest of the time, or I'll have you removed from the Hall until you're needed. The Council appointed me judge, and I *will* do what I need to do to make that possible. Do I make myself clear, Dominic?"

"*Hai*. I'm old, not deaf. I heard you." He sniffed, his cane tapping angrily on the floor. There was a brief tittering from the audience in the Hall—it subsided quickly when Kyra turned back.

"All right," she said. "Then here's who will be testifying today: Micah, Dominic, Hui, Elio, and Máire, in that order. Is there anyone else that feels they have facts that I need to hear at this time—and I do mean facts, not hearsay and gossip. No? All right, if anyone changes their mind as we go along, let me know."

Kyra closed her eyes, taking in a long, slow breath. "I'm ready, then. Micah, if you'd come forward..."

VOICE:
Anaïs Koda-Levin the Younger

I THINK I SPENT MUCH OF THE FIRST PART OF THE hearing still in a dazed state, half wanting to believe that all this commotion was a cruel joke or a particularly vivid nightmare from which I couldn't wake. I don't think I really believed yet that Máire and I had been caught *en flagrante* and dragged here.

I know Micah got up and told everyone in graphic detail what he'd witnessed in Gabriela's cave—how he and the others had caught us in the act and what I'd looked like—but I don't really remember the words. Well, that's not entirely true. I know that at one point he said I was a "deformed sexual monster" and that "anyone who could be aroused by her must be sick themselves." I didn't say anything; I just sat there, numb. I know that Kyra stopped Micah a few times and asked me if I wanted to respond, but I just shook my head. There didn't seem to be any point. No point. I felt heavy, dull, and tired. Very tired.

I remember Micah grinning at me as he left the witness bar. I should have been angry, should have glared back at him. I didn't. I didn't feel anything.

"Anaïs... *Anaïs*."

I became aware that Kyra was calling my name. I looked up, like a startled wizard, only I couldn't fly away. "I'm sorry, Kyra," I said. "What did you want?"

"Do you want to offer any rebuttal to what Micah's told

us? Do you want to give us your version of what happened?"

I shook my head. I saw Kyra look over at my Geema, then at Hui. A silent communication passed between them, and then Kyra nodded. "We'll take a short break," she said. Dominic started to protest, but Kyra was already rising. "I'm old, and my bladder isn't as big as it used to be. Anaïs, you may retire to one of the anterooms, if you'd like. I'll send for you when I'm ready again."

With that, she left the dais. The rest of the Elder Council looked momentarily confused, then they left also. Geema Anaïs came up alongside me, with Elio and Máire. "Come on," Geema said, her voice graveled and somehow sad. "Come on, child. We need to talk."

In the anteroom, Geema Anaïs sat with a loud sigh. She took my chin in her wrinkled hand and brought my face up. "You listen to me, girl," she said firmly, her face close enough to me that I could smell the spice of her breath. "I don't like what you've done, and I'm not happy that you've dragged our Family into this, but I still love you. So do others here, and I'm not going to let you disappoint them by sitting there like a damned stationary target for Dominic and his poison arrows. Do you hear me? Snap out of it *now*, girl, and fight for yourself."

Geema let go of me and I looked at them, mouth open but without words. I spread my hands, searching. "I..." I started. "...you can't..." I started to cry again. Máire put her hand on one shoulder; Elio the other. I sniffed and rubbed my sleeve across my face. "They've already made up their minds, Geema, most of them. I can see it in the way they look at me."

Geema shrugged. "Some of them have, *hai*. Not all. You only need eight supporters on the Council. Eight people, and they can't do anything to you, and our Family has four of the votes. You know I won't vote to shun you." She sighed again, and looked from me to Elio and—with a lingering examination that ended with a slow nod—to Máire.

"Talk to her," she told them. "Make her listen. Ana, I will see you out there."

With a grunting effort, Geema rose from her seat. Her rheumy, pale eyes regarded me, and the slightest hint of a smile tugged at her lips. She patted my cheek once, softly, as she had when I'd been a girl in the Family creche. Then, shuffling away, she left us alone. As soon as she was gone,

Máire dropped to her knees in front of my chair and put her arms around my waist, hugging me tightly. "I'm sorry," she whispered into my ear. "It's my fault. If I hadn't—"

I shook my head and held her away from me. "No. Everything I did, with both of you, I wanted to do. There's no blame."

"I agree," Elio said. "And that's why your Geema's right, Ana. You need to fight. Hui's on your side, and so are a lot of other people you've helped over the years. So are Máire and I."

"I know," I said, holding each of their hands. "I know." I *did* know. I could feel their support, a warmth that eased the chill of the carvern, but I also knew that as soon as I walked back out into the Hall that the warmth would be overwhelmed and lost in the cold that rolled like a glacier from the glares of the Council. I knew that this pale flame of optimism was no match for Dominic's hate. But I nodded because they expected me to, and I squeezed their fingers and hugged them. When one of the younger Martinez-Santos kids cleared her throat and stuck her head in to announce that the Council was coming back, I kissed both of them, not caring who saw or who watched. I tried to burn the soft caress of their lips into my memory, and then I took a deep breath and nodded.

"All right," I said. "Let's go back."

CONTEXT:
Dominic Allen-Shimmura

DOMINIC DIDN'T CARE IF KYRA WANTED TO TRY THE impossible as judge and offend no one. He didn't care if she played at being fair and evenhanded. Let her do as she wished—so long as the end result was that the monster who had degraded and then killed Ochiba was cast out.

That *would* happen. He could not envision any other future.

Dominic tapped his fingers on the head of his cane—Patriarch Shigetomo's cane. Like the patriarch, the cane was simple and utilitarian, the shaft a tapering length of local hardwood, the head the knobbed end of an oaken branch from old Earth, polished by generations of use but otherwise left as it had been. Over the years, Dominic had often wondered where the fragment of oak had come from, and why Shigetomo had bothered to bring it along on the *Ibn Battuta*'s voyage, but none of the Family knew the anwer to that. There were times when Dominic had meditated on the rich hues of the wood, on the knobs and swirls and dark hollows, imagining the hands who had taken hold of it so long ago, listening as if—having absorbed the silent thoughts of its maker—the wood might speak. Whatever secrets there might have been, whatever tale might have been behind the artifact, had died with Shigetomo.

By all accounts of those who had known him well, Shig had been obssessive when taking on a task, whether that was clearing a field or making certain that the rules needed to ensure the survival of his people were created and then enforced. Dominic was much like Shigetomo in that single-mindedness—his mam had told him so, even when he'd been a child. He hadn't changed.

As Shig had ensured that Gabriela was cast out, so Dominic would do the same with Anaïs. The thought made him press his lips tightly together, and brush the documents spread out on the witness bar before him, his vestigial sixth finger dragging on the thick, handmade paper.

"You told me to stay with facts, Kyra," he began. His fingers tapped the papers once more for emphasis. "All right, then. Here are facts: figures and statistics gathered by Ghost and by my own research. I've shown these to all of you on the Council during our initial decision to bring Anaïs before judgment; there's no reason to belabor them now. But I'll reiterate the bare facts once again, the facts that speak so plainly: since Anaïs reached menarche and became sexually active, since she's begun working at the clinic, we have experienced a lowered fertility rate, increased mortality and a higher percentage of mutations."

"Ghost has also said that there is not enough data there to prove anything," Kyra interrupted. "While all that is true, Ghost has reminded us that it could as well be only a normal statistical variation from the current trends."

Dominic gave an exhalation of disgust. "And I say that when you see snow falling, and your muscles shiver and you feel the cold wind in your face, those events tell you that winter's coming. They're not just a 'normal variation' from the usual weather. Even if I'm wrong—and I'm not—I'm not willing to gamble the survival of our colony on a 'variation.' To be blunt, I'd rather make a mistake that hurts one person than a mistake that kills us all."

"That sounds unnecessarily dramatic to me, Dominic."

"It sound *logical* to me, Kyra. And to a lot of us." Dominic tapped the cane for emphasis. "Even if that were all the evidence we had, it would be enough. But it's not. It's not."

"Dominic," Kyra said. "I want to warn you again: I won't tolerate rumors here."

"Facts." Dominic spat out the word. As far as he was concerned, it *was* a fact that Anaïs had murdered Ochiba. He longed to just shout it out anyway, wanted to see the *rezu's* face when she realized that he knew, but he swallowed the impulse. It tasted acid and sour. Most of the Elder Council already knew his feelings, and there was enough here already to convict the bitch. "I know. Facts. Micah has already given us all the facts we need. It's bad enough that Anaïs's presence has lowered our fertility rate, but she's also stolen at least two women from the childbearing pool: Ochiba and Máire."

"I never 'stole' Ochiba," Anaïs interrupted. It was the first time she'd spoken, and Dominic's head swiveled hard to the right at the sound of her voice. "Yes, Ochiba and I were lovers. I'll admit that—but Dominic, *she* came to *me*, not the other way around. We also started *before* she became pregnant with Euzhan. Ochiba still had other lovers among the men, the entire time. You knew that, too, Dominic—it's the only reason you tolerated our relationship."

"That's what you say," Dominic answered. "But she lived with me, and I know what goes on in my Family's house and who visits, and once she began seeing you, she stopped seeing anyone else."

"That's not *true*," Anaïs declared.

"And I say it is," Dominic said imperiously. Anaïs started to protest again, and Dominic hurriedly continued. "And the same has happened with Máire. I've talked to Gerard and Eleanor, and they tell me that no men have slept with Máire in their compound in months." Dominic gestured to the crowd watching. "Ask any of them. Have any of you men been with Máire recently? Come on, speak up. Go on. Any man who's been with Máire in the last three months, please say so."

Dominic lifted his cane, waiting. His disdainful sniff was loud against the dark silence. "There. If anyone here doubted I told the truth, there's your answer. I say that we don't need to know more than that. I agree with Kyra—just look at the *facts*. Look at facts, and look at our history, and suddenly there's no question at all concerning what we need to do."

Dominic slammed the end of the cane down for emphasis. The hall had gone silent once more, and the report was startlingly loud. Dominic nodded to Kyra and started to leave the witness bar.

"Dominic." Anaïs's voice was barely audible. When he ignored her, she spoke again, more loudly this time. "Dominic, I loved her as much as you did. Maybe more. She was as special to me as she was to you. I would never have done anything to hurt her. Part of me died with Ochiba, just like part of you died also. Don't hate me for that. Don't hate me for loving her."

Dominic looked at Anaïs. A tear was tracking down the woman's face, sliding from cheek to chin. For an moment, Dominic wavered, hesitating. His fingers wrapped around the cane's head. "You make a fine speech when your own skin's on the line," he said. "You made a fine speech at her Burning, too. Very tearful and moving. But was it sorrow or your guilt that upset you more?"

"*Dominic!*" Kyra's sharp quaver brought his head around. "I told you, I'll have none of that. Ochiba died from complications of childbirth. There's no evidence indicating anything else."

Dominic smiled grimly. It didn't matter—he'd said it. He'd reminded the Elders who had killed his lovely Ochiba. The shocked look on the abomination's face was payment enough. "I apologize, Kyra," he said, but there was too much satisfaction in the words for them to sound contrite. "I've nothing more to say, then."

Looking at the faces of the Elder Council, he knew the damage had been done. He nodded to the judge, to the rest of the Council, and left the bar.

CONTEXT:
Hui Koda-Schmidt

IT WAS NOT HUI'S WAY TO WASTE TIME WITH niceties. He didn't do so now. He gripped the witness bar, looked at the Elder Council and Kyra, and shook his head as if facing shoddy work by one of his apprentices.

"You want facts?" Hui spat out. "Here's one for you pack of idiots. If you decide to shun Anaïs, you are sending away the only competent doctor you have in this colony. You'd also be demonstrating that the Elder Council's collective IQ could freeze water—Fahrenheit."

"You'll still be here, Hui," Kyra said quietly, ignoring the sarcasm. "We'd have one doctor, and you have Ama and Hayat to help you and in time take over for you. Another apprentice or two can be assigned to do the drudge work. We can give priority to the medical staff."

"Kyra, I am half-blind with cataracts and getting worse every month. I know everyone here wants to deny that, but someone with the brains of a verrechat must have realized that I haven't done any of the real surgery for over a year. Ama and Hayat might—*might*—one day be half as good a doctor as Anaïs already is, but that day is *years* off. At the moment, I wouldn't trust either of them to diagnose a cold, and that's simply the brutal truth. Here another one of those facts of which Dominic seems so fond: send Ana away, and the next person whose appendix goes south, who shatters a rib and starts bleeding internally, or who needs a cesarean section, will die."

No one said anything, and Hui gave a harsh chuckle. "*Hai*, that's something to think about, isn't it? You're worried about our future with Anaïs here? Well, *I* worry about it with her gone, and if any of you are sane, you'll do the same."

Through the cataract-haze, he could sense Dominic glaring at him. That was fine, Hui just glowered back. Dominic might intimidate others, but Hui had no patience with the man. Kyra shifted in the judge's chair. Hui felt sorry for her—she was trying to find that place of ethical fairness that would end up offending no one. Unfortunately, Hui was convinced that there was no such location. One faction or another was going to end up angry here today. Hui planned to make sure it wasn't his.

"Hui," Kyra said, "we all appreciate your views on this, and I assure that they'll be taken into consideration. However, we've asked you here not as an advocate for Anaïs, but as the person who can tell us the most about her. Please understand that I'm asking this question only because of what I've heard today. You are her physician, and according the records, you've examined her regularly. Is Anaïs a functional female?"

"What the hell does that matter? She's a damn good *doctor*, no matter what sex she is. Aren't you *listening* to me?"

"At your current volume, I'm certain *everyone* in the Rock is listening to you." Kyra's retort sent nervous chuckles rippling through the crowd. "And you still haven't answered the question. Is Anaïs a functional female?"

Hui shrugged. "Anaïs has certain hermaphroditic qualities, all of which are far more minor than the gossip I've heard lately. But I would call her female, yes. All the secondary sexual characteristics are there: breasts, the lack of facial and body hair, her basic bodily shape, her pelvis. She can perform sexually as a female, in an entirely normal manner. She menstruates, though in a limited, erratic way. With the lousy medical equipment we have here, I can't check her chromosomes, and there's no way I can tell whether she can actually bear children or not—which is something I can say for *any* woman here who has yet to become pregnant. Yes, I'd call her a functional female, if I had to." Hui lifted his chin defiantly and looked more at Dominic than Kyra. "Does that answer your question, or is it your intention to embarrass Anaïs further? Maybe you'd like to have her strip and display herself? Wouldn't *that* be fun?"

"Enough, Hui," Kyra snapped. "You've made your position abundantly clear; you don't need to mock us to make the point."

The cutting edge of her voice made Hui realize he'd gone too far, but the realization didn't change his tone or his manner, nor was he even slightly tempted to apologize. "Someone needs to do something to shock the Council out of this folly," Hui answered. "Because frankly, I think you've all gone senile."

"That's *enough*," Kyra shouted back, her wart-studded face a rictus, the veins standing out on her neck. "Please step down, Hui. We've heard all we need from you."

"No, you haven't," Hui persisted. "You haven't even come close. But I can see you're not going to listen to me any more. If you don't like the messenger, fine, but you'd better pay damned good attention to the message. Dominic's right about one thing: our lives *are* at stake here."

With a mock gravity, he nodded politely to Kyra, then to the ranked Elders behind her. "You really need to think beyond your petty Family concerns and see the larger picture," he told them. "If you don't, I guarantee you'll see a real disaster."

VOICE:

Anaïs Koda-Levin the Younger

"ANAÏS?"

They questioned Elio, treating him like he was some kind of freak himself that he'd even think about making love to me. They grilled Máire until she wept, trying to make her say that it was me who initiated the relationship, and wringing from her the admission that, no, she hadn't been to bed with any men for months.

It was ugly, and the pain of having to sit there and endure it was worse than the weight of Masa when he tried to rape me.

Then they sent everyone away while the Council went into deliberations. No one bothered to watch or guard me—where could I run, where was a sanctuary for me? Elio, Máire, Geema, Hui—they all came up to me, but I just told them that I wanted to be alone right now. Ironic, that need for solitude now when I was facing isolation from everyone for the rest of my life . . .

"Ana, please?"

Somehow, sometime later, I ended up in the clinic, standing in front of the body of the poor murdered Miccail midmale. My warped mirror, my reflection. I touched the leathery shell of her body. "Was it this way for you?" I asked her. "Did they do this to you as a punishment for being the way you are? Is that why your kind died out?"

"Anaïs, they've asked for you."

For the first time, I realized that someone was standing at the door watching me. I touched the misshappen cheek of the midmale, and slid it back into its compartment before I turned, wondering if I'd ever see her again, if I'd ever untangle more of the mystery of her death.

It was Elio. He was looking at me the way he might a sick child, a smile perched precariously on his lips. "They sent me to find you. I . . . I kinda figured you might be here."

"How do they look?"

"I can't tell. Not really." Elio stepped into the room and put his arms around me, drawing me into him. "They can't shun you, Ana," he whispered into my ear. "After what Hui told them, how could they?"

"You think Hui's speech made any difference to your Geeda?"

His arms tightened. "No," he answered at last. "But he's only one vote, Ana. One vote." I felt his lips brush the top of my head. "Come on," he said. "I'll stand with you. So will Máire."

We walked out of the clinic into the cold air, wet with flurries, then through the main entranceway into the Rock. The Gathering Hall was more crowded than before. The Elder Council were already in their places, and Kyra moved to the judge's chair as I entered. As Elio promised, he walked with me, and Máire also came up on the other side as we passed her Family. None of the elders for either of their Families was happy with that; Dominic looked nearly incandescent, in fact.

People parted to let us pass as if we were diseased and our touch might infect them. When I stood at the witness bar, I looked from the grim-faced Kyra to the Elders behind her.

Dominic was staring at me. As soon as I saw his face, I knew what Kyra would say.

INTERLUDE:
KaiSa

AbriSa moaned as Kai cleaned ker wounds with astringent *kapa* juice. "I know it burns," Kai whispered to ker. "But the cuts are deep and I need to disinfect them before they get worse. . . ."

When ke finished, ke bandaged Abri with strips torn from a spare *shangaa*. Then ke slid down on the floor of the tent beside the cot. He cupped Abri's hand in ker own, squeezing ker fingers gently. "How, my friend?" ke asked. "How did you come to be there?"

Abri lifted ker head weakly. "When you didn't return, JaqSaTu asked for another volunteer to go and contact DekTe. After all you and I have gone through together, I said I would go. I passed through NeiTe's territory and spent a few days with him. He told me how DekTe had threatened to kill his daughter, and that there had been a Sa with DekTe and CaraTa. I sent one of NeiTe's Jc back to AnglSaiye with a message to the Tu that there was a good chance you were still alive. He'd been gone a hand of days, and I was waiting for instructions from ker when DekTe attacked."

Abri closed ker eyes and a shiver passed through ker frame as ke lay back again. "I've never seen anything so awful, Kai. All around me, they were dying, and there was nothing I could do about it. LirXa, she may have been pregnant through me, and they killed her, stabbed her as I was holding her. Her blood splattered all over me, and I thought I was going to die myself . . ."

"Hush," Kai said, stroking ker forehead. "It's over. For now, at least."

"Over?" a deep voice interrupted from the tent flap. "No, Sa. There is much more to come, unless your SaTu comes to ker senses."

"DekTe . . ." Kai scrambled to ker feet, putting kerself between DekTe and AbriSa. DekTe seemed not to notice the

215

protective move. He looked down at Abri, and Kai could see concern and sorrow in his dark eyes.

"How is your friend?" he asked Kai, his voice soft, solicitous. "When I found ker, I was afraid that ke was dead."

"When *I* saw ker with you, she was bound and helpless," Kai answered. "Is that how you normally express your concern for someone's health?"

"Ke was bound when I found ker," DekTe answered. His hand touched Kai's shoulder, lingered for a moment, then fell again. "I stopped my people from killing ker outright. Most of them have no love for the Sa. They feel you are there only for the TeTa, and sometimes for XeXa, but never for JeJa."

"And you?"

"I think the Sa have too much power, but . . ." DekTe's hand lifted, his lips pursed. "I don't hate any one Sa for that. I think . . . I think I could love a Sa, if that Sa could see behind the mask ke's made for me." His eyes had snared ker, trapped ker like a *marset* in a hunter's noose, wriggling and helpless. "KaiSa, will you come with me?"

Ke retained enough of ker defiance to shake ker head. "I can't leave AbriSa. Not now."

DekTe glanced again at the cot. "Ke's sleeping, and you've done all you can. I'll send one of my healers in to see to ker. I promise that no one will harm ker."

"Where are we going?"

"You're needed elsewhere. Come." There was an urgency in his voice that Kai had never heard before. "Please," he added, and that word decided ker. Ke nodded, tugging the covers over Abri.

"All right," Kai answered. "I'll come."

DekTe only nodded at that, but the relief was visible in his face, in the way he touched his *brais* as they left the tent. DekTe led Kai through the encampment, set up just outside the smouldering ruins of NekTe's village. The smell of woodsmoke, once so fragrant to Kai, now threatened to turn ker stomach, the odor freighted with the horrors of the previous evening. DekTe's soldiers were laughing, talking, eating—Kai wondered at that. *How did they find joy in such destruction?* ke wondered. *How did they deal with the ghosts of those they'd killed?*

Kai could feel them, the restless spirits. They drifted in the campsmoke, cried in the breeze through the tent poles, clutched at the heels of their murderers from the mud. Kai knew they would never rest, not when the honor of death in *xeshai* had been denied them, not when the rites of their gods had been ignored. NeiTe's dead couldn't return to the gods; they would stay here, infecting this place and making it unlucky.

The people of DekTe didn't care. Either they didn't believe in the gods, or their god was so strong that they didn't care.

There was no hunger in KaiSa, no laughter. Ke wondered how long it would be before ke would find a reason to smile again.

Too long, ke suspected.

When Kai saw PirXe's figure before the tent, ke stopped. DekTe looked back at ker. "What do you want of me in there?" Kai asked. Ke expected DckTe to smile sardonically, or perhaps to flash anger. Instead, he spread his hands wide, the long fingers curled almost in supplication.

"You're needed," he said simply. "I need your help, nothing else." Then, again, he repeated the soft "Please . . ."

KaiSa slipped past the lifted flap and into the tent.

The old Miccail was inside, as he had been when Kai had first seen DekTe, fussing with linen strips soaking in a pot of steaming water suspended over the central fire. As he wrung out the rags, Kai thought ke saw a tint of red in the heated water. "How is she, DaiXa?" DekTe asked as he entered behind Kai.

"The bleeding's worse," the old one grumbled. "Otherwise, the same. The healer's been here and gone; she didn't seem to help much."

DekTe sighed. His hand touched Kai's shoulder, guiding him toward the interior of the tent, where a gauze curtain hid the rear. Kai's shoulder seemed to burn cold at DekTe's touch, but ke moved with him, stepping inside as DekTe held aside the curtain. Ke went inside.

CaraTa was there, reclining on a bed of pillows. She seemed asleep, or perhaps half-unconscious. Her head was beaded with sweat, rivulets sliding down from the matted fringe of hair high on the skull. The fabric covering her *brais* was dark, soaked with perspiration, and she moaned, her head lashing from side to side. Kai saw the blood then, staining the bedclothes and spotting her *shangaa* at the groin.

"This is why I brought you here, Sa," DekTe said. "It started last night, while we were setting up the tents. She rode her *konja* all day, and then the fighting . . ." DekTe shrugged. "I'm told the Sa know about these things."

CaraTa's eyes had opened. Her mouth opened slightly, and she squinted, trying to focus. She gave a hissing intake of breath when she saw Kai. "You..." she began, and stopped. She licked her lips, swallowed. "You said this child in me would never live. Does it make you happy to see me now and know you were right?"

"No," Kai said truthfully. "The truth came from VeiSaTi, not me. I wish Ke had been wrong."

CaraTa's face wrinkled in pain, furrowing the ridge of her long nose and drawing the tendons rigid in her neck. "It hurts so much," she said.

Kai felt sympathetic tears start in ker own eyes. "I know," ke said. "Will you let me help you?" CaraTa nodded, mutely. Kai turned back to DekTe. "Tell DaiXe that I'll need the linen he's boiling, some fresh *bai* root ground into a paste, and a needle and thread. Have someone find your healer and have her bring me her kit. Then leave me alone with her. Go quickly!" he added when DekTe still didn't move. DekTe blinked as if awakened from a trance, nodded, and left them.

"He's in love with you," CaraTa said softly as Kai lifted her *shangaa* and began a slow, gentle examination.

"He doesn't know me at all."

"I know. But I can see it. I saw it the first day you came. You feel it, too."

"Yes," Kai admitted. "But nothing will come of it."

CaraTa grimaced as Kai probed, all her muscles tensed. "That's not an answer he will accept," she said, then cried out as Kai's fingers moved. DaiXe came shuffling in with the boiling water. "Over there," Kai said. "The *bai*?"

"It's coming, along with the healer's kit. Is she...?"

"She's hemorrhaging. The baby's already lost. We need to get the child out and stop the bleeding. I'll need your help..."

CaraTa's hand grasped Kai's arm, and ke stopped. "Save the child," she said. "I don't care what happens to me, but save the child."

"I can't," Kai answered. "You already know it, if you listen inside yourself. I'm sorry..."

"Can't save it, or won't, Sa?" CaraTa hissed back, her claw digging into his skin with the effort.

"If there was anything I could do, I would do it," Kai told her. Ke touched her hand where it clutched him. "Believe me."

218

Slowly, the hand relaxed. Where the claws retracted, there were three bright spots of blood. CaraTa lay back again, exhausted. "Then do what you must," she said.

It was much later that Kai emerged from the curtain. DekTe was there. He looked at the small wrapping of cloth in Kai's hand and his eye ridges lifted in question. "It was a male," Kai told him. "Badly deformed. He would never have lived, even if she'd taken him to term."

DekTe only nodded. Kai gave the wrapping to DaiXe, who left the tent. "How is she now?" DekTe asked.

"Sleeping. Very tired. But she'll recover, in time. She could still have other children."

"It would be easier with a Sa's help."

Kai brought ker head up, locking ker gaze with DekTe's. "No Sa will do that for you and CaraTa until you return to the Laws, DekTe."

"That's Sa arrogance speaking. That's why I began this, because of the Sa's arrogant Laws."

"The Laws of VeiSaTi have kept peace, DekTe, a peace you've now destroyed. Our Laws have allowed the Miccail to prosper. Because of the Sa, the population's grown and there are TeTa with territories far beyond where any Miccail have ever lived before. DekTe, there is a madness in you, a bitter rage that I don't pretend to understand, but you blame the wrong people when you blame the Sa. We've done nothing to hurt you. I wish . . ." Kai stopped, unable to look anymore into DekTe's face, which had gone to cold and stone. "I wish I could help you, because there's also a great power within you. But I can't."

"You flatter yourself, Sa. There are many Sa. I don't need you." Though Kai knew that DekTe intended the words to hurt, they didn't. Ke could sense that there was no truth behind them. Even DekTe's face revealed the lie.

"All other Sa will give you the same answer, DekTe."

"Even if it would mean the death of a fellow Sa?" DekTe asked, his voice deceptively calm. "I believe you when you say that you would refuse, no matter what I threatened to do to you. But I am not threatening *you*, KaiSa. I care for you—see there, I admit what we both know but are reluctant to say. But I don't have that feeling for your friend."

Kai shivered. Ke started to move past DekTe. "I need to see AbriSa," ke said.

"Yes," DekTe said. "Go see ker. And while you're tending

to ker, remember that I hold *both* of you, and I only need one."

There was pain in his words, and in his face. Kai nodded in acknowledgment of that pain, and of ker own part in it. "You wouldn't want me that way, DekTe. Please don't force me to make that kind of choice."

DekTe only stared at ker.

"Sometimes," he told ker, "there are no good choices to make."

JOURNAL ENTRY:
Gabriela Rusack

BEING TRUE TO YOUR OWN PATH IS RARELY THE RE-sult of following along in someone else's footsteps.

Choices: I came down to northern Mictlan base because I wanted to see the Miccail ruins for myself. I could have stayed happily in orbit in my role in NetOps, but that wasn't my way. I always tried to step outside the boundaries, always pushed at the confining envelope of my official duties. I'd requested that I be attached to the archeo-xenological team because I found myself fascinated by the mystery the planet had left us; Captain Roberts had reluctantly agreed to let my assistants take over some of my responsibilities so I could do that. I'd pored over the holographs and the orbital surveys, had written programs to pull hidden details from the data for the team, argued and fought with them over the meaning of dry facts we were uncovering.

It still wasn't enough for me. I wanted to *touch* the stelae, wanted to feel them with my fingers and see them with my own eyes. "Go on down," Elzbieta had said the night before, as we lay in bed. "You know you want to. Roberts will okay it; she'll figure that when you get back to NetOps, you'll work twice as hard to pay her back for the favor."

"Planetside teams are only rotated out once a month. I'd be gone at least that long."

"Gab," Elz laughed, "I love you dearly, and I'll miss you,

but I think I can survive a month or two without you. Besides, we can talk through the net anytime we want."

So I went. I stepped off the shuttle onto Mictlan, and watched the shuttle leave again, carrying with it those returning to the *Ibn Battuta*.

Several hours later, we all felt the explosion in our heads, as the shuttle's collision with the ship destroyed the neural network to which we were all linked. I would never hear Elzbieta's voice again, never touch her soft skin or sink into her warmth at night. Unknowingly, I'd traded that for a cold world and dead race.

Choices.... Had I known, I'd have stayed behind. I remembered how mundane, how fucking *normal* our goodbyes had been, how damned *casual* our last few minutes together were. That bothers me more than anything.

If I'd known ... but then we never can know such things, can we? We make our life choices in inevitable ignorance of the consequences, and we live—or not—with the messy results.

INTERLUDE:
KaiSa

ABRISA WAS STILL ASLEEP WHEN KAI RETURNED. KE changed ker bandages, then rummaged through ker pack until ke found the packet of dried *jitu*. Ke set a pot of water to boil over the fire, emptied the packet into a mug, then poured the steaming water in. Sitting alongside Abri, ke sipped the bitter, sour brew, inhaling the acrid vapors and waiting.

Ke didn't know how long ke waited. Slowly, ke became aware of a presence in the tent with ker. Ker head lifted, ker nostrils widening as ke sniffed. There were movements in the flickering fireshadows, shapes and figures, and a sense of Presence.

"VeiSaTi ..." ke whispered, and the breath that contained the word became a wind, a gale that tore open the flaps of the tent and ripped the canvas from the poles. DekTe's soldiers gaped in awe, and then ran before the apparition that was revealed, the great, indistinct figure of the Eldest God, Ker *brais* gleaming sapphire, Ker eyes cold white.

The god turned and held out Ker smoky hand to KaiSa, and ke reached out in turn. When their fingers touched, they were simply . . .

. . . gone. Kai blinked, and saw that ke was back in Angl-Saiye, standing in the White Temple before VeiSaTi's immense shell. NasiSaTu was there also, ke who had founded AnglSaiye and organized the Sa, and who had given ker own life in sacrifice during KeldTe's attack on the island. Kai knew who it was without asking. The Great Tu was oblivious to their presence as ke prepared a sacrifice on the altar: a squirming *guffin*, mewling and struggling against the bonds that held its feet. "For life, I feed you," Nasi said to the *guffin* as ke smeared a paste of grain porridge on its mouth. "And with your death, I feed life: with earth, with air, with water." Nasi reached for a stone axe that lay next to the *guffin* . . .

. . . but Nasi and the sacrifice were gone. They were still in AnglSaiye, but Kai could feel the emptiness here. Standing in portals of the White Temple, ke looked out and saw the buildings of the island barren, falling, and empty. It was raining, a cold sleet that ran in frigid rivulets down ker spinal mane and over ker eye ridges. "Where are they?" ke asked VeiSaTi, but the god didn't answer. "Where are the Sa?" Kai asked again, but there was only the rain, and silence, and ruin . . .

. . . another shift, and there was now another presence with VeiSaTi in the White Temple, a brooding, ruddy thing of flame and smoke that emanated a sourness, a carrion smell. This presence grasped for VeiSaTi with a long arm of fire, and Kai screamed. Ke tried to thrust kerself between VeiSaTi and the attacking god, and ke was engulfed in searing heat and choking smoke . . .

. . . and when it cleared, Kai could see that VeiSaTi was lying motionless before the altar. Kai crept closer, terribly afraid, and looked into the god's face. The seeing eyes were closed, the *brais* was dull and faded. Yet . . . Kai sensed life in Ker still. It was buried deep, and nearly gone, but ke could feel it. Shadows flitted across Ker face, and Kai glanced up at the sky. The sun streaked past overhead, a fiery wisp, and then the double moons raced through a momentary darkness, and then the sun once more: days and years passing faster than Kai could imagine, their alternating light and dark reflecting on VeiSaTi's face. In the racing time, the god waited, asleep. *You can make this possible.* The words came unbidden into Kai's head. *Without you, there will be no hope at all.*

"What do you mean?" Kai demanded, but VeiSaTi slumbered on, and the days raced past. In the strange flicker of time, Kai sensed someone approaching, and VeiSaTi seemed to stir slightly. Kai squinted out into the world, and saw a form, a figure. Ke thought for a moment that it was another Sa, but ke was different, shaped strangely . . .

. . . and . . .

. . . and . . .

Kai started, coming awake with a sudden grunt. For long moments, ke sat there, blinking.

Ke must have been out for hours. Abri was still asleep, but the fire had dwindled to orange embers, and the encampment outside the tent was still but for a few muffled snores and the sound of the night insects. The cup of *jitu* was still in ker hand, the dregs cold. Ke set it down carefully and leaned back, ker knee joints cracking from being in one position for so long.

I think I understand what You have shown me, ke told the silence. *But is this what You truly want? Is this really what I must do?*

There was no answer, unless the breeze ruffling the canvas was an affirmation.

Kai nodded.

Then I'll do as You ask, ke answered, and was surprised at the ease with which the words came to ker. There was no fear in them, no apprehension, only warm, unfrightened acceptance. *I will do it.*

VOICE:

Anaïs Koda-Levin the Younger

*"WE DECLARE YOU SHUNNED. YOUR PERSONAL BE-
longings and your supplies are at the entrance to the
Rock. From this moment on, no one here will talk to you, no one
here will help you. We no longer see you, Anaïs Koda-Levin the
Younger. We no longer hear you."*

223

With those words, they made me pariah.

I remember shouting "No!" I remember that no one answered.

From the anguish on Geema's face, and from the looks from several of the Elders, I knew the verdict had been split. In the audience gathered to hear the pronouncement, I heard Hui give a loud "Fools!" as he turned and left, but I heard many more mumbles of agreement.

Elio grasped my arm; Máire sniffed and hugged me. Their faces were serious and grim. I was entirely surprised when both of them stepped away from me. They left me, pushing through the front ranks of the crowd and vanishing before I had a chance to react or speak. I opened my mouth to call out after them, but couldn't. The sudden abandonment by the two people I felt closest to hurt me the most. Their actions told me how complete this isolation was to be, told me that even those I thought I knew best would abide by this unfair judgment and never speak to me again. I was left there, with everyone staring at me and no one saying anything, the silence already imposed, the shunning already in effect. I was no longer a person to them. For a moment, acid burned in my throat, and the room started to wheel drunkenly around me. I closed my eyes, forcing some semblance of manic calm on myself.

You have to be strong, I told myself. *You're the only person you have to rely on now. Just yourself.*

I wanted to cry, wanted to scream at them that they were stupid and that they were cold and that they were like the ghouls who found entertainment in the guillotine, but I took a breath and set my face. I wasn't going to let any of them see how much they'd hurt me. I wasn't going to give them that pleasure.

I gave Kyra a curt nod, tried to smile bravely at my Geema and halfway succeeded, and stalked out of the Hall with what I hoped was a dignified pace, my head up. They parted to let me pass, silent faces I knew so well: Elena with her baby, Miat, Micah, Havala, Chi-Wa, Thandi . . . I saw little Euzhan, standing with her *mi* and *da*, her face a mask of confusion, and I wanted to go to her and hug her and tell her that I would be all right and not to worry, but the stern glares from Micah and the others held me back.

No one followed me as I left the Hall. I walked down

the laser-smoothed corridors alone, accompanied only by the padding of my footsteps.

I wondered whether I'd get used to the silence, to the aloneness.

As Kyra had said, they'd put a large pack at the entrance, with my coat, gloves and hood piled on top of it. The Rock's main doors were closed, but I could feel the cold drifting from underneath the wood, waiting for me. I checked the pack, checked that the rifle they'd given me was loaded. I put on the coat and gloves, pulled the hood up and shrugged on the pack.

"Going somewhere?"

I know I couldn't have been used to the quiet already, but somehow in my mind I'd convinced myself that I wasn't going to hear a voice again. "Elio? Máire? I thought—"

"You thought we were going to let you go alone?" Máire finished for me. "You thought we'd abandon you like that?" She shook her head. "They shun you, they shun us all."

"You can't do this. Your Families . . ."

Elio grinned. "*Hai*. Geeda Dominic might have a coronary. Right now, I wouldn't consider that a tragedy. Unfortunately, when he finds out I'm gone, he's more likely to celebrate than have a fit. Maybe he'll choke on his dinner." They were both dressed for the cold, both had packs to rival the size of mine. "So . . . where are we heading?"

"Elio . . ."

"Hush, Ana," Máire interjected. "We both made the decision—separately, actually—when this fiasco started. I'll admit I'd hoped we wouldn't actually have to follow through, but . . . I couldn't live here anyway, not after this. And you haven't answered Elio's question. Where are we going?"

I tried to shrug under the weight of the straps. "I haven't exactly had time to think about that," I began, but even as I spoke, I remembered the bog body and the map inscribed on his chest. "The island at the end of the Miccail roads," I told them. "That's where I'm going." I looked at the two of them. "You should stay," I said. "You really should."

"So should you, but they won't let you," Elio answered. "So we don't really have a choice. But we'd better get moving before someone sees us and decides that our leaving with you doesn't qualify as a proper shunning." He pushed at the doors—they opened, and the cold air hit us as we looked out over the snow-wrapped panorama of trees, hills, and lake. "Let's go," he said. "The sooner we're moving, the warmer we're likely to be."

They followed me from the Rock.

CONTEXT:
Bui Allen-Shimmura

"He did *WHAT*!"

"It's true, Geeda. I was watching from the tower window, and I saw Anaïs leaving the Rock, and *da* Elio and Máire were with her."

Bui watched Geeda Dominic's face as he gave him the news. Bui wasn't certain how Dominic would react—no one was ever certain how Dominic would react when he was angry. It had been two weeks after Euzhan's accident before Dominic would even speak to Bui civilly. Bui figured that Dominic was going to get angry now, and he was prepared to move backward quickly if it looked like that cane was coming his way.

But his geeda surprised him. Dominic snorted, as if he'd just heard something that amused him. He tapped over to the chamber window with his cane, and looked out over the landscape. "*Hakuchi!* The boy never was much good at listening to those who know better," he said to the glass. "And he *is* a damned fool if he thinks this will change my mind. I hope he manages to survive his dose of reality, but it's a choice he made. The *kami* will help him or not, but I won't."

Bui watched Dominic's thin shoulders lift and fall, then the old man turned around to him again. His lined face was solemn, but the network of furrows around the eyes—the ones Bui thought of as "madmarks"—were relatively untouched. When Dominic spoke, his inflection was calm.

"Let the Koda-Schmidts know—they may want to go haul Máire back here, though I doubt it. Then find out from Ché Koda-Levin when Ghost is due back; we're going to need to assign a new historian if Elio hasn't come to his senses and come back by then—oh, and you might as well let old Anaïs know about this, too. I don't want her to find out second-hand. You understand all that?"

Bui nodded.

"Then what are you waiting for, boy? Get moving, get moving! And make sure you come right back here and tell me what they say!"

This time the cane did come slashing through the air, but Bui was already at the door and heading down the stairs at a run.

VOICE:

Anaïs Koda-Levin the Younger

WE CROSSED THE RIVER AT NEW BRIDGE, BEHIND the Rock. It was snowing fitfully, and dull orange chunks of ice piled against the foundations of the bridge, the water churning around them noisily and foaming at the delay in its rush to the sea. The hills looked as if a giant had pricked his sole and bled on them, and the sun was being coy, peeking out flirtatiously from behind the clouds then quickly ducking back again. It was not an auspicious day to begin a new life.

Then again, I doubt there's ever a good day for that.

The bridge led to a cleared section of the forest, where snowmounds hinted at buried piles of cut whitewood logs, waiting for someone to take them back to the Rock to be dried out, cut for lumber, or burned for fuel. We pushed on through a meandering path that led through tartberry bramble and down a steep incline to a frozen creek bed, and about another half a kilometer—up the other side of the weed-choked hill—we stumbled, almost literally, across the half-buried flagstones that marked the old Miccail road.

"If we're following the map, then we go left," I said. "That also takes us past Gabriela's old cabin, about two klicks up. We should be able to make that in four hours or so. That'll be about dark. It'll give us some kind of shelter, anyway."

An hour or less away from the Rock, and I already felt cut off. I looked at us—three figures hooded and cloaked, with

227

mud-splattered boots and snow-matted pants. A flurry hissed through the globe-trees; a wizard muttered incantations in the tree above us. The full import of the situation threatened to overwhelm me then. We weren't going to make it. No one could make it like this, with no resources except what we carried on our backs.

"Gabriela survived out here for years and years," Máire said, as if she'd read my thoughts, then added: "It wasn't hard to figure out. You looked like a kid who just broke her favorite toy." She smiled at me. "There's three of us—we don't have any room to complain."

"Yes, we do," Elio interjected. "I'm damned cold, and standing here isn't helping. Gabriela's cabin sounds good to me. Let's get going before my boots freeze to the ground."

Elio didn't wait for any of us. He headed out, leaning into the wind that snaked among the trees alongside the road. We followed without a word: breath was better saved for the effort of walking.

The old Miccail road was overgrown and at times invisible. Often, the only evidence of it was a minor gap between the taller trees. A few thousand years ago, I could imagine, it had been impressive—a wide path of flat stone arrowing through wilderness. Gabriela had believed that the Miccail settlements were widely separated, and the roadway we followed would once have been the link that made travel between them convenient. Time had eroded most of it away. The flags were often covered with dirt, overgrown with meadow grass, or lost beneath the roots of young trees which had sprung up where the Miccail had long ago walked. Here and there were hints of an old grandeur: the supports of a tall bridge that had once arched over a ravine, the broken columns thrusting upward above the trees; a quarter mile where the flags lay relatively unbroken and untouched, with the remnants of mortar still holding them together; the circular foundations of a Miccail wayhouse, overhung with creeper vines.

This far away from the Rock, the path we followed was the only sign that any sentient beings had ever worked this land and tried to tame it.

The sun silhouetted the peaks of the hills sooner than I would have liked. As we started down a hill toward a fog-draped valley where the river awaited us again, I heard a low, throaty call from the hills to our right, answered by another highly modulated yowl from the other side.

"Khudda," Elio cursed. He was already unslinging his rifle. "Grumblers out hunting. Just what we need."

"I've never been out this way. How far's the cabin?" Máire asked. Her voice was outwardly calm, but concern lifted it a step higher than usual. Elio shrugged in answer and looked at me.

"I was there once when I was a kid," I told them. "I went along on a foraging expedition, and we stopped there for a rest. It was near where the path crossed the river again, as I remember, so we don't have much farther to go. I think." I unslung my own rifle and checked the clip.

"You think?"

"It was a long time ago, Elio. Hey, you're the historian—you never came out here yourself?"

"Historians don't actually investigate anything; we just write up what other people find out and try to make it sound halfway interesting. It's a great occupation for otherwise useless people." Elio grinned and shrugged again. "Aren't you glad I came along?"

Another grumbler howl—close by, this time—ended any answer I might have made.

We moved downslope with the sound of grumblers hurrying our footsteps. There must have been a pack of them in the valley, because now we heard them from all sides, calling and answering, though we didn't see any of them. I once thought I caught a glimpse of movement just off the path, but when I turned, the rifle's muzzle down and the safety off, I couldn't see anything but thornvines netting a grove of amberdrop trees. Yet I could feel them watching. There was always the sense of eyes peering at us. They knew we were here, and from the sounds, they weren't happy with the intrusion. Getting to the cabin quickly was beginning to seem imperative. None of us wanted to be caught out in the open without shelter tonight.

My memory had been fairly accurate. Gabriela's cabin was visible before we reached the floor of the low valley. The dwelling had never been a model of architecture, and it hadn't been inhabited for over thirty years, since Gabriela's dessicated, skeletal body was found lying on the bed in the single-room building. I seemed to remember a larger clearing around it, but either my memory was mistaken or the forest had crept in closer in the intervening years. Vines drooped from the nearest trees to the swaybacked roof, part of which had collapsed. The log walls were hand-hewn, the ends rough with lighter-hued axe marks—I could imagine Gabriela struggling to move the tree trunks by herself. She'd built a shingle roof over the door; it had collapsed, and the door itself was missing. If there'd ever been glass in the windows, that was gone, too. One wall was seared black from an old fire around the tumbled chimney: Gabriela had been lucky that the whole cabin hadn't gone up in flames. The entire structure leaned as if weary. In another thirty years or probably less, the land would reclaim it entirely, absorbing Gabriela's labor back into itself.

The cabin looked better than anything I'd seen in a while.

I started toward the door opening, but Máire grabbed my arm, shaking her head. She put a finger to her lips and pointed at the ground. In the failing, low light, I could see the footprints of grumblers in the snow around the cabin. "*Khudda*," Elio whispered behind me. "House guests."

As if Elio had conjured them, they stalked out of the darkness of the cabin a moment later: two grumblers, a male and female. We were no more than twenty feet from them, a distance a grumbler could cover in a few seconds. The female snuffled in our direction, her nasal vents widening, though I wondered how she could smell anything through their own musk. The male waggled his dreadlocks at us and snarled, double tongues lashing. At the same time, both of them clenched their hands and their retractable claws emerged from matted fur. Golden-brown eyes glared at us while their central lenses glinted above and between them.

There was something about the male that tugged at me, and with the sense of strange familiarity came a memory: *Masa bearing me down into the cold marsh, his hands tearing at my clothes, his fingers violating me, his cock thrusting—and then his weight suddenly gone from me, torn away as I heard him scream. The grumbler stared at me as I lay there, as if confused by the sight of me . . .*

I couldn't be certain, but this one might have been the same animal. The way it cocked its head, the eyes, the streak of white in its spinal mane . . .

The male took a step toward us, and I heard Elio's safety click off. "No," I told him. "Elio, don't."

"Ana, we can't take any chances right now." His breath clouded around us.

"I know, I know. It's just . . ." I took a breath. None of us moved: grumbler or human. "Wait. Just wait a moment. Please."

Footsteps scraped through dry leaves and snow behind us. We all turned. Another grumbler had emerged from the cover of trees. It saw us at the same moment and shrieked a challenge, its claws sliding out of their fleshy sheaths. Before any of us could respond, it charged, leaping high into the air with a spray of snow. Elio brought his rifle up and fired, but the shot only tore foliage behind the beast. I heard Máire stuggling with her own gun, and I tried to bring mine up, but I could see that the grumbler was already too close . . .

Something moved past my shoulder, a blur of mottled gray fur.

The male from the cabin slammed into the attacking grumbler, sending it sprawling on the ground. He stood over the creature, slashing once with its claws as the grumbler tried to rise and attack again. They shrieked at each other, spitting and howling, claws out and striking air. Finally, the attacker's voice quieted to a mumble, and it slunk away into the trees again. The male stood watching the retreat, occasionally sending a snarl into the dusk.

We'd all forgotten about the female. I suddenly realized that she was nearly alongside me, still sniffing as if my odor confused her, and I took an involuntary step backward as Elio and Máire both recoiled. The grumbler's lips curled back, exposing her teeth, and she hissed, the claws lifting. The male was looking back at us now, but we were between them and the cabin now.

Neither one of the grumblers, despite the help the male had just given us, looked particularly friendly. I could see the large ripping claw on the male's right foot quiver, as if he were imagining gutting me with it.

"Go on!" I shouted at them. "Get out of here!" I waved my arms, taking another backward step. They stayed where they were, mumbling and snuffling. "Get *out*!" I raised the rifle and fired into the air. They stumbled backward at the report. I fired again, and they turned and ran.

"What the hell was it doing, protecting its supper?" Elio asked after they'd disappeared into the growing dark.

"I guess," I told him. "I guess." I shuddered, the cold making itself known as the adrenaline rush subsided. Máire's cheeks were blotchy and red, and Elio had a frost moustache on the stubble of his upper lip. "We need to get warm and eat something. Let's get inside and make a fire," I said to them. "And we'll hope we've seen the last of our guests for the night."

JOURNAL ENTRY:
Gabriela Rusack

I MISS SO MANY THINGS ON MICTLAN.

I miss music, being able to call up any piece in my head through the database whenever I want to hear it—the implant's still there, of course, but all it gives me is white noise unless Ghost's in range. I miss holography, videography, and photography—all those marvelous ways of capturing snippets of reality and preserving them: drawing and painting are wonderful skills, but they're also skills I don't have. I miss flying and being able to see the great, glorious and wide landscape far beneath me—looking down from several thousand feet and seeing how small and insignificant we really are on the great scale of things. I miss the smell of the ship—a miasma of thousands of humans, bearing with it the realization that every molecule I breathed in had also been breathed in and exhaled by everyone else in the community. I miss steel and glass constructions—I thought they were ugly then, but there was a sterile grandeur to them that wood and stone lack. I miss the entertainments, the thousand grand ways of wasting time that were available on the *Ibn Battuta*—here we waste nothing.

We especially do not waste time.

I miss being able to go to someone and say "Make me this" and know that it would be made. I miss being able to play with the computer and have my own creations awaken to walk and talk and interact with me, almost human themselves (though at least Ghost, my favorite among them, still exists). I miss the old familiar foods, the ones that never flourished here and are now gone forever: corn (lost to the maize blight early on), tomatoes (which were scheduled to be brought down on the very next flight of the shuttle that destroyed the *Ibn Battuta*), apples (the trees never flourished, no matter what we tried), chicken (which the local predators liked even more than we did).

I miss chocolate—oh, by all the *kami*, let's shout the glorious lost word: CHOCOLATE!!—rich and dark and so incredibly sweet. Just the dusty memory of it starts my salivary glands working and conjures long forgotten tastes and smells: steaming cups of hot chocolate, chocolate cake with frosting, frothy chocolate mousse, chocolate bars, chocolate ice cream, chocolate candies . . .

Oh, I swear I would *kill* for one taste of chocolate again. . . .

CONTEXT:
Elena Koda-Schmidt

ELENA STROKED THE HEAD OF HER BABY AS IT nursed, slurping noisily as it suckled. Feeling Elena's hand, the baby stopped feeding, let go of Elena's nipple, and smiled toothlessly up at her. Elena could only grin back, laughing. She touched the baby's hand with her index finger and felt the tiny fingers curl around her and hold.

"Oh, *hai*, you're showing off now, aren't you, you imp," she crooned. "That's right, I'm looking at you, baby. Are you full? Is that what you're telling me, eh? Fine, come here, then. . . ."

Elena lifted the baby to her shoulder, cradling her head. She leaned back in the rocking chair, patting the infant gently as she rocked in the candlelit twilight of her room. The chair creaked gently as they moved, and she remembered that she'd intended to get Derek Koda-Levin to reglue the supports. She'd thought to talk to him yesterday, but then the business with Anaïs had come up, and she didn't want to bother the Koda-Levins right now.

The baby stirred, snuggling against her neck. "Hush, hush," she crooned, but thinking of Anaïs put an edge on her voice. *Poor Máire, and Elio, too. I feel so sorry for all of them . . .*

Elena hugged her daughter tighter, suddenly frightened. "What will they do to you?" she asked, and ice gripped her heart at the thought. "It's not fair. It's not. You can't help the way you were born. It's not your fault."

The baby began to cry—she must have been holding her more tightly than she'd thought. Elena patted her, rocking harder now, a new tightness in her jaws and shoulders. "Shhh, shhh, little one. I'm sorry. Your mam's just a little scared for you, that's all. A little scared. But don't worry— I'll protect you. I'll be there for you. I will. I promise. Shhh. . . ."

The baby's wail subsided to a cry, a sob, then a sniffle. A few minutes later, when her breathing deepened and slowed, Elena stopped rocking and took her over to the cradle. She tucked the covers around her.

She watched her child sleeping for a long time.

VOICE:
Máire Koda-Schmidt

MY STOMACH CHURNED AGAIN, AND I KNEW I WAS going to be sick. I went to the farthest corner of the cabin and tried to throw up as quietly as possible. I obviously didn't succeed very well. Elio stirred in his sleep, got up on his elbows, and struggled out of his sleeping bag. He didn't say anything, just stroked my back while the last spasms passed.

I wiped my mouth on my sleeve.

"You all right now?" he asked.

"*Hai*," I told him. The taste in my mouth was wretched. Elio handed me my canteen. I took a mouthful of water, swished it around, and spat it out, then kicked dirt over the mess. "Sorry. Guess the rations last night didn't agree with me. I feel better now." Elio looked concerned and worried, and I smiled at him in reassurance. I've never found Elio at all attractive, but I understand why Anaïs considers him a friend, and I was glad he'd come with us. I touched his cheek softly. "Thanks," I said. "You helped."

"We could wake Ana. . . ."

"I'm fine. Let her sleep a little longer. My stomach's just upset."

I went back to the fire. Dawn—long fingers of light slicing

through chinks in the logs into the misty interior—had chased away some of the fears of the night. I could still hear a distant grumbler or two out in the valley, but their calls were no longer haunting, overlaid with those of wizards and the morning insects. "Try to catch another hour's sleep," I told Elio. "I'm still on watch, and we've got a walk ahead of us today."

Elio shrugged. "I'm up now." He grabbed his rifle from alongside his pack and shouldered it, going to the makeshift door we'd made the night before from scraps of wood. "Gotta pee, anyway," he said. "Be right back."

"Be careful."

Elio grinned. "I'll just piss on the damn grumbler if he shows up again. That'll send him running." Elio moved out into the mist.

I listened to the sound of his footsteps crunching through the crusted snow. He whistled softly, a tuneless melody. I sat on my pack, hugging my knees to myself and trying to ignore the nausea that was threatening to return. I played the calendar game women had played for time eternal, wondering . . . What was today? The fifteenth? sixteenth? How long had it been now since?

I told myself it wasn't possible. It couldn't be.

You'll know, eventually. All you have to do is wait. . . .

So I waited.

VOICE:
Elio Allen-Shimmura

IT TOOK US THREE MORE DAYS TO REACH THE SEA, none of them pleasant. I spent most of them whirling around at strange sounds in the landscape and jumping every time I heard a grumbler howl nearby. That happened fairly often—two or three times a day we'd have to send them running with gunshots. Once, a particularly persistent male wouldn't be deterred by the warnings. Máire finally dispatched him with a shot to the head.

Grumblers were only part of the problem. There were

packs of proto-wolves in the forest, one group of which shadowed us for half a day while we picked off the occasional too-bold one before the remainder of them decided to go after easier game. Sawtooths—carnivorous seabirds who were only occasionally spotted near the Rock—were prevalent, and their periodic strafing missions at our heads caused us to sometimes abandon the roadway for the shelter of the trees. The first day out from the cabin, a horde of spidery insects the size of my hand crossed the road in a crawling mass a good two meters wide. None of us had ever seen anything like them before, and we weren't interested in finding out if they were poisonous or not, so we watched and waited. Not long after, a nik-nik fawn standing about as high as Euzhan tried darting through them. They swarmed up its thin legs and over its body as the fawn squalled in distress, and then it went ominously silent and collapsed. It took over an hour for the column of insects to cross our path and disappear into the woods again, and they left behind only the skeleton of the nik-nik.

The land itself was our worst enemy. Past Gabriela's cabin, the old Miccail roadway deteriorated almost entirely. At times, we lost it completely as we crossed a valley or forded a stream. The river, widening as it neared the ocean, laid its serpentine coils across our path on the second day, and we had no choice but to follow the bank for a few kilometers until it abruptly curved away to pour widening waters into a massive river that would—I remembered from the survey photos—eventually empty into the sea.

We found the Miccail road again, and now it traipsed up one ridge and down another. I think we covered more kilometers vertically than we did horizontally. We pitched tents in protected hollows, building campfires that seemed to attract more local fauna than they repelled. Máire and I, without speaking to each other about it, found ourselves revolving around Ana. While Máire was on watch, Ana slept beside me; when I was up, I'd look over across the fire to see the two of them snuggled together. When it was Ana's turn on watch, Máire and I slept apart and alone. Máire said nothing to Ana, but I think the stomach virus still bothered her. Ana, as we approached the road's terminus, became quiet and contemplative. She'd go hours without saying anything, and when I spoke, she'd give me a faint smile that seemed to come from a distance.

It was in the late morning of the sixth day after we'd left

the Rock that we stood on a low cliffside and looked down at the long rollers breaking against a pebbled beach: Crook-jaw Bay. A salty breeze tangled our hair, and the smell of brine and seaweed was strong. A notch had been cut in the cliff wall nearby, and where the opening widened onto the beach, there were two large, weathered stelae with indistinct carvings on them, seaweed draped around their bases. The land curved around on either side of the horizon to form a large bay, and out near the mouth, the steep-walled, flat-topped island threw its shadow on the waves. We could see the distant foam of waves crashing against the rocks, giving the island a shifting white bottom.

"Looks like we've hit the end of the road," I said. "Now what?"

Ana was staring at the island, lost in her thoughts. I glanced at Máire, who shook her head at me. "I'm going down the cut to the beach," I said. "We're going to need a shelter tonight—maybe there's some caves above the tide line we can use until we figure out our next step."

Ana didn't answer beyond what might have been a nod. She let her pack fall from her shoulder and sat, leaning back against it at the cliff edge and staring out at the island. "Stay with her," I said to Máire, and then went exploring.

The cut in the cliff wall was a stepped incline that went down at a sharp angle. I could see the marks of the tools that had chiseled away the rocks, long ago. Here and there, the walls had collapsed, leaving piles of boulders that had to be carefully stepped around and over. I spent a lot of time wondering what in the hell I was going to do if I broke an ankle down here, but eventually I reached the bottom with a few minor scrapes and bruises. I examined the stelae—the wind, surf, and water had weathered them severely, and I could barely make out the hieroglyphics on the surface. The beach was narrow, about five meters from the bottom of the cliff to where tidal pools gathered in the rocks. At low tide, it might have been twice that size. A double line of sizable flat slabs followed the beach out and disappeared under the surf; I assumed they were the remnants of a pier or dock. Any wood that had been part of the structure was long gone over the millennium or more since the Miccail had walked here: washed away, broken, or decayed into pulp.

"Anything?" Máire called down to me from above.

I turned around to look at her. Stopped.

"Hey, Elio! Can you hear me?"

"*Hai*, I hear you," I answered. "I think you and Ana ought to come down here."

"Did you find something?"

"Just come on down," I said. "You have to see this."

Máire disappeared, and while she and Ana made their way down toward the beach, I stared at the boat that was lodged on a ledge a few feet up from the beach. I hadn't seen it until I turned around to talk to Máire. Placed upside down on the rocks, it was flat-bottom and squarish, like the river boats Ana's *da* Jason makes, the planks well-planed and fitted together with wooden pegs, and the seams caulked with a blackish tar. It had been there a long time—the wood was gray with age and unpainted, and a glossy black knot of limpets had taken up residence at the bow. When I looked underneath it, I found an unshipped mast and a set of oars, along with some rotted vine-rope and a pile of decaying cloth that may once have been a sail.

I heard the two women coming up behind me, boots rolling the pebbles about. "Someone left us a little gift," I said.

"Gabriela." Anaïs almost whispered the name.

"Probably," I agreed. "It's definitely been here for some years, and I don't remember any stories about someone from the Rock exploring this bay. Still, that's a hell of a lot of work for one person, especially someone who—as far as we know—didn't know how to build a boat."

"She had all the time she needed to figure it out," Ana answered, and bitterness soured her voice. She looked away from the boat out to the island. "As interested as Gabriela was in the Miccail, she'd have wanted to go there to explore the ruins. I know she would, whether Ghost thought so or not."

"Well, if we're heading for the island, she may have saved us a lot of aggravation. What matters is whether we can use this boat or not," Máire said. "And whether we want to. We won't know that until we stop talking and see if she floats or sinks. I suggest we get her down on the beach and find out."

JOURNAL ENTRY:
Gabriela Rusack

❧ WHEN I WAS GROWING UP ON THE MOON, WATER was something to be conserved. You might drink it, cook with it, wash with it, but you never wasted it. When I was sixteen, I was sent down to Earth for university, and there, to my utter amazement, water was so common that it fell unwanted and unremarked from the sky. During certain seasons, people actually complained about how often it rained. Water was so cheap and plentiful that you could let it go swirling down the drain to oblivion. Water was so ubiquitous that there were more places than not on the planet where it was all you could see in any direction.

Despite the fact that during that time I lived within spitting distance of the ocean, some perverse reaction toward the utter obliviousness of the groundlings to their wealth of water ruled me. I never learned to swim, never waded in the surf, never took a boat ride, never snorkeled or scuba-dived or even reclined on an inflatable raft in a pool. As much as possible, I lived on the Earth as if I were living in the middle of Copernicus Central.

So it was an ironic inevitability that the one place on Mictlan I wanted most desperately to get to was an island.

CONTEXT:
Tozo Koda-Shimmura the Younger

❧ TOZO PACED, PANICKED AND UNABLE TO STAND still, as Hayat worked on the baby. "She was having trouble breathing, and I was doing the back pats to get the gunk out, but she was choking on it..." A deep, wrenching sob wracked her, leaving her unable to talk. Hayat was hunched over the baby, his hands busy. She couldn't see what he was doing. "Hayat, I don't hear her. Hayat . . ."

Tozo's mam, Hannah, took her arm and pulled her close, holding Tozo as she cried. "Mam, she can't die. She can't. I have a name to give her on her Naming Day. I was going to call her Zoe. She can't die."

"I know, *mojo ljubav*," Hannah said, but Tozo could hear the resignation in Hannah's voice, a dullness that came from her mam's own past: the multiple miscarriages, the early deaths of Tozo's three siblings. Tozo suspected that what her mam knew was that children died all too frequently on Mictlan, and that Tozo's nameless girl would be no different. Tozo glanced at Hayat's back, angry now.

"Damn it, where's Hui, Hayat? I want Hui in here!"

Hayat didn't answer. Ama came rushing in, and she and Hayat conferred in hushed, urgent whispers before Ama ran out again. "Hayat!"

"He's coming, Tozo," Hayat said over his shoulder, his voice muffled by the mask he wore. "He'd been here thirty some hours already, and we sent him home. Faika's gone to fetch him. Now let me work . . ."

Ama came back in with a tray of instruments, setting them down on the table next to Hayat. Tozo saw Ama putting a tube down the baby's throat, and then attach a bag to it, which she began squeezing rhythmically. Once, Ama looked up at Hayat, and from across the small room, Tozo saw the hopelessness in the woman's eyes. She began crying again, and a fist seemed to have grabbed her chest, crushing it.

Hui did come, then, rushing into the room with a gruff, tired "What have we got?" Tozo listened as Hayat outlined what had happened and what he'd done while Hui plunged his hands into the thorn-vine sap to coat them. Tozo didn't understand much of it. Then Hui went over to the table as Hayat moved aside. After a few minutes, Hui put his hand on Ama's, still squeezing the bag attached to the ventilating tube, and shook his head. Ama's posture sagged, and she stopped. Hui patted Hayat's shoulder. "It's over," he told the young man, and with the words, Tozo wailed.

"No!" she cried, lunging toward the cold steel table that held her baby. Hui caught her. "I'm sorry, Tozo," he said. "I really am."

"No . . ." Tozo said again. "No . . ." and the words dissolved with her tears. She beat at Hui's chest once with her fists, then collapsed into him. "Damn it, why weren't you here when I brought her? You could have saved her."

Tozo felt Hannah pull her gently away from Hui, and she saw the apologetic look that passed from Hannah to Hui. "I'm sorry," Hui said again. "I really am, but there's nothing more we can do. Hannah, please take her out of here while we clean up."

He wouldn't look at Tozo, and that sparked the anger again. "You weren't here," Tozo said. "It's your fault. You should have been here."

Hui pressed his lips tightly together, grimacing as if in pain. "I wish I had been," he said. "Hannah . . ."

Hannah urged her to the door of the room. As they left, Tozo heard Hui talking to Hayat. "You did what you could. Get over it, because it's only the first of many. Too many . . ." he said, and then the door to the room closed behind them, shutting Tozo off from her daughter forever.

TRANSFORMATIONS

VOICE:

Anaïs Koda-Levin the Younger

"OVER THERE!" MÁIRE POINTED TO A TONGUE OF black rock that extended from the base of the island, creating a small harbor. A zigzagging series of steps cut into the cliff face ran upward from the natural dock toward the summit of the crag. "Let's head in. The waves on the seaward side are going to be too much for us."

It had taken us a week to get the craft into shape. Several of the boards were rotten and had to be patched or replaced, and with the limited tools we had, that took time. When we first tried the boat in a small, quiet inlet, water had streamed through the seams, all of which had to be resealed with tar from the stink-flower trees. We didn't have the spare cloth to make another sail, so Elio carved another set of oars and notched out a pair of additional oarlocks so that two of us could row at a time. We added a rudder to the stern for steering and stability.

Even with all of our work, I was afraid that we were going to capsize as soon as we reached the long, rolling waves of the bay. I'd been out in *da* Jason's boats on the river—this was another experience altogether. We took in water over the sides until Máire got the bow heading into the waves and we moved out into deeper water. The persistent offshore wind chilled our hands and faces despite the bright sun. I was alternately freezing from the cold and sweating from the exertion of rowing. I think we all *thought* about turning back, but no one said anything, and so we kept on. The island rose slowly, looking higher and more ominous the closer we approached. Until Máire spotted the steps and the small docking area, we were wondering whether our efforts were going to be futile. The cliffs were steep and jagged, well over a hundred meters high and plunging straight into the sea.

We maneuvered into the natural harbor and calmer water, and the boat scraped bottom on a tiny sand beach near the bottom of the steps. Elio jumped out, then Máire and myself, and we dragged the boat up from the water, pulling it past the line on the rocks that marked high tide. Elio craned his neck back and squinted into the bright sky, peering upward at the top of the cliffs. "My bet is that there's five hundred steps or better, and there's not a railing in sight," he said. "Anyone here have a problem with heights?" Nobody answered him; I don't think he expected us to.

It was certainly not a staircase for the timid. Cut into the cliff wall itself, the stairway turned and twisted with the natural flow of the rock, each step about two meters wide from where it met the cliff to the precipitous end, and the height of the step was a little more than was comfortable for humans. As we climbed, we were only rarely sheltered by a screen of stone; most of the time we stood exposed on the cliff face, with nothing between us and a long fall but air. The view was spectacular as we rose, the churning sea gnawing at the foot of the cliff, the panorama of the bay spread out in front of us, orange-tinted water glinting in the sun. It didn't appear there'd ever been a railing or other protection on the stairs; at least we didn't see any evidence of holes where supports could have been embedded—evidently the Miccail that came to the island weren't bothered by the precariousness of the climb, or they spent much of it with their backs pressed against the cliff wall, as we did. In winter, with ice and snow, it would have been suicidal. There wasn't much room to pass—if someone was coming down at the same time as someone was coming up, they'd have to trust each other. The staircase had seen much use during its time, for the feet that had trod it had worn down the center of the steps over the centuries, hollowing the hard stone. Trying to ignore the wind that insisted on trying to fling us off the precipice, we continued the climb.

My calves and thighs were burning when we reached the top. I collapsed onto the grassy plateau of the summit, exhausted and relieved. Máire and Elio sprawled out beside me. After I'd caught my breath, I knelt up to look around. "By all the *kami* . . ." I exclaimed.

Even in ruin, it was gorgeous. The top of the island was a huge, overrun garden, maybe three kilometers across. The plateau tilted gently upward from where we sat, and the ground had been landscaped in long, wide terraces from which flowering vines curled. Honeydippers flitted through the vines, darting from flower to flower with their wings buzzing energetically; a bumblewort glanced at us curiously and then skittered off under the nearest screen of leaves. Wild verrechats yowled somewhere nearby, unseen, and a groundslug the size of my arm humped its way along the stones of the first terrace. To either side the tumbled walls of ancient buildings rose like the stumps of teeth, fragments of bright paint still clinging to the deepest pores of the stone.

In the center of this immense natural amphitheater was the largest building, with the walls still mostly intact and rising a dozen meters or more high. The building had once been painted white, judging from the few stubborn flecks of paint that still clung to the pores of the marble walls. It sprawled over an acre or more of the first terrace, parts of the walls rising higher than the lip of the island. The front, facing us, had the remnant of a frieze, carved with detailed figures, and columns framed the main entrance. Once, this edifice would have dominated the plateau, a beacon that could be seen even from the shore.

I knew I had to go there. The ruins pulled me to my feet.

As we approached the entrance, I stopped, overcome for a moment by an intense sense of reverence, like entering the Kami's Grotto in the Rock for the LastDay ceremonies, only far more powerful. "Think of it," I said to Elio and Máire, "the Miccail gathering here over centuries, praying to their gods . . ." I touched one of the columns, feeling the bite of cold stone through my gloves. Above us on the frieze, the strange, thin figures of the Miccail stared down at us. I heard Máire take her rifle and click off the safety as we crossed into shadow.

I stopped.

We stood in what once must have been an outer walkway, with columns flanking us and leading further into the interior. There'd originally been a wall here, shielding the view of the main hall until you reached an archway further down, but the wall had fallen, as had most of the roof. Sunlight played on rubble and fallen stones, sparked from mica-spotted columns and dust.

And spotlighted in the noon glare about fifty meters from us was an enormous shell placed on a crystalline altar in the center of the building. Untouched, unbroken, its surface reflected a soft luster, pearls of multicolored light glancing from the whorled exterior, and rainbow hues shimmering in its gigantic mouth.

"It's gorgeous," Máire whispered alongside me, with almost a laugh in her voice. "It is frigging gorgeous."

Mesmerized, we went toward it. I'd seen shells similar to it, brought back to the Rock from exploratory jaunts to the ocean. "Nautilus," they were called, after an Earth mollusk. But the nautilus shells I'd seen were tiny in comparision. This one was more than an armspan across, and I could have comfortably sat in the opening to the interior. I took my glove off and touched it, stroking the enameled, pinkish surface, as smooth and glossy as ice and as cold. Standing in front of it, the sound of my breathing and the sounds of the island were transmuted into white noise, a tidal garble.

"Hello," I called softly into the shell, and a long, crashing echo returned. Máire and Elio circled the altar, with the same sense of awe. We all felt the sense that we were intruding on sacred ground, and we talked in hushed tones and walked softly and carefully, not wanting to disturb the silence.

I was standing close to the shell's trumpet mouth, listening to the altered resonance it gave the world, when a new chord sounded in the atonal chorus. I squinted, glancing behind me to see what had changed. "Damn!" I said, and Elio and Máire both whirled around.

"What?" Elio asked, still whispering, shading his eyes against the glare from above. I pointed to the entranceway, where sun poured into the building. There, a quartet of figures stood silhouetted in a shaft of dusty light.

"Grumblers," I said.

INTERLUDE:
KaiSa

ABRI'S FEVER BROKE THAT MORNING, AND THOUGH the tracks of ker several wounds were red and angry, they had already begun knitting well and there was no sign of infection. Kai helped Abri sit, helped ker walk around the tent, and fed ker grain mixed with *kavat* milk. When ker *brais* had cleared and ke could sit up without pain, Kai sat on the bed alongside ker.

"We can't stay here," ke said, and told ker about taking the *jitu* and the visions that VeiSaTi had gifted ker with. "I know now what we must do," Kai finished. "VeiSaTi has made it clear to me, and I will need your help. We must leave, AbriSa. We must leave as soon as we possibly can."

Abri nodded without protest. "Then we go," ke said, but there was pain and weariness in ker voice. "Let me help you get our packs. We'll leave now, if they'll let us."

Kai smiled at ker friend. "Not yet," ke said. "Rest for now. Tonight or even tomorrow night will be soon enough, and we'll need the darkness. Gather your strength now and sleep. I'll wake you when it's time. . . ."

Despite the advice, Kai couldn't rest kerself, even though ker body ached for sleep. The residue of the *jitu* still burned in ker blood, and knowing what must happen today, ke did not want to lost what little time remained to sleep.

But ke could also not sit there and watch Abri. Ke rose and went out into the encampment.

Ker eyes seemed newborn—the colors around ker were brighter and more saturated, the wind prickled the skin of ker arms as if someone had brushed across them with a feather. Ke could smell the woodsmoke of the funerary fires as the dead were burned and the odor was rich and varied, scented with spices anointing the dead. Kai would have sworn that the day seemed warmer because of the pyre's heat. The pall of smoke smeared across the sun twisted and curled, an endless, fascinating pattern. Kai stood watching the wriggling column of smoke for long minutes, and then walked closer.

The fire had been started in NeiTe's dwelling, and the dead among the village defenders had been the first to be fed to the flames. Now that their remains had been turned to ash and the house itself was a pit of glowing coals, the dead of DekTe's army were being given to the fire with full ceremony. Kai heard the name GhazTi invoked; on Angl-Saiye the Sa had been taught the names and attributes of the gods, and Kai knew that GhazTi was a deity worshipped in the south, a god of dark needs with a voracious appetite for sacrifice. Kai was not surprised to find Him worshipped here, and ke realized that it had been GhazTi's aspect who attacked VeiSaTi in ker vision. The thought made ker shudder, and ke turned from the priests and their incantations, half afraid that if ke listened to their chants ke might see that ghastly apparition once again.

To one side of the main pyre, a smaller fire had been lit, and there Kai saw DekTe himself, standing with PirXe and the older Miccail. The fire lapped around a small, cloth-wrapped offering, and Kai realized that it was the stillborn child ke'd delivered the night before. Kai felt a sudden re-luctance, but before ke could slip away without being seen, DekTe's head turned and their gazes met. The lost sadness in those eyes pulled ker, and ke approached, wondering why part of ker was so eager to be with him again.

As soon as Kai started toward him, DekTe had looked away again. PirXe and the old one watched ker approach, then stepped away from the pyre, leaving the two of them alone. DekTe stared now into the hungry flames, his nostrils quivering at the sharp odor of deathspice. "How is CaraTa?" Kai asked him.

DekTe didn't move. He watched the flames consuming the linen wrapping of his child, the edges of the cloth curling and blackening before floating away into glowing ash. "She is as well as I could expect, but still very weak," he said at last, and he finally turned to Kai. "I . . . I spoke badly to you last night, KaiSa. You saved CaraTa's life, and you tried to save our child. I want you to know that I'm grateful to you for that."

"I know," Kai answered. Ke could get lost in the strength of his gaze, ke knew, yet ke didn't really want to look away. "I couldn't refuse you, DekTe. Not in that."

" 'Not in that.' " DekTe repeated the words, and the cor-ner of his mouth lifted, his beaded locks clashing together softly. His strange blue eyes pierced ker. "But certainly in other things. I can't let you go, KaiSa," he said. "You realize that."

"You also can't keep me. In the end, I will never be what you want me to be, and CaraTa doesn't care for me."

"Then what is the solution?"

KaiSa had to laugh at that, a short bark of amusement. Ke swung ker arm to indicate the encampment and the wreck-age of NeiTe's village. "Give this up," ke said. "Then I would refuse you nothing." Ke remembered VeiSaTi's vi-sion, and a note of sadness crept into ker voice. "Then my fate might change."

"You think highly of yourself."

"I'm only the smallest piece in this game, DekTe. I know my role." Kai shivered. In the pyre, ke could see the form of the child now, dark as the flames consumed it. "You won't listen to me or to anyone else, DekTe. You will pursue this to the end, no matter what it costs. I'll tell you this, as well—you won't find satisfaction in your triumph."

"What, you spout prophecy as well?" DekTe's laugh had an edge of unease to it, and he glanced at the fires around them. "You have more talents than I ever suspected."

"I'm only what you see in front of you," Kai answered. "Nothing more." Ke turned slightly, so that ke could watch the pyre, and ke said a silent prayer to VeiSaTi for the spirit of the little one, asking the god to take care of him in the shadow-world. DekTe's hand touched ker shoulder, and for a moment, ke inclined ker head so that ke trapped his hand, enjoying the touch of him and wishing that it could be more. DekTe's claws extended slightly, as a lover's might. Kai turned again, taking a step back from him so that the hand dropped away. "I'm truly sorry for your loss," ke said. "Tell CaraTa that I wish it could have been different."

"There will be other children for us."

"No," KaiSa said with certainty, knowing that ke was speaking truth. "There will not." With that, ke turned and walked away. Ke could feel DekTe's gaze as hot as the coals of the pyre on ker back, and ke expected him to call out to ker, but he didn't. When ke turned back, just before returning to ker tent, ke saw DekTe still at the pyre, his back to ker as he watched the glowing ashes spiral into the sky.

JOURNAL ENTRY:
Gabriela Rusack

I NEVER SERIOUSLY CONSIDERED THE OPTION OF SU-icide during my final shunning. After all, suicide is just giving your enemies what they want without making them work for it.

All right, I'll be honest here, since the only one likely to ever read this journal is me. The thought of suicide *has* drifted through my mind, off and on. But I've never gone to the point where I actually had the gun in my hand, or stood at the edge of the cliff waiting for the right moment to take a last, long step.

I came closest in the awful months after Elzbieta and the

Ibn Battuta died. Already the Crow, I couldn't imagine how it would be possible for the few of us left to survive, and part of me longed to be with Elz in death, if we could not have life together. I missed her that much, and a raw, putrescent wound pulsed in my soul where her presence had been ripped away from me.

What kept me from following through then was the way we survivors clung together. I don't think I was ever alone for long enough to do the deed even if I'd had the courage, and we worked so damned hard: converting the storage caverns the shuttles had carved in the Rock into living spaces; getting crops planted so we could survive the coming winter; shepherding the few animals we'd brought down from the ship; commiserating with the other stranded folks on the southern hemisphere whenever we could get radio contact with them. Eventually, a year or two later, I realized that the soul wound had scarred over, and I was still alive and there were things I still wanted to do.

When I was shunned the first time, I thought of suicide again, angrily. I wanted to punish the bastards for doing this to me, and I thought (irrationally, I admit) that finding me dead would make them feel acceptably guilty for the rest of their miserable lives. Of course, I'd be dead and not able to *savor* their guilt. . . .

I managed to avoid the temptation.

You'd think that being shunned for the remainder of my life would make me start thinking about suicide again, but it hasn't. Over the decades, I've found the parts of me that can actually enjoy solitude. I don't think I'm whole or entirely sane anymore—but I can live this way. I can even, in some warped and small fashion, be happy.

INTERLUDE:
KaiSa

"IT'S TIME, ABRISA."

Kai whispered the words, and Abri simply nodded ker acceptance of them. Kai handed ker a pack, and Abri slipped the straps around ker shoulders with a grimace, hissing once in pain. The only light in the tent was from a small pile of glowmoss; in the green-blue, pale illumination, Kai moved to the rear of the tent. The blade of a small knife flashed as a support rope was slashed, and Kai lifted the cloth. The blue-white light of Quali entered, splashing a bright triangle on the ground, but otherwise there was only darkness. Kai nodded to Abri, and the two slid from the tent as quietly as possible.

They made their way through the tents, glowing eerily in the light of the moons, toward the ruined village and the road. For a time, Kai thought that VeiSaTi's power had overshadowed that of GhazTi and that they'd escape undetected, even though ke knew that guards had been set around the perimeter of the tents. They slipped past the final row and ran crouched toward the half-toppled village wall, stopping there a moment to rest. Abri was already limping, and ke held ker side as they crouched with their backs to the broken rock. "Can you keep going?" Kai asked, and Abri nodded grimly. Kai motioned toward the open gates of the village, then slipped along the wall to the opening. Abri followed, hobbling.

Kai stopped.

One of DekTe's soldiers lounged there, leaning against the opposite side of the arch. They saw each other at the same time. "Sa!" the guard said, reaching quickly for his spear. "What are you doing out here?"

Kai heard Abri moving softly away so that the guard could not attack them both at once, but ker breath was ragged, and the guard's eyes glanced at ker and dismissed ker. "You haven't answered me, Sa," he said again to Kai.

"We're leaving," Kai answered, and took a step forward. As ke had expected, the guard swung his spear toward him to block ker path, and at the same time, Kai moved. Ke grasped the shaft below the blade and thrust the butt end back into the guard's stomach. At the unexpected movement, the air went out of him with an audible *umphh* as he doubled over. With a twist, Kai ripped the spear from his weakened grasp and slammed it hard against the back of his head. The shaft cracked, one end pinwheeling away into the night.

The guard toppled, unconscious.

"I see you remember your lessons," Abri said, grinning quickly at Kai. Back on AnglSaiye, Abri had been one of those instructing the acolytes in the fighting arts. "We'd better move before he wakes up, though. He's not going to like the way his head feels."

Kai tossed the remaining half of the spear on the ground alongside the guard and nodded. They moved out of the village and into the cover of trees.

Once they'd escaped the encampment itself, Kai expected to have no pursuit. Even if DekTe decided to come after them, he would almost certainly assume that they would make for AnglSaiye and refuge. He would be wrong. Kai turned away from the scent of the ocean and looked instead to the hills from where they'd just come, to where the Black Lake beckoned.

The journey took them the rest of the night and all of the next day. If Abri wondered what Kai was doing or why they walked in this direction, ke made no protest, hobbling with Kai along the High Road. They stopped a few times to rest, but while Kai prepared food for Abri and urged ker to eat, Kai ate nothing kerself, and would drink only a few sips of water. As they approached the Black Lake, Kai became silent and withdrawn, and though Abri tried to get ker to talk, ke would not be drawn out.

The Black Lake was quiet and still in the wake of the passage of DekTe's army. Kai walked along the shore, ker feet sinking into the swampy ground. The marsh grass had sprung back up again, as if a thousand feet had never trampled it under only two days before. The bluewings had settled back into the net-branches and were feeding in the lake shallows, plucking out the clawed shellfish that inhabited the dark waters. Across the lake, the great outcropping of bare stone that sheltered the lake was reflected in the water's quiet surface, and its shadow just touched Kai and Abri.

The chill of the shadow stopped ker, as if ke had run into an invisible wall, and the vision of the *jitu* returned, shimmering against reality. Kai felt ker stomach lurch, and ker breath caught.

"Here," Kai said abruptly, with a shiver. "This is where it must happen."

Ke slipped the pack from ker shoulders. Crouching in the muddy flat, ke let the contents fall out: a mortar and pestle, a stone axe, a length of cord made from spindleleg gut and knotted three times, with wooden handles on either end. Abri knew the implements well, knew what they signified— any Sa would. Ke cocked ker head toward Kai inquiringly.

"We came here to sacrifice?" ke said. "Kai, we could do that in AnglSaiye."

"Yes, but this is where VeiSaTi told me that this sacrifice must happen," Kai answered. Ke hunkered down alongside the upended pack, ker arms around ker legs, staring at the water and the rocky slopes on the other side. Ke was sweating, though the day was cold. *You can do this*, ke thought. *You know that you must.* Ker stomach rumbled, and that woke ker from reverie. Ke began gathering sweetgrass and nettles, as if foraging for breakfast.

Abri watched ker, puzzled, wondering what was wrong with ker friend. Ke had never seen Kai so pensive. "And what are we going to sacrifice, some of these bluewings?"

Kai didn't reply. Ke only looked at Abri somberly, and the realization came to ker slowly.

"No," Abri said, sinking to the ground in front of Kai. "Oh no, Kai. I can't do that. You can't ask it of me."

Kai nodded. "You can. And I don't ask you; VeiSaTi does," Kai replied.

"But why? Why does Ke ask this?"

Kai laughed at that, the dark amusement a release. "I only know what I saw in the vision, what VeiSaTi revealed to me. I'm to die the triple death so that VeiSaTi will not die completely Kerself. It's what Ke demands of me. I don't know why, and Ke didn't explain it." Ke stopped, ker arms lifting then falling to ker side again. Ker voice trembled as ke spoke. "AbriSa, I'm terribly frightened of this, and I need you. I can't give VeiSaTi my life without your help. Please."

"Kai—"

"AbriSa, my friend . . ." Kai took Abri's face in ker hands. So warm, Abri was. So alive. "I've thought about this for a long time. I've argued with myself, tried to convince myself that the *jitu* vision was wrong, that I misinterpreted it, but . . ." Kai huddled on the ground, hugging ker knees to kerself and not looking at Abri. Ke shivered. "I told Ker that I was frightened, that I was afraid that I couldn't do this, but VeiSaTi tells me that I must. I must. And I've accepted that. In my mind, it's already happened." Now Kai looked up at Abri, and ker eyes pleaded with ker companion. "I'm afraid, AbriSa. But I can obey VeiSaTi—as long as you're here to help me."

Abri started to protest, but ke saw the resolve in Kai's face and knew that it was useless. Sa were trained from the beginning to sacrifice. They were taught that, on extremely rare occasions, VeiSaTi demanded the sacrifice of one of Ker own. This was no different than what NasiSaTu had done kerself, under similar circumstances. "Kai, DekTe—"

"DekTe will win, AbriSa. He has already won."

"Then why this sacrifice? If he's already won, then there's no need for a sacrifice."

"The time of Sa has passed, but if I go into the ShadowWorld now, VeiSaTi has promised that the Sa will return. But I must die here, and I must die now." Kai reached out; AbriSa took ker hands—they were chilled as if death had already come to ker, and they trembled.

"And afterward?" Abri asked. "What then? What am I supposed to do?"

"You have the hardest task. You must return to AnglSaiye and tell them all what you've seen. And you must tell them this, most importantly." Kai leaned forward, and spoke softly into Abri's ear. When ke was finished, ke drew back and looked into ker eyes. "You understand?" ke said. "You'll tell them what VeiSaTi has commanded?"

Abri nodded through the sudden, awful weight in ker chest. Ker head dropped, and ke shielded ker *brais*, as if the sun bothered ker. "KaiSa, this is terrible. I never thought . . ."

"AbriSa."

Ke looked up.

"One day, I'll come back to AnglSaiye. That's what Vei-SaTi has promised me. The Sa will return. One day. Ke has promised us."

Abri nodded. "Then I have the strength to do this," ke said.

Kai nodded, then stooped down to grind the grains ke had gathered, mixing in a few drops of water from the lake. Ke dipped ker fingers into the paste and ate it. "For life, I feed myself," ke said, and with the ritual words, the landscape seemed to shimmer around ker, as if ke were already lost to the shadow-world and this were a dream. "And with death, I feed life."

Kai stripped off ker clothes, standing naked in the warm sun. Kai handed the axe and the garrote to Abri. Ke stepped out into the lake until ke stood knee deep in the water, and then ke knelt, the water lapping at ker waist. "Now," ke said. "Please. You finish it, my friend: with earth, with air, with water."

Abri lifted the stone axe hesitantly, and Kai, still kneeling, bowed ker head to accept the blow.

256

"Kai . . ."

"With earth, AbriSa. Say it. Do it. Before I lose my courage."

Abri lifted the axe high. "With earth," ke repeated, and brought the heavy, sharpened stone down on the back of Kai's skull. Blood gushed from the wound, and Kai gasped and swayed, still kneeling. Abri quickly stepped behind the stunned Sa and slipped the garrote around ker neck.

"With air," Abri said, ker voice breaking, and ke twisted the garrote tight. Ke heard the neck snap under the pressure. As the body began to fall, ke pushed it into deeper water.

"With water . . ."

The murky waters rippled and closed over Kai's body, black and opaque. Abri waited until the water was still once again, and then, with a cry of pain, ke flung the bloodstained axe far out into the lake. It splashed once and was gone, the ripples slowly fading.

Abri stood there, silent, until dusk sent the bluewings searching for their nests. Then, at last, ke turned and left the Black Lake, making ker way to the High Road and Angl-Saiye.

VOICE:

Anaïs Koda-Levin the Younger

WE MOVED QUICKLY AWAY FROM THE ALTAR OF THE shell, hurrying into the deeper shadows of the interior to crouch behind tumbled columns, hoping the grumblers hadn't seen us. The grumblers stood at the entrance to the temple for several seconds, then moved toward us with their crouching, old-man gait. "Damn!" I heard Elio exclaim as he sighted down the barrel of his rifle. "Let's pick 'em off before they get close."

"No," I told him. "Hold on. I don't think they're really interested in us. Look . . ."

We were well off to the side of the altar and the great shell. As the grumblers approached, it was evident that their destination was the shell itself, not us. One of the grumblers was an ancient, with a long mane of silvered hair and a bend to his spine that indicated advanced arthritis. Two others were younger adult males, and the fourth was a very pregnant female, her belly swollen with child and her young-pouch distended. I knew they had to have seen us, but though the old one glanced toward where we hid, they ignored us.

The quartet went up to the shell, which the old one touched with an obvious reverence. He reached inside the mouth of the shell, deep into the interior. We couldn't see what he was doing from our vantage, but his mouth opened and he gave a low, throaty growl. After a few seconds, he brought his hand out again, splaying his long, webbed fingers on the shell's exterior. His claws extended slightly—we could hear them scrape against the smooth surface—and he gave a series of low, articulated grunts.

Taking the female's hand, he placed it, palm out, on the same spot on the shell he'd just touched. His hand still over the female's, the silverbacked elder extended his claws, pressing down until the sharpened tips just broke the tender skin of her palm. I heard the hissing intake of breath as the claws punctured skin and drew blood. The old one released the hand, and the female smeared the blood over her young-pouch, leaving a streak of dark wetness in the short fur. One of the males, standing alongside her, took her hand in his and brought it to his mouth. The twinned tongue darted out, tasting the blood, and then he pressed her palm against his own abdomen.

"Grumblers aren't sentient," Máire whispered to us. "They don't *have* ceremonies. They don't have a language. They're just dangerous animals, cunning but not particularly intelligent."

None of us answered, though we all agreed with the marveling sarcasm in her voice. Each of us had been taught the same mantra—it was the experience we had of grumblers. We'd hunted them; we'd killed them whenever and wherever we'd found them. But this. . . . The glimmer of a revelation came to me, one that I felt sure Gabriela had once experienced long before.

The grumblers had turned away from the shell and were shuffling toward the open doorway. As they passed us once more, the old one looked in my direction again. For a moment, our gazes locked. I was certain that he saw me. I knew he realized that we were there and had watched. His fingerclaws extended slightly, and I saw the large ripping claw on the foot quiver, lifting. His nostrils widened, and I heard him sniffing in my direction. His head lifted, as if he were appraising the scent and judging what danger we might represent. He regarded me, the head still up, that strange, lidless third eye staring at the open sky above him.

Then he sniffed, grumbled something, and continued on toward the exit. The males followed, but the female also glanced at me, pausing. She lifted her bloodied hand toward me, palm out, as if displaying her wounds for me. Then she folded her hands under her abdomen—a gesture I'd seen a hundred times with pregnant women back on the Rock— and followed the others from the building.

When they'd left, we sat there stunned for long seconds, just looking at each other. When we did talk, it was all at once.

"By all the *kami*, we were so *wrong* . . ."

"That was a rite, I know it was . . ."

"They saw us, but they didn't do anything . . ."

. . . and then we were silent again, as if the sound of our voices might shatter the memory and destroy the moment.

"They saw *you*," Elio said to me. "Not us. You."

"He's right," Máire agreed. "It was you they were interested in, Ana. They didn't care about Elio and me."

"I don't know," I said. *But I did. I did.* I went over to the shell, touching it where he'd touched, and then putting my hand into the shell's mouth as he'd done. My fingers touched something, hidden around the curve in the shell, and I explored the shape of the object, finding it familiar. I could feel others like it, shoved into the space. "I'll be damned . . ." I pulled one of them out. "Look at this."

The leather cover was soft and blotched with old stains. The paper was stiff and thick, handmade, and stitched together with dark thread. "I know what it is," Elio said before I could open the book. I looked at Elio, who shrugged. "I'm the historian, remember. I've seen other ones like it."

He took a breath, shaking his head. "It's one of Gabriela's journals," he said.

CONTEXT:
Sabina Allen-Levin

❧ "Mam, why did they send the doctor woman away?"

Sabina tucked the covers around her three-year-old son, slowly, using the task to give her time to think about how she wanted to answer the question. "Well, she did a really bad thing, Beiri."

"But I liked her. She was nice to me, not like that grumpy old Hui. And you told me she was the one who made me better when I was really sick, remember? When I was little."

"*Hai*, I remember." Sabina would never forget that night. It still haunted her dreams sometimes, and she'd get up in the middle of the night and go to the creche just to make sure that Beiri was still there, still sleeping. Still alive. She saw the long scar on his abdomen, every night when she undressed him. If she let herself, she could still hear him screaming, hysterical with the pain; she could still feel that sickening, empty helplessness, of not knowing what to do or how to help him or how to make it stop hurting . . .

"Mam, what did she do?" Beiri had reached out from the covers to touch her arm. His own arms and hands were diminutive, too small for his body, as if they belonged to a child half his age. *It could be much worse*, Anaïs had told her during one of his first checkups. *From all indications, he has normal motor functions in the hands. They're just undersized, that's all. He'll learn to adjust to them, and I think he'll do fine. He's a good kid. Just love him. That's the best thing you can do for him.* "What'd she do, mam?" he insisted.

"It was something only grownups can do, Beiri. When you're older, you'll understand."

Beiri made the face he usually made when she gave him that excuse, his lower lip sticking out in an exaggerated pout. "I don't care," he said. "I don't care what she did. I liked her."

Sabina leaned down and kissed him, brushing his hair

back from his forehead. "I know you did. It's okay to feel that way. Now, you need to get to sleep. Goodnight, love."

She tucked the covers around him again and got up from the bed. Meghan was in charge of the creche tonight; she nodded to Sabina from across the large room where she was reading to Cheri and Omar. Sabina went to the door of the creche, turning around again to look at Beiri.

"Good night," she called out to him again.

But he was already asleep.

JOURNAL ENTRY:

Gabriela Rusack

I'M LEAVING THESE BOOKS HERE FOR TWO REASONS. First, I doubt that anyone back on the Rock is particularly interested in anything I have to say, especially regarding the Miccail. "But they're *dead*, Gab," was Jean's constant rejoinder to me whenever I tried to interest him in my findings. "And they've *been* dead for over a thousand years. Who the hell cares about them?"

Even Adari, who loved me so briefly, might sit there smiling patiently while I prattled on about my precious Miccail, but I could see that she didn't care and I was really only talking to myself. So I leave my journals here because—if someone ever reads these words—then you (whoever you are) were *here* too, and I have some small hope that you came because of curiosity, because you thought that the Miccail, even dead, might teach us something.

Because you might have some *passion* for the past.

And I leave them here because, frankly, I don't trust the others. Because I fear—perhaps egotistically—that the writings of the Crow, the *rezu*, the *una tortillera*, might one day be considered too dangerous to read and they might destroy them.

I don't want to see my words, which are the only offspring I leave to Mictlan, burned like the bodies of the dead.

VOICE:
Máire Koda-Schmidt

❧ "SO . . . IS IT INTERESTING?"

Ana sat cross-legged on the stone-flagged floor, reading Gabriela's journal in the light of the fire, while Elio slept nearby. I came up behind her, wrapping my arms around her shoulders and pulling her back against me. Ana let the book go and leaned back into the embrace. "Mmm, that feels nice. *Hai*, it's interesting. Very."

"What's she say?"

"A little bit of everything. Whatever came to her mind. There's no real structure; it's a hodgepodge collection of her thoughts and observations, all jumbled together. But some of it . . ."

I could hear the excitement in her voice, which for a moment banished the uneasy state of my stomach. I gave her a quick hug, then sat in front of her so that I could see her face alight with that animation. I held her hands in mine, enjoying the feel of them. "So tell me," I said.

Ana shrugged, looking around. We'd spent the rest of the afternoon exploring the ruins of the temple without finding anything quite so dramatic as the shell and Gabriela's journals, though I'm sure an archeologist would have been endlessly fascinated by the pottery, the remnants of furniture and other everyday minutiae of the Miccail strewn through the site. I'm sure they could have gleaned a few thousand conclusions from the rubble, but to me it looked like so much broken and ancient stuff. With dusk, and knowing that grumblers were lurking about, we'd decided that one of the smaller rooms within the temple complex would be the most defensible site, and we'd set up a camp there. Elio had taken the first watch, then awakened me. Ana, from all appearances, had yet to get any sleep. "I think I would have liked old Gabriela," she said.

"Uh-oh. Now I'm jealous."

Ana smiled at that. "Hush," she said. "And listen. From

the datings in the journals, she spent a lot of time here over the years. She believed that this island was sacred to the Miccail, and she was working to decipher some of the writings on the walls and on the stelae. In fact, she was convinced that the island was where—"

I wasn't listening to Ana, too intent on the rising acid in my throat. Ana noticed, stopping, and her hands pressed mine. "Are you . . . ?" she began, and then touched my forehead. Her hand felt cold, but I was sweating.

"Excuse me," I said, and rushed away. I ran outside the room and bent over a pile of stones as my stomach heaved. Sometime in the middle of it, I felt Ana's hands rubbing my back and shoulders—as the spasms came and then subsided. When I finally spat out the last of it, she handed me a cup of water to rinse my mouth and a soft cloth.

"Thanks," I said, still gasping for air and hating the taste in my mouth. "I'm sorry."

She was staring at me the way she stared at someone arriving in the clinic. "Is this the first time you've been sick since we left the Rock?"

"No," I admitted. "I've had this, off and on, for ten days or so. It started before we left."

"And you didn't tell me."

"You had bigger problems. I thought it would go away by itself."

"Come on back inside where I can see. I want to look at you." She escorted back to the fire, and made me lie down. She probed my abdomen, pressing. "Does it hurt here? Here?"

"No. It doesn't hurt anywhere. Ana, I feel fine now. Really."

Ana sat back on her heels, a strange look on her face. "How long has it been since your last period?" she asked, her voice soft.

I sat up. "Ana, I haven't been with anyone but you."

"How long, Máire?"

"I've skipped a period before, Ana. I have." She didn't answer, waiting for me. "It's been at least forty, fifty days," I told her finally. "Maybe more. I'm not really sure." I gave a mocking laugh. "It wasn't anything I worried about, considering."

Ana nodded. "Lay back," she said, "and let me have a look at you . . ." When she glanced up again, her face was drawn and tight, and the color had drained from her cheeks.

Her hands reached for mine, and our fingers intertwined, clutching tightly. Her eyes searched mine, as if looking for something lost. Her voice, when she spoke, trembled like her hands.

And she told me what I think I already knew but hadn't wanted to admit, hadn't dared to believe. She told me what I both wanted and was afraid to hear. She said words that would change me forever. Looking at her face as she spoke, I know the words changed her as well.

"I think," she said, "that you're pregnant, Máire."

Anaïs let go of my hands and sat with shoulders slumped, stunned with her own diagnosis. She blinked, and a tear tracked down her cheek; I reached out to wipe it away and found myself crying as well.

"Máire," she said, clutching at me, her clinical composure gone now and my name quivering on her lips as if she wanted to say more but didn't know how or what. "Oh, Máire . . ."

I held her, cradling her to me like a child.

JOURNAL ENTRY:
Gabriela Rusack

EVERYTHING WE KNOW ABOUT BIOLOGY SAYS THAT "there must be a reason." Back on Earth, with a few minor variations, most higher-level animal life had settled on the usual two-sexed reproductive strategy, as has almost all Mictlanian life. Yet the Miccail stirred another sex into the mix. Evolution might operate on chance mutations, but the midmale clearly gave some evolutionary edge to the Miccail or they wouldn't have come into prominence. At one time, anyway, there were thousands of them here, and after they all disappeared, so, very quickly, did the Miccail civilization.

My hypothesis, in a nutshell, is that the midmale served as some kind of "mutational stabilizer" for the Miccail. This is supported by simply looking at the Mictlanian life, with its rapid genetic changes and evolutionary shifts. Two-sexed animal life *alters* here, very quickly, and for at least several thousand years while the midmales were around, the Miccail did not. Also, much like us, the Miccail evidently suffered from frequent miscarriages and congenital defects in off-spring conceived in the conventional way. Perhaps the mid-male served as a filter for the male ejaculate, culling out the defective sperm and then redepositing the remainder in the female. Perhaps they added some totally unknown hormone to the seminal fluid, or perhaps the Miccail male was missing a few DNA strands that the midmale supplied. Maybe the midmales never made use of the male sperm at all but simply passed on their own genes to the females, serving as a "biological condom" against pregnancy from the regular males.

Or—and perhaps most likely, given my ignorance in biological matters—the reason was something else entirely. I really don't know. What I *do* know is that once the midmales arrived on the scene, the Miccail civilization thrived. Once they were gone, the Miccail fell. Whatever purpose the mid-male served, it seems to have been a rather necessary one.

Which brings me to one last observation, again in a nutshell. *The Miccail are not gone.* Not in the strict biological sense, anyway. Their civilization lies in ruins, the midmales have vanished, and there are no more grand stele-makers and builders left on this world. But . . . I believe the Miccail still exist: much different, and like all Mictlanian life much changed in this world over the centuries.

The grumblers are the Miccail.

Even as I write that down, I'm shaking my head, not wanting to believe it. After all, we considered them nothing more than beasts, treating them no better than our ancestors may have treated wolves, bears, or lions—tolerated as long as they left us alone, but dumb creatures to be killed if they become a threat to our safety. I must have killed a half dozen grumblers in the first few years of my shunning, and for each one, I cut a small notch in the wooden stock of my rifle as a reminder. I thought I was marking my prowess, changing my weapon into a totem of power—as gunfighters and soldiers had done since the dawn of time, as the Miccail did with their stelae.

When I came here to the island, I found grumblers. For the most part, we left each other alone, but I watched them, and the grumblers *here*, at least, were more than the two-legged beasts I saw near the Rock. I saw a complex tribal organization. I heard language, and I witnessed them performing rites in the temple building where the midmales once gathered—simple rites, *hai*, but definitely not animal behavior.

I realize now that each of those cuts in my rifle was a notch in my own soul, that I had whittled away something of myself each time, and that—like the chips of wood I'd discarded—those lost pieces could never really be put back.

We've been murdering the Miccail all along, unknowing.

CONTEXT:
Tozo Koda-Shimmura

"WE SHOULD GO GET THEM AND BRING THEM back," Tozo declared. "I know that I voted with you on this, Dominic. You were very convincing with all your charts and graphs and your zeal. But ever since I've had troubled dreams. I believe the *kami* are telling me that I made a mistake."

Tozo knew that Dominic had always seemed a little frightened of her, as if her devotion to *Njia* and her claims that she could actually hear the spirit-voices of the land somehow threatened him. That attitude showed now in the way his gaze kept finding her eyes and then sliding away again. But he also wasn't about to admit it. His six-fingered hand curled around the knob of his cane, and the corners of his mouth tightened and turned down. The smell of Tozo's incense, burning atop the Miccail stele in her room, seemed to bother him—and that made Tozo less inclined to snuff it out, as she might have with someone else. She leaned forward and touched the stones in front of the stele, enjoying the way the firelight played through the translucent webbing between her fingers.

"*Bah*," Dominic grunted, his eyes watching her movements suspiciously. "You and your *kami*. What you're saying is that you're feeling guilty, that's all. The decision was correct. It was the only good decision we could make under the circumstances."

Tozo's wrinkled, snouted face tightened. "I've listened to

the *kami*'s voices," she persisted. "I've meditated. And I've heard the whispering of the spirits. We've made a mistake that's still within our power to correct."

"And who are these *kami* that talk to you so often?" Dominic answered derisively.

"I don't know," Tozo answered quietly. "They're just . . . there."

"Or would this have something more to do with the fact that you're Adari's daughter? Maybe you're just feeling guilty because it was your mam who caused Gabriela to be Shunned."

"Next you'll be digging out those old rumors about me actually being Gabriela's daughter by a transplanted egg."

"No," Dominic sniffed. "I don't believe that any more than you do. That's garbage. But the truth is that your mam Adari was once Gabriela's lover. So it doesn't surprise me that you're having second thoughts."

"And you're not?" Tozo smiled gently at him, mostly because Dominic usually expected his confrontational demeanor to spark anger in return, and he always seemed so annoyed when people reacted calmly. "Elio's out there with her, Domi."

The reminder brought Dominic's head up sharply. "The damn pup made his choice. He'll live with it, or die with it. I don't care which."

"I don't believe that's the way you really feel, Dominic. He's Family, and I know you care about that, if nothing else."

At that, Dominic's back went stiff in his chair. The cane tapped once, twice on the floor. "That's what you believe, eh? Then your precious *kami* have told you wrong again, Tozo. Elio has chosen that abomination over his Family. Indeed, because of their decision, he and Máire have become a threat to all the Families. They are no better than grumblers to me."

Dominic leaned back in his chair again, his face grim. "So, Tozo, tell me. How do your goddamn *kami* feel about that?" he asked.

VOICE:
Anaïs Koda-Levin the Younger

I LOOK AT MÁIRE, AND I FEEL SO LOST, SO CONFUSED. She tells me that she hasn't been with anyone except me for months, and I believe her. And she is pregnant. I'm as certain of that as I can be without running the blood work.

But *that* means . . .

Oh hell, I don't know what that means, and that's the frightening part. I'm *female*. That's the Anaïs I know, the Anaïs I understand. I've spent my life fighting to create that identity and denying that it could be any other way—that's what Geema Anaïs told me, that's what Hui told me. If Máire's child is also mine, then I really don't know who I am or what I've become, and I feel very, very lost. I don't know how to live with an Anaïs who is also a male.

I know that I look at Máire, and she smiles with our secret, happy with it, comfortable with it, pleased with it. There's a child growing inside her, curled in the tidal heat of her womb, connected to her and with her, and that's something she welcomes. She smiles at me because she's happy and because she believes that somehow, impossibly, it must also be *my* child.

I smile in return, but it's a lie.

I can't be the father. I don't have the biological equipment. No testes; therefore, no spermatozoa. The miniature clitoral penis doesn't mean anything. I'm not a male. I'm not. I can't be the father.

I can't be the father, but I know who must be, then. I'm certain of it.

Elio.

It's Occam's Razor. The simplest explanation. Simpler, anyway, than divine intervention, which would seem to be the only other possibility. I've been making love to both of them. Since I can't produce the sperm myself, I must have somehow transferred Elio's to Máire. And having autopsied the midmale bog body back at the clinic, and now reading Gabriela's journal, I'm half convinced that I even know some of the how.

Not why. Not any of the other half a hundred questions that come to mind.

But how.

And that scares me more than anything else. Because then I'm not female, nor am I male. I'm something else. Something else. And there's no pattern for me, no ground, no center.

VOICE:
Elio Allen-Shimmura

ANA AND I SLEPT TOGETHER WHILE MÁIRE WAS ON watch, and for the first time since we came to the island, we made love. During our lovemaking, Anaïs was fierce, almost desperate. She pushed against me, her legs around my waist, clutching me with her arms, her eyes closed so tightly shut that skin furrowed from the corners. When she found release, she gasped almost as if she were in pain, burrowing her head into my neck.

Afterward, we curled together. I kissed her forehead and the tip of her nose, and she gave me a wan smile. "You look so sad," I said. "Was it that bad?"

"No." She attempted another smile, with pretty much the same results. "It was fine. Really it was."

"Uh-huh. Does your mood have to do with what's going on between you and Máire?"

She looked startled at that. Her eyes widened as if I'd just touched a nerve, and then, a second too late, she tried nonchalance, giving me a quizzical "What do you mean?"

"Well, I'm not sure what's going on with you two, but I know something is. First, Máire's been acting oddly happy and satisfied for someone who's abandoned everything and everyone she's known for subsistence living outside the Rock. And you . . . you're totally distracted, Ana. We've spent, what, four days here now, and ever since the first night, your mind's been somewhere else. In the last few days, I've found you crouching before a Miccail stele or sitting with Gabriela's journal on your lap, but you're not looking at the stele or reading. You're just staring. Thinking. What are you thinking about, Ana?"

"Nothing," she answered, then bit her lower lip and shrugged. "Everything. I'm just trying to make sense of it all. That's it."

"Make sense of what, Ana? The Miccail? Gabriela's journals?"

"Just . . . everything." Her hands trailed down my side, stopping warm on my hip. "Elio, I can't tell you anything more. Not right now, anyway."

"So there *is* more. Hah."

Again, the smile. This time it was nearly successful. "*Hai*," she said. "There's more. I promise you'll be one of the two people I tell."

"Oh, right. That makes me feel special." I said it lightly, not wanting her to take offense. I was rewarded with a short, quick laugh that faded all too soon.

There was a rustle at the opening of the room we'd commandeered for our own, and I saw Máire's face appear, ruddy with firelight. "I hope you two are finished. We have some company: our grumblers are back. Bring your guns and come on." With that, she was gone again. Ana and I scrambled out of bed and into our clothes, snatching up our rifles on the way out.

Máire was just outside the room, behind a tumbled pile of stone that had once been a wall of the main temple. "Over there," she whispered, pointing toward the temple's main entrance. "See them?"

Longago and Faraway were both up, coating the ruins in silver and giving everything a double shadow. For a brief instant, the sight of the moons reminded me that back on the Rock, there'd be a Gather tonight, but then I saw the shell's polished surface glinting hypnotically, and it brought me back. In the moons' light, we could see two grumblers. They were muttering to each other just inside the broken archway. One was the old silverback male; the other might have been one of the two males that had accompanied the ancient one before—I couldn't be certain. Silverback was flinging his arms wide, as if making some point, gesturing toward the shell and—just coincidentally, I hoped—us.

"Whatever he's saying, he's being damned emphatic about

it," I said. My voice sounded hoarse from the effort of trying to be quiet. I resisted the impulse to clear my throat. "So what's the plan here?"

"We watch," Anaïs said. "There's no reason to do anything else."

She was right. In the last several days, we'd surveyed the island, at least superficially. I wasn't comfortable as we roamed, knowing that grumblers were living somewhere close by, but though we saw them once or twice a day, they never came too close, never made a threatening move toward us. They watched us much the same way we watched them now, warily.

"How long have they been there, Máire?" Ana asked.

"Not more than a few minutes. I came and got you two as soon as I noticed them."

The grumblers had stopped arguing, if that's what they were doing. The old one made a final gesticulation toward the interior of the temple and began walking toward the shell and us. After a moment, his companion followed. I put the barrel of my rifle on top of the stones and sighted down the barrel, keeping them in the notched sight. I thought they'd stop at the shell, as they had the last time. Silverback did pause there, running his hand across the shell's surface, and I heard the distinct *clack* of his claws stroking the hard mother-of-pearl exterior, the sound loud in the night stillness.

But then he let his hand drop, and he took a few more steps toward us, though the younger male hung behind.

He stopped, midstride.

His nostrils quivered. I couldn't see his normal eyes, too shadowed under the heavy ridges of his face, but the open third eye stared blindly, lidlessly upward, stark white in the moonlight. Ana, Máire and I stood motionless, holding our breaths. The grumbler was not more than six or seven meters away. I could have dropped him, one shot, and taken out the other with the next. My finger hugged the trigger, the metal briefly cold but warming quickly.

The old one was staring at Anaïs. I swear he was. Without otherwise moving, he raised his left arm palm up toward us, toward her. His long, slightly webbed fingers were curled, and I could see the tips of the claws in their knobby sheaths at the end of those fingers. His hand trembled slightly, as if with some palsy. He croaked something: a word, maybe, or maybe just a sound. When none of us moved or reacted, he

271

repeated the sound, louder this time. *Sa-ah*, a throaty breath.

I heard the rustling of movement alongside me. "Ana . . ." I said, not taking my eyes away from the rifle. On the other side of her, I heard Máire's urgent whisper: "Ana, stay down."

She didn't listen. Ana was standing now, the moonlight washing over her. The grumbler seemed to hiss, the double tongue snaking out over its lips and then retreating. He repeated the word once more, softer now—*Sa-ah*—and he brought his hand together over his stomach, as if holding a large ball in front of him. He leaned his head back and howled once, as if in pain, and sank to his knees. His arms came together, a cradling gesture, and then he held his hand out to Anaïs once more.

"*Sa-ah*," he said.

"He's asking me to come with him," Ana said.

"That's one interpretation," I told her. "My bet is that they probably need a main course for dinner. *Sa-ah*: that means 'tasty entrée.' Ana, you're not seriously considering this, are you?"

"He's telling us something about the pregnant female," Máire said. She was looking at Ana strangely. "That's what it looks like to me. Maybe she's in labor."

"Tell him to find his own damn doctor," I answered. "Ours is taken."

The grumbler still had his hand out. He rose awkwardly, stiffly, to his feet again. Anaïs took a step away from the cover of the stones. "Ana, don't," Máire said. "Ana . . ."

"You read Gabriela's journal, both of you. These aren't animals, these are the Miccail." Another step, toward the grumbler this time.

"*Khudda*," I muttered, hugging the rifle tightly and trying to keep one eye also on the younger male, who was still back by the shell. "Ana, don't get too near him."

Seeing her, the grumbler let his hand drop to his side. He made no move as she approached behind a widening of nostrils. I watched Silverback's hands; I watched the terrible ripping claw on his feet. If he'd so much as twitched, I'd have blown him into history, no matter what Gabriela might conjecture about them.

Anaïs took two more slow steps toward the grumbler as we held our breaths. I glanced quickly at Máire, who had her own rifle up to her shoulder. "Ana, remember what happened to Euzhan," I called out. "Come on back here." If the grumbler laid Anaïs open the way Euzhan had been, she would die here. I suddenly realized how precarious *all* our lives were out here, and how even more fragile they'd be without Anaïs. "Ana, please . . ." Máire called.

"I'm okay," she answered without looking back. "Just don't do anything back there to alarm him." The grumbler's head was shifting from Anaïs to Máire and myself, and his snout wrinkled as he exhaled in an explosive *huff*. "It's fine," she crooned to the grumbler in the reassuring tones she might use with her verrechat. "Everything's just fine."

Anaïs lifted her arm, imitating the grumbler's gesture and reaching out toward him. The grumbler blinked, and then he brought his arm up in kind. Only a few centimeters of air separated them, and Anaïs shuffled forward again. Their fingers touched.

The grumbler's hand lifted as if he was shocked by the feel of her skin, and I saw the knobby ends flex as his claws emerged slightly from their sheaths. "I'm fine," Ana called again, sensing that Máire and I were both about to remove the threat. In the moonlight, I could see the claws dimple the skin of her fingertips, but he didn't extend them fully or dig in. The claws flexed, almost kneading, pulling her toward him slightly, and she went easily with the motion, taking another step. She was now standing directly in front of him. The grumbler could have slashed her with one motion, or kicked out with its feet to eviscerate her. My whole body was trembling from the strain and adrenaline rush. Anaïs had blocked off my shot to the grumbler's chest, and I didn't know now if I even dared to fire for fear that I'd hit Ana. I heard Máire cursing and trying to move to the side to get a better line.

"Ana, I'd really, really like you to take a step back," I said. "Slowly. You're way too close."

"I'm fine, Elio." The grumbler was hunching over, looking at her, his head tilting from one side to the other. His hands moved to touch her, and Anaïs stood still and unprotesting as his fingers roamed her body, touching breasts, waist, and crotch. He seemed frustrated by her clothing, and finally stopped. He cupped his hands around an imaginary pregnancy once again, grimacing with his lips drawn back from his snout, and then shuffled away from Anaïs until he reached the shell and his companion. There, he waited.

"I'm going with him," Anaïs said. "That's what he wants."

Máire and I glanced at each other. "You think you can stop her?" Máire asked me. "I know I can't."

"Then we all go," I said. "You hear that, Ana? All of us."

She glanced back at us finally. Her face was pale, and the moons laid soft shadows like scarves over her shoulders. "I don't know. . . . The grumblers—"

"Don't have a choice," I finished for her. "He gets all three of us, or none. Agreed? Máire?"

"*Hai*," Máire answered. "Anaïs, I'm not losing you. Not now." Máire's voice sounded choked, and she was blinking hard. Anaïs sighed and nodded.

"All right. Máire, please go get my medical pack and bring it along. We may need it."

We followed the grumblers out of the temple. The young one darted ahead and was gone, but Silverback moved slowly and deliberately, glancing behind now and again to make certain we were behind. For us, we followed at a few paces back. I half expected a pack of grumblers to leap from cover, attacking us from all sides. Even out in the open, the feeling wouldn't go away. The double moons drifted in clouds, and the tumbled ruins of the island looked surreal, like a stage setting in a play. I just didn't want us to be the hapless victims killed off in the first act. We moved from the main temple level to a set of jumbled steps leading up to the next terrace. There, the old one ducked into an ancient, doorless building and disappeared. I stopped. "I'll go first," I said.

"They want me, Elio," Anaïs said.

"I know, but if I get hurt, you can fix me. If *you* get hurt, we're in trouble." Anaïs didn't argue with that, and Máire hadn't made any protest in any case. Wishing my altruism didn't make so much damned sense, I took a breath and stepped inside, poking the snout of the rifle into the interior first.

The smell was the first thing that hit me: a warm, animal musk. There were three grumblers in the large room: Silverback, the young male, and the female. She was crouching in one corner, legs widespread, with splatters of dark blood staining the ground below her. She didn't look up as I entered. Panting, she moaned softly, a keening mewl of pain. Her furred skin was matted with sweat, and her body trembled, shivering. The male went over to her, sitting behind her to give her support, leaning her body back against his own. The old one just stared at me. I stared back. Without losing eye contact and keeping my rifle discreetly aimed somewhere around his knees where I could pull it up quickly, I called out: "Anaïs, Máire, come on in."

Anaïs entered, hesitated only a few seconds, then rushed over to the female. "Poor thing," she said. "Máire, I'll need the kit; El, can you get a fire going so I can see better?"

"Do you know what you're doing?" I asked.

"Not really," she answered. "But I figure I'm going to learn." She looked at me. "You're not going to be much help holding that rifle."

"Ana . . ."

She didn't answer, just turned toward the female again. I sighed, eyeing the ancient. He didn't look like an immediate threat, watching Anaïs intently with his odd triple gaze. I swung the rifle to my back and made sure that the strap was loose enough to make it easy to bring forward again. "What can I do?"

"Get the fire going, first of all. Máire, is there an everlight in the pack? Shine it here, please . . . Oh damn, I see the problem. The pup's breech and stuck. I'm going to try to turn him. Elio, give me a hand. I think this will be easier for everyone if mam's laying down."

Anaïs reached for the female's legs, trying to ease them out so the grumbler could lay down. The male holding her suddenly hissed, and I saw claws. Ana tumbled backward, and I scrambled away, trying to get to my weapon. Behind me, I heard Máire rushing for her rifle, on the ground beside Anaïs's medical pack. "No!" Ana shouted. "Take it easy, everyone."

The male's claws were still out, but he hadn't moved away from the female. Silverback barked something angry and short, but he was looking at the male, not us. There was an exchange of barks and hisses, and then the younger male's shoulders drooped slightly. The claws disappeared into the fingertip pads again.

"Good," Anaïs said. "That's better. Now let's see what we can do . . ."

Half-crawling, she moved forward again and started to ease the female down. I went and helped her, keeping one paranoid eye on the male. Anaïs crouched between the female's legs, while Máire focused the everlight for her. I gathered a few sticks into a heap over some dried grass for tinder, and fumbled in my pocket for a packet of matches. The sulfurous flare, when I struck one against stone, caused old Silverback to grumble and put his crooked spine to the wall. I blew on the flames, gently coaxing them to life, until a slow warmth and flickering light filled the room. "Ana?"

"Getting there. Almost . . . *Hai*. That should do it." Her hands were bloodstained halfway to the elbows. The female howled, and then arced her back in a quick spasm. "That's it," Anaïs said. "Just once more . . ."

The female grunted again, bearing down, and then gave a long, warbling cry.

"So much for the idea that the Miccail were true marsupials," Ana said softly. "They're definitely placental. If this one's any example, the babies are a lot smaller than ours, though—but I guess they need to be fairly small to fit into the youngpouch. Máire, could I have scissors? Thanks." Anaïs cut the umbilical, tied it, and then wiped the newborn with the cloth Máire handed her. The infant looked like it had been dipped in curdled milk, and its chest heaved with the effort of breathing. When Anaïs slid a finger inside its mouth to clean it, it suddenly cried, sounding far more feline than human in its distress.

"Everything all right?" I asked, noticing that Anaïs had abruptly stopped cleaning the grumbler infant. She was frowning, tight lines at the ends of her mouth. She didn't answer me. She gave the infant to the female, who took it eagerly with soft grunts, and then started her own examination of the infant. "Boy or girl?" I asked.

Ana looked at me. At Máire. "Neither," she answered. "And both."

Before I could make sense of that, the female howled excitedly. She was holding up her child, who wriggled in her spidery hands, squawling softly. Silverback came rushing over as her mate leaned down, taking the child from her, cradling it for a moment and then handing it carefully to the old grumbler. Silverback turned the infant front to back, and then placed the crying infant against his chest. He repeated once more the word he'd said back in the temple: *"Sa-ah!"* Still holding the baby, he lifted back his head, sending a long, articulated yowl into the night. As he gave the child back to its mother, we heard the call repeated, faintly, from outside, echoing in darkness. It danced from terrace to terrace, taken up by new voices each time, and the sound of the grumbler chorus bristled the hair at the back of my neck.

I stared down at the tableau in front of me—the female and her child, the male and the ancient silverback—and I shivered.

CONTEXT:
Ghost

THE SHRILL PIPING OF THE GATHER'S MUSICIANS INterfered with the audio pickup, as if the audio connection was loose. Ghost adjusted the input filters, dampening the worst of the distortion. A large smear trailed over the projector's main lens, and everything Ghost saw swam by slightly out of focus. She'd have to mention to someone that it was definitely time for some maintenance work.

She had deliberately chosen to appear as Gabriela this evening, and was pleased when Dominic did a slow doubletake when he first saw her standing at the edge of the crowd watching the dancers. "Ghost," he said, hobbling over to her. "I didn't know you'd be here tonight."

"Just trying to see if I can get lucky with one of our young women."

"That's in incredibly poor taste."

"So were the files I downloaded a bit ago. So you've shunned her, finally."

Dominic couldn't keep all the satisfaction from showing in his face, but at least he seemed to try. "That was the decision of the Elder Council, not just me." He watched the people dancing for a time, nodding his head to music and clapping when the tune ended and the dancers changed for the next song. "Do you know where they've gone?" he asked finally.

"Is that concern I hear in your voice, Dominic? Is it for Anaïs and Máire too, or only Elio?"

Dominic's nose wrinkled, his eyes narrowed. "Just answer the damned question, Ghost. I didn't ask for conversation."

"I don't know where they are. I don't have any remaining optics on the *Ibn Battuta* that can resolve down to that scale. Sorry."

"It doesn't matter." Dominic sniffed. "It's cold tonight," he said. "I heard grumblers out near the river earlier, and they seemed louder than usual. Is there a front coming in?"

"Ahh, so we're on to weather now. That should be safe. Dominic, really—it's all right if you care; it shows you're human."

Dominic rounded on Ghost, so quickly that he had to steady himself with his cane. Around them, people turned to watch, suddenly curious. "What we did, we *had* to do," Dominic said loudly. "I acted to protect my Family, and all the Families on the Rock. I don't need to make any apologies for that. I *won't* make any."

With the anger, dampers cut in and Ghost's voice went soft and almost conciliatory. She let her image fall away into static for a moment, then returned as Dominic's brother Marco. "I understand, Dominic," he said. "You obviously convinced the Elders of that, too. You did what you saw as your duty, and no one can blame you for that. And by the way, there's a strong high coming in from the west, and I expect you're going to have a few unseasonably warm days . . ."

JOURNAL ENTRY:
Gabriela Rusack

SIMPLE FAITH ISN'T ONE OF MY ATTRIBUTES. FAITH takes the soul by its lapels and shakes it; faith is thunderbolts and lightning and a hurricane wind; faith grabs your gut, shivers your vision, and paints bold patterns on your world. *Believe me!* faith shouts inside you, and the reverberation makes your heart ring in answer. Faith drives your actions whether they're right or wrong, not because what you're doing makes sense, but only because it resonates with your beliefs.

Faith doesn't need or even desire knowledge. In fact, knowledge is often its mortal enemy.

Faith is dangerous, both for the believer and those who fail to believe as you do.

Some of us (of all sorts of various and contradictory beliefs) obviously possess that ability. I'm not one. I am Skeptic. I am the Crow, my voice the ragged *caw* of scorn.

But I know the Miccail midmales believed. They had a faith, and that belief in their role within the greater span of life allowed them to build upon this island, and that same faith in a world that transcended their own individual lives allowed them to depart from it.

I know this because I found the last stele the midmales carved. It's a small thing, tiny in comparison to its vast importance in the history of the Miccail. Placed near the main temple at the cliff's edge, the stele mutely speaks of the last days of the midmales.

It speaks of faith. Dangerous faith.

INTERLUDE:
AbriSa

DEKTE'S ARMY CAME TO THE SHORE OF ANGLSAIYE Bay later that summer. He and CaraTa stood on the rocky beach and gazed outward at the foggy crags of the island. They blinked at the gleam of the White Temple at its summit, and they heard the sea bells clanging muted in the tides.

They'd expected resistance. They had thought that they'd be confronted by the massed Sa with as many of the TeTa and XeXa as could be mustered, all screaming curses at the conquering invaders. They had expected the smoke and grim fear of battle, the wordless clamor and chaos of war. They'd prepared for stern, unforgiving resistance and many casualties.

They'd not expected silence and emptiness.

PirXe had directed the building of boats while they were still three days' travel from AnglSaire, and the army had come to the Endless Water on the back of the river, floating quickly between the trees. There were no Sa boats waiting for them on the salt waves. The bay was quiet and alone. DekTe motioned, and they rowed out to AnglSaiye. Each moment, DekTe expected the silence to break and the inevitable battle to begin, but it never happened: not as they entered AnglSaiye's harbor, not as they cautiously made their way up the frightening cliff stair, not as DekTe and CaraTa themselves reached the summit.

The doors of the White Temple hung wide open, as did the doors of the Sa dwellings. There were no cookfires burning, no noise, no bustling. Only the quiet of emptiness.

"They're gone, all of them," PirXe reported to DekTe and CaraTa. "We've searched the buildings, and it's as if someone came and snatched them up. The furniture's there, all their possessions . . ." PirXe shivered. "I don't understand," he said. "They're gone, all of them."

"All but one," a voice called loudly.

They turned at the sound. A Sa had appeared, standing at the cliff's edge alongside a *nasituda*. "AbriSa," DekTe called. "Where is Kai? Where are the rest of the Sa?"

Abri smiled. "Gone," ke said. "Congratulate yourselves. You've won, you and CaraTa. But the Sa won't be the spoils of your victory. KaiSa has gone to VeiSaTi—I performed ker sacrifice myself at Black Lake. And all the rest of the Sa have followed ker. You'll find their bones down there, in the sea."

"No!" DekTe roared. "It's trickery. A trap. You've hidden yourselves somewhere until you can strike back at us. This is a lie."

Abri shook ker head. "There's no reason for the Sa to lie to you, DekTe. KaiSa never lied to you, nor will I. The Sa are gone."

CaraTa stepped forward to stand next to DekTe. "It doesn't matter," she said. Her *shangaa* fluttered in the wind, the cloth snapping—dark red, the color of mourning for a child lost. "There will be other Sa born, and we will know of them because we rule the lands. There will be no Angl-Saiye to corrupt them and make them think that they're better than the rest of us."

"There will be other Sa born, perhaps," Abri admitted. "But they'll be very few, and you'll fight over them and try to hold them for your own, and you'll have few children of them. Remember that Sa are almost always born only of Sa relationships, and then only rarely. In another generation, maybe two, there will no longer be any Sa at all. VeiSaTi will not permit it."

"VeiSaTi's power has waned. We follow GhazTi, and we are standing on AnglSaiye as its conquerors," CaraTa answered. "Look out there, AbriSa. Turn your head and look at all the lands spread out below: they are ours, AbriSa. Ours." She pointed out over the bay. AbriSa turned to glance at the landscape for a moment before turning back to them, ker mane rippling in the gusts coming from the ocean.

"For a time, perhaps. But not forever." AbriSa took a step backward, so that ke stood on the brink of the precipice. Stones clattered under ker feet and spilled over the cliff's edge, falling into oblivion. "I am the last of the Sa," ke said to them, and ker smile was fierce and terrible. "But I give you this promise from VeiSaTi. The Sa will return when it is time for KaiSa to return to AnglSaiye."

"But you've said that KaiSa is dead." An inner pain marbled DekTe's words, an undertone that brought back to Abri the pain of losing KaiSa, for ke knew that DekTe felt that pain as well. With that empathy came the realization of just how charismatic and powerful DekTe was, and how easy it must have been for KaiSa to be attracted to him. The sadness deepened in Abri, knowing that such incredible power had been wasted.

"Yes, KaiSa is dead," Abri answered. "As I am. I am the last Sa, and I have given you the message I stayed behind to give. You have the TeTa lands, you have AnglSaiye. We leave you to enjoy them while you can."

Still facing them, AbriSa took another deliberate step backward. For a long moment, ke seemed to hang there, one foot on rock, the other trodding air, and then—silently—ke fell. DekTe and CaraTa rushed forward to look down, but there was nothing to see.

At the foot of AnglSaiye, there was only the shifting ribbons of seafoam as the waves crashed against black rocks in their futile, endless rhythm.

VOICE:
Anaïs Koda-Levin the Younger

I CLEANED UP WITH THE WATER ELIO HAD HEATED, and watched as the grumbler female placed the child inside her youngpouch, reaching her hand in to direct him/her to a nipple. Silverback had disappeared outside; the male was still sitting alongside his mate, smoothing her fur with a gentle hand.

They looked happy. They looked as I suspect our own ancestors might have looked back in prehistory. "What now?" Elio asked as I started to pack the medkit.

"We leave," I said. "We're done here."

"They seemed to like what they got," Máire said. I could feel her staring at me. "So will I," she said after a moment. "Whatever the baby might be."

I hadn't expected that. I knew Máire would end up letting Elio know, but I hadn't counted on it being here and now. I thought it would be when we were all together, so that I could say what I needed to say to both of them. But I smiled at her—what else could I do?—and Elio raised his eyebrows. "You're . . ." he began, and Máire nodded.

"*Hai*, I am."

Now Elio was looking at me more than Máire. "Well," he said. He rubbed the pale, blotchy skin of his cheek, and I saw the sudden uneasiness in his stance. "I guess . . . ummm . . . congratulations," he said. "To the two of you."

"To the three of us," I corrected him, and the quizzical look on his face deepened. I could feel the pressure of Máire's gaze as well, but I didn't dare look at her. This wasn't how I wanted to tell them. I'd wanted to think about it further. I'd wanted to do some more investigation to verify my suspicions, but . . .

"The *three* of us?"

"You've both read Gabriela's journals," I told them. "You know how the Miccail reproduced, and you've seen how my body works—both of you have. You can make the same connections and extrapolations I did. As unlikely as it seems on the surface, I'm willing to bet—"

Silverback saved me from further conversation. He came back into the dwelling holding a small hollowed-out gourd. He proferred it to me, indicating that I should take it. I did so; there was liquid in the gourd. I sniffed the herbal scent as Silverback watched me, his head cocked slightly to one side. "Sa-ah ji-tu," he growled.

"You're the doctor, you get the refreshments," Elio said. "You really going to drink that?"

The gourd at least looked clean, and the smell wasn't offensive. "Why not? I don't want to insult them. Besides, I just delivered a midmale; are they going to poison me for that?" *Besides*, I thought, *it keeps the conversation safe for a few more minutes.*

I sipped the brew—it was tepid and bitter, and fragments of whatever herb had made this tea clouded it. There was a sharp aftertaste, but it was no worse than some of the medicinal teas Hui and I made for our patients. Silverback was still watching expectantly, and I drank it down, wondering if that was approval I saw in his eyes. I handed back the gourd, which he took and then tossed absently into a corner. He hobbled arthritically over to the female, who opened her youngpouch and let Silverback reach inside to stroke the infant. The grumblers then proceeded to ignore us entirely.

"I guess we're done here," I said. "I think . . . I guess we need to talk. I especially think I owe you an explanation, Máire, but I want to wait until we're back where we're comfortable. Let's get the—" I stopped. The fire was still glowing, but the flames leaping up from the logs looked to be frozen and the shadows stood still on the tumbled stone walls.

"Ana?" Máire asked. Her voice sounded distant and thin.

No, everything was normal. The flames were licking at the wood once more and the shadows shuddered and moved. "It's nothing. Nothing. Let's get back to our place," I said. I suddenly wanted to be out of there. I felt claustrophobic and closed in. We quickly finished packing and left. Silverback watched us leave; the parents paid us no attention at all.

Outside, the night seemed both brighter and colder than I remembered. The air shattered into crystalline knives in my lungs. Longago had set, but Faraway was like a small, burning sun in the darkness, almost too bright for me to look at. And the stars . . . I'd never noticed the *colors* of them before, so saturated and brilliant, like someone had spattered glowing electric paint across a black canvas. Strangest of all, I could see their movements, too. I blinked hard to make certain, but yes, the stars were moving, a barely perceptible Brownian motion. I couldn't stare at the glorious display for long; it made me dizzy. Still gazing upward, I tried to take a step and stumbled.

"Hey, careful!" Elio cried, and caught my arm.

"Sorry, Elio. I must have tripped over something. Sorry. Isn't the sky beautiful tonight?" I took a breath, leaning on him. The temple was just ahead of us, but it wasn't the ruin it had been. It gleamed white and whole in the moonlight, with strange angles and a tall, knobbed spire that lanced out and up. I thought for a moment that I saw robed figures moving at the entrance, the doors of which were made of thousands of shells arranged in intricate patterns. I could hear them talking, their words just on the edge of understanding. Somewhere inside, a small, centered voice whispered: *The drink . . . some type of hallucinogen . . .*

"Get me inside," I said to Elio and Máire. "I need to sit down . . ."

They rushed me into the temple, one at each arm. None of the robed Miccail paid us the slightest bit of attention, which for some reason didn't strike me as odd. As I collapsed into the blankets and Elio rushed to get the fire going again, I closed my eyes, leaning back. "I'll be fine," I said to Máire's concerned ministrations. "There was something in the drink . . . a psychoactive . . ."

"Ana—"

I waved her hand away, but my hand seemed to pass right through her arm. I could see a red pulsing in Máire's chest, and a smaller, more rapid one in her belly. Small bloody stars in the universe. "It'll pass, but the next few hours might be difficult. Just . . . just don't let me hurt myself or any of you. Do you understand?"

"*Hai*. The grumblers—"

I shook my head, but it felt like I was dragging a cannonball through water. "Leave them alone. I don't think they meant to—"

I stopped talking, since Máire wasn't there anymore. In the darkness in front of me, there were only two throbbing points of scarlet. I thought that if I reached out just a little bit, I could touch them—and I did, taking one into each hand. They were warm, and beat in my palms with their two varied rhythms, like drummers playing different songs. Their light brightened with each beat, enveloping me in a ruddy air, and then shattered into white, falling away like petals of ice. The hoarfrost slowly melted in front of me, and I saw the midmale bog body as it had been when we first pulled it from the peat, dark and folded. I reached out to touch—my hand encountered no resistance, going into the skin like I'd reached into a pan of water . . . blood-warm water, for its skin was the same temperature as mine. I tried to pull my hand back, but I couldn't—it would let me go forward, but not back. Never back.

Because I had no choice, I closed my eyes and dove into the bundled skin. . . .

... I came to the surface for air, bubbles cascading around me. In my hands, I held a large wriggling eel, and I heaved it into the boat. The midmale there smiled at me, helping me out of the salty swells ...

... and onto the Rock. I was standing naked on the peak above the Compounds, near where the Miccail stelae leaned into the wind, and my body was not mine, but that of a midmale. Dominic was there also, and a grumbler. They were fighting, the two of them, bloodied and furious, and they rolled on the stony ground near the cliff edge. "No!" I cried to the two of them. "Stop it!" but they were at the cliff's edge. I ran forward, grasping both of them, but they were already falling, and as they clutched at me, I clutched at the Rock in desperation. The Rock shuddered under my desperate grip and broke asunder ...

... and we fell into the sea and the part of the Rock I held became an island, *the* island, and I stood on it. The temple was there, gleaming white, and one of the midmales came out to join me at the cliff's edge. I recognized her/him, somehow. I felt comfortable in her/his presence. Together, we held hands, and leaped from the cliff ...

... soaring over the land ...
... the highroads whole beneath ...
... the sounds of laughter, of children ...
... of children ...
... and more ... much more ...

"Anaïs?"

I blinked, gasping as if I'd been holding my breath. A face drifted in front of me, almost colorless after the dazzling hues of the dreamscape. "Máire?" I felt someone touching my forehead with a soft cloth. "How long?"

"It's daylight," she said softly. "You were out for several hours. How are you?"

"I'm..." I took inventory. "... fine." My voice sounded weak and ragged. I wondered if I'd been shouting in my dreams. "I think so, anyway. Where's Elio?"

"Here," he answered. I turned my head to see him sitting near the door, the rifle across his lap. His face was grim and exhausted, dark circles under his eyes, and I knew he hadn't slept all night. "Now that I know you're all right, I'm going out," he said. He rose, checking the clip on the weapon and slamming it back into place.

"No, Elio," I said, struggling to rise. My legs didn't seem to want to cooperate, having gone to sleep. I gritted my teeth against the tingling. "They didn't intend to hurt me. That wasn't why they gave me the drink."

"They have a fucking odd reward system, then."

"Did you expect them to act human? They're not. I'm all right, Elio. Better than I was before. I finally know what we have to do."

"And you got your answer from hallucinations? That's comforting."

I was too tired to be irritated with him. I took Máire's hand in one of mine, and held the other out for Elio. He grimaced, then finally came over and touched my fingers with his own.

"We have to go back to the Rock," I said, looking at each of them. "We have a gift to give them—whether they want it or not."

CONTEXT:
Euzhan Allen-Shimmura

BECAUSE THE WEATHER HAD BEEN WARMER FOR A few days, several of the adults had gone down to the river to seine for fish before the river iced over completely for the winter. Gan-Li had taken Euzhan and Hizo down to watch. Euzhan thought that the flotilla of boats with their nets was interesting for a while, but not much happened and Gan-Li was more interested in flirting with some of the young men on the riverbank than in entertaining Hizo and her. For a while, they tossed rocks into the river, but Hizo was older and could throw farther and it wasn't much fun after the first few times. They began to explore the riverbank, with Gan-Li keeping one eye on them and the other on the boys.

Euzhan found a nest of spindle-legs. She called Hizo, and they hunkered down in front of the nest, teasing the long-legged, palm-sized insects with sticks. They poked them until they reared up with their front two legs, batting back and snapping at them as they glared with their huge, multifaceted triple eyes. Hizo leaned too close, and one of the spindle-legs nipped his finger.

"Ouch!" Hizo shook his finger, sending the spindle-leg flying while Euzhan laughed. "That's it," Hizo said to the insect, sucking at the droplet of blood that oozed from the puncture wound. "You're shunned."

The offending spindle-leg was trying to get back to the nest; Hizo flicked it away with his stick. The insect returned again, and Hizo sent it tumbling again. And again. Euzhan giggled. "It doesn't like being shunned."

"Huh." Hizo looked around and found a large flat rock. Lifting it, he held it over the spindle-leg as it crawled back toward the nest. "You stupid Anaïs," he told it.

He dropped the rock.

"There," Hizo said. He looked at Euzhan, who was staring at the rock. "What's the matter, Euz?"

Euzhan lifted the rock—the spindle-leg was crushed and dead, a greenish goop seeping from the thorax. She let the rock drop again and then threw away her stick. "I don't think I want to play anymore," she said. "This isn't fun."

VOICE:

Anaïs Koda-Levin the Younger

HUI HAD OFTEN TOLD ME THAT IN LIFE, AS IN MEDicine, there was rarely a single right choice. "No decision I've ever made has been totally black or white, good or bad," he said. "That only happens in fairy tales. Every damn *real* judgment contains shades of gray and adverse consequences. Every decision is to some extent the wrong one. You can go with the percentages or you can go with your heart or you can just roll some goddamn dice—it really doesn't matter. Just be prepared to deal with things if it goes sour."

We argued about my decision to return to the Rock. Elio agreed that we had information that the Rock needed to hear, but he wanted to go alone to tell them. "You don't know what Geeda Domi might try to do to you," he said. "You're a nonperson now. If you're lucky, no one will talk to you. If you're not, they may hurt you or worse."

I scoffed. "Come on, Elio. I don't believe that."

"Believe it. If Masa had raped and then killed you, Geeda would have said that it was just the *kami* balancing the scales for Ochiba. Don't underestimate his hatred, Ana. I know him, and that's always a dangerous tactic."

"We don't need to go back at all," Máire interjected. "None of us. Fuck them. They ran you out and they won't welcome you back, Ana. Elio's right about that. But there's only three of us—soon to be four—and we can't *afford* to split up. I say we all stay here."

" 'Soon to be four,' " I quoted back to her. "And what then, Máire? What do we do with your son or daughter? Down the road when they become sexually active, where do they go, who do they see? We can't stay out here. At the very least, *you* can't. I want you back in the Rock: where Hui can look after you, where there's a Family for you."

"Then send Máire back, and I'll stay here," Elio said.

"And then there's only two of you, and Ana's my lover also," Máire retorted. "I don't like that idea at all."

And on and on. . . . In the end, I could see that Hui was right, and so I listened to my heart and the lingering vision the grumbler had given me. *I'm going back*, I told them. *You can come with me, or you can stay. But I'm going back.* . . .

As I'd hoped, as soon as Elio and Máire realized that my decision was firm they simply loaded up their packs and prepared to leave. I don't know if I really would have been strong enough to go without them. I certainly didn't care to try it.

And we picked up a companion as we departed.

Even though we'd waited another day, I still felt some residual disorientation from Silverback's potion. Every once in a while, I'd hear a sound or see something out of the corner of my eye, and I wouldn't know if it was real or fantasy. When we noticed the old grumbler waiting for us outside the temple, I'd thought perhaps that he was a hallucination as well, except that Elio and Máire both saw him. He shadowed us over the broken ground to the top of the stairs, maybe ten paces behind.

Silverback followed us down the cliffside steps, shambling slowly behind us, never too close, never too far away. Elio kept glancing back over his shoulder despite the height and the precipitous drop to his left, and he grumbled more than the old grumbler. "All he has to do is rush us and we're all dead," he said. "All he has to do is *stumble*."

"Worry about yourself, Elio," I told him. "We can't do anything about him. Just keep going."

I think the descent was worse than the climb up. We looked down over the entire impressive expanse of the stairs, from clifftop to the mist of the breaking waves far, far below. The black rock sparkled and shimmered in the sunlight . . . at least I think it did. Real or not, it was still unnerving. I hugged the cliff wall and moved slowly, trying not to think about the several hundred meter sheer drop just a step away. We didn't talk, any of us, just concentrated on getting down safely.

It took just a few minutes short of forever to reach the bottom.

The boat was still there and still dry—a definite plus, since I had no idea how we'd manage to build another craft here. Máire was already in, waiting for us. Elio stepped onto the docking area a minute later. "He's still back there," Elio said.

"Then let's get moving," Máire said. "Come on!"

We threw our packs in, Elio and I grabbed the oars and we shoved away into the rolling swells. As we paddled away from the island, we saw Silverback reach the bottom of the stair and step out on the flat rocks.

"All right," Elio crowed. He stopped rowing to gesture obscenely to the grumbler. "You're damn lucky I didn't kill you, you son of a bitch." The grumbler bellowed something. He waved his arms back at Elio, looking at us and then back at the stairs. As we continued to row away, he paced the docking stone, going to the very edge where the bay lapped at the ancient workings.

And then he jumped in.

"*Khudda!*" Elio shouted. "Damn it, he's in the water."

And he could swim. I stopped rowing to watch, and we saw the grumbler put his head down and begin to paddle toward us with strong strokes. The long-fingered and webbed hands pulled him through the water with surprising ease. "Row!" Elio shouted to me, and we dug at the choppy water with our oars.

We pulled away, but the grumbler continued to follow—as we moved from the shelter of the small island harbor, as the first long swells of the bay hit us and the wind pulled foamy whitecaps from the water. Silverback followed, persistent, but falling further and further behind. He stopped once, treading water and obviously tiring, and I thought he might turn back then. A moment later, he was churning water again in pursuit, but more slowly now, his strokes erratic.

"He's in trouble," I said. "He's exhausted."

"Then he'll go back," Elio said.

"No, I don't think he will."

"Ana, you can't be seriously thinking about going back for him." Salt spray had dappled Elio's beard, and he blinked the stinging spray away. "We can't bring him in the boat. It's too dangerous."

"As dangerous as going back to the Rock?" I asked him, and then glanced at Máire, holding the rudder. "Máire?"

"Elio's right," she said. "If he's in the boat, and he decides to attack . . ."

"Not to mention the whole problem of getting him *in* the boat," Elio added. "I don't want to capsize out here—I swim a whole hell of a lot worse than that grumbler."

"Then he can at least hold onto the side for support. Elio, you can keep your rifle ready. If he makes an aggressive move, you can deal with him. But I don't want to just let him drown. Look at the poor thing."

I gestured out to where Silverback was floundering, flailing at the water rather than swimming. Elio looked at Máire, who shrugged. "All right," Elio said. "But I want you to know that if he so much as looks at us wrong, I'm going to send him to the fishes. I don't trust them, Ana. I especially don't trust *him*, not after what he did to you."

"He gave me a vision," I told Elio. "Maybe it was what I needed." I picked up the oar again. "Let's go get him," I said. "Though I have the feeling wet grumbler isn't going to smell very good at all."

JOURNAL ENTRY:
Gabriela Rusack

I WONDERED WHAT WOULD HAPPEN IF I JUST WENT back. What if I just strolled up the Rock and into my old chambers and pretended that I'd never been shunned at all?

I started to do exactly that one day—I think it was on the

second or third anniversary of my last shunning. I packed the essentials into my pack and started off toward the Rock. I was just at the edge of the fields when Dominic Allen-Shimmura saw me. He was out sowing the newly tilled ground with his brother Marco and Adari's brother Kahnoch. Dominic nudged the others, pointing. Kahnoch dropped his bag of seeds and reached for his rifle.

"Hey, a fucking grumbler!" he called out, supposedly to Domi and Marco but mostly to me. He cocked the rifle. "You see it, Domi? A grumbler, a piece of *khudda*, a festering sore." He brought the rifle up to his shoulder and sighted down it. I started to tremble—I had no place to hide, not out here, and Kahnoch had once tried to attack me after he found out about Adari and me. He'd been stopped by Shig, but out here . . . out here I wasn't certain what he'd do. My quixotic idea suddenly seemed very stupid. Dominic had picked up his own weapon. Marco just watched.

"What do you think, Domi? Marco?" Kahnoch said, still speaking so that I could hear him. "Should I kill it? After all, I need to protect my sister and my Family. No one cares if trash like this lives or dies. Why, they can't even shun me for killing a thing, an animal, something that's not even human anymore. What do you think?"

Domi and Marco didn't answer; they knew Kahnoch wasn't talking to them but to me. Domi just watched, his own rifle in his hands. Marco said something softly to him that I couldn't hear, but Domi shrugged. Kahnoch continued to sight down the barrel of the rifle.

I saw the puff of smoke just an instant before I heard the percussive *kkkree!* of the shot. Soft earth splattered my feet—and I realized that Kahnoch had fired. Belatedly, I jumped to Kahnoch's bitter, sour laughter. "I wonder if grumblers are smart enough to learn," he said, and he fired again. This time I heard the whine as the bullet passed close to my head. "Or are they stupid enough to stay where they're not wanted."

Another shot—I'd turned sideways, caught between being afraid to move and wanting desperately to run. The slug hit my backpack, the impact spinning me around like someone had punched me. I fell, and scrambled back to my feet as quickly as I could, really scared now and breathing hard. I started to run, thinking that any second he'd fire again, and this time I wouldn't hear it, because I'd be on the ground with my skull split open, dead and pouring blood out on the ground. I heard him laughing as he saw me fleeing in stark terror.

"That's it," Kahnoch called out after me. "Run, you fucking bitch, you goddamn cunt-licking *rezu*. You come around here again, and I promise I'll kill you. I promise. Now run!"

I ran. As if all the *kamis* of the lower world were after me, I ran.

CONTEXT:
Miranda Koda-Shimmura

GEEMA TOZO POKED HER HEAD INTO THE CHAMBER. "How are you doing, Kit?" Kit had been her geema's name for Miranda since she'd learned to talk, when the elder Tozo had told her a story about old Earth and Matriarch Akiko and the animals she'd once had as pets. The story had fascinated her and for a week afterward she had called anything small that moved a "kitten." After that, she'd become "kitten" herself. Most of the Family and her friends called her that. It was almost more her name than Miranda.

"I'm fine, Geema," she answered. "Just laying here thinking about getting up."

"Need company?"

Kit shrugged, and the Family elder came into the room to sit on the bed alongside her. She placed her ancient, wrinkled hand on Kit's swelling stomach and smiled softly. "Your mam tells me that you felt him move yesterday."

"You know it's a him?"

Another smile. "*Hai*, I'm fairly sure. The *kami* have been talking about it the last few days. They can tell when a child quickens, you know."

"A boy . . ." Kit closed her eyes for a second. It felt right. It would be good to have a boy. Her other two children had been girls: Michele, seven now, and the unnamed one who had died from the Bloody Cough at three months, two years ago now. Kit had wondered if she'd ever become pregnant again, after that; she wondered if she'd ever *want* to. She'd been pleased to find that she did, on both counts. It would help the Family, especially after the loss of little Tozo's baby a few days ago. "He's probably Peter's—the timing was about right. Maybe Umberto, though. I was with him once. I don't know. What else do the *kami* say to you?"

A brief flicker passed over her geema's face at the question. "What, Geema?" Kit asked, suddenly worried. "Is the baby . . . ?"

Tozo smiled again and patted her cheek. "No, child. No. It's nothing about your baby. Other things. There are . . . currents."

"What currents?"

For a moment, Kit thought that Tozo was going to tell her. Geema Tozo was generally closemouthed about the *kami*, about the specific whisperings she heard in the smoke and incense of her meditations. "It's just . . ." she began, then took a long breath. "The world has changed, and we don't know quite why or how yet." Geema Tozo smiled down at her again and patted her stomach. "Change is always a little frightening, isn't it?"

Geema Tozo groaned as she pushed herself up from the bed. "Come and get up, *lavativo*. There's work to do, and that little boy growing inside you doesn't give you an excuse to miss it."

VOICE:

Máire Koda-Schmidt

"DOES IT HAVE TO DO THAT?"

Elio glared at Silverback, who was singing. I don't know of any other way to describe the sound. This wasn't a short hunting call, a quick shriek or series of low hoots like I'd heard the grumblers around the Rock make a thousand times, or the mumbling nonsense they'd spit out when they looked at you. Just at the edge of our campfire's light, Silverback was crouched on the ground, his head lifted to the array of stars in the evening sky, and he *sang*: a strange, warbling drone that seemed to have words embedded in its long flow. The sound woke echoes in me, made me want to wrap my arms around my stomach protectively. Though I knew it was too early, I thought I could feel the baby inside stir at the chant.

The grumbler had also given us this little concert just after dusk on the night before, as we camped on the shore of Crookjaw Bay. The grumblers from the island had joined him from across the bay, faintly. Tonight, he had other accompaniment. As he paused for breath, there was an answer from the hill to the south, and another from further up the river valley. I saw Elio reach for his rifle, and Ana placed her hand on his, shaking her head. "It's okay," she said to him, and to me. "It's okay."

Silverback cocked his head, listening to the dissonant harmonies floating in the dark. He snuffled to himself, as if discontented, and came back to the fire. He stayed near Anaïs, which bothered me and Elio as well. One unexpected slash from those claws could kill her before we could stop the attack, but Ana didn't seem worried.

I wondered how much of that was an act for our benefit.

I watched Elio watching the grumbler. I thought about what Ana had said, that Elio was the ultimate father of my child. Ana was right; I'd known it as soon as she spoke the words, back in the grumblers' dwelling. I felt the truth of it, the way you feel when you're contemplating a problem and the answer comes to you in a sudden, rushing epiphany, all the walls of resistance collapsing inside.

I wondered how Elio felt about it. Probably he felt very little; men in our society on the Rock are taught to protect and care for the Family into which they were born, not to concern themselves with any family they might create. Many times, they don't know for certain if they're the father of any one child, and they're also taught not to ask—because the child will be raised by the mother's Family, not the father's. If they speak about it at all, it's to boast about their virility in hopes of luring their way into someone else's bed.

I wondered . . .

. . . and sat up with a start. I could see eyes reflecting firelight in the dark between the bubble-trees. Twigs snapped underfoot, the light shifted on gray-black fur, and the breeze held a trace of a familiar scent. "Grumblers," I said loudly, and reached for my weapon. I heard Elio scramble for his rifle across the fire.

There were at least a half-dozen in the grumbler pack, and Anaïs's weapon was still strapped to her backpack. Silverback had sensed them also. He was already on his feet, standing between us and the intruders. I could see the tips of his fingerclaws, and the large ripping claw on each foot was extended. He growled something in their direction, and they emerged from the shadows: four males and three females, one of whom was obviously pregnant—I touched my own belly in unconscious sympathy: would I really be swollen and bloated like that? I didn't like the odds here, and didn't like the way the grumblers spread out as they approached our fire. I was contemplating whether a warning shot was going to necessary to keep them together when Silverback approached one of the males. They sniffed at each other appraisingly, and then Silverback launched into a long series of modulated barks and yowls, in which I heard the word "Sa-ah" interjected several times. At the end, he pointed directly at Anaïs through the twisting column of sparks and flame, and the grumblers stared at her. Two of them—male and female—started toward Ana, and both Elio and I brought our weapons up, and the grumblers paused, hissing in irritation.

"No," Ana said. "Look at them—aren't they the ones who were in Gabriela's cabin? Remember that white tuft of hair on the male?"

"Maybe," I answered. "But what possible difference . . . ?" I stopped. I wasn't sure if I did or didn't recognize the grumbler. Maybe, maybe not. I didn't see that it made that much difference. *Hai*, that grumbler had saved us from another's attack, but I didn't know whether the grumbler had been protecting us, his mate, or whether he just found another male in his territory more threatening at the time than our presence. I didn't particularly remember the white hair. Anaïs started to take a step toward the grumblers, but Elio put his hand out and stepped in front of her.

"Don't," he said.

"Trust me," she answered, and gave me a look that told me that the words were for me as well. "Please." She gently pushed his arm aside and took another step. The grumblers had stopped near Silverback. As Ana approached, they drew themselves up slightly. Another of the males from the pack started toward her, and Silverback pushed him back. The male howled in protest, his claws slashing out from his fingertips; Silverback howled back, his own claws out now.

They exchanged a series of angry mutterings, with some of the other grumblers interjecting occasionally. It was obvious to me that there were two disagreeing factions here, about evenly split, with our Silverback and the grumbler pair from Gabriela's cabin on one side. Ana watched the argument—too close to them for my comfort. I moved around to the other side of the fire; Elio and I put ourselves between the grumblers and Ana.

Without warning, one of the males suddenly kicked at Silverback. For the first time, I actually saw how powerful and awful an offensive weapon that kick was. Silverback must have sensed the attack coming, for he'd moved back at the same time. The kick should have laid his abdomen open; instead, blood spurted from a long, jagged cut from his ribcage to just above his groin, and the old grumbler shrieked in pain. Whitetuft darted in and slashed once with his claws across the attacker's shoulder and chest, and then leaped back himself from another kick, which missed entirely. The pregnant female ran forward and raked the attacker's back with her claws, and he turned on her next. I saw the foot lifting, ready to tear her open . . .

There was a sharp explosion and the male went down in a sudden heap, his chest a bloody ruin. I could smell gunpowder and see the blue smoke trailing from my rifle, and I realized that I'd been the one to fire. My ears rang with the percussion, and for a second no one moved. "She's pregnant," I said to no one in particular. "He was going to hurt her."

Anaïs put her hand on my shoulder silently. Elio moved back, making a tight cluster with me and Ana. The grumblers, all but the one I'd shot and Silverback, had faded back into the darkness. Ana pushed through the two of us and rushed over to the old grumbler, who was kneeling on the ground staring down at his bloodied front. "He's shocked," Ana said. She was in doctor mode, all business. "Elio, please get my pack; Máire, check on the other one and see if he's still alive." She looked up at the two of us; neither of us had moved. "Go on!," she said.

"Ana . . ." I said, motioning with my rifle toward the trees. Whitetuft and his mate had returned, along with the pregnant female. They slunk in cautiously, watching me and Elio carefully and moving toward the stricken Silverback. Anaïs didn't move as they approached. Whitetuft's mate crouched down alongside Silverback, her long, agile fingers exploring softly as she crooned words to Silverback, who grunted softly in return. She barked something at the male, who turned and disappeared into the darkness again. Then the grumbler looked at Anaïs, kneeling on the other side of the silverback. "Sa-ah," she said. She put her hands protectively around the old grumbler.

"I know," Anaïs said. "I want to help him too." Elio placed Ana's medical pack carefully alongside her; Ana opened and brought out a bottle of disinfectant. She opened it and spread a little on a swatch, holding it out to the female. "This will help," she said. The female leaned down to sniff; her nose wrinkled at the smell, but she didn't otherwise react. Anaïs started to clean Silverback's wound, who howled at the first touch of the astringent stuff. His claws came out and he tried to stand, but the female put her hands on him and spoke, and Silverback knelt again, and then finally lay back on the ground. Whitetuft returned with a handful of leaves. The female crushed the leaves in her hands and held the resulting brownish dust out to Anaïs. I could smell the sharp odor from where I stood, and I could see the skepticism on Ana's face.

"She trusted *you*," Elio reminded her softly. Ana glanced at him almost angrily, but Elio only gazed back at her and Ana finally sighed. She leaned over and sniffed at the grumbler's finger, and nodded. The female grunted approvingly. She let the crushed leaves in her hand trickle over the section of the wound Anaïs had cleaned. Where they touched, the bloodflow quickly stopped. Ana's head lifted in surprise. "By all the *kami* . . ." she half-whispered, and then laughed. "I want to know what plant those leaves came from. We could use a good coagulant."

Watching Ana and Whitetuft's mate work on Silverback, one with human medicine, the other with her alien skills, I'd forgotten about the pregant female. I suddenly realized that she was standing almost next to me. Her face was long and pointed, delicately furred around the chin but otherwise hairless, with a long mane that started high on the forehead and continued down her back, spreading out once it reached the shoulders. Her two seeing eyes were large and otherwordly, golden flecks floating in the large, pale brown pupils; her third, lidless eye was nearly blue-white, with no discernible pupil at all. Along the snout three nasal vents flared, and I could hear her breath through them. She had a roll of skin around the diaphragms that served as her ears, set low on her head. Her hands, in an almost-human gesture, rested on the mound of her belly.

I think it was the first time I really *looked* at a grumbler, the first time I actually believed what Gabriela had said, that they were the fallen remnants of the Miccail.

She was looking at the rifle, and I could see fear in her face, mingled with . . . I don't know. If she'd been human, I would have said that she looked grateful. I let the stock swing down and swung the strap around my shoulder, holding up my empty hands to her. "See? No weapon." Slowly, I let my hands drop, and reached out to touch her belly. We watched each other's eyes, both of us, I think, unsure of each other. Her skin was warm and soft, and the belly was hard and taut under my fingers. She laid her own hands on top of mine, pressing down, the claws emerging just enough to dimple my skin.

Underneath my hands, I felt the child within her move.

CONTEXT:
Micah Allen-Shimmura

THERE WERE MORE GRUMBLER TRACKS THAN MICAH liked near the old Miccail road. They'd already seen too many of the creatures or heard them howling around in the dusk. Last night, two of them had blundered into their campsite—he and Ben had killed them both. They'd yet to see a single jaunecerf since they'd left the Rock two days ago—the whole hunting trip so far had been an unmitigated disaster.

"Look at this," Micah said. Yesterday had been unseasonably warm enough that the ground had been muddy at midday before refreezing overnight. He pointed at the prints in the frozen turf. "There must have been a half dozen of the bastards up here yesterday. A frigging convention."

"No wonder the jaunecerf have disappeared. Between us and the grumblers, their life expectancy's not particularly high." Ben sat down on a mossy, frost-covered boulder that overlooked the valley to the west. The old Miccail road cut a narrow swath through the trees, down the valley and up the other side. Wizards cursed them from the trees above them, and ice-borers honked plaintively from some creek nearby. "I hate coming back empty, especially after Gayle swore we'd find one of the herds out this way. She's not going to believe us."

"If she wants to eat grumbler, it's the land of plenty. Otherwise . . ." Micah shrugged and sat on the boulder next to Ben. He pulled a pair of battered binoculars out from his belt pack. They weren't shipmade—he'd heard it claimed that the ship binocs didn't use lenses at all, but connected directly to the neural web and the user's own eyes—but they'd been crafted by Ranjan Martinez-Santos over two decades ago. Ranjan still oversaw most of the glass-making in the colony, though worsening emphysema had made him too weak to do much of the actual work. The binocs were good, though, the glass clear and undistorted except for the inevitable scratches of time.

"I'll tell you, if we don't find anything today, we're going back, empty or not," Ben said. "I was with Karin the night before we left, and I'll tell you . . ."

Micah scanned the valley, twirling the knobs and half-listening to Ben talk about Karin. The globe-trees, white-woods and amberdrops on the far side swam into focus as he panned from right to left. He thought he saw a flicker of movement near the old Miccail road. He brought the glasses down, squinted into the sunlight. ". . . if you ever get the chance—"

"You see that?" Micah interrupted Ben. "Look—just coming over the ridge." Micah focused the lenses on the hilltop and on the figures moving out of the cover of trees. "By all the *kami* . . . " he breathed.

"What is it?"

Micah brought the binoculars down. "We'd better head back to the Rock. I have to talk with my Geeda."

Elio Allen-Shimmura

GRUMBLERS HAVE A UNIQUE BOUQUET.

They emanate fish and old earth and perspiration that has been generously stored in bodily hair for far too long. They wear the perfume of life.

In short, they fucking stink.

You do get used to it. That's the frightening part. The *kami* know I've had enough chances. We've picked up an entourage of them now: Silverback from the island, and Whitetuft and his mate, who we've nicknamed Dottó. The pregnant female that Máire tentatively dubbed Okáasan didn't stay, though—she slipped away a few hours after we saved her life.

Surrounded by grumblers, I hardly notice the smell anymore. In fact, considering how long it's been since we've had a chance to bathe or shower, we're probably almost as ripe as they are.

Dottó definitely deserves her name. After she and Anaïs did the initial repair work on Silverback's nasty wound, Dottó disappeared for several hours, and came back with a regular pharmacy of herbs and roots and powders, from which she mixed a couple noxious mixtures to administer to Silverback. They worked: he was up again and moving, if a bit stiffly, the next morning. Ana looked both surprised and I think a little embarrassed. She also managed to snag samples of most of the stuff, I noticed, and now she watches carefully when Dottó stops along the road to examine some plant or another.

With Silverback mobile again, we continued on toward the Rock, and the grumblers kept us company. I'm glad of it, honestly. We've seen several packs of grumblers in the area, and though they come around us, curious, the presence of "our" grumblers seems to keep them away. Even Silverback and the others seem nervous when they hear the packs calling at night—they obviously don't trust the reactions of their own kind.

Much like us. *Hai*.

We stayed last night at Gabriela's cabin; a half day from the Rock, a half day from whatever reception is waiting for us there. While Anaïs, Máire and the grumblers slept in the cabin, I sat on the broken stoop and watched the snow falling, worrying. Ana was insistent that we all stay together, but I still wasn't sure that was the best strategy. Leaving Ana and Máire alone with grumblers was also not something I was entirely comfortable with, but after four days with them now, I was more sure of how the grumblers were going to react than of how the Rock might respond to Ana's return.

I thought . . . well, I thought that if I went in alone, ahead of them, I could get a sense of their mood. I could prepare the Families for what she was going to tell them. I might be able to diffuse whatever reaction Geeda Dominic was going to have—and I was certain his reaction wasn't going to be pleasant. If Dominic was going to play nasty, well, then I could be the lightning rod that took the first hit.

I thought it was the right thing to do.

The first few steps away from the cabin were difficult; after that, each one became easier and by the time Gabriela's old dwelling was no longer in sight, I'd mostly convinced myself that this was exactly what was needed to be done. I moved along the path of the ancient Miccail road under the light of Faraway, trying to ignore the nagging, uneasy voice inside.

A few hours later, I came to the path down to Old Bridge and turned right onto it, moving downhill toward the river. In minutes, I'd be at Stelae Rise, just on the other side of the river, and from its bare top studded with Miccail-scrawled stone, I could look across the valley and see the Rock.

It was snowing harder and I was cold despite the walking, so I started to pick up the pace. So close to the Rock, to what I still considered "home" despite all the troubles, I wasn't really paying much attention to what was around me—the familiarity of it all was comforting, lulling me into complacency.

The noise came from just behind me: the crunch of hurrying footsteps in the snow. I started to turn, but something hard and solid smashed into the side of my face as I did so. I went down in slow motion in a whirl of snowflakes and bright, circling lights. I felt the ground cold against my cheek and the blood hot on my temple, and then, for a long time, I didn't feel anything at all.

CONTEXT:
Micah Allen-Shimmura

❧ "GEEDA DOMINIC SAID WE WERE SUPPOSED TO BRING Elio back."

Micah shrugged at his older brother, Dominic's namesake. "And we will," he answered. "Later."

"You smacked him pretty good with your rifle butt," Domi insisted. "He bled a lot, and he's still out. What if he's really hurt bad? We should take him back so Hui can look at him."

"Fuck, Domi, I've knocked my head harder in some of the old passages in the Rock," Micah scoffed. "And scalp cuts always bleed like that. So he has a headache when he wakes up—he's going to have worse when Geeda gets hold of him with that cane of his. Elio'll be fine, and we'll get him back soon enough." In the cold moonlight, the fog of his breath was almost luminescent. "After we've dealt with the rest of them. He wanted to run away with that *rezu* Anaïs—well, he doesn't get any sympathy from me. A cracked skull is probably less than he deserves. What's it matter, brother? If we escort him back now, that bitch Anaïs and her lover might sneak back to the Rock. Máire'd go right to Hui and Ana to her Family, and who knows what happens then. I saw them yesterday—they're out there with goddamn tame grumblers. Geeda told us to wait here and make sure they didn't cross the river. I say we do exactly that. My bet is that Ana's going to be right behind our Elio."

Micah could see that Domi was wavering. He smiled and clapped his brother on the shoulder. "Come on, come on. . . . Another day at the very most. Elio'll keep that long. Hell, we didn't kill him." When Domi took a long breath, Micah grinned. "*Hai*, that's it, Domi. Hey, you know that wooden flute of mine you're always lusting after—the one Marcus carved? I'll bet you that against your good knife that we'll see the *rezu* by FifthHour. What do you say?"

Domi nodded. "All right," he said. "You're on."

VOICE:
Elio Allen-Shimmura

MY HEAD WAS SMALLER THAN MICTLAN AND LARGER
than the Rock, and asteroids had been smashing
continually into it for the last millennium, leaving behind
bleeding craters and a cracked surface. I opened my eyes,
and comets whirled and all the neighboring stars went nova
all at once. The universe throbbed and screamed. I decided
that, overall, oblivion was preferable, and closed my eyes
again.

Somewhat later, I opened them once more. My headache
hovered somewhere on the scale between excruciating and
sheer agony, but at least the celestial light show had ended.
I seemed to be lying on my side, and my body didn't work.
I tried to stand up and only succeeded in lifting my head,
which immediately flopped down again when the rest of me
didn't follow. This brought the return of the light show for
several minutes and inched the headache up the scale closer
to unbearable.

I reminded myself to move much, much slower next time.

This time I contented myself with looking around first,
without moving my head at all. Only one eye opened completely; the other was crusted shut with old blood. Didn't
matter—there wasn't much to see: a dusty, rough wooden
floor, and racks of woven baskets. Through the odor of dirt
and dust, I could smell an overlay of ripe fruit. The sun was
shining through the cracks in the plank walls, and I could
see a pear-nut tree standing in snow outside. I was in the
orchard shed, then, just across the river from the Rock.

My jaw seemed to be out of socket or broken; I couldn't
shut it all the way. I tried wiggling my fingers; I could feel
them move, but they were stuck behind my back. Same with
my feet: the toes moved, but I couldn't move my feet away
from each other. I risked moving my head a bit to look down
the length of my body and saw twine winding around my
ankles: someone had tied me up, then. That was good—a

much better option than paralysis. It also meant that whoever ambushed me was from the Rock.

I definitely had a debt to repay, there.

It also meant, probably, that the same person or persons who got me would be going after Anaïs and Máire next. With some effort, I managed to roll over toward the wall—I could at least move that way. Once I had the wall's support, I managed to sit up, though the effort cost me a few minutes where I thought I might black out again. Once I had my back to the wall, I was able to use my legs and push myself up to standing. I leaned against one of the tables used for sorting and packing.

Evidently whoever stuck me here hadn't been overly worried about me getting up and around—there were at least three old knives lying on the table from the last time people had been in here working, along with a bobbin of the same twine they'd used to bind me. Working blindly with my hands behind me was awkward, but I managed to snag one of the knives; kneeling, I cut the twine around my ankles. Once my legs were free and the feeling had returned to them, I put the handle of the knife between my feet and starting sawing at the twine around my wrists. I must have nicked myself a half dozen times on the edge, but at last the twine parted. I rubbed feeling back into the hands, and then stood again. I pushed at my aching, locked jaw, ignoring the pain; it snapped loudly and the pain was twice as bad as before, but the hinge was back in its socket and I could move my jaw again: another small victory.

I went to the door and pushed it open. That almost made me angry—evidently I wasn't considered enough of a potential threat for my assailants to even lock the damn door. I blinked into the cold sunlight. The glare made my head pound worse than ever. Above the pear-nut trees, the Rock loomed.

Trying to ignore the sledgehammer crashing against my skull from inside, I started toward the Rock.

VOICE:
Anaïs Koda-Levin the Younger

I LOOKED AT THE BLURRED FOOTPRINTS IN THE snow and wasn't sure what to think.

"He went back to the Rock," Máire said behind me. "You know he did. He was worried about the reception you were going to get, and he wanted to defuse it as much as he could. He didn't want to see you get hurt; that's the way Elio is."

I scuffed at the nearest mark with my boot, smearing it. Máire was right; I knew where he'd gone, and had a good idea why. As I stood there trying to decide if I was angry, worried, or both, Whitetuft and Dottó came out of the cabin, holding their hands over their top eye until they adjusted to the daylight. Silverback followed just behind them. None of them seemed concerned about Elio's absence. I wondered whether they even noticed.

"It doesn't matter," I said, trying to sound unflustered. "Let's just get going. We still have a long walk today. You feeling up to it?"

Máire nodded. "*Hai.* I'm fine." Her grimace told me how tired and sore she really was, but she also wasn't going to admit it. I hugged her, and we kissed. I cupped the slight swell of her belly with my hand. "Come on," she said. "We'd better go rescue Elio."

The snow might have stopped, but the day was cold and the sunlight only hurt our eyes without warming us at all. We slogged through the orangish drifts the wind had piled up, following the old Miccail road back toward the Rock. Each curve in the road revealed something familiar, and the knot in my stomach grew larger and more twisted with each step. A hundred different scenarios played out in my head as we walked; none of them were pleasant. Yet the vision I'd had under Silverback's potion kept returning, and each time the conviction that I *had* to return to the Rock was reinforced. I had to: because of Máire's unborn child; because of all we'd learned about the Miccail; because, damn it, they'd been *wrong* to shun me.

We reached the path to Old Bridge, and turned down it. A half a kilometer further, and we stood on Stelae Rise. From the bare-topped hill, above the winter-dry foliage of the amberdrops, we could see the summit of the Rock, its own stelae-crowned head a kilometer away, dark against the sky. We stopped to gaze at the sight, and even the grumblers seemed entranced by it. Somehow, the Rock looked larger than it actually was from here, the perspective making the steep walls appear to loom over us like a brooding mountain. Silverback and Dottó said something in their growling tongue; Máire and I just stood side by side, her arm around my waist as we regarded our old home. After a few minutes I sighed—I wasn't going to untangle the emotions I was feeling until we got there and met whatever it was we'd meet. I hugged Máire again and started toward the opening in the trees where the path moved down toward the river and the bridge.

Which was when Micah and the younger Dominic stepped out from the shadows. "Welcome back, Anaïs," Micah said, and his voice was as sharp and dry as a scalpel's edge. "I hope you don't mind our little advance reception party."

CONTEXT:
Micah Allen-Shimmura

"HAI, THAT'S RIGHT," MICAH DRAWLED. HIS RIFLE leaned casually on his shoulder, muzzle up, but his finger wrapped the trigger. He looked from Anaïs to Máire, standing beside her. Máire's hand went to Anaïs's shoulder, and the gesture made Micah grimace. "You didn't think that you could just walk back into the Rock unnoticed, did you? We don't like your kind, especially with the stinking friends you've brought along."

"Micah—" Anaïs began, but he put his finger to his lips and shook his head into her protest.

"Just listen," he said in his blurred voice. "I want you to

306

turn around and leave. You understand me? You're shunned, and Máire has chosen to become shunned with you. That's fine. But it means we don't hear you, we don't know you, and we don't want you. Get the hell out of here."

"Where's Elio?" Anaïs asked. "He—"

Again, Micah brought his finger up warningly. "Elio is Domi's sib and my sib. We've dealt with him. That's our concern, not yours."

With that, Anaïs took a step toward them, her eyes flashing angrily. "Damn you, Micah, if you hurt him—"

Micah snapped his rifle down, holding it at his hip with the blackened barrel pointing at Anaïs's stomach. Alongside him, he heard Domi unshouldering his own weapon. "Back off, *rezu*," Micah snapped. "I don't care . . ." but what happened then occurred so quickly that there wasn't any more time for words.

Micah heard one of the grumblers—the old one with the nasty half-healed wound down the front—howl threateningly and start to charge. Micah pulled his rifle quickly up to his shoulder: the beast had its claws out and would be on him in a few seconds. Anaïs screamed "No!" and he saw her move at the same time, stepping between Micah and the onrushing grumbler. "No!" she shouted again, but it was too late—at least that's what he would tell himself afterward.

Too late. The grumbler was coming for him and there was no time for him to do anything but react.

He'd *already* reacted. He couldn't stop.

It was too late.

The rifle slammed against his shoulder, the sound of the shot echoed from the hills, and Anaïs grunted: a startled "*Umpphh.*" Her eyes went wide, and she looked at him in startled amazement. He would remember that gaze—that accusing surprise—for a long time. Then, suddenly, she crumpled like a doll dropped from a child's hand, and the snow underneath her was bright crimson, not dull orange, steaming in the cold air. The grumbler let loose a howl of mad grief, standing over her.

"Fuck!" Micah shouted. "Oh, *fuck!*" He turned wildly to Domi, standing stunned. "I didn't mean to do that," he told him, half-shouting the words. His breath was a cloud in front of him. "You saw it. I didn't mean to do it." He whirled around, kicking up snow, hoping that when he turned he would see Anaïs standing, unwounded.

But she wasn't. The still figure lying curled and unmoving in the snow seemed unreal. Máire huddled over Anaïs, looking about the stele-pocked hill desperately, searching for help that wouldn't ever come. The female grumbler dropped to her knees alongside her, pushing Máire away. The two males were glowering, their claws out, and the young one started to attack, but Máire pushed herself to her feet and stood in front of him even as Domi started to bring his weapon around, belatedly. She fumbled with her own rifle.

"No!" Máire shouted wildly, the barrel of her rifle swinging. "No, damn you! You've done enough already."

They looked at each other. Domi started to take a step toward Anaïs. The old grumbler moved to block him, the slashing claw on the foot rising, and Domi stepped back. The younger one had pushed Máire aside, and looked as if it were gathering itself to attack again, and Máire looked furious enough to start shooting herself. "Let's get out of here," Domi said. "Micah, come on. Let's just go . . ."

Micah hesitated. He stared at Anaïs's body, at Máire's accusing face.

He nodded to Domi.

Not daring to turn his back, he retreated to the trees, Domi ahead of him. The grumblers watched, but stayed where they were. When he was finally in the shadows of the trees, he turned and ran.

The sound of Máire's angry weeping pursued him.

VOICE:
Elio Allen-Shimmura

WE HEARD THE RIFLE SHOT FROM THE GROVE, echoing off the Rock.

The sound hit me square in the chest; for a moment, I stopped breathing. Hui, alongside me, looked at me strangely. I tried to shake my head in denial, and then we both started to run.

Halfway up Stelae Rise, we met Micah and Domi coming down, fleeing as if all the *kami* of the woods were pursuing them. Micah pushed past us, but Hui set down his medical bag, snatched up Domi and shoved him back against a tree trunk with a strength I'd not thought he possessed. "What the hell happened up there, boy?" he roared at my sib, and Micah looked from him to me with round, frightened eyes.

"Anaïs . . ." he said, and that was all I needed to hear. Hui smacked Domi backhanded across the face, and then shoved him downhill. I heard him stumble and fall, but I didn't care. I was already running up the path, ignoring the pain in my head and my lungs, just trying to get there as fast as I could and afraid of what I was going to see. I heard Hui panting and toiling after me through the snow, but I didn't wait for him.

"Ana! Máire!" I called as I broke into the open field at the top of the rise, but I saw them at the same time, and the despair that had clutched my chest deepened. I saw Máire and Dottó crouched over a dark, fallen shape, and I saw Silverback and Whitepatch . . .

"Ana . . ." I breathed the word and surged forward. I dropped to my knees in the blood-smeared snow next to Máire. Máire saw the question in my eyes, and she shrugged.

"I don't know," she answered. "She's alive, but I don't know." Máire's voice cracked; tears marked her cheeks. I reached down to touch Ana's face, but Dottó sniffed, grunted, and slapped my hand unceremoniously aside. She had ripped away Ana's shirt and was sprinkling a tan powder over the gunshot wound, the powder turning an ominous black as soon as it touched the oozing, ragged edges. Ana's injuries looked terrible to me, a ragged, deep hole the diameter of my thumb torn in the side of her right breast. I thought I could see the white of bone in its depths, thought I could hear the wheezing of her lungs.

Hui came huffing up, stopping short as he saw the grumblers. "Damn it, get those animals away from her!" he shouted. He evidently then noticed Dottó, for his face flushed and darkened, as I'd seen him do with Ama and Hayat. "What the hell do you think you're doing? Máire, are you trying to kill her? Get that grumbler *away*."

"She's helping, Geeda," Máire answered. "You have to trust her."

"I'll do no such thing, child. Get up, Elio, and let me in . . ." Hui pushed his way to Anaïs's side, slamming down his bag, and I heard the hissing intake of breath as he saw the wound. Dottó was still sprinkling her powder, and I saw Hui start to push her hand away much as Dottó had done to me a few seconds before. He stopped in midmotion, his eyes squinting. "She's not bleeding," he said, and he looked at Dottó, who gazed silently at him for a moment with her strangely colored eyes, and then silently pulled a pinched roll of leaves from her pouch. She crushed them with a finger in the palm of her hand, and then held them under Anaïs's nose. Ana coughed, gasped once, and her eyes fluttered open.

"Elio," she said, her voice wet and raspy. Flecks of blood spotted her lips. "You sure look like hell."

I touched my puffy, bloodied, and bruised face. "Believe me, it matches the way I feel. And you haven't seen yourself lately."

Ana smiled weakly, her head turning to the others. "Máire, I'm so sorry, so . . . And Hui. This isn't the way I expected to see you again, but I'm glad. How am I, old friend?"

"I don't know yet," he answered gruffly. "Ana, I need to turn you over. Think you can stand it?"

"Are you giving me a choice?"

"No." Hui glanced at Máire and me, and then, warily, at the grumblers watching us. "I need your help," he said to us. "Elio, you take her legs; Máire, roll her at the hips. Over to her left side. That's it . . . gently . . . *gently* . . ." Anaïs groaned as we turned her. Hui grunted as he saw a larger wound just below her shoulderblade. The ugly hole pulsed thick, bright blood. "Okay, we have an exit wound, and it's bleeding heavily. We need a pressure bandage. Elio, get into my pack and . . ."

Hui stopped. Dottó had padded around behind us, and she mumbled as she reached into her pouch. She dusted the wound with more of the tan powder. Ana cried out, as if the touch of it burned her, but the bloodflow visibly thickened and then stopped. Hui turned his head to look at the grumbler, a grudging acceptance carving furrows around his eyes. "I guess that works," he said. "I hope like hell it's antiseptic." He reached into his bag and brought out a bottle of surgical solution. He splashed it generously into the wound, and Anaïs cried out. "All right, let her down again . . . slowly . . . We don't want to tear it open . . ."

"Well?" Ana asked, her eyes clouded with pain. When Hui didn't answer, she lifted her head slightly. "Hui, talk to me."

"I can't say," he said. "You've lost a lot of blood—but you

would have lost more without your grumbler friend here. You've broken or shattered ribs, and I don't know if you've lost lung tissue as well. We can worry about infection and pneumonia later. I've got to get you into the clinic right away, and with my eyes . . ."

Anaïs nodded and closed her eyes. "Ama has good hands and good eyes. All she needs is your knowledge and experience. You won't let her make a mistake. I know." Her voice was little more than a whisper, and she grimaced. Her eyes opened again. "Hui, the grumblers . . ."

"I know. I saw what the female did for you. You know what she used?"

"Some of it. Hui, they have things to teach us, and I have a lot to tell you. You're going to be surprised."

"Evidently," Hui agreed. "But it needs to wait until later. Right now, we need to get you back to the Rock." He stood, his knees cracking. His clothes and hands were stained brown-red. "Máire, child, run to the clinic and tell Hayat to bring a litter. Quickly. We need—"

Dottó had stepped back, and now Whitetuft crouched alongside Anaïs. Carefully, his claws masked under the thick fingerpads, he slid his arms beneath her, and then lifted her up, his powerful legs flexing as he stood. Ana groaned softly, then wrapped her arms around the grumbler's neck. "You can trust him, Hui," she said. "I do. You have to also."

Whitetuft stared at us, waiting. Finally, Hui nodded to the grumbler. "All right," he said. "Let's go then. If your intention was to make a grand entrance back into the Rock, this will certainly do it."

VOICE:
Anaïs Koda-Levin the Younger

I KNEW FROM SEVERELY INJURED PATIENTS OVER THE years that the mind often has a merciful forgetfulness when it comes to the pain of trauma. A few years ago, Yves fell from one of the pilings while putting up New Bridge and cracked his skull on an inconvenient rock in the middle of the river. Morihei dragged him out of the water, but Yves was unconscious for several hours. When he finally woke, he swore that the last thing he remembered was leaving the compound for work that morning.

I suppose I shouldn't be suprised that I remember almost nothing of what happened immediately after Micah confronted us. I have dim memories of trying to put myself between him and Silverback, but not much else. I'm actually grateful—very little of what happened afterward would have been pleasant. I have no recollection of being shot. I don't recall talking with Hui, Máire, and Elio afterward, though I think I can recall the discomfort of being carried in Whitetuft's arms down the path, being jostled and bumped.

I remember wondering some time later why we'd stopped all of a sudden, and opening my eyes to find out. I saw Dominic standing like some ancient guardian at the main entrance to the Rock, with Micah, the younger Dominic, and several of the Elders arrayed behind him. Micah and at least a few of the others were armed. Familiar faces peered from shadows behind them—I think most of the population of the Rock was there: Elena and her child, Euzhan, looking concerned and puzzled, my *das* Derek and Joel, Ben, Faika, Phaedra, Hayat, my sib Ché . . .

"You're not bringing her in here, Hui," Dominic rumbled, his cane tip jabbing in my direction. "She is *shunned*, and she's not to be here. If you want to help her, I suppose that's your business, but you'll do it elsewhere."

"Get out of our way, Dominic," Hui half-shouted back at him. I could hear his voice rebounding from the rock walls. "I don't have time to argue with any of you. Move!" He started forward, then must have seen Micah and the dull glimmer of the weapons. He stopped. "There's already been enough of this nonsense. Are you going to shoot *both* your doctors?—go ahead and be damned for it. I'm coming inside anyway."

Dominic didn't move. "This isn't just my decision, Hui. She was shunned by a vote of the Elder Council. Be reasonable, man—that's the only law we have, the only thing that stands between us and anarchy. Is that what you want to destroy, Hui?"

"I have a person who was shot and nearly killed by one of the two young fools standing behind you, and that's all I'm thinking about at the moment. I'm sorry if that doesn't

312

meet your high standards, but frankly, I don't really give a damn. Now . . . stand aside."

"*Nei*. A shunned woman, those grumblers . . ."

"Dominic, get out of the way." The voice was familiar to me, coming from deep in the crowd. I saw Geema Anaïs shove her way unceremoniously toward the front. "If my Ana's hurt, then by all the *kami* you will let her in."

"She is *shunned*," Dominic repeated in his stentorian voice. "You already had your vote in this, Anaïs. If it bothers you to abide by the decision, leave. But it *will* be enforced."

Dominic wasn't moving, and Hui wasn't going to change his mind, either. I could see another confrontation coming. "Let me down, Whitetuft," I told the grumbler holding me—strange how we'll talk to someone or something even when we know they can't possibly understand the words we're saying. I pushed feebly against his furred chest, and that evidently communicated the idea. The grumbler lowered me down, and I managed to stand, wobbling. I couldn't have taken a step, and my right arm hung limp and dead at my side, but I stood, the world seeming to turn slowly in front of me. I closed my eyes for a moment, trying to shake away some of the pain and disorientation. I felt my knees start to buckle. Hui started toward me, but I looked at him and managed to straighten up again; he stopped, glaring at me the way he always glared at patients who dared to disobey his orders.

"Dominic," I said, surprised at how my voice sounded, so weak and graveled. I could hear it inside my head, sounding like someone else. "You shunned me for the wrong reasons. You had me shunned because I was a woman who would dare to love your Ochiba and Máire." I paused, both to let the Rock stop wobbling in my vision and to consider my next words. I couldn't think of any other way to say it other than to simply state the truth: "I'm not a woman."

Disbelief rippled noisily through the onlookers, and I saw Geema frown and clamp her mouth shut. Even Hui looked at me strangely. Dominic turned slowly to face me, his glance sarcastic and freighted with hate. "So you're claiming to be a man now, *rezu*? Do you think that changes things or that it makes any difference? Do you think any of us even believe you?"

"I'm not claiming to be a man, either," I told him. "I'm neither one, but something else entirely. Something that was necessary for the Miccail, and I think something necessary for us."

Dominic sputtered; the crowd noise rose. "This is nonsense."

Despite the pain, I wanted to laugh, because part of me agreed with him. "For the longest time, I thought the same thing," I told him. "Unfortunately, I've found that whether I want to believe it or not, it's still the truth."

Máire stepped up alongside me, linking her arm through mine; I was grateful for the support, because Dominic was shivering in my vision and I wasn't sure how much longer I could stay standing.

"Here's some more truth for you, Dominic," Máire interjected before I could speak again. "I'm pregnant. With Elio's child, even though I've never slept with him. I've never been with Elio, Dominic. I'm pregnant because of *Anaïs*. Through Ana."

If anything, Máire's statement garnered more of a reaction than my statement. For a moment, everyone was talking at once. "Máire!" one clear voice cut through the uproar, and Elena pushed between Dominic and Micah, still holding her child. She approached us, though I saw her watching the grumblers warily. Her eyes searched Máire's face wonderingly, and she stroked her baby's head, clutching her close. Máire smiled back at her, and touched her sib's cheek. The unnamed infant turned her head to look at us with the wide-eyed, open-mouthed curiosity of the very young. Behind me, I heard Dottó make a crooning grunt in response.

"She's so gorgeous, Elena," Máire told her. "She's still doing well?"

Elena nodded, silent.

"I told you she was special," Máire continued. "Now I know she is."

Elena turned to me, and nodded down at her baby. "She'll need someone who is like her when she's older," Elena said. "To help her understand."

I smiled, feeling tears burning in my eyes. "Then I'll help her. As much as I can."

Elena nodded.

Hui stepped grumpily forward. "Come on," he said. "Ana—"

"*Nei!*" Dominic roared. "Hui, I told you. She doesn't enter the Rock." He motioned threateningly toward me with the cane, and Silverback grunted and slid forward, claws exposed. Dominic scowled, but took a step backward. Micah brought his rifle to his shoulder, little Domi belatedly following suit. "If the grumbler takes another step, boy, put it down," Dominic told Micah.

I put my hand on Silverback's shoulder: a futile gesture, since I could no more have held him back that I could have held back a storm. But he seemed to understand; I felt his powerful muscles rippling, but he held. "Dominic," I said hurriedly. "That's another mistake we've made. The grumblers aren't just animals; they're what's left of the Miccail. At least some of them share a language and a society, and they know more about this world than we do. Kill them, and we're killing the last of another sentient race."

"Bah!" Dominic spat. "You can say that after what they did to Euzhan, after what we've *all* seen of them? They're animals. Disgusting, dangerous beasts."

Silverback must have understood the tone of Dominic's words, because he growled loudly, and Whitetuft, behind me, echoed him. This time it was Elio who stepped forward, his hand in front of Silverback. "*I* say it too, Geeda. Believe it—because I've *seen* it. There's more proof in Gabriela's journals, if you'd dare to read them."

Dominic wouldn't even look at Elio. He ignored him, as if he'd never spoken; instead, he glared at me with a steady hatred. "You are no longer of the Rock," he said, the corners of his mouth drawn tight. "You are no longer even Family. I tried to save you, but I see now that it's too late."

I was leaning heavily on Máire, forcing myself to remain standing, but I knew that I wasn't going to be able to manage it for much longer. I could still see Dominic in the center of my vision, but the edges of my sight were going dark, as if I were staring into a narrowing tunnel. I couldn't see the crowd watching us anymore. My mouth was incredibly dry; I had to lick my lips before I could speak. The memory of the vision I'd had on the island came back to me, and I surrendered myself to its words, too weak to form my own.

"Dominic, let me offer a compromise. I didn't come back here to stay. All I wanted was to tell you what we've learned, to share the knowledge. If you won't or can't accept the changes I bring you, that's fine. But I'm telling you that changes are all around you, and they offer us new life. All we have to do is accept them. You misunderstand me if you think that I came crawling back to the Rock to beg forgiveness and ask to stay here again. I didn't. Máire, Elio, and I will stay on the island, and anyone who wants to stay there also or to visit there will be welcome. What we ask is the same from you—open the Rock to us. Let us visit our Families. Let us grow together, not apart."

The effort took what little strength I had left. I was standing only because Máire held me up, and I had no more words. I was empty.

"Nei," Dominic answered, and I nearly collapsed at the finality of the word. "No," he repeated, harsher and louder. "You are shunned. Stay on your island if that's what you want, because we won't have you here."

"Then I'll go with her," Elena said unexpectedly before anyone else could answer, her voice defiant. "You were wrong, Dominic, you and the elders who voted with you. If you won't admit that, then I don't wish to stay here, either."

"Neither do I." Geema Anaïs's voice quavered, but her step was firm as she came and stood at my side.

"Geema . . ." I began to say, and she shook her head at me, like I was a child. Others of my Family pushed their way through the crowd then: Derek, my mam Maria, Ché, Joel, Shafiqul. A few of the Koda-Schmidt's followed, surrounding Máire: her mam Morag, and then Máire's sibs Wan-Li and Arap. Last came old Tozo, shuffling forward and shaking her head at the members of her family who tried to convince her to stay. As she passed Dominic, she turned to him.

"The *kami* tell me that it's time, Dominic. Can't you hear them, or has all that old hatred made you deaf? Do you think that Ochiba's *kami* would be proud of what you've done? Do you think she'd understand or agree? You can end Anaïs's shunning now. Just say it."

"We all made the decision, Tozo," Dominic answered. "It was the right one."

Tozo only shook her head.

"I want to go with Anaïs, too," a small voice said, a young child's voice: Euzhan. Her *mi* Sarah had been holding her, but Euzhan wriggled free. Before anyone could stop her, she was standing beside me. She smiled at me, then looked solemnly at Elio. *"Komban wa, da* Elio," she said. "Your face looks horrible. Does it hurt?"

"Hai, Euzhan," Elio answered, ruffling her hair. "It hurts."

"Euzhan, come back here," Dominic said. He tapped the ground in front of him with his cane. "Now, girl." Euzhan shook her head, shrinking against Elio.

"Geeda," Elio said, "let us in."

"*Nei*," Dominic persisted. He gestured with the cane toward us. "Do you think this makes any difference? Do you believe this changes everything that's happened, everything we've built? I tell you that it doesn't."

I was fighting to hold onto consciousness. Máire sensed it, for she looked at me and I saw the pale concern on her face. "Hui—" she said, who took one look at me and gestured toward the Rock. "Get her in," Hui said. "Now."

Elio started forward at Hui's command, but Micah moved to intercept him. Elio looked down at the rifle aimed casually at his stomach, and at Micah. "You shot Anaïs and then you ran, sib." He pointed to his own battered face, and I was surprised to see how bruised and puffy it had become. "I figure you did this because Dominic told you to, but it's one thing to hit someone and another to kill them deliberately. Can you pull that trigger—right here and now—if Geeda asks you? With everyone watching?"

"Shut up, pup!" That was Dominic. "I'm Eldest in our Family, and you will damned well give me respect." The cane poked at Elio's chest. "You made your choice, boy." The cane jabbed at Elio again.

It never reached him. Elio grasped the end and snatched the cane from Dominic's hand, sending Dominic stumbling forward and nearly falling. Elio held Patriarch Shigetomo's cane, the knob in one hand, the tip in the other. Then, with a sudden motion, he brought the ancient stick down and broke it in two over his knee. The pieces clattered on the stones in the stunned silence that followed.

Micah stared unbelievingly at the pieces of the broken cane in front of him. Elio pushed the rifle's barrel aside and pushed past him. The crowd parted to let him through. Hui gestured to us to follow Elio, and we did, Whitetuft snatching me back up again. Dominic gaped at us, his fists balled.

"Elio! Hui!" he shouted at our backs. "Damn it, you can't do this." He turned to the watching Families. "Stop them!" he shouted at them, gesturing wildly. "You can't let them do this."

But none of them moved. No one spoke, but they moved aside silently. I saw their faces as I passed: wondering, curious.

With the strangest entourage our little colony had yet seen, I entered the Rock again.

REFLECTIONS

JOURNAL ENTRY:
Gabriela Rusack

TAKING UP THE PEN TONIGHT, I REALIZE THAT THIS will be the last entry I make. I'm fighting my body to shape the words and mark them down. I'm old, I'm sick, and sometime soon after I write this, I'll give up the fight and finally discover whether I live on as a *kami* or not.

This epiphany is strange, and yet I find that the realization leaves me peaceful. I feel transparent; I feel that if someone could look at me now, they'd see through me as if I were glass.

But there's no one here, of course. No one on the Rock will know I died. Probably only Adari will care when they eventually find out, and dear little Tozo. I'm glad, Adari, that you disobeyed the shunning and came to see me every so often. Those visits gave me sanity. I love you, Adari. I love you as I loved my poor Elzbieta, and I wish I could have been more to you. Kiss Tozo for me, and Bryn and Eric. Keep them safe, and teach them to choose carefully what they believe.

By the time I'm found, all that will be left of the Crow is whatever bones the scavengers have tossed aside. I'll have finally entered into the endless cycle of Mictlan—me, the alien, who should never have been part of this world. With each death, we become more deeply part of whatever world-spirit moves around and between us here. She will take us in and She will either kill us or make us part of Her.

We are bound to Mictlan now, bound by flesh and dust and death. And also by new, ever-changing life.

I give myself to Mictlan-Gaia. Gladly.

Take me, and make of my poor offering what you can.

VOICE:
Anaïs Koda-Levin the Younger

I WAS TWO MONTHS RECOVERING IN THE ROCK BE-
fore I returned to the island. Between Hui's
knowledge, Ama's fledgling surgical skills, and ministrations
by Dottó, I survived. Six months later, I still can't lift my
right arm above my shoulder, my fingers sometimes feel
numb, and my side aches and throbs, but I'm alive. When I
undress at night (in front of Rebecca's mirror, which Geema
Anaïs allowed me to bring here), I see on my breast the
puckered skin and the hollowed scar where the bullet entered.

It's a reminder I'll carry the rest of my life.

As I'd promised Dominic, I left the Rock as soon as I was
able to safely do so, as winter started to give way to spring.
Leaving the Rock was best for everyone—my continued
presence there would have inevitably led to more confron-
tations. Dominic is stonily unrepentant. I doubt that he'll
ever forget the hatred he has for me, and there are many in
the Rock who still agree with him. When it came time to
depart, only a very few others made the difficult decision to
leave behind everything familiar and come with us: Elena
and her child, my sib Ché, Faika and Wangari Koda-
Shimmura, Thandi Martinez-Santos. Euzhan wanted to come
also, but Dominic wouldn't permit it. Maybe one day, when
she's past her menarche. . . .

I've never been back to the Rock myself, though Máire and
Elio have, a few times. I don't think I ever *will* go back, at
least not until Dominic is gone.

As summer approached, I asked Elio to bring back the
bog body, still lying on its slab in the clinic coldroom. We
built a pyre at the highest point of the island and lit the
oiled wood as the sun touched the ocean in red and orange,
watching the sparks go wheeling off into the darkening zenith as the flames consumed the body of the ancient Miccail
midmale. I didn't pray—the Miccails' gods are unknown,

and I really didn't know if I still believed in mine, either. Silverback and the other grumblers came and watched with us—I don't know what they felt, or whether they spoke words of farewell for their long-hidden ancestor, but I took comfort in their presence, and they remained behind after I left.

Late that night, when the fire had gone to embers and most of the humans and grumblers were finally asleep, I came and gathered what remained, carrying it back down to the temple. The lone projector we'd brought from the Rock was set up there, and Ghost was waiting for us, wearing Gabriela's body.

"Hello, Anaïs," she said quietly, almost subdued. "Are you pregnant yet?"

I nodded to Ghost. "No, but others soon will be, the *kami* willing," I told her.

"Then that's all we need."

"I'm glad you could be here, Ghost."

"Sometimes things work out—if only so that later we'll be properly disappointed when they don't."

"You know, you're still an utter pessimist."

"It's not my fault. Blame the person who wrote me."

Elio had dug a hole, lifting the stone flag in front of the altar of the shell and shoveling into the stony dirt underneath. I'd brought along a large jewelry box my *da* Jason had carved long before I was born, and I placed the cremains of the bog body into that improvised casket. With the moons and Ghost watching from above, Elio and I lowered the small burden into the earth.

I looked at the shell, brilliant in moonglow. "I feel like we should say something, but I don't know what the Miccail believed or how they did things," I said to Elio and Ghost. "Odd, to feel this sad about someone you never really knew at all."

"You knew him or her better than anyone here," Elio said. "I'm not surprised that you feel the way you do. I'd be a lot more surprised if you felt nothing."

"Maybe. You're probably right. I don't know."

Elio didn't answer. Stone scraped stone as he placed the flag back over the hole, and he stood, putting an arm around my shoulder. From the temple's entrance, a baby cried, and I turned to see Máire standing there, rocking side to side softly as she cradled her child. "That's where she belongs," she said. "You did the right thing."

I smiled at her, softly. "How's Gab?"

"She's fine. Keeping her mam awake. Here, you want to hold her?"

I took Gabriela—my child, Elio's child, Máire's child. I looked into her chubby, round face, and I touched her hand, feeling the tiny, flawless fingers close around my own. I marveled that such perfection could come from us, who were not. As I've mentioned, when we'd first returned to the island, few others accompanied us. It was Gabriela's birth—our perfect girl, unmarked by the genetic scars of Mictlan—that truly sparked an exodus from the Rock. Over twenty people now call the island home, and others travel regularly back and forth from the Rock. I have new lovers now, male and female.

We are all learning, slowly, a different sexual dance.

"*Hai*, you're beautiful and you know it, don't you," I whispered to the baby. She'd stopped fussing. Her wide, dark eyes blinked and stared at me, so huge in her round face, and she suddenly smiled, wriggling. Helpless, I smiled back at her.

I took her over to where Ghost shimmered, bright in the darkness. "Look—there's what your namesake looked like. She was pretty, too, wasn't she?" Gab reached for Ghost, and looked surprised when her hand went right through the projection.

We laughed, delighted in her curiosity, and the sound set her to crying again. "Here, I'll take her," Máire said. "She's hungry."

We sat in front of the shell, watching as Máire opened her blouse and held it aside for Gabriela. She took the nipple, sucking hungrily and loudly. None of us said anything. Someone was snoring loudly nearby. In the middle distance, I heard another child cry: Elena's child, my special charge. We heard Elena's voice calling out comfortingly to her baby a moment later. Somewhere higher up on the island, a pair of grumblers were singing, their voices warbling strange harmonies into the night.

The island sounded alive, even at night, full of the noise of humans and grumblers.

And that seemed right to me. It seemed proper.

I went up to the flagstone and put my hand on the cold stone. "Rest well," I said. "You're home."

Leaving Máire and Elio behind with Gabriela and Ghost, I went out into the night.
To listen. To feel alive.
To feel at home.

APPENDIX

THE BACKGROUND AND LINEAGE OF MICTLAN'S MATRIARCHS AND PATRIARCHS

The racial/national makeup of the nine original colonists was relatively diverse given their numbers, in part because people of known mixed-race background were preferred by the designers of the *Ibn Battuta*—a deliberate tactic to lower any latent racial tension aboard the ship. Given the social structure the unintentional colonists devised in face of their situation, the humans of Mictlan were an aggressively hybrid race by the time of the third or fourth generation. Epicanthal folds around the eyes were common but not the usual; the skin color was usually a pronounced golden-brown, though there were some who had significantly darker or lighter skin. Eye color was almost universally dark, though again there were the rare individuals with light eyes; hair color was the same, generally dark brown to black, with occasional lighter hues.

Here is what is known of the genetic makeup of the original nine colonists:

Rebecca Allen: Rebecca was from South Africa, and was of nearly equal mixtures of Caucasian and African heritage, still euphemistically referred to in South Africa as Colored.

Akiko Koda: Akiko was a US citizen. Her mother was Japanese, while her father was a Caucasian who shared with many Americans a diverse national background. "A real mongrel," Akiko reported him saying. "You name the nation; I have an ancestor who lived there."

Maria Martinez: A Brazilian citizen. Maria was mostly Porteguese/Spanish, though her grandmother was a full-blooded Inca.

Jean Delacroix: French, of mixed Caucasian and African heritage.

Guy Levin: A US citizen of German/Jewish descent on his maternal side. His father was African-American.

Antonio Santos: Despite the name, an Australian whose paternal great-grandparents had emigrated from Spain. Antonio claimed that one of his maternal grandparents was an aborigine.

Robert Schmidt: His father was a caucasian of German extraction living in Great Britain. His mother was Hindu.

Shigetomo Shimmura: A Japanese citizen with no known admixtures.

Gabriela Rusack: Although Gabriela Rusack produced no children of her own womb, there were persistent rumors that she contributed to the gene pool of Mictlan via implantation of one of her fertilized eggs into another woman's uterus. This is highly unlikely, given the extremely limited medical resources of the colonists, but Rebecca Allen was an OB/Gyn specialist, and so we cannot discount this tale entirely. The most persistent version of this myth implied that Adari Koda-Shimmura received the implanted egg, resulting in the birth of Tozo—after all, it was Adari who became Gabriela's lover, for which act Gabriela was irrevocably shunned. For the sake of completeness, then: Gabriela was half Syrian, half Serbo-Croat.

MATRIARCHS AND THEIR OFFSPRING
(female names in boldface)

Rebecca Allen (d.64)

- **Kaitlin Allen-Levin (b.0–d.57)**
- Thomas Allen-Levin (b.2–d.23)
- **Alicia Allen-Shimmura (b.6–d.85)**
- Robert Allen-Delacroix (b.7–d.96)

Akiko Koda (d.23)

- Morihei Koda-Shimmura (b.0–d.66)
- **Adari Koda-Shimmura (b.1–d.68)**
- Hirokazu Koda-Shimmura (b.3–d.23)
- Hideyoshi Koda-Schmidt (b.6–d.7)
- **Eleanor Koda-Schmidt (b.7–d.61)**
- **Rebecca Koda-Levin (b.8–d.76)**
- Kahnoch Koda-Levin (b.10–d.77)

Maria Martinez (d.23)

- **Anita Martinez-Santos (b.1–d.7)**
- **Consuela Martinez-Santos (b.2–d.84)**
- Antonio Martinez-Santos (b.3–d.23)
- Gunter Martinez-Delacroix (b.6–d.86)

Gabriela Rusack (d.66?)

- none

LINEAGE OF PRIMARY CHARACTERS

Anaïs Koda-Levin (b.80–):

Mam: Shawn (b.59–)
Grandmam: Keri (b.37–)
Great-Grandmam: Anaïs (the Elder, b.22–)
Great-Great-Grandmam: Rebecca (b.8–d.76)
Matriarch: Akiko Koda (d.23)

Elio Allen-Shimmura (b.74–):

Mam: Stefani (b.53–)
Grandmam: Diana (b.29–)
Great-Grandmam: Alicia (b.6–d.85)
Matriarch: Rebecca Allen (d.64)

Máire Koda-Schmidt (b.81–):

Mam: Morag (b.62–)
Grandmam: Safia (b.39–)
Great-Grandmam: Tami (b.26–)
Great-Great-Grandmam: Eleanor (b.7–d.61)
Matriarch: Akiko Koda (d.23)

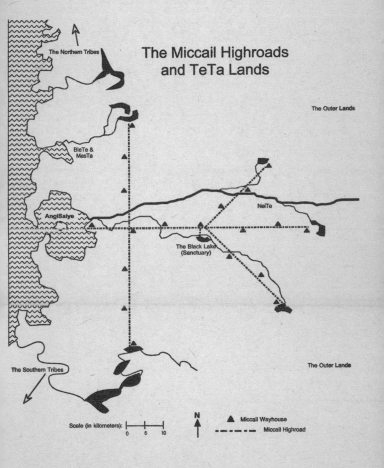

The Miccail Highroads
and TeTa Lands

The Northern Tribes

The Outer Lands

BieTe &
MasTa

NeiTe

AngiSalye

The Black Lake
(Sanctuary)

The Southern Tribes

The Outer Lands

Scale (in kilometers):
0   5   10

N

▲ Miccail Wayhouse

—— Miccail Highroad